Praise for Machir

'.... a fast moving plot full of suspense it becomes a real page turner.' *Jean Cook, Women Together magazine*

'Machir Bay is quite excellent and worthy of your attention' *Ileach*

'I really, really enjoyed this book. The descriptions of Islay (you could be there!), the distillery chapter (you can taste it!), the very detailed and very accurate historical threads, the plot, the lot! I was particularly taken by the dynamics of this story. Tense, wistful in bits, day to day, violent, romantic, even racy and then, particularly during the car chase, edge of seat gripping. Ideal read. Winter's night + log fire + dram.'

'...excellent descriptions of the places and believable characters mixed with a plot full of suspense made for a great read'

'...fantastic read kept me entertained till the very end with its twists and turns. Would highly recommend and am looking forward to the sequel.'

'...a real page turner difficult to put down'

'Fast moving, good character development and compelling stories linking war time tragedy with modern crime. Well worth a read and if you like Peter May, you will enjoy Machir Bay.'

BAC MOR

Alasdair Wham

Greenan Publishing

Bac Mor

First published in Great Britain in 2019 by Greenan Publishing, Ayr.

ISBN 978-0-9933400-2-4
Copyright 2019

Also by Alasdair Wham:
Machir Bay

A catalogue record for this book is available from the British Library.

For further information please contact info@greenanpublishing.co.uk

This book is dedicated to:
Calum, Chloe and Kacey

Prologue

Ross of Mull

The figure appeared on the far side of the small bay, out of the mist which swirled around the settlement of Fionnphort, picking his way between the granite outcrops, their red colour muted by the mist. His yellow cagoule easily spotted, as he made his way down the steep rocky slope to the beach. Between the rocks the ground was saturated, as a result of recent heavy rain and the conditions were soft underfoot, slowing him down, his boots sinking in the soft ground. His cagoule added a dab of colour in what was a bleak scene of monotone grey. Driving, gusting rain was sweeping in from the south-west threatening to obscure the view of the island of Iona, a mile offshore, but he never glanced in that direction. The sea was choppy, a fast current sweeping up the Sound of Iona, temporarily stranding the ferry at Fionnphort for the next few hours.

Once he reached the beach he walked directly across the sand, not attempting to avoid the many puddles left by the receding tide. Bypassing a large boulder, which had been cleaved in two, a local landmark, and splashing through a stream, engorged by the rain, he reached the grassy slope which led up to the road. Due to the weather there were few cars and no tourist buses in the parking spaces which straddled both sides of the road. Having made his way up to the road he turned towards the only shop, a general store for the community, his pace picking up on the firmer ground disturbing a sheep wandering along the road, which startled, ran away bleating, its woollen coat glistening, heavy with water. Arriving at the store he took the few steps up to the shop in his stride, entering the porch past the empty paper racks, the papers not arriving until mid-day, this being a remote part of the island of Mull. He picked up a hand basket and took a pint of milk and a tub of margarine from the refrigerated section and some bread from another shelf. He smiled briefly at the assistant, who was stacking shelves, and made his way to the counter.

'The usual, Tommy?' said the owner, from behind the post office counter, looking at the bearded man with the long straggly wet hair, streaked with grey. Tommy nodded and the owner reached behind her for a quarter bottle of vodka and tallied up his purchases.

'A stamp - first or second class?' The routine had become established over several weeks.

Tommy spoke quietly with little discernible accent.

'Second,' and the owner moved to the post office counter and gave him a stamp which Tommy stuck on a postcard.

'See you soon?'

'Probably', replied Tommy, not ungraciously but giving little encouragement that he wanted to continue the conversation and prolong his stay. He shoved the postcard inside his cagoule ready to post in the red pillar box outside.

As Tommy went to leave the female assistant stopped him and spoke to him quietly and offered some out-of-date bananas which he accepted. As the shop door closed the owner looked across at the assistant.

'I am not sure that we should be encouraging him, Linda, but I suppose the bananas would have gone in the bin anyway.' The owner shrugged, 'It's his life, not one I would want. But I

10

would love to know who he was sending his postcards to. He always keeps it, never letting me put it in the bag and posts it himself in the pillar box outside. Just being nosey, is that bad of me?' but she didn't really expect an answer.

'When he smiles his teeth look in good condition,' said Linda, after a pause, 'not your typical tramp.'

'Should that man of yours be worried?

'No, but you can't help but feel sorry for him, especially in this weather,' Linda replied, returning to stacking the shelves.

Outside Tommy walked along the road in the direction away from the ferry slipway, passing the road end signposted to the Columba Centre and Fidden, quickly reaching the outskirts of Fionnphort. As he did a black Mercedes saloon turned onto the road from the junction, slowing as it passed him. Tommy noted the rear window being lowered slightly but the gap was small and the tinted glass prevented him from seeing inside the vehicle. He stopped, took the quarter bottle of vodka from his cagoule pocket, unscrewed the top and took a slug.

The car drove on and after a minute Tommy put the bottle away and continued along the road, with a loch now to his right and after passing a small church located between the road and the loch he took a left turn, the road to Kintra, a small hamlet located on a tidal bay, a couple of miles away.

This was his routine, repeated every few days, which in the weeks he had been here people had noticed. Someone living rough, not causing any problems - a curiosity.

The rain had now stopped. As he approached a farm, some young boys, wearing Manchester United strips appeared, enjoying the freedom from school that a weekend offered, riding their bikes glad that the rain had ceased. They shouted at him as they passed, not unfriendly, aware that he was different, but he ignored them and saw a woman looking out of the window, alerted by the noise, keeping an eye on him. Even in Mull strangers and young children were not an accepted mix.

As he walked on the sun came out and steam rose from the rutted tarmac surface of the road. Just as the road dipped down steeply towards a row of cottages along one side of a bay, he left the road, picking his way over boggy ground, until he reached a rocky ridge. From the ridge he descended to reach a roofless ruined cottage, hewn from the local red granite, its edges rounded as if to streamline it from the wind - a fisherman's cottage long abandoned like many around the area, surrounded by ferns and nettles.

There were two rooms, one for the people who once occupied it and the other for their cattle. In-between was a small storage area where Tommy had hung a tarpaulin to protect himself from the elements. Inside were his few meagre possessions, a sleeping bag, a few utensils, a primus stove, a kettle, a pot and some tins of food. Some kindling wood was stacked, bought at the Fionnphort store, because there were few trees about, augmented by some drift wood salvaged from the shore. A nylon rucksack contained more personal possessions and in one corner were discarded vodka bottles, mostly empty.

Tommy put down his purchases and went over to a rusty corrugated metal sheet held down by small granite boulders and removed them and the metal sheet which gave to access a well. He used a bucket on a rope to collect water.

Dover Harbour

The articulated truck slipped into gear and eased through the gates of the Dover Harbour Authority, security check completed. The driver showed no emotion, aware that there were numerous cameras scanning him, looking for anything unusual. Behind him built into a compartment in the refrigerated section were six stowaways - women from Eastern Europe. Conditions, by now he knew, would be horrendous in their confined space, lined with polystyrene, to mask their heat signature. Four hours since their insertion, with only bottled water and a bucket, the atmosphere would be stuffy and the channel crossing in stormy conditions would have added to their discomfort.

It amazed him that people were willing to risk everything to enter the country, but he was paid well and the decision was theirs, he believed. It would be another hour before he could stop. Lay-bys on the A2 road out of Dover often had security cameras and he didn't want to be caught. The women would know that they were back on the road, successfully inserted in a foreign land, the expectation that gave them would have to do.

An hour later, near Rochester, following his sat nav, the driver reached the Peninsula Way and left it near a golf course, following a track to a farm. There were no lights on in the farmhouse, as usual, until he stopped, the squeal of the air brakes bringing the truck to a stop, sounding loud in the night air. A small light came on over a barn door and two figures appeared. As he jumped down from the cabin of the truck a torch light shone in his face.

'No problems, Jimmy? No one following you?'

Jimmy grunted - shaking his head.

'Better let those women out – it's been a rough journey. You get them out I need a comfort break,' and Jimmy headed around the side of the barn. He had been here before, many times.

Within ten minutes the men were aware of a sickly smell and the cabin within the container had been exposed and minutes later the women staggered out, dignity lost, gasping at the fresh air, drawing deep breaths, clearing their lungs.

'You've made it, ladies', the taller of the two men stated, no warmth or sympathy in his voice. 'You all speak English?' A quick glance and he gave his next instruction.

'Go through the doors, there are showers at the far end and some clothing. Freshen up and there's coffee - help yourself.'

The women looked disorientated, a dark haired one showing more interest in her surroundings.

'Hurry along, luv, you don't want to be spotted,' he said, encouraging them to get inside.

The woman remained defiant, taking her time, but she was covered in sickness, her long hair matted and eventually, slowly, she followed the others.

Inside the barn was a small wooden hut, with a mirrored one-way window. From inside two men were observing the arrivals closely as they left the showers, still looking exhausted, collapsing on the chairs scattered by the coffee urn.

'I expected better, Sean.'

'Sorry Mr O'Brien but the authorities are getting wise to our games and we are not welcome. The Romanians want a better image for their country - times are getting tougher.

'The one with the long hair, is that the one.' stated O'Brien, impatiently, interrupting Sean's excuses. Sean stared at his companion, the black leather jacket O'Brien wore seemed to add an extra air of menace to him, like a Gestapo officer - not that he needed to try hard. Must be three years and I still don't know his first name or even if O'Brien was his real name, Sean mused. Certain things you didn't probe.

'I believe so', and then realising he had to be more certain or the situation might get worse, he added, 'Bruno is sure.'

'You better be correct. You don't want to disappoint my client any further.'

O'Brien looked through the window, watching the women, who were unaware of his presence, his eyes coldly assessing the women, subconsciously playing with a gold earring.

'Maybe also the girl by the coffee urn just now, with the long legs, but the rest are...' and he didn't complete his sentence. The silence hung in the air, a distance between the two men, a disappointment for both.

Sean cast an anxious glance at his companion and bit his lip. This was money and he had people to pay.

'The sedative in the coffee will work before long,' Sean muttered, 'they'll soon be compliant.'

O'Brien shrugged, fastening another button on his jacket against the cold.

Twenty minutes later, assessments complete, the hut door opened and the two men emerged, O'Brien leading. They attracted only a few glances, the sedative having now taken effect, the women sitting silently some slumped on the floor exhausted.

O'Brien approached the woman with the long hair.

'Stand up,' it was not a request. The woman frowned and O'Brien shouted at her, repeating his demand. He gave her no time to respond and grabbed her pulling the hair back from her face. The woman responded angrily, her English failing but the intent of her oath was clear.

O'Brien smiled. 'I like it', and he nodded towards the barn door where a group of six men had now appeared, some yawning, trying to focus, be alert.

'This one,' and looking again at the girl with the long legs for a second more, he nodded.

Both women looked startled but strong hands grasped them, the sleeve of the loose top that the long haired girl wore was pulled up, a rubber tube tightened around her arm, and she screamed as a syringe was produced.

'If what you say is right, she'll do my boss.'

Sean looked relieved.

Ross of Mull

By evening, the clouds had started to clear away, a pale sun had appeared with dampness hanging in the air, the ground wet. Tommy shivered and grabbed his rucksack, making his way up a small hill, offering views of the sea. Only a few sheep shared his space. He found a familiar hollow, above the beach, and spread a ground sheet on the damp ground. Below him the tide had brought in the usual flotsam - plastic bottles, fishermen's nets and drift wood. The view out to sea always enthralled him, the vista superb, looking across the Sound of Iona the short distance to the north end of Iona, and further out the Treshnish Isles to the north and west - a scattered group of islands, uninhabited, rocky outcrops, remnants of a distant volcanic era. Nearer to him was Staffa and its famous cave with its basalt columns. Of Mull itself, clouds still obscured the peaks and also other islands to the north and west. Tommy was pleased that he could still appreciate scenery - that natural beauty could still touch his soul; that there was still life within him, even if it was usually well concealed.

He watched and waited as the hours past. Few boats were out at sea, given the rough conditions earlier. The excursion boats heading to and from Staffa and any yachts traversing Mull's coastline seemed to have found shelter for the day. Time passed, over to the west as the sun set some shafts of light shone through the cloud, briefly creating patches of light on the sea, a shimmering tapestry. With the setting of the sun the detail on Iona was gradually lost, with eventually only the twinkling of house lights adding illumination on what was a starless night sky.

Tommy struggled to stay awake, the cold damp making him uncomfortable. Then from the south passing through the Sound of Iona, a sailing boat emerged, its billowing sails capturing the wind, driving it forward. Tommy scanned it with his binoculars, noting the cabin lights on its lower deck and its navigation lights. Now alert Tommy watched as it sailed past the rocky headland and pitched anchor, out to sea, near the entrance to the tidal bay at Kintra. He noted people clambering down steps to a rowing boat. It was time to get a closer look.

As he edged down the hillside keeping low, he saw the rowing boat heading towards the shore, with what he thought were four people on board, two rowing and the other two sitting in the back, the bow raised as it cut through the waves. By now he was at ground level aiming towards a narrow gully which led directly to the sea.

Suddenly, there was a shout and he was aware of someone to his left. Breaking into a run he entered the gully but slipped on seaweed, momentarily losing his footing, his leg gashed on a rock. Before he could recover his balance a fisherman's net was flung over him impeding his movement. The net went tight and he was aware of people pulling it, his face straining through the mesh. He glimpsed someone else raising what looked like a baseball bat and felt the thump in his stomach. Tommy doubled up gasping for breath and someone kicked him hard in the chest. He collapsed.

Now he heard voices, some sounded foreign, but struggled to make out what was being said. He was grabbed roughly whilst bound in the net and as the ends of the net were yanked up he was trapped, being carried over the rough ground, his body twisting in pain as it hit rocks.

Tommy realised that he was being carted back towards the cottage and aware of torch lights at it. A few minutes later he was dropped outside the entrance of the ruined cottage.

'Free him', and hands grabbed at him untangling him. Freed from the net he sat up but a well-aimed kick made him gasp for breath and he slumped.

'Not so good, Tommy,' he heard a voice and looked in that direction trying to focus but the scene was blurry.

'I expected more fight.' The same voice again. Peering in the direction of the voice he could make out a man sitting on a boulder, near the corrugated metal cover of the well, his face lost in the shadows. Beside him he could see that someone had lit the primus stove, the roaring sound of the lit gas, the only other sound. Silence, as his attackers waited in expectation to see what was going to happen next, what further orders would be issued. He couldn't make out how many were involved in his capture. His vision began to clear and he could now see the man sitting on the rock his legs apart, leaning forward, staring at him. The eyes were unblinking, the gaze steady, a narrow face, with thinning hair, the tip of his tongue flicking repeatedly at a purple spot on his lower lip.

'What are you doing here, Tommy? Looking out for us?' The accent was Irish, south of the border. Tommy was trying to control his breathing, trying to get a grip on himself and the situation he found himself in.

'I wanted space, broke up with my partner,' he eventually answered.

'Why did you run away? We are reasonable, we could have accepted that explanation.' Tommy knew that was a lie.

'Some locals don't like me.'

Tommy saw the man lift up a quarter bottle of vodka and

pour out its contents.

'It's just water.'

'I don't drink all the time. It's handy to carry with me. Recycling.'

'Tell the truth, Tommy,' now there was a sinister edge, and with a slight movement of his hands, the figures lurking behind him grabbed Tommy roughly by his arms in a vice like grip.

'Now, tell the truth.'

'I am...' but before he could finish the man stood up quickly and smashed him in the face. Blood trickled down Tommy's face. The man lent down and picked up a radio transmitter.

'Drunks, tramps, call yourself what you like, don't have these. Nick might have a radio like this. Are you one of his?'

'I don't know who you mean.' The response was again savage and Tommy's body sagged.

'What were you doing near Fidden?' Again silence. 'It could be a long night, Tommy. Each time you lie I'll break one of your fingers.'

The man leaned forward, inches from Tommy's face and shouted at him.

'What are you doing here?'

Tommy shook his head and immediately his hand was grabbed and the pinkie bent back hard. He screamed. There was a sickening crack and his head swam.

Time passed. Eventually Tommy broke, his screams muffled by a rag stuffed in his mouth.

'I could send you back to Nick with a message but that would be foolish, wouldn't it? I'll be gone soon and by the time he finds your body it will be too late to be of use to him.'

'You know what happens to those who cross my path.' It was a statement. Tommy couldn't help but flinch. For the first time a smile crossed the man's face.

'Word gets around doesn't it.'

The man fished in his pocket and produced a small plastic container, from which he produced a two inch metal rod, quarter inch in diameter, pointed at one end, and a silk cloth from which he took a pair of tongs. Slowly, for effect he used the pliers to grip the rod and held the metal rod over the flame from the primus stove. Slowly, the metal turned red.

'You will have heard of how people can identify my victims,' and he brought the glowing rod towards Tommy's face, whipping the rag from Tommy's mouth, as strong hands held his head back.

'This can be quick or slow. Answer my final question and it will be quick.' He paused to check that Tommy was still capable of responding. 'Tell me about Peter Meldrum and his son?'

Part One

Search and Rescue

1

I had mixed emotions as I stood on the sand dune overlooking Machir Bay. The view was so familiar, and as the time for our departure approached I felt an increasing appreciation of the raw natural beauty of this island, Islay, that had been my life so far. There was a sense of timelessness, expressed in the never ending breaking of the waves on the beach. Nature's metronome would continue long after I had gone, only to be appreciated by others, not me.

The crashing waves, the freshness of the air, the sheep chewing the grass on nearby fields, even the trickle of smoke from Kilchoman distillery, all added to my restlessness. So familiar and somehow not really valued until you were leaving. Maybe this was how you felt at the end of life: where had all the years gone, suddenly bunched up together, over so quickly. Soon all this would be replaced by a house, a clone of many on a street like many others - cheek by jowl with neighbours - so unlike Machir Bay.

Jenny stood beside me, snuggled in, my arm wrapped around her body, her long black hair cascading down her back. Neither of us needed to speak, our shared emotion part of our ever growing intimacy. She more than me would miss this; she needed the power of nature to stir her artistic talent, capture and explore the natural beauty to share with others in her paintings. In a room overlooking a small garden, surrounded by a high wooden fence, she would feel trapped, her imagination struggling to compensate for the inspiration of the wild places.

But, as I said, my emotions were mixed. As I replayed, no, churned over in my mind, the events of the last six months I had bitter regrets. Why did I go to the Robinson's farm that night? Life would have been so different. We would have had a choice about leaving Islay, even though the outcome might have been the same, the circumstances would have been easier.

Recent traumatic memories especially involving Ben had changed us both and we were still recovering. We both watched carefully as Ben played on the sand below us, no more than ten yards away, using a plastic spade to dig up the sand, imposing a temporary structure before the next tide washed it away. Jodie, our ever faithful black and white Border Collie, hung around him, tempting him with seaweed and waiting for it to be thrown. More than ever, it seemed, we were unable to forget how Charles Robinson had tried to abduct Ben, the memories leaving scars in our minds. I glanced south looking, at the rocks in the distance, where Robinson had held a knife to his throat. The psychologist had been hopeful. Ben, she suggested, would have absorbed the emotion but maybe not realised the danger. The fact that Jenny and I were there and had been able to support him immediately would have helped, but, she warned, we had to look out for signs of delayed trauma emerging. Starting school had helped him and we ensured that someone dropped him off and picked him up. Hopefully, he could take the impending change of home and school in his stride.

'He's resilient,' Jenny said, breaking the silence.

'Probably better than me,' I replied.

'Don't be too hard on yourself. You didn't have a choice to

be involved.'

We had been here many times.

'But I made wrong decisions.'

Jenny turned towards me her expression softening, a smile emerging. She lifted her head to reach my face as she kissed me gently, her way of saying that she didn't hold me responsible. I knew how much she was suffering herself, her constant nightmares, her weight loss, told a story. Then she held my face in her hands, forcing me to look into her green eyes, 'I don't blame you, Peter,' she said. I kissed her gently on her forehead and she released her hold.

A minute later, I shouted, 'Come on Ben,' and saw him lift his head in my direction and wave. 'Malcolm and Alison will be here soon, we need to go back.'

We wandered back from the sand dunes, through the car park and up towards our home, a bungalow overlooking the beach, that we called we called Mable's Cottage, after an aunt whose estate had made the purchase possible.

...

Malcolm was enjoying his wine: Alison was driving. It was a last chance to catch up before we all left the island. Malcolm had got a new job at the Strathclyde Evening Echo, in Glasgow, as a junior crime reporter, and was looking forward to it. Alison was quieter, looking tired. She had got a nursing post at the Royal Infirmary in Glasgow. They would live about twenty minutes away from us when we moved over to the mainland.

After the meal we sat down ready to reminisce about Islay life; it was going to be an evening of nostalgia, old stories probably embellished, hopefully, much laughter. As I refilled the wine glasses, I saw Alison glance at Malcolm and he sat up, putting down his wine glass, clearing his throat. Jenny was immediately alert, turning towards Alison, who blushed slightly.

Jenny squeezed Alison's hand and Alison nodded. Even I was catching on. Malcolm cleared his throat again. I wasn't sure if it was for effect or because he had drunk too much wine. 'Alison is expecting a baby. She has just had her twelve week scan.'

'So that's why you couldn't meet up last week,' said Jenny, moving even closer to hug her friend.

'That's great news,' I said, getting up, going to the cupboard to produce a bottle of Islay malt whisky and two glasses.

'Look at them,' said Jenny laughing, 'we have only to carry the baby, give birth and they are congratulating each other, job done.'

Jenny and Alison got busy talking, heads close together, leaving the two of us alone. We had much to remember, our friendship going back to school days.

'Let me have a last look at Machir Bay,' said Malcolm, unexpectedly, putting down his whisky glass, which had by now been filled and emptied several times.

We got up and wandered out through the small porch at the front. The sun had set some time ago, the familiar crash of the waves could be heard clearly, the sea black. We wandered over to the low stone wall that surrounded our house.

'I'll miss all this,' he said, breathing deeply, the stars offering some illumination as our eyes adjusted. 'I'll be back but it won't be the same.' It was a side of Malcolm I hadn't seen before, but it was comforting, I could understand his feelings, empathise. He took off his wire rimmed glasses and wiped them with his hankie. I looked the other way. Why is leaving so hard?

'I know that we'll keep in touch, look forward to it.' I needed that reassurance as much as he did.

'What will your new job entail?'

'Plenty of whisky tastings, talking about the Islay distillery, its new ranges, expressions, travelling home and abroad. Pretty tough. And I can't really touch too much of the stuff,' I added with a smile.

There was a lot more to the job than that, but that is what people expected me to say. Why disappoint them?

Malcolm laughed. 'There had to be a drawback. When are you going?'

'Another fortnight, the house isn't ready yet. The house is owned by the distillery and had tenants in it until recently. Pence Gifford told me that there is some decoration required. He has been wonderful to us, one of the all-time iconic figures in the whisky industry, and he has even organised to rent out our house here at Machir Bay.'

'He rates you, Peter. We've given up the lease on our house in Bowmore but we are taking out a mortgage for a new build. Real responsibilities now. I am going to be junior in the crime department but it will be good experience; the team are highly rated. They broke the story about the Paterson gang and their threatening of the jury members at the murder trial of Bob Paterson's son.

I vaguely remembered it. The trial had dominated the news for a few days.

'I didn't want to say in front of Jenny, but I will often have to research backgrounds, dig up information. If you like I can try and find out a bit more about Jason. Maybe give you closure. I haven't told Alison,' he added, knowing that it was a sensitive subject.

It says a lot for the strength of our relationship that Jenny had so readily accepted that I had had a child with Catherine Robinson. It had been a big shock to me, when I heard the recording on my mobile phone that evening in Ayr Police Station. Catherine had given birth to Jason, my son not long after she left the island. And then crushingly, I learnt that she had lost him.

No detail, no explanations, just plenty of emotion. Jason looked like me, it seemed. I would have been a good dad, she said. He would have been around ten now. It was so hard to take in. The Robinsons and the Meldrums lives had been so entangled here on Islay. My relationship with Catherine, my first love, so dramatically stopped when she and her parents had been taken from the island, now I understood, because of their involvement with Desmond McGrory's drug smuggling gang, which had used their farm as a staging post for smuggling drugs in from Ireland.

I nodded affirmatively as it bothered me. What had happened to Jason? I reckon if I knew, then I would cope better.

'Yes, I would like that, but we will not tell the girls our plans. They have enough to deal with. Any word about Desmond McGrory?'

'Nothing, everything was hushed up. I doubt that we will see him again.' The attack on Ben was the Robinson's attempt at revenge, for his sons being imprisoned as a result of the drug bust and losing Catherine. Charles Robinson, Catherine's father, had been a nasty brute with a vicious temper. I remembered looking down on his bloodied body, further along the beach feeling elation realising that he was dead.

I hoped Desmond McGrory had decided to move on, forget about us, but I couldn't drop my guard yet, maybe never. The whole family still had the emergency contact app on our phone that Nick, who was in charge of the drug busting operation, had placed there.

Ben's safety was the major concern for us, neither of us wanted to let him down. A major drug dealer had power of life and death or worse. He wouldn't take kindly to his smuggling chain been disrupted. Woe betide anyone who got in his way and I had. How I cursed the Americans for making me go with them to the Robinson's farm, in return for releasing a recording that would prove my innocence about malicious claims that I had attempted to rape Catherine. Even now looking back over the recent traumatic months it all seemed surreal.

We walked back in and Malcolm poured himself another whisky. Later they left, earlier than usual, but Alison was tired, her face pale.

We waved goodbye and returned to the house as the phone rang.

'Hello,' I never gave out my name as I had been advised.

'Mr Meldrum, this is Gordon Parker, Beattie's son. I am afraid that I have sad news for you. My father passed away peacefully yesterday. We are still making the arrangements. The final details will be in the local newspaper, the Ileach, but it will probably be late next week.'

'I'm so sorry,' I replied, and I saw Jenny stop as she was about to go into Ben's room to check on him for a final time. She turned towards me, an anxious look on her face. I gave my condolences and put down the phone.

'Beattie's passed away,' I said, blinking.

2

The wind swept in over the Rhinns of Islay, across Loch Indaal, chilling the air, making those heading up to the Round Church in Bowmore grateful for their warm clothing. The Round Church perched at the top of the Main Street appeared like a place of pilgrimage with a steady stream of people heading towards the entrance at the base of the church tower. We had had to park the Golf near the Islay distillery at the bottom of the hill; so busy was the Main Street.

With Ben safely deposited at school, we had arrived slightly late and were now hurrying towards the steps of the church pausing as we saw the coffin being carried the short distance from Beattie's house towards the church. Those carrying the coffin kept a slow pace in step with the chiming of the church bell. We waited until the funeral party entered the church through the porch, passing the two monuments to previous local lairds, and quickly followed them in. The church was packed; mainly downstairs, but there were even some sitting in the horseshoe shaped gallery. There were few on the island who had not journeyed in Beattie's taxi at some time, who had not experienced his warmth, kindness and had had a safe journey, who didn't want to pay their final respects.

The Rev Walker, the local minister, greeted the funeral

party and bowed his head as the coffin was placed at the front of the church. We waited until the pall bearers, in turn bowed and retreated and found a seat at the rear near the twin chambered sarcophagus, but with a view past the dominant central pillar which supported the roof.

Mary, his wife, looking frailer, more shrunken by age and grief, than I remembered, stood between her sons, who both towered over her. She had glanced at the coffin as it had drawn level with her, her eyes fixed on it: so many memories to draw on but none masking the grief of parting

Welcoming everyone to what the Rev Walker proclaimed was a celebration of a good life, well-lived, the service began. I allowed my mind to wander partly to help me cope with the emotion which was gripping me. I had been very close to Beattie. I thought of the taxi runs to primary school with Catherine when I was younger. Happy days; despite subsequent events. I remembered talking to him just a few months ago, probing him about the Robinsons and the gold watch he had returned to me, plundered from the Chief Officer of the ship the *Empire Constellation*, which was sunk off the Islay coast during the Second World War, and now safely back with the Chief Officer's family.

And then there was the Rev Walker, who appeared older, his hair now white, having let age finally make its mark. He had visited us several times after Charles Robinson's failed abduction of Ben. Not forcing any theology on us, just listening, supporting us, especially Jenny who now struggled to let Ben out of her sight. Jenny had suffered, becoming tense, anxious, her creative artistic spark dimming as a consequence, struggling to finish orders for clients.

A final rousing hymn - 'Would your anchor hold?' was uplifting and heartily sung. The funeral party then left the church and moved into the adjacent graveyard where the council workers hung around by the stone wall having previously dug the grave.

The pall bearers helped lower the coffin, the brass handles momentarily reflecting the sun, which had briefly appeared, before the coffin was lowered into the grave. A brief prayer from the minister, his white hair and clerical robes ruffled by the wind gusting in from Loch Indaal. People hung around, some who were not going to the hotel for refreshments, bidding farewell to Mary and her sons, others shuffling away.

'It was a beautiful service,' whispered Jenny.

'Yes,' I replied lying, having been lost in my thoughts during it.

I noticed one of Mary's sons looking in my direction, his mother pointing me out. He came across smiling.

'I'm Gordon, I spoke to you the other evening.'

Beattie had spoken of him. He had left the island many years ago to study at university and like many from the island had never returned.

'My mother is anxious to have a word with you. Are you coming to the hotel?'

I looked across at Jenny, who nodded.

'We will be pleased to but we can't stay too long. We have to pick up Ben, our son, from primary school, in just over an hour,' I added, by way of explanation.

'That's good, Mum will be pleased. Dad often spoke warmly of you.'

Gordon turned away and walked back to his Mum. People were now filing out of the graveyard, heads down to avoid the biting wind.

We walked briskly down the hill to reach our car and then drove quickly the short distance to the hotel, parking across the road near the petrol station, in Bowmore. A waitress offered us a drink, as we arrived, which we accepted and moved into the lounge bar. I noticed that Ronnie, an old school friend, who had helped me escape from the clutches of the drug smugglers, was there with a man that I didn't recognise.

'Were you at the funeral?' I asked, going across to join him, pleased to see him, wondering if I had missed him earlier. Ronnie shook his head and then gave Jenny a kiss on the cheek.

'No, I've been having lunch with Gil, talking about a business proposal. I didn't really know Beattie, only heard about him from you.'

Gil, Ronnie's lunch companion smiled. He was even shorter than Ronnie, who was not the tallest. Shaven head, piercing blue eyes, he had an intensity about him; giving the impression that he was someone who meant business.

'I'm, Peter, this is my wife, Jenny,' I said by way of introduction.

'Ronnie has told me about recent events. A tough time, hopefully it is all in the past.'

Ronnie looked slightly uncomfortable; Gil was very direct, it seemed, his brusqueness and demeanour suggesting a military background, I decided. Most people avoided talking about our recent troubles, feeling that it might upset Jenny.

'Gil is going to be working around Jura,' where Ronnie and his wife Maria lived, 'running a survival course,' he explained. 'The plan is that I will be taking him and clients to parts of Jura, like Jura's deserted west coast, not usually reached, using my boat.'

'I'll be working for myself, with the estate owners' permission. I already have a few clients willing to pay for a unique experience.'

Gil was certainly the confident type but it seemed reasonable. The north end of the island was recognised as one of the last wilderness areas in Europe, largely untouched by man, a perfect area to test yourself against nature and discover your real self.

'I'll no doubt see you around on my return to the islands. We're leaving soon for the mainland.'

'It must be a special job to attract you away from Islay.'

'Promotion and a change of scene will do the family good.'

Gil looked at me, as if assessing all that he had heard. 'Good luck,' he replied, after a brief pause.

'Please excuse us; Mary, Beattie's widow wants to speak to us and then we must pick up Ben from school, ' I said, making my excuses, noting that she had just arrived and was now sitting by the coal fire, alone, while her sons went for some food and a cup of tea for her.

'We better go across,' and I put my arm around Jenny guiding her away.

'Send Maria our love,' Jenny said turning briefly to Ronnie. 'You are both down to be our first visitors,' and she followed me towards Mary.

Up close Mary seemed even frailer, her hands badly twisted with arthritis. Despite the difficulties of the day she managed to smile and invited us to sit down. Gordon brought across a cup of tea and then left. I wondered what she was going to say.

'You were both very special to Beattie.'

I smiled but I could feel the resurgence of the emotion I felt during the church service. I swallowed hard. Mary knew that the affection was mutual.

'He also loved your paintings, Jenny. What a talented girl.' She continued after drawing a deep breath. 'I have prepared in my heart for this day for a long time so don't feel sorry for me. I've lived a full life. But that is not what I wanted to speak to you about,' and she leant forward.

Mary spoke softly. With the background noise I struggled to hear what she said.

'Last week, Jimmy,' who I knew as one of Beattie's taxi friends, 'called in. Afterwards Beattie was agitated. Wanted me to phone you, but,' and she paused again, seeking composure, 'events took over.' Jenny instinctively put her arm around Mary.

'I wish I could remember clearly but my mind wanders. Beattie wanted to warn you about Barry More. Or I think that is what he said. Jimmy had overhead two men talking in the back of his car when he was taking them to the airport. They mentioned your name and also someone called, Barry More. Jimmy was concerned, didn't feel that it sounded good. I'm sorry I don't know why and Jimmy has now gone on holiday to Tenerife.'

Jenny didn't need to hear this. She would only become more agitated.

'Thanks,' I replied, 'I'll speak with Jimmy when he gets back.'

I smiled reassuringly. Mary seemed relieved to have passed on Beattie's enigmatic message and I changed the subject.

We talked for a few more minutes and then noting the time I said that we had to leave. Gordon came over offering his mum something to eat and we made our farewells. I looked around the room for Ronnie, but he was at the bar collecting drinks talking to someone I recognised from school. As I turned I saw Gil, nursing a whisky. He was looking at me and nodded in my direction, little emotion on his face. He raised his whisky glass, not denying that he was observing me. A cool character, slightly unnerving. Then I noticed that he suddenly put the glass down forcibly on the small table beside him, some of the whisky spilling and I saw that his hand was trembling. So, not so cool, I mused, hoping that Ronnie wasn't rushing into something he might regret.

'What did Mary mean?' Jenny demanded, as soon as we reached the car.

'I haven't a clue. Beattie was always very protective of me, especially after everything that happened. He was probably being over anxious and let's face it everyone on Islay knows most of the story by now.'

As I suspected Jenny looked unconvinced and neither was I

by my statement. It seemed odd. Why was I being talked about? And who was Barry More? And why was Beattie anxious to let me know - what had troubled him? I knew Beattie a lot better than Jenny and his mind was always sharp, even in declining health. It worried me.

I drove on in silence glad when we picked up Ben, pleased when Ben's chirpy conversation enlivened the mood in the car. The gossip of the playground was a good antidote to Jenny's mood and Jodie's welcome, when we reached home, was as enthusiastic as usual.

· · ·

The next morning, our last day on Islay I drove into Bowmore on a final visit to the Islay distillery. The shop staff were wishing me all the best and made a small presentation of an 18 year old bottling, finished in a sherry cask, which was lovely. There were lots of hugs and kisses and expressions of good will. Even Mrs Hall, the personal assistant to the distillery manager, Pence Gifford, managed to smile and I reciprocated. After all she had her reasons for contacting the police about the allegations made against me by Catherine, even if it had complicated matters and made life more difficult for me.

When I eventually got to his office, its shelves lined with whisky samples, Pence Gifford looked please to see me, a broad smile on his face as he came from behind his desk to shake my hand, his trademark large glasses, for once, left on the desk. He looked quite different without them, his eyes blinking but his expression just as warm.

'Sorry to see you go but when you return I am sure that you will have a more senior position.'

I smiled and thanked him for all he had done for me.

'The least I can do, Peter. We must encourage potential.

38

Hector McAlpine will be your line manager. He's a good guy. I'm sure he will look after you.'

More than that, at six foot six, with a long red and white beard, which resembled a hairy sporran, and a ponytail, Hector was certainly conspicuous and with his penchant for wearing a kilt and matching tartan waistcoat he cut a dramatic persona. But what really made him remarkable was his love for expounding the wonders of Islay distillery. I was in good hands.

We spoke for a short while before he smiled and selected a small bottle from a nearby shelf. 'Try this,' he said, ' if you ever feel nostalgic for these shores then its peatiness will immediately connect you with Islay. Sip it slowly though, it's pretty powerful - cask strength.'

Buoyed by the expressions of goodwill I drove back to Machir Bay. Jenny was still busy packing up, her long black hair tied back. The house looked different. We were leaving our furniture, for what it was worth, but our personal possessions were filling several large cardboard boxes and, of course, Jenny's paintings and materials filled several more. The distillery had organised a van which had collected most of our possessions the day before and they would be waiting for us on our arrival. The rest would fit into Jenny's campervan and the Golf.

Later, I collected Ben from school for the final time and handed in a present for his teacher. He seemed upbeat, excited probably because he didn't know how different his new surroundings would be.

. . .

Once he was in bed and while Jenny was finishing off packing her paintings, I took Jodie down to the beach for a final walk. The car park was empty, the beach deserted. I wandered towards the seaweed covered metal remnants of the shipwreck exposed by the receding tide. Different stories existed about it, the most dramatic being that its cargo of alcohol had resulted in several islanders prostrate on the beach having over imbibed. It was, as if I wanted to say goodbye to an old friend, a mute observer of my time at Machir Bay.

I walked north, crossing the burn which fed into the bay, splashing through it not concerned that my feet were getting wet, enjoying the moment. This evening I wanted to experience everything that Machir Bay had to offer. I looked out to sea, the water bronze in colour the sun by now low in the sky, the light diffused through layers of cloud. As I sat on the rocks, at the north end, throwing seaweed for Jodie, I allowed the peace and solitude to permeate my body, reach for my soul. I looked south towards the ridge of hills, which marked the southern end of the bay, with the old radar station buildings and the modern transmitter masts on top. The view so familiar. I consciously didn't look towards the rocks at sea level where Charles Robinson had taken Ben.

Slowly, I made my way back, not in any hurry, although aware that I should be helping Jenny, my footsteps leaving a trail in the damp sand. As I crossed the burn, the sun appeared weakly through a gap in the clouds. It was then I saw a flash of light reflecting off something in the sand dunes. Probably a bird watcher arriving to watch the birds settling for the night, I thought, even though there were surprisingly few birds about this evening. I saw the light flash again and was now more curious, especially when I saw a figure arise and quickly slink away keeping low, not wanting to be detected. A bird watcher wouldn't have needed to conceal himself in these circumstances.

I picked up pace, calling on Jodie, reaching the base of the sand dunes and quickly scrambled to the top, gasping for breath, just in time to see a man running to the car park towards a van which had arrived after I had walked through the car park earlier.

Why did he need to run? Why did he not want to be seen?

I had now reached the path at the top, beside a low wire fence, Jodie thinking I was playing a game running ahead, circling me. With only a brief glance in my direction the man, dressed in jeans and a dark coloured anorak, opened the door, throwing in what looked like binoculars, and jumped in. Starting the engine he reversed fast from where he was parked near to a fence, and then turning headed up the rough track to the road, leaving a trail of dust. By now I had reached the car park and was close enough to make out the markings on the van. The van was black with a yellow panel on the side with what looked like picture of a dripping tap, so a plumber's van. There was a name and what looked like a telephone number on the side but I couldn't make them out. I took out my phone, turned on the camera app, and tried to zoom in on the side of the van taking a few photos as the van sped away.

Annoyingly, the photos were out of focus. Was I being paranoid? The driver's behaviour did seem suspicious but... Why did he make such a fast exit? Life had changed, I realised. Now I was jumpy, anxiously scanning my surroundings, looking for danger wanting to protect my family. Maybe the anonymity of the big city would be welcome after all and I never thought that I would say that about leaving Machir Bay.

3

I was awakened by Jenny thrashing about in the bed, lathered in sweat, shouting out. Gently, I held her offering reassurance but it took a few minutes for her to come around and then she clung to me breathing deeply, beginning to sob, her nightdress soaked in sweat. Another nightmare.

'It's okay,' I said, trying to calm her, but Jenny replied quickly, her voice becoming more shrill.

'No it's not. These men could come for Ben at any time.'

'It's unlikely now. They have bigger issues to deal with. Remember Pence has alerted the company that no one is to give out our new address and he personally will look after our house here.'

'Oh, Peter, I hope that you are right.'

'I am,' I replied, trying to sound more confident than I felt.

Neither of us could get back to sleep. Later Dad phoned from Iona to wish us well. It was a strange day for him, his family home temporarily in new hands, but he was his usual upbeat self.

'It's a beautiful morning in Iona,' he said, 'and the red granite of the Ross of Mull is sparkling in the sunlight. You must visit me soon, it would be good for Jenny, provide inspiration for her paintings, the light is special, artists love working here. I am just off to the Abbey for the morning service,' he continued without pausing, 'I'll phone you tomorrow in your new home.'

Dad knew what had happened, knew about Jason but his support never wavered. He appeared to see life differently. Temporary troubles were just that; it was eternal matters that inspired him.

We left the house in convoy, me leading in the Golf, Jenny following in her light blue WV campervan with Ben and the dog. I couldn't look back. We would return someday, I promised myself.

Our journey from Machir Bay to Bowmore was so familiar. Inland Loch Gorm was, as usual, enticing, a deep blue colour, a gentle ripple on the surface. As I passed the Robinson's farm, a short distance on, which was still deserted, I refused to let my mind dwell on the many vivid memories it held for me. We wound our way over the hill towards Loch Indaal and the view across the loch to Bowmore and the Islay distillery. This morning Islay was tugging at me, reluctant to let me go. The feeling was mutual but I couldn't dwell on the emotions, instead I had to be practical, look ahead to the fresh challenges.

We waited in line at Port Ellen to embark on the *Hebridean Isles*, one of the older boats on the route. Several cars had already been loaded with a couple of large trucks centrally positioned up at the front. We waited our turn and were directed to the side of the trucks where there were presently no other cars.

With no one allowed to remain in the cars during the journey we headed up steep stairs to the lounge area with Jodie straining on the lead, and Ben with Jenny. We heard the ramp going up and the ferry edged out of the narrow confines at Port Ellen. I left the dog with Jenny and took Ben to collect breakfast, an important tradition, one of the few occasions that Jenny allowed me a full cooked breakfast. I made the most of it and indulged Ben.

The journey was uneventful, the seas calm and we slowly headed up the narrow confines of West Loch Tarbet towards the ferry terminal at Kennacraig. When the announcement for passengers to return to their cars was made, Jenny led the way back to the car deck, with Ben and I waiting to let others go down the steep stairway before taking Jodie down. I let Jodie into the back of the campervan and returned to the car. On the car deck the lorries were already prepared to move, the ramp down, the docking having been completed.

As the first truck pulled out I spotted the plumber's van on the far side. I immediately grabbed my phone to take a picture.

I could now make out the writing on the side of the van.

The driver saw me and quickly turned his head away, lifting his arm to block my view, but not before I saw him glare at me and his expression reminded me of someone, but I couldn't think who it was. I recognised him, he had been ahead of me in the queue for breakfast. Now I was alarmed, who was he? His reaction suggested that he was aware of who I was and that gave him a big advantage. Fortunately, Jenny was unaware, busy talking to Ben in the campervan, Jodie panting sticking her head between the two of them.

The deck hand indicated to the van driver's side to proceed and within a minute the van was gone.

The deck hand eventually called me forward and I turned away to concentrate on leaving the ferry, Jenny in the campervan following behind. There was no sign of the plumber's van on the road and after a few hours, and a stop at Inverary, we were approaching Glasgow along Great Western Road, reaching Anniesland Cross. This was home territory for the Meldrums, dad having been brought up in the west end of Glasgow. I had found his old house when I was a student at Strathclyde University. Now I could show Ben my family roots. The sat nav proved useful especially after we reached Canniesburn Toll and after ten minutes we reached our destination. The street was long, with detached houses stretching down each side. This was suburbia, a long way from Islay.

My first impression of the house was neutral, although I didn't think that Jenny would be so positive. The roughcast appeared damp giving a rather dowdy impression to the house. There was a garage separated from the house by a narrow passageway. Some of the roughcast was missing on the garage making it look run down and the paving slabs were uneven, weeds growing between the slabs.

I unlocked the front door. The hall was tiny with a stair way immediately behind the door. It was no more cramped than our bungalow at Machir Bay, and we had no upstairs before, but the experience was so different. Somehow the house seemed smaller, not helped by piles of boxes everywhere. Jenny made no comment, her long hair tied back somehow making her expression more severe, accentuating the lack of colour in her face. Ben was excited, Jodie busy sniffing about, at least she was eager to explore. Upstairs there were three bedrooms or rather two bedrooms and a tiny box room. The trade description people might have quibbled about the description of the third bedroom. The kitchen was bigger, just, and Jenny at last smiled when she saw the conservatory and assessed its potential.

'The light is quite good and I can see some hills. I can cope,' she proclaimed, trying to sound perky, and she turned flinging her arms around me her suppressed emotion released.

'And,' she added, 'surely no one can find us here.'

I hugged her tight and kissed the top of her head. The van driver, somehow, had shaken my confidence in that.

Then we got busy unpacking, making up the beds and I went out with Ben searching for fish and chips, which at least were easier to find than on Islay.

4

Jura

Ronnie looked across the table at Maria, studying her face intently. It was easier now that she had cut off her long tresses, which highlighted her high cheek bones. He could detect the exhaustion which revealed itself in the hollow cheeks, the tired eyes. He knew that she would be defensive, not wanting him to raise the topic, again.

'Did you get to bed?' he asked, his voice non-confrontational, already knowing the answer.

'I got up early,' Maria replied, not making eye contact.

'Very early. I woke about two and you weren't there.'

'I couldn't sleep,' not attempting this time to deny the allegation.

'Maria,' but she held up her hand, stopping him making any further comment.

'I'll go to bed early tonight,' and she grabbed his hand, stroking it, smiling.

'It's something that I have got to do, you know that.'

'I understand, but the search is becoming all consuming,' he replied, and she acknowledged that he had a point by lowering her head, not meeting his gaze.

'I love you,' and Ronnie leant across the small breakfast table and kissed her tenderly on the head as he rose.

'I don't know when I will be back, probably late afternoon. Hopefully, Gil and I can work out some arrangement.'

Maria knew that the meeting was important; finances were tight after they had extended themselves with the new boat.

'Good luck,' and she smiled, her face lit up. Something always clicked with Ronnie when she did that. Issues were just that - they would work through them.

Ronnie chose to walk into Craighouse, the main centre of population on the island, it was only half a mile and it was a bright sunny morning. Passing the red metal roofed Jura Hall, he saw two noisy seagulls perched on the roof, squawking over territorial rights, hoping that wasn't a metaphor for the two of them, before he called in at the Jura Stores, the only stores on the island, to collect some chocolate biscuits and milk. From there it was a short distance to the small stone pier, where his boat was moored. With only two hundred residents, most of them in Craighouse, Jura was never busy. The island was more remote than its near neighbour, Islay: either reached by an additional short ferry crossing from Islay or the passenger only service from Tayvallich, which ran only in the summer months. It also had only one whisky distillery to attract tourists, unlike Islay's nine and counting. In the morning sun the Jura hotel and the distillery, both overlooking the pier, looked their best, their white painted surfaces, gleaming in the sunlight. It was a familiar scene, one that never failed to enthuse Ronnie - he loved the island.

He walked along the pier to where his boat, *Casablanca*, named after his favourite film, was tied up and clambered aboard, unlocking and pulling the sliding door open, to enter the cockpit. He decided to extend the awning over the rear of the boat, which gave more shelter from the sun. This was a new boat for him, a second hand, Jeanneau Merry Fisher 755, which had used up all the funds and more, left by an uncle who had passed away. He also had had to approach another relative, who hinted that there was a limit, but as long as he got two weeks fishing when he wanted, he would subsidise the venture. Gleaming white, with the cockpit fully enclosed, most mod cons and a powerful Yamaha 150bhp engine, it met the needs of Ronnie's clientele: fishing, trips around Jura and beyond. He filled the kettle, turned on the gas and waited while the water boiled, getting out the coffee and sugar.

Gil would be here soon, years in the military having trained him to be punctual. Ronnie prepared the boat while he waited removing the cover from the outboard, switching on the VHF and going through the usual routines, prior to departure. Everything seemed fine. On time Gil wandered down the pier towards the boat, a neat figure in a tartan shirt and cargo trousers, a small rucksack on his back, he clambered aboard.

'Welcome, on board,' Ronnie said, and directed him into the cabin. 'Coffee?' and Gil accepted. 'Good weather for our trip, the sea's calm, the tides favourable.'

Sometimes Gil was very quiet, lost in himself, other times more verbose. Old habits die hard it seemed, because his eyes roamed the interior checking everything out, reconnaissance. He could imagine Gil surveying some small Afghan village preparing for a night time raid.

'I'll explain how everything works later: all the capabilities of the boat.'

'It certainly looks the part,' Gil said, speaking for the first time, 'I look forward to the trip, thanks.'

Just two days ago Ronnie had gone with Gil to the Jura Hotel, shared a few whiskies, probing, trying to fill in something of Gil's background. Gil had talked a little about Afghanistan, guarded in his comments, mostly generalities and Ronnie had added little to his knowledge of this far away country or what Gil did whilst he was there. He wasn't surprised soldiers often disliked talking about their experiences, his grandfather being one who never talked about the war, only later did they discover that he had been a hero.

It was from the laird's factor, Torquil that Ronnie had discovered that Gil was staying at one of the small estate lodges, originally built for a gamekeeper, rent free. Torquil had hinted that the Laird was returning a favour, giving space to Gil encouraging him to develop his own business, hence the trip today. Knowing of the Laird that was quite a gesture and Torquil agreed but the Laird had made it clear to Torquil that Gil was to be supported. He had speculated that it was something to do with the Laird's son, who was a major in the same regiment as Gil, but Torquil knew that his boss was very private and the factor respected him too much to probe.

'So you want an adventure experience, Gil, for a small group of clients - survivalist in nature. I take them out in my boat, through the Gulf of Corryvreckan, to the west coast of Jura and drop you off, collecting you later, at an agreed time. You live rough, observe the wild life, live off the land.'

'That's about it. I use my training, show them how to gather food from the land, cook it and camp out under the stars, or build a camouflaged shelter if the weather is poor. I have had a good response from adverts I placed in outdoor magazines, including interest from the States. My prices don't seem to put them off.'

Good, thought Ronnie, hoping that his cut would be worthwhile. He certainly looked the part Ronnie surmised - wiry, shaven head, very fit. The guy had leadership qualities Ronnie felt, seemed in control, knew what he was doing, although he had noticed the occasional facial tic or trembling hand which hinted at inner turmoil.

Minutes later, life jackets on, the mooring ropes tidied up on board, the boat edged away from the pier, trailing a small dingy, heading out to sea through the Small Isles, between Eilean nan Gabhar and Eilean nan Coinein before turning north, no other boats in sight, the Sound of Jura their own to explore, the mainland to starboard, lost in haze. The radio crackled with a message from the coastguard and Ronnie gave details about their trip.

Out at sea the red roofed Jura Hall remained prominent for a while, as Craighouse slipped from view and Ronnie provided Gil with binoculars and talked about Jura's crowning glory, the Paps of Jura, the island's own mountain range, which dominated the southern end of the island. The three mountains with their distinctive steep scree lined slopes glistening in the sun, their conical tops meaning that they were well named; 'pap' being derived from the Old Norse word for breast. It was a perfect morning, their peaks shorn of cloud.

As the boat proceeded up the Sound of Jura, Ronnie pointed out Lowlandman's Bay and the former Lighthouse keepers' houses, the shore station for the now automated Skervuile lighthouse, which was to starboard, marking a subsea hazard. Ronnie took his time sailing up the coast, conserving fuel but also giving Gil time to appreciate the surroundings. Lagg Bay followed then Tarbet Bay. Gil studied the coastline, turning his attention to basking seals on the shoreline, porpoises and the sea birds overhead, asking a few questions. This was an information gathering trip.

'Jura only has one road,' Ronnie explained, as the boat past Lussa Bay, 'known simply as the 'Long Road', which stretches for over thirty miles, all the way from the ferry slipway for Islay, at Feolin, to end at a bridge near Inverlussa, where it crosses the Lussa River. From the bridge a road winds down to Inverlussa and Lussa Bay,' which Ronnie pointed out as they reached it. 'Branching from it, a rougher road continues north where Jura's first gin distillery, Lussa, is located - very nice too, the botanicals foraged locally. Beyond there you soon need a four wheel vehicle, especially if you want to reach Barnhill, four miles further on, where George Orwell wrote *1984*, or to reach the north end of Jura, another three miles.'

The boat passed Barnhill, sometime later, Orwell's former rented house, set on a hill overlooking the Sound of Jura.

'So isolated, peaceful, don't know how he could use this environment to conjure such a nightmarish vision,' Ronnie said, trying to make conversation, which had been sparse, so far.

He didn't want to intrude on Gil's space but neither did he want to be unfriendly. So often he felt that his words hung in the air, echoing back to him, unsure whether they had been received.

'You would be surprised,' Gil replied, suddenly breaking his silence, startling Ronnie, 'you can carry a nightmare anywhere, difficult sometimes to get rid of them,' and he stared out to sea again lost in his thoughts.

Two dolphins were now swimming near the boat, their snouts and fins breaking the surface, curious about us. Ronnie relaxed, this is what he had wanted. As he came closer to the shore he scanned the hillside for deer and pointed out a herd.

'Stalkers will never be out of business on this island,' Ronnie claimed, 'only two hundred people but six thousand deer.'

Even Gil smiled, at that familiar description of Jura and its inhabitants used by the whisky distillery in one of its adverts, with the punch line of, 'imagine the stag parties'. The reality of this long, sparsely populated island was beginning to sink in, much of it a wilderness: ideal for what Gil was proposing.

Shortly after Barnhill, Ronnie started to steer the *Casablanca* round the northern tip of Jura. 'Now this is where the trip gets exciting. We are about to turn into the Gulf of Corryvreckan which separates Jura from Scarba, a small island to the north.

You might have noticed that the Sound of Jura is narrowing, as we head north, the gap between Jura and the main land reducing, funnelling the water. The water has to go somewhere and can flood through the Gulf between the islands and as it passes through the gulf of Corryvreckan the tide can race at eight and a half knots, nearly ten miles an hour. What makes it interesting is that there is a deep hole in the Gulf of Corryvreckan; 111 metres deep. You could stack forty four red London double decker buses on top of each other before you would break the surface. The water from the Sound of Jura pours into the deep hole, turbulences are set up by the crags and crevices the water encounters deep under the surface. What exaggerates these is a basalt rock pinnacle just off the north-west side of the Gulf, near Scarba. Seventy metres high, but still thirty metres below the surface, when the water from the Sound of Jura hits it, it can create further turbulence and a whirlpool. It is the third largest whirlpool in the world, one of nature's spectacles. The time of year, the direction of the tide can all combine to create a maelstrom - the water seems alive. At full flow the water races along, with waves reaching thirty feet. Your guests will enjoy the spectacle.'

'How close can we get,' asked Gil.

'Pretty close, depends on the tide, but that is my responsibility. I make these type of decisions.'

'Of course, I expect that,' he replied.

'Today, you might be disappointed; the tides are not combining together to create much turbulence.'

Ronnie took the *Casablanca* into the Gulf keeping close to the northern tip of Jura, pointing out a sea eagle hovering above the hills.

'A lot of caves on this side of Jura,' and Gil seemed to absorb the information, using his binoculars to scrutinise the coastline, 'mainly full of spiders, goat droppings and decaying dead goats.'

Gil seemed unconcerned.

'And don't forget the adders. Few natural predators, shy as they are you will have to be careful not to tread on them or they will strike at you. I once came across an injured adder lying on the road. I thought that it was dead but as I approached it reared up and went to bite me. Got the fright of my life, fortunately its injuries caused it to flop to the ground. I gave it a wide berth.'

Ronnie knew he was still doing most of the talking, not sure what Gil was wanting, but felt that he had to explain the hazards.

Not long after traversing the northern tip of Jura they reached a bay where the waters were not so turbulent. 'We are in now the Bay of the Glen of the Pigs, and that is Eilean Beg,' he pointed out a small island at the mouth of the bay. 'The bay is one place that you could go ashore.'

'Take me in closer, Ronnie, let me see,' and Gil again studied the coastline with his binoculars.

The *Casablanca* then continued west through choppy seas, passing Eilean Mor, another small island, and Ronnie pointed out more turbulence - a waterfall at sea created as the water levels in the area tried to level out, fairly modest today.

'George Orwell almost came a cropper near here, having misjudged the tide times. His boat was being sucked towards the whirlpool, not helped when the outboard sheared off but fortunately he managed to row to Eilean Mor, where the boat capsized, stranding him, before he was picked up by a passing lobster fisherman who saw a fire that he had lit. Might never have been a *1984*. I wonder how we would have described a dystopian society without Orwell's phrases like 'big brother'.

'We would have found plenty of other examples,' Gil replied tersely.

Eventually as the water subsided, Ronnie's boat reached Glengarrisdale Bay.

'Gil, I wanted to especially show you this bay. There is a bothy here, which might prove useful, if you need shelter and there are several caves. You can also trek back up Glen Glengarrisdale which will bring you down eventually to the long road. Useful to know.'

'Thanks, most useful. Good to get an appreciation of the coast. It will help me to plan my activities. I'll come back by foot and trek the area over the next few weeks. Your choice of route back,' and with that the exploration was over.

'Fine, I'll take you around the island. We'll head south to the Sound of Islay and back to Craighouse that way.'

The rest of the voyage was taken mostly in silence, as Gil wrote in a small notebook, a look of concentration on his face, as he tried to commit his thoughts and plans to paper.

5

We had settled in quite quickly to our new house. The empty cardboard boxes were now stacked in the garage and Jenny had taken over the conservatory for her painting. The conservatory, while too small was east facing and that pleased Jenny who wanted the morning light to paint by. A view of the Campsie Hills to the north also pleased her. Light and views were so important to her. She also seemed more relaxed now and was sleeping better with only the odd nightmare.

I had started working, only a twenty minute drive away, at the distillery's main administration and bottling plant, near Glasgow. I worked in a room with four other brand ambassadors, all older but welcoming, and Hector McAlpine, my line manager, a slightly intimidating but warm personality, his persona exaggerated by the bold tartan kilt and tartan waistcoat that he always wore, along with a long mane of white hair usually tied back in a ponytail. You might have expected him to be about to toss the caber at Highland games, but give him a glass of 12 year old Islay and he could caress it gently, describing its virtues in poetic terms that would not have embarrassed Robert Burns himself.

At this stage my job involved visiting groups displaying the wares, letting customers and clients sample the different expressions in our current range; creating an image of quality and heritage to woo them. Hector McAlpine, his presence dominating every room that he was in, had accompanied me on my first few trips, giving me little tips, telling many funny stories. He would tactfully withdraw from the room at times, making an excuse, to leave me to develop further my own skills. He must have liked what he saw as I was being allowed to go to Dumfries in a few weeks to a whisky show on my own.

Ben was on good form having settled into the local primary and loving his teacher, Miss Thompson. She was probably learning a lot about pirates and dinosaurs.

So far so good and after the pain of leaving Islay, we all sensed that there was a life beyond the island. Malcolm had phoned me to ask how we were. He seemed busy and had not had a chance to find out anything about Jason. In a way that was good at the moment. I was desperate to find out more about my son, but if things were easier at home then I didn't want to rock the boat.

As promised Ronnie and Maria were our first guests and arrived, in their blue Mondeo, to stay over. Jenny had been busy preparing a meal, I had prepared the desserts, my banoffee pie, made to my mother's special recipe was highly regarded, and looked out wine to accompany the different courses, and I was intending to open Pence's special whisky sample.

The big change, when they arrived, was in Maria who I had not seen for several weeks. Her hair was now cut short, completely changing her appearance and making her look older. Maybe that was the intention as there was I reckoned eight years between herself and Ronnie. Ronnie had definitely inherited his father's hair genes - he was rapidly thinning on top. We showed our guests to their bedroom - the small box room and warned them that they would have to share the room with some of Jenny's packaging materials, intended for wrapping around customers' orders, and that the walls were paper thin.

The meal went well and the drink flowed. Jenny's chicken casserole was highly praised but so was my banoffee pie. It was good to catch up among friends. To begin with all the talk of what had happened on Islay and in Ayr was avoided and both of us tried to be very positive about the changes; after all a move to the mainland would have happened some time.

After the meal we all settled down with Ben now safely tucked up in bed. Maria was commenting on Jodie's blue eye and tickling her stomach. Pence's bottle had been opened. It was certainly Islay, more heavily peated than usual for our distillery, I thought, more assertive but very pleasant.

We were relaxed, it was a good feeling. Before we could pick up on our conversations from the table, Ronnie coughed and pulled out his iPhone. Maria raised her eyebrows and made a face at Jenny. Jenny laughed and I groaned. We knew what to expect.

'Another film quiz?'

'Yes,' replied Ronnie, 'this time about Scottish locations used in films.' Ronnie certainly was a film buff and we knew what to expect, it was now an after dinner ritual among us.

'First question. Where was the opening sequence in the 1981 film the *Chariots of Fire* filmed?'

'Easy,' said Jenny, and I looked surprised.

'On the beach at St Andrews. I drew some sketches there.'

'Correct,' said Ronnie.

'In the 2006 film the *Da Vinci Code* where were the end sequences filmed.'

'Rosslyn Chapel, south of Edinburgh.' This time it was me.

'Impressive stuff,' said Ronnie, but disappointing stuff from my wife.' Maria playfully kicked him.

And so it went on.

'The next question is definitely one for Peter,' said Ronnie. 'Give the others a chance to answer first.'

'Hey, that's not fair, you're changing the rules,' I complained laughing.

'In the 2012 film the *Angel's Share* filming was conducted at three distilleries. Name two of them.'

Ronnie looked expectantly towards the girls. Jenny shook her head, Maria looked blank.

'Okay, Peter,' he said after a pause.

'Certainly, Balblair distillery.' After that I was stumped.

'Your boss better have a word with you. The other distilleries were Deanston and Glengoyne.'

'Name two castles used as locations in the 1975 film, *Monty Python and the Holy Grail*.'

'Castle Stalker,' said Jenny confidently. 'I also took photographs there and did some sketches for a painting.'

'The other one.'

'I should know this. I had watched the film.' Ronnie waited.

'Castle Doune,' I said, suddenly remembering.

Ronnie looked disappointed.

'Okay, final question, a tie break. Jenny and Peter are level. Maria is nowhere,' and he shook his head at Maria in mock exasperation.

'Ask me some questions about European films,' moaned Maria.

'What was the location used as a backdrop in the film *Monty Python and the Holy Grail*, where the Knights meet Tim the Enchanter?' asked Ronnie ignoring his wife's request.

Ronnie looked around confident that no one would be able to answer.

'Duke's Pass,' I said without hesitation and Ronnie looked surprised.

'I am correct, yes?'

'How did you know?

'Ben and I were walking in that area, near Aberfoyle, with Malcolm and the walking club he has joined, who explore disused railway tracks. One of them was a big Monty Python fan and told us. Also Jenny has an exhibition of her work at Aberfoyle in the next few weeks and that is where the Duke's Pass starts.'

Malcolm had taken up this hobby as soon as he had arrived in Glasgow. It was certainly something that he couldn't do on Islay and as he explained every time he tried to climb a hill it rained or the mist descended, so walks along old railways were more productive.

'I win?'

Ronnie totted up the scores.

'Yes.'

Not often did I beat Ronnie's encyclopaedic knowledge of films, so I continued. 'And there was another film made near there, partly at the village of Gartmore, south of Aberfoyle,' and I looked at Ronnie, who appeared stumped. I waited a minute and then said, 'It was called *Geordie*, a film, made in the 1950s, about an athlete going to the Olympic Games. He leaves for the games from Gartmore station, which they renamed Drumfechan for the film.'

'I'm impressed,' conceded Ronnie.

'Malcolm told me as we walked past the former station site - the railway and station are long gone, just some houses,' triumphant that I could get one over on Ronnie.

Game over, the ritual complete and Jenny and Maria began talking together and I was pleased to see Jenny, slightly flushed with the drink, appear so relaxed. Ronnie began to tell me a bit more about his latest venture and spoke positively about Gil, his new accomplice. Maybe I was wrong, too critical of him, having now learnt about his military background. Afghanistan sounded horrible and while Gil hadn't revealed too many details, he had seen plenty of action.

Maria stood up to pour herself more coffee and sat down again beside Ronnie and turned her attention towards me.

'So Jenny and I have caught up. How are you doing, Peter? Enjoying your new job?'

'Very much so. It's interesting and varied and I am getting about the country a bit more. My line manager, Hector is very helpful, which is good. Living here we feel safer and it is not forever. At the moment that idea seems important,' and I saw Jenny nodding.

Maria paused, briefly looking at Ronnie, but turning away quickly, ignoring what looked like a warning glance from him, determined to raise something, which they must have talked about before this evening.

'Tell me,' she said sitting down with her cup of coffee already half drunk, 'have you found out anything more about, Jason?'

It was my turn to catch the eye of my partner and I saw Jenny draw breath. Maria seemed determined. Ronnie took a quick sip of his whisky.

'Not yet,' I replied, not sure how to respond. I don't know if I wanted this new direction of conversation to be pursued. Jenny understood about Jason, she had told me. The event was in the past, sadly. There was little more to say.

'You know that I am Polish,' Maria said, 'but maybe you didn't know that my family moved to Romania in the mid-nineties, when I was baby, to allow my father to take up a post at Bogdan Voda University, as professor of Economic History. The university is situated just to the west of Cluj-Napoca, one of many universities in the area and Cluj-Napoca itself is one of Romania's largest towns, located to the north-west of Bucharest, in the heart of the Transylvania region - Dracula country. It was big promotion for my father. The university was a new one and had just been opened a few years before and already had a good name for Economics studies. He was, what do you say - head hunted.'

'The university buildings were new but the housing around it was post war housing blocks, Communist era - ten storeys high. We had plenty like that in Poland, I have since discovered. Not well insulated in the cold winters. In Cluj-Napoca there was an attractive old town and given its position equidistant between Bucharest, Budapest and Belgrade, it was quite popular for tourists - a busy nightlife, though obviously it took me many years to discover that.'

Ronnie was staring at his whisky glass, wrapped in his own bubble, which slightly alarmed me. Jenny was intrigued I could see by Maria's tale, which she obviously had not heard before. I was trying to jump ahead wondering where her tale was going, given that it had started with an enquiry about Jason.

'My name is really Marianna but everyone in Romania called me Maria, it is the most popular name there. I was brought up in the country with my older sister, Hanna. She was four years older than me and very attractive. Long dark hair, deep set eyes, long legs, attractive smile.' And to reinforce the message, not that we disbelieved her, she opened her handbag and searched in it, producing a picture of her sister. A beautiful face framed with long dark hair and an attractive alluring smile. Maria was correct and went on. 'What would Ronnie say - a stunner. She was also very clever. My father had arranged for her to study economics abroad.'

'Had,' I thought. A hint of where this was going. Jenny had also picked up on Maria's wording and a look of concern played across her face.

'My parents were strict Catholics, loving and full of faith. They wanted the best for us. Protected us and brought us up as good Catholic girls. They escorted us around the area to church, dancing classes, everywhere. We had to use public transport, since dad had no car for many years; which usually meant long waits at bus stops, freezing in winter and sweltering in summer. We understood their concern because the area we lived in was quite rough. People went missing, especially young girls. We were well warned.'

'In our teens you rebel, don't you,' and Maria looked at us for confirmation. 'By the time that we were allowed to make our own way home from school, we used to linger, talk to our friends, mainly girls, the boys were just football daft. But we always had to be in for a certain time or we would be in trouble.'

'Hanna was the first to go to college and it became clear very soon that she was very bright. My Dad, in particular, was pleased. He arranged for her to go to Bogdan Voda university and was delighted when she chose economics. Hanna was a natural student; the university saw her as a star student.'

'I was more of a rebel and certainly not as bright or good looking. Hanna was special, my dearest friend.' Again I noticed the use of the past tense. 'However, I got into the same course at university when she was in her final year.'

'We started to go into the old town shopping, looking at clothes, the latest fashions, having coffee, enjoying ourselves. I don't think that my parents ever relaxed about our trips, they were more aware of the dangers.'

Maria stopped and I saw Ronnie touch her hand. I offered her more wine to fill the silence, but she shook her head, holding her hand above her empty glass.

Having regained composure she continued. 'One day we met a couple of young men - Vasile and Ion both dark good looking, although Ion had a strange accent, was not a native of our area. They were very good fun. We laughed and joked they even offered us cigarettes. Hanna liked smoking, I hated it but

I liked the glass of wine that they offered. We all met up several times and I could see that Hanna was really interested in Ion - it was mutual, I believed. They would cuddle and kiss each other, but it was light flirty stuff.'

'Our parents soon detected the smoking and were unhappy. Dad was curious about the boys and probed me. I convinced him that it was innocent, although he cautioned me that young men were more forward in sexual matters. That was the first time that he had directly mentioned sex. I just smiled, we had no internet, but there were libraries and TV programmes, so we were not unaware of these matters. We were aware that our bodies had changed, but, let me say, not very wise in the way of the world.'

'I liked Vasile, but he was not a proper boyfriend, and I am not just saying that for Ronnie's sake - we were good friends but I had no further interest. The main deal was between Hanna and Ion. We would leave them and Vasile and I would wander around the central square in the town with its dramatic statue of King Matthias Corvinus, on a plinth, a fifteenth century king, surrounded by knights in armour. We explored the Gothic style St Michaels church, the church towering above the many distinctive red tiled roofs around the square. For me, Vasile was company, nothing more.'

'Our trips gave space for Hanna and Ion or I wouldn't have kept seeing Vasile. We would all meet up again in the early evening and Hanna and I would travel back together. It was then I slowly realised that Hanna was in love. She talked of her feelings and I could see that she was wanting him. I told her to be sure. The thing was that Ion was charming, good looking, good fun, the type that I thought would appeal to Hanna. We shared all secrets, she knew little about his background, his accent explained by spending time in Italy when he was young. We never questioned that.'

'By now my father had used contacts to get Hanna a place at Glasgow University for a one year masters degree. Everything was wonderful. I wondered if she would go, such were her feelings for Ion.'

'One night Hanna came home from seeing Ion, by now she would see him on her own. She had wanted to sleep with him, she told me, but he had refused.'

'Wait until we are married,' he said, and Hanna was frustrated but touched by his manners and knew that Dad would approve. They arranged to go away for a night to visit his parents.'

Maria now held up her wine glass and I filled it quickly. She slurped some of the wine, a few red spots falling on the table top, like drops of blood. She drew breath and I noticed that she and Ronnie were gripping each other's hands, her knuckles white.

'Hanna never returned. She disappeared. That was nearly two years ago. I weep every day but I find it difficult to talk about. My parents are devastated, mum now very ill. Dad a broken man. Their prayers not answered. Why is God so cruel?'

'There was no answer to Hanna's phone or Ion's or Vasile's mobiles, despite many frantic messages being left. We told the police, who were useless. We scoured the streets, put up posters. Hanna had vanished and so had Vasile and Ion. They had said that they lived out of town, and so we had never been to where they stayed. Now that seemed odd, but at the time we just accepted it. A few months later I was walking the streets of the old town and I saw Ion walking with another man, not Vasile. I immediately ran across the street angry.'

"'Where is Hanna?" I screamed in his face.'

"'I don't know you," he replied, lying.'

'I slapped him hard. The other man immediately grabbed me.'

"'What do you want to do with her, Bruno?" he said, gripping my arms tightly as I struggled kicking out at him.'

'Bruno stared at me. "Look Maria if Hanna has not come back it is not my problem. Maybe she has found someone else, wanted away from home." '

'I knew that wasn't true, couldn't be.'

'"He called you Bruno. Who are you?" By now a few people had stopped.'

'"Take my advice," he said, "remember I know where your parents live. They can easily disappear." There was such menace on his face, his personality had changed, the charm had gone. It had all been an act to draw in two gullible girls, one of whom had now disappeared.

He turned laughing to the curious onlookers. "She's pregnant and thinks that I am the father. How would she know who the father is? Go whore, don't bother me."'

'I was pushed roughly to the ground. Bruno knelt over me. "Don't attempt to follow me," he said, and he picked me up holding me tightly, until I felt the outline of a gun under his jacket.'

'"Do you feel that," he said.'

'Turning to the few anxious onlookers, he shouted: "I must be good she still wants me," and he laughed. The people dispersed, one old man looking disgusted at me and spat, on the pavement at my feet.'

'"You should be locked up," he said, and turned away.'

Ronnie's arm was around Maria, a tear was rolling down Jenny's face and I was silent. I knew why she had told the story, but she reinforced it.

'Find out what happened to Jason, it will stop a lot of heartache. Up to now only Ronnie has shared my heartbreak - our secret. My poor Hanna, abducted. Where is she? Is she alive? If so, what are they doing to her? You hear stories. It tortures my mind. I must find out.'

I saw Jenny nod her head slightly. More than ever she understood my inner turmoil. I had to have answers.

6

Malcolm was clear: he didn't wish to talk on the phone but he wanted to meet up for lunch. I noted down an address he gave me, of a bistro in Glasgow's Merchant City and I did a quick calculation - I could make it during my lunchtime.

The eatery was small and private and Malcolm had booked a small cubicle. He was already waiting for me and indicated to the waiter that we wanted to order immediately.

'I recommend the liver pate for starters and the pasta dish on special today.'

I accepted his advice and nodded my agreement to the waiter who then proffered a drinks menu. In unison we shook our heads.

'Soda water and lime, no ice,' I ordered and Malcolm concurred. At least we were making the waiter's job easy.

'I know your time is limited, so is mine but I have something to show you.'

Malcolm seemed suddenly hesitant and studied my face for a minute before producing a brown envelope from his jacket pocket and placing it in front of me.

I picked up the envelope, which wasn't sealed and pulled out two folded pieces of paper. Malcolm was still watching me carefully. I unfolded the first folded sheet of paper: it was a birth certificate - Jason's.

'Oh,' I said involuntarily, my stomach tightening. Here was the proof - I had a son and from a quick calculation - a ten year old son or a son, more correctly, who would have been ten.

The mother was Catherine Robinson and I was listed as the father, occupation student. Catherine must have been determined to get my name on the birth certificate. I wasn't exactly 'Mr Popular', with the Robinsons. Knowing the family, she would have suffered for her loyalty. I had always wondered why the Robinsons loathed me, but that was before I had found out about Jason. To them I was a loafer, with few prospects, a simple island laddie. Catherine had certainly stood by me and while I knew that there was nothing I could do I still felt guilty. I hadn't been there for her.

Jason's full name was Jason Quinn Robinson. I didn't know the relevance of the middle name.

I was still lost in thought when the waiter arrived with our first course.

After a few minutes, studying the birth certificate, I put it to one side and picked up the fork and started to eat. I was still grappling with my thoughts.

Malcolm talked lightly, even inviting me for one of his old railway walks in Galloway on an upcoming Saturday. I think he knew my answer but I felt that he was just trying to be supportive. We talked about his job, which he obviously enjoyed, until the waiter took away our plates, mine half eaten.

I then picked up the other folded sheet and opened it. It was photocopy of a school photo. A class of smiling kids. This time my stomach turned. I didn't need to look at the names underneath the photo - I saw him immediately. Second row, third from left, a smiling face, brown hair, unmistakeably related to me. My son, very like Ben in appearance. I kept my eyes on the picture, partly to hide my emotion, but Malcolm would have seen my eyes when the waiter returned with the next course. This time he made no attempt at small talk and gave me space taking off his glasses and polished them with his hankie, looking into the distance.

I just kept staring for a minute, then confirmed that I was right by checking the names under the photograph - Jason Robinson. I made an attempt to eat the pasta but couldn't have told you any flavour other than an overpowering taste of garlic.

'I found the photo whilst searching through old copies of the local Lanarkshire newspaper on microfiche,' Malcolm explained.

I knew that the Robinsons had moved to Douglas when they had left Islay, a name that meant very little to me. A mining community with a nearby castle, Douglas Castle, now demolished, that was the seat of the Douglas-Homes, one of whom, Alex, became the prime minister in the 1960s. That much I had found out from the internet. It was ironic that their castle had been undermined by mine workings and had become unsafe. Given the wages paid to the miners and the riches of the Douglas-Homes there must have been some sort of justice there.

I didn't know where the Robinsons had lived in the village but the village was obviously big enough to have its own primary school. I looked at the teacher, who must have been nearing sixty, judging from her appearance - carefully coiffured white hair. She would have known Jason, could talk about him, put flesh on the bones, could tell me what happened to him. I hoped that he didn't suffer. I read the caption at the bottom of the photograph - a Mrs Barker, a lady with a kindly smile. Did she like Jason? What were his likes and dislikes? So many questions.

I noticed that Malcolm was finished. I tried to surface from my racing thoughts. He glanced at his watch and finished his drink.

'I have not found out anything else. Can't find any other

details, but I will keep looking.'

I knew what he meant - no death certificate, yet. I wondered what that would reveal. Part of me didn't want to know.

'It's obviously had a big impact on you. I understand. Take time to absorb the information. It must be very hard,' and he leant across, briefly put his arm on my shoulder, a supportive gesture.

'I'll be in touch soon. Okay?'

I nodded.

'This is on me,' he said, as he got up.

I sat on for a few minutes, after Malcolm left, looking at the documents until I heard a cough. It was the waiter and I realised that the bistro had filled up. They needed the cubicle for the next customers. Life goes on whatever happens.

I thanked him, fumbled in my pocket for a tip, and left. Outside the sun was strong, I felt its warmth on my face, which was already flushed. I glanced at my watch, it was time to get back to work. I hoped that Hector would not realise how distracted I was. Ben had a brother - a half brother, but they would never meet. Jenny would probably not want to show him the photograph or tell him until he was much older. I agreed, but as I walked along the busy street, I desperately wanted to know what had happened to my son.

7

Jenny had been very supportive when she saw what Malcolm had found out. 'This is not easy,' she said, adding quickly, 'for you, especially,' but also for her, I understood.

'The picture really brought it home to me. I hadn't expected that, and the birth certificate somehow makes it official. I was surprised my name was on it.'

'I'm not,' said Jenny, 'Catherine was very determined, and she loved you. It was her family's behaviour that drove you apart, not her.'

'She did love me but she was no longer part of my life, even before her death. You are my life along with Ben and I love you.' I said it firmly. This wasn't the time to be too introspective. I needed to respect Jenny.

'How was your day?' I asked, steering the subject away from Malcolm's discoveries.

'Not too bad. I am making progress with the paintings for the exhibition at the Fairy Dell Gallery in a few weeks. Probably, because they had all been started on Islay and I know what I want to do, I can finish them on time.'

It was a good opportunity to exhibit, bring her paintings to a wider audience. The gallery was on the outskirts of Aberfoyle, a village in the Trossachs, close to the Duke's Pass, an important tourist hub, only a half-hour journey to the north from where we stayed. In many ways it was ideal and there was to be an opening social, when Jenny could discuss her work and, hopefully, sell some paintings. We needed the money, Jenny had no other income, her expenses on materials; paints, canvasses and framing were high and my pay was modest.

But the implication of what she said was also clear - there was no fresh inspiration since she had been here. That worried me. Dr Khalid, the GP on Islay, before we left, had warned me to watch Jenny carefully for signs of depression. The events with the Robinsons had taken their toll.

'I almost forgot,' she said, 'Colin phoned,' and a big smile broke out on her face, which I noted with pleasure. It made me realise how infrequent that was these days. 'Mandy is pregnant. Baby due in six months.'

'Wonderful.'

It hadn't been easy for Colin and Mandy. When I first visited them in Ayr, a few months ago Colin had been unfriendly, suspicious of our motives for visiting, had deliberately avoided Jenny over the years. He surprised us by announcing that his father was Charles Robinson, his mother, and Jenny's, having had an affair with Robinson. In a complex family history it also meant that he was a half-brother of Catherine. His treatment of his wife Mandy, was another concern, a typical Robinson trait, when I recollected how badly Charles Robinson had treated his wife, Linda. Colin and Mandy were about to start divorce proceedings when we first visited, but their relationship had since improved and now she was pregnant. They had visited us on Islay, not long after our visit to them, and had been there the day that Charles Robinson had abducted Ben. We were now good friends.

'It is good news, we must visit them soon,' Jenny announced.

We had discovered that their house in Ayr, at the sea front, had partially been bought with gold stolen from the Robinson's farm. The gold bullion that had been brought to Islay on a life raft after the *Empire Constellation* had been sunk by a U-boat off Islay's shore, had been discovered and hidden by the Robinsons, who had lived of their ill-gotten gains for many years. Colin had discovered and taken some of the gold, as a boy, and ultimately sold it, using the proceeds for a deposit on the house in Ayr. He had been pleased by our reaction when he announced the source of the deposit for his house - anyone who stole some of the Robinson's ill-gotten gains gave us satisfaction and we let him know that.

'And,' Jenny added, 'I meant to show you this,' and handed me an air mail letter, from North Dakota.

It was unopened.

'From Sally?'

'I presume so, but given what she and her two American friends did and the consequences, I am not interested,' and she let the letter drop on the coffee table.

Sally, it turned out was a half-sister of Jenny's, another twist in the tale of our recent times on Islay. Their father Ryan Loudon III had died in a plane crash on Islay, but not before making Jenny's mother pregnant. Her American friends, Brian and Jonathon, along with Sally, had blackmailed me into going to the Robinson's farm and exposed me to Desmond McGrory's gang of drug smugglers, the consequences of which, continued to haunt us. Jenny had ruled Sally out of her life, bitter about what she had done, the dangers that she had exposed us to.

'Enough revelations for today,' I suggested, 'let's open a bottle of wine.'

Jenny hesitated but I knew her well enough. Alison was

pregnant, Mandy was pregnant and I knew she wanted another baby. So did I, but maybe this wasn't the best time. And Jason, well that was an added complication.

8

We were on our way, firstly down the M74 and then turning off for Douglas on the trail of Jason. I suddenly understood why the Robinsons moved to Douglas - it was ideally placed for the motorway - drug shipments could quickly be on their way in either direction along the motorway - south to England, north to Glasgow and the central belt of Scotland. Handy location.

Jenny sat beside me, with Ben and the dog in the back. I wanted to go alone - Jenny wouldn't hear of it. I appreciated her support and I hoped that we would get answers. The distance between the motorway and Douglas was only a few miles. We drove through the village, reaching the primary school at the western end, slowing for the traffic calming chicane in front of the school that Jason must have attended.

I soon turned around, finding a cafe behind a petrol station, where we stopped. It had been a long journey, we needed a break.

I had Googled house sales in the area and had identified the Robinson's house. I wanted to see it - curiosity, I suppose. The house had been on the market for a few months and so far no takers. I wondered what had happened to Charles Robinson's wife, Linda, the only one left not dead or in prison pending trial. I had also found an address for Mrs Barker and I was going to pay her a visit.

The Robinson's house was only a short distance away from the cafe and I left Jenny to take Jodie and Ben down to the nearby river, whilst I walked the short distance. We were still close to the primary school. This must have been the route that Jason walked home from school, which gave me a strange feeling and I wanted to absorb each step, follow in his footsteps, as if that might bring me closer to him. Daft, I know.

There was a mixture of detached and semi-detached houses on the left, with a housing development screened by a fence and trees on the right. At the top of the street, up a slight incline, another road joined at right angles and there it was, a detached villa overlooking the village, the 'for sale' sign protruding out of a hedge, which badly needed trimmed.

I looked around, no one was out and about. I walked past it looking in. There was a small garden at the front with a long driveway ending at a detached garage, to the rear of the house, but connected to the house by a secure door and high fence. Empty refuse bins, their lids having been blown open by the wind, one on them on its side, suggested no one was around. At the front of the house was a bay window to one side and a central porch.

A few houses down there was a path leading to the rear. I followed it to the back where there was a grassy slope. I climbed to the top of the slope and walked until I was level with the rear of their house.

There was a swing in the back garden, which touched me. Was this as close as I would get to Jason, who must have played on it? There were no distinctive features to the rear of the house. I hadn't known what to expect and I took several pictures on my phone and continued to study it for several minutes before I noticed at each corner that there was a camera. I also noticed a barred window to the rear of the garage. The house was what I would have expected given what I knew went on there.

I retraced my steps and met Jenny who was waiting for me in the car. I shrugged as I got in and explained what I had seen, which wasn't any great revelation but at least I knew where Jason spent his short life and that somehow was important.

Now for the Barkers, and this would be harder, I wondered what her reaction would be. Mrs Barker's house, a detached bungalow, was part of a small development just off the main road. There were no garages just parking bays in front of the houses. Jenny wished me luck, as I got out the car clutching the brown envelope that Malcolm had given me.

I approached number three, and opened the low gate into a neat garden. I was tense as could be, clearing my throat which was very dry, so that I would speak clearly. I glanced towards the lounge where I could see the light from a television.

I rang the bell and waited. Inside I heard a sound of someone approaching the door and shortly a man opened the door, stooped and very white haired. He smiled pleasantly.

'I wonder if I could speak with your wife, Mr Barker.'

He didn't seem bothered and turned towards the lounge, shouting,

'Sheila, a visitor for you.' he turned back to me: 'Are you from the church?'

I shook my head. The television was muted and presently Mrs Barker appeared, older than the school photograph but still very recognisable and studied me for a minute, looking puzzled.

'You remind me of someone, but I don't think I met you before,' she said eventually, reserved but warm.

'My name is Peter Meldrum and I am the father of one your former pupils, Jason Robinson.'

Her expression changed and she studied me for a minute.

'A lovely boy, very like you in appearance.' I had a sudden thought - I bet that upset the Robinsons, being reminded of me every day. I quickly dismissed the thought.

'I'm not sure how I can help but please come in.'

Her husband who had hung around turned and went into the kitchen where I could see that he was making what looked like jam, in a big metal pot.

From here on I had no script. I sat on the edge of the couch facing Mrs Barker.

'I wanted to find out about my son, Jason.'

Mrs Barker smiled, 'You are very much as Miss Robinson described.' She saw my startled expression.

'She always spoke warmly of you and so did Jason. You were on a long-term assignment abroad - oil industry, somewhere in south-west Asia, I believe.'

I had never heard Islay, so described. I was flummoxed not sure what to say.

'I've missed him, how is he doing?' It took a minute for the words to sink in.

'What!' I sat up straight, confused, 'he is dead.'

'Oh no,' and her eyes filled with tears, her hand covering her mouth, as she gasped.

'Richard,' she shouted, 'come here,' and her husband quickly appeared at the door.

'Mr Meldrum is telling me that his son, Jason Robinson, is dead.'

Something was happening, something not right. I looked from one to the other trying to interpret their expressions.

'How did he die?' asked Richard. Now I was puzzled. I always assumed that he had died here, in Douglas.

'I used to take the football team. He was a good goalkeeper.'

I covered my face with my hands, gradually pulling my hands down until they supported my chin, my heart was thumping.

'Is anything wrong, Mr Meldrum?'

'I am pleased that Catherine spoke well of me, talked about me positively to Jason, but the rest of her family would have nothing to do with me. Until last year I didn't know that I had a son and then I heard that he had died, but I don't know how. I thought that you might be able to help,' and I showed them the birth certificate.

The Barkers looked stunned.

'Did you know that Catherine had passed away?'

Mrs Barker looked very shocked.

'No,' she replied. The news had been hushed up.

'How did Jason die? Was it in an accident with his mother?'

'No, at different times. I was hoping that you would tell me how Jason died.'

'Jason left school just before I retired a year ago. He was fine and healthy then. Miss Robinson explained that he was going to Ireland to live with an uncle. She seemed very worried about him but very vague. I thought that they were going to follow him...'

'You mean he might still be alive?' I interrupted, confused.

'Why not, I never heard from his new school, never got a request for his files. But that often happens if someone moves abroad.'

'Richard get Mr Meldrum a cup of tea. He is upset.'

I was struggling to take all this in.

'Whereabouts in Ireland,' I asked.

'They never said. Miss Robinson did say that she would inform us. She didn't, which was not like her. I saw her once in the village thereafter and she said that there had been some sort of delay. I never saw her after that. But she never said that he had died. I think I would have known.'

I accepted the cup of tea and sipped it.

'Is there someone in your car?' Richard asked, looking out the window, 'your wife?'

'I'll invite her in,' and he left the room.

Minutes later Jenny came in holding Ben by the hand.

'I'm Peter's wife, Jenny,' she said and this Ben our son. What's happening?' She looking anxiously at me, puzzled, as well she might.

I looked at Mrs Barker and then at Jenny.

'Mrs Barker says that Jason left for Ireland to stay with an uncle over a year ago. He was fine then and she hasn't heard otherwise.'

I looked at Mrs Barker for confirmation and she nodded.

'You mean he might still be alive?' Jenny inquired.

'Yes'

'Oh my God. Where in Ireland?'

'I don't know,' said Mrs Barker, 'I wasn't told.'

Jenny stood, clutching the door handle, struggling like me to take this all in.

'Sit down, please,' said Mrs Barker.

'Richard get the lady a cup of tea and the wee boy a glass of orange squash.'

I heard further rumblings in the kitchen.

'Would anyone know where Jason might be?

'His grandparents, I suppose.' And I suddenly realised that she wouldn't know anything about Charles Robinson. It would take too long to explain. No court case yet. Nick, who was in charge of the operation, had imposed a strict embargo. Charles Robinson, it was declared had died, the result of a fall, but he hadn't been named in the national papers.

'But I noticed that they have moved, the house is up for sale. Not Mrs Robinson, of course...'

'Why not?'

'She is in a care home, suffering from dementia. Has been for many years.'

'Whereabouts?'

'Not sure.' She thought for a minute. 'I think Kathy, the school secretary, said that she came across her when she was visiting her Mum. Cumnock, that's the place, a small town, in Ayrshire, about twenty miles west of here. Not sure which care home. There may be several, but it won't help you, I believe that she was pretty bad.'

So Jason was lost not dead. But why would a family send away their son? Even for the Robinsons that seemed cold hearted, but for Catherine it just didn't ring true. We left the house, an hour later, our trip back made in silence, neither of us able to absorb what we had just learnt. Jason was alive but lost somewhere in Ireland and the only person who might be able to tell us had lost her mind.

9

I took time out during a coffee break to phone around the various care homes in the Cumnock area, and on the third attempt I was successful. The woman who answered, the manager who was called Ella, took my name, said that she would pass on my best wishes to Mrs Robinson, and gave the visiting times.

An hour later she phoned back asking to speak to me, but Hector picked up the phone. I was just coming back into the office, from lunch, when I heard him say, 'Sorry, but we can't give out personal phone numbers of staff,' and he hung on the phone while the other person presumably continued to speak, before repeating what he had said about giving out personal numbers and put down the phone. He looked up at me, rubbing his long beard thoughtfully.

'That was Ella from the care home where Mrs Robinson resides. She was following up your recent enquiry,' and his eyebrows rose slightly, 'wanted to inform you that Mrs Robinson is not too good and it would be better if you phoned in advance, so that they could have her ready.'

Then he added as an afterthought, 'Something about her I didn't like. Not sure what, just instinct.' Hector was no one's fool, a shrewd judge of character.

I picked up on his concern. 'I'll arrive unannounced.'

Hector responded with a smile and nodded.

He must have made the connection with the Robinson's name and I know that Pence had spoken with him about recent events but he said nothing more.

. . .

It might be a wasted journey but I had to try and decided to go down the following weekend on the Saturday afternoon. Partly, because Ronnie and Maria were again staying for the weekend and he offered to drive me to Cumnock especially when he heard the latest revelations about Jason, like me anxious to find answers. It also allowed Jenny to visit her brother, in Ayr, taking Ben, Jodie and Maria with her.

After an hour we were approaching Cumnock, entering the heart of Ayrshire's former coal field. I even spotted an A-frame of an old pithead on the approach to the town. This area was all new to me. We turned off the main road and following the sat-nav quickly finding the Glaisnock Water Care Home, located on the outskirts of the town, at a junction, beside traffic lights. The care home was at the end of a cul-de-sac, the area around the home was still being redeveloped, according to a sign, and the care home was the first fruit, the rest of the land looked like it had been occupied by former industrial buildings, rubble, bricks and concrete, littering the uneven ground.

The care home was a low single storey brick building based on a central hub with residential wings fanning out from the hub, set in landscaped gardens, surrounded by a low stone wall. Several small trees were planted in the gardens and there were several benches, one of the benches occupied by an old man, leaning on his walking stick, an auxiliary sitting beside him.

It was unlikely that Linda Robinson would make much sense, but and it was a big but, maybe there would be photos or some memorabilia that could help me in my quest.

Ronnie turned the car around at the end of the cul-de-sac and parked by the main gate, ignoring the car park to the rear of the nursing home.

'I'll wait outside in the car,' said Ronnie and I agreed. There was no point in him coming in and I felt anxious glad that he was waiting for me; ready to get away.

'Maybe afterwards we can join the girls in Ayr, it is not a long detour. See you shortly,' I said, as I left the car, walking up the path towards the main entrance, a sign gave visiting times, which had just started, although there were, as yet, no signs of visitors.

I pressed the intercom. 'Visitor for Mrs Linda Robinson,' I stated, and after a brief pause there was a click and I was able to pull the door open.

The main desk was to one side, beside toilets, and seating for visitors and as I approached it, I saw a board giving patient names and rooms. I scanned the board until I saw Linda's name. I was also aware of a smell of disinfectant, quite strong, not too pleasant. There was an office behind the main desk. A woman, probably in her fifties, hair harshly dyed, came out from an office to the rear of the main desk and her name badge confirmed that it was Ella.

'Are you, Mr Meldrum?' she was clipped, quite cold, as if she was annoyed.

'Yes.'

'I asked you to let me know when you were coming, we are short staffed.'

'I didn't receive any message,' I lied, taking an instant dislike to her, picking up on Hector's instinct.

'Have a seat, you will have to wait, I'm afraid,' and she pointed to a seat beside the main desk and went back into the office quickly. I sat down for a minute, looking around and then spotting information leaflets I got up to collect one, and saw that she was on the phone her back turned to me. As I leant over the desk to get the leaflet, I noticed a post-it note stuck to the surface by a computer terminal. The message made me shiver.

'If a Peter Meldrum visits immediately contact this number. Delay him!'

Alarm bells rang in my head. I snatched the leaflet and sat down.

Ella came out of the back office and briefly looked flustered, before she smiled, regaining her composure.

'The auxiliaries say that she is sleeping. Hasn't been too good recently, her dementia is far advanced. Can you wait a few minutes, I'll order you a coffee. What do you take? Do you want biscuits?'

'Yes coffee, black, no sugar. No biscuits.'

She disappeared out another door at the back of the office to collect the coffee. I was worried now, not sure what to do. I decided to text Ronnie, telling him to be vigilant, but I had come this far, so there was no going back.

It was five minutes before she returned with the coffee. Was that deliberate?

I accepted the coffee, smiled at her, but there was no small talk, she seemed nervous. I drank the coffee quickly and put the cup down.

I got up: 'Can I use the toilet?' I half expected her to say no.

She nodded and curtly turned away.

Inside the toilet I waited a minute, then eased the door open and saw that she had gone back into the office. I slipped out and ran along the corridor - Room 6A, west wing. I glanced around but didn't see any cameras. I only had a few minutes before she would rumble what I had done.

I reached the door, which mercifully was unlocked and

85

quickly entered it. An old woman was lying on a single bed, asleep, her face lined and her hair pure white. It took me a minute to realise that it was Mrs Robinson. Age and no doubt her husband had taken a savage toll on her. She lay motionless, her mouth half open, breathing deeply, occasionally snoring. She wasn't capable of telling me anything, but I need to discover if there was something in the room, an address book, a diary that might be useful. I looked in the bedside drawer, nothing other than a Gideon's Bible. I looked under the bed, just a spare blanket. I looked around the room. There were patio doors, but they were locked and a small ensuite toilet and shower. I glanced in the ensuite and there was a window partly open for ventilation. No old person could get through that space but I reckoned with a squeeze that I could. I opened it fully, escape insurance. On the corridor wall there was a fitted wardrobe with sliding doors. I slide back the door. There were a few clothes hanging from a rail and a top shelf. I stretched up to look at it - a few folded towels, some incontinence pads and then at the back I noticed a cardboard box and I jumped up and grabbed it.

My phone went ping and I stopped to look at the message.

It was from Ronnie.

'Car drove up very fast and what I could only describe as two thugs got out. Be careful.'

I didn't have time to reply. I took the lid off the top of the box and examined the contents. There was an address book and I flicked through the pages and saw my old number from Machir Bay. I stuffed it in my pocket as it wouldn't be of use to Mrs Robinson. There were a few sheets of paper, but they were blank and bizarrely a knitting pattern.

I put the lid back on and shoved the box back on the shelf.

Then I heard feet running along the corridor. I had no time to get out the bathroom window and slipped into the wardrobe crouching down, pulling the sliding door almost shut, leaving just a crack, but hiding myself behind the hanging clothes, trying to control my breathing.

The door was flung open and two men burst in and through the gap in the door I could see that one was tall and lean, and carried an attaché case; the other was also tall but more thick set with cropped hair.

'Where is the bastard?' the tall one proclaimed.

He flung open the sliding door, fortunately at the opposite end, but the other man shouted, 'He's gone out the window,' and he ran into the toilet jumped on the toilet bowl and manoeuvred himself quickly through it and a second later I saw him running across the grass outside the window, looking around.

The other man calmly placed the attaché case on the bed and opened it and took out a vial of a colourless liquid and a syringe, removed the protective cap from it, and drew some of the liquid into the syringe and put it on the bed. I felt sick. I could only imagine my fate.

Then there was a ping and another message on my phone.

Immediately, the man turned around. I had to react instantly. I pushed back the clothes on the rail and the sliding the door so hard it hit the stop at the far end and bounced partly back. I ran out shouting and jumped, kicking him hard on his knee, which made him stagger. He grunted and I punched him in the face, blood spurting from his nose. He rocked but didn't go down, so I grabbed the syringe from the bed and plunged it into his arm, disgorging some of its contents. Why should I bother what it did to him, after all it was intended for me.

The effect was immediate, and dramatic, he simply slumped and fell to the ground. I grabbed the vial, capped the syringe and stuck them in my pocket. I didn't want the other man getting it and it might prove useful.

I almost screamed as a hand suddenly grabbed me. Mrs Robinson was sitting up in bed and was clutching my hand. In what, I imagine, was a rare moment of lucidity, she said, 'Peter, how nice to see you, have you come to see Catherine?'

I looked up to see that I had been spotted by the other guy, who was racing towards the bathroom window, to scramble though it. I left Mrs Robinson looking momentarily puzzled as I quickly turned and opened the corridor door sprinting towards the end of the corridor where there was a fire door. It was alarmed, but I didn't care. I pushed the release bar and ran out around the side of the building, emerging not far from Ronnie's car. There was a bench against the outside wall and I pulled it quickly from the wall forming, I hoped, an obstacle for my chaser. I saw the auxiliary, who I had seen earlier, with the old man, getting up shouting at me, but stopping as my chaser shouted something, pushing the bench aside as he chased me, and she grabbed the old man, not sure what was going to happen next.

Ronnie was just getting out of the car anxious about what was happening. I screamed, 'Get in,' as I heard a shout from behind, it was the other man catching up, ten yards behind, picking up speed.

Ronnie saw the danger and jumped into the car, starting the engine. He stalled it in his haste and I could see him trying again as I vaulted the low wall and I jumped in, locking the door. The engine roared as Ronnie put his foot down, as the man, his face snarling in fury, reached the door tugging at the door handle. The car sped away and the man ran after us as we headed towards the traffic lights, which were set at red. As we approached the traffic lights they started to change and Ronnie flung the car around the corner leaving the man well behind. I was shaking, wanting to be sick. Ronnie was ashen.

'What is it about the bloody Robinsons, they're always

trouble.'

I didn't need to say anything in reply, just panicking about the possible consequences.

10

We were both silent for the first few minutes, Ronnie anxiously looking in the rear view mirror for signs of pursuit. When I had controlled my breathing I quickly explained what had happened.

'They are going to be as angry as hell,' said Ronnie.

'They must have put a message on the care home's system, to alert them if I turned up. The manageress was also fishing for my mobile number, but Hector wouldn't give it.'

I buried my head in my hands when I realised the pressure this would put on Jenny.

Ronnie must have read my mind.

'Don't tell Jenny, certainly not at the minute. It wouldn't do her any good. Maria is worried about her.'

So was I.

'Let's head to Ayr and catch up with them,' and Ronnie agreed. We took a different road passing Dumfries House, a local stately pile and after twenty minutes we were approaching the outskirts of Ayr.

It was only then when I had calmed down that I suddenly remembered the address book that I had taken from Mrs Robinson's room and fished it out of my pocket. It was old, some of the telephone numbers even had letters, as a prefix, not numbers. Jason's name didn't appear, not surprisingly. Quinn was his middle name so I thumbed to the back of the address book and looked for 'Q'. There it was - Quinn with a long number, which started 00 353..., an international number.

So Mrs Robinson knew someone called Quinn in Ireland. This was worth checking, maybe they knew the whereabouts of Jason.

I took out my mobile and phoned Malcolm.

'Hi Malcolm,' I started.

'Peter, you are lucky to get me, I've just been walking an old railway track and have just reached Creetown, come down out of the hills. I had no signal until a few minutes ago when messages started arriving. How can I help?'

I quickly explained.

'I'll get back to you tomorrow,' he replied,' it shouldn't be difficult.'

We arrived at Colin's house in Ayr a few minutes later. It was a beautiful day, the sea blue and the island of Arran with its rugged high peaks appearing very close, although almost twenty-two miles away. As Ronnie parked the car Jenny came out in tears, not a good sign. I said nothing about Jason, I agreed with Ronnie, it wasn't the time.

'Jodie has injured her right hind leg - I think that it's a cruciate ligament injury. She was just running along the beach, when she pulled up and started to limp.'

I hugged her and saw Ben come out, very subdued.

'She'll be fine,' I said, trying to be reassuring.

'The vet's been,' Jenny said, ' and it will be expensive. I don't know how we can afford it,' and she was close to tears.

Nor did I, but I would worry about that later. Dogs were too important, we would do it somehow. 'We'll find a way,' I answered, and I saw Ben who had now joined us smile.

I remembered my last visit and the cold welcome from Colin, but this time was different. He was smiling and warm and Mandy appeared, no bump showing yet, but her face radiant, infused with happiness. What a contrast.

I shook Colin's hand and embraced Mandy and congratulated her.

'We have a lot to thank you for,' she said. 'Your visit gave us a fresh start, got us talking.'

Maria appeared shyly by the door and waited for Ronnie to join us.

Inside Jodie was lying on the floor her tail beating the carpet, pleased to see me as I bent down to pat her and stroke her gently. If she had been fit, her face would have been buried in me, nuzzling against me, welcoming me, but not today; she was in pain not moving. The soft expression on her face was melting my heart, her blue eye, if anything, making her appear more vulnerable.

'What did the vet say?' I asked, once the greetings had been made.

'She'll need an operation,' said Jenny, 'what was it the vet called it?' and she looked around at the others.

'TPLO,' said Maria.

'Sounds complicated, whatever it means,' I answered.

'The local vet, who seems to be very good, young and yet experienced, can do it, but will need to keep an eye on her,' said Colin.

'We'll pay for the operation,' he announced, unexpectedly, and held up his hands as Jenny started to protest. 'We can afford it,' and Mandy agreed refusing to take no for an answer.

'We will look after her here and bring her back when she's deemed fit.'

Jenny hugged Colin. 'Thank-you,' she said.

'That's wonderful,' I added, 'it's a massive help.'

'Settled then, and I will phone the vet. The operation can be done tomorrow.'

Colin and Mandy had prepared a meal and while they were setting the table I told Jenny, something of the visit, emphasising that I had got a phone number in Ireland for somebody called Quinn. Jenny was beginning to relax and seemed pleased for me. Little did she know - I had stirred up a hornet's nest. What a nightmare. I so wanted to find out the truth about Jason, but I certainly hadn't wanted to place Jenny or Ben in further peril.

The meal was almost over, when I felt my phone ping. I glanced at the message. My heart sank - it was from Alan Siviter, the app on my phone which connected me to Nick and his team, who had been involved in busting Desmond McGrory's drug ring on Islay.

'Contact me,' it read, 'immediately.'

Jenny noticed my reaction.

'It's a message from Hector,' I lied, 'I'll take it outside.'

The connection was made immediately.

'I'm Steve,' said the voice at the other end.

'Nick is not here at present. I work for him. The app allows us to locate you at any time. You are standing in front of your wife's half-brother, Colin's house. Why were you in the Cumnock area this afternoon?' he added, getting to the point.

'Visiting Mrs Robinson to see if she had information about, Jason, the boy I fathered with Catherine Robinson.'

'What happened at the care home?

I explained.

'The police were called, something about a running fight and a man collapsed on a bed in one of the rooms. He has recovered, claimed that he had taken a funny turn. Neither wants to say anything more. I have spoken with the police inspector. A report will be filed and forgotten.'

'Thank-you,' I replied.

'You were very fortunate. You will need to be more careful, make sure that everyone carries their phone with them at all times. McGrory will be less than pleased and he is not a nice man. You have come to his attention again. Need I say more. I will let Nick know what happened,' and the phone went dead.

I was concentrating so hard that I hadn't realised that Jenny was standing behind me.

'Don't lie to me, ever,' she said, biting her lip, trying to suppress her anger.

11

Life had not been easy since we returned home. We didn't talk in the car, other than a few words about Jodie, not wanting Ben to overhear. Ronnie and Maria were still staying with us, and indeed had extended their visit, and that prevented the two of us being able to talk through the issues, especially with the thin walls in the house.

Malcolm phoned the next day. 'The number belongs to a Quinn O'Halloran, who has a farm, north of Dunquin, in County Kerry.' He gave me the details that he had. The farm was located in the south-west of Ireland on the Dingle peninsula.

I thanked him.

'I suppose that you'll want to check it out and see if they know about Jason.'

'I have to find out,' I replied.

When I got off the phone Ronnie and Maria had taken Ben out to the local swing park, something that I am sure had been arranged on our behalf, and as soon as the door had closed, Jenny grabbed me putting her arms around my neck but holding me at a distance so that she could study my face.

'I had no problem with you going to see Catherine's mother and I know that you were doing what you thought was for the best. You didn't want to frighten me about what happened at the nursing home, I understand that, but we must always tell each other the truth. Promise,' and she looked me straight in the eyes, holding my gaze, her green eyes probing me, waiting for my response.

'Yes,' I replied, leaning forward slightly kissing her head. I knew how much I loved her, but also how much she was suffering, anxious that something bad might happen again.

'You must go to Ireland and find Jason, if he's there. Maria said that Ronnie will go with you. Colin has invited Maria and me down to Ayr with Ben next weekend, which is a holiday weekend, fortunately. We can be with Jodie and I can paint down there. I need to get more paintings finished for the Fairy Dell exhibition, it starts in less than two weeks and I still need to frame some of the paintings.'

Jenny had it all worked out. What could I say, as I drew her closer; she was remarkable.

. . .

Back at work on the Monday, I explained to Hector, something of why I was going to Ireland and requested a couple of days off. It was a long journey, nearly 350 miles from Larne, in Northern Ireland and that after a two hour trip in Scotland. Even leaving on the Friday evening, it would be late on Saturday before we arrived in the area. Hector gave me a searching look but agreed and we then joined the others in our meeting room which was separated by a glass partition from our communal office.

Hector started our regular weekly team meeting by saying not to be distracted, but while we were in the meeting our computer systems were going to be upgraded. Soon he was talking about some new Islay bottlings that were about to be launched, the markets they were aimed for and the taste profile that made them different. I soon was lost in the nuances of whisky tasting, mainly by nose and then by sips of the different bottlings, being tutored in a master class by a real expert. My confidence in understanding the subtleties of whisky was improving but I still had a long way to go. It was not a bad way to spend a Monday morning and as we returned to the office, the computer technician, a young woman, in her twenties, with short blonde hair and wearing a blue sweatshirt with a company badge displayed on it, was just closing her case.

'All upgraded as requested,' she stated to Hector, as she got up to leave. 'You're machines should be working faster.'

At lunchtime I had the bonus of a chance meeting with Pence Gifford who was coming out of the blending room as I passed. He stopped immediately to speak with me, warm as usual.

'I am pleased that you are doing so well. Hector can be a hard man to please with his passion for promoting whisky but he sees potential in you. Stick in. I hear that you are going to Ireland?'

I explained about Jason.

'If it works out you'll get closure. I almost forgot,' he added, 'I've managed to rent out your house to a young Geography teacher and his wife - a Johnnie Galbraith. He'll pay rent to the company at the end of each month and the money will be transferred into your account the next day. I'll deal with any problems, but I don't suspect there will be any.'

I thanked him again and told him I had enjoyed the whisky sample that he had given me as a parting gift when I left Islay, but he almost seemed embarrassed.

'Only too pleased to support you,' he replied, 'and take care of Jenny and Ben. Pass on my best wishes,' and he turned away.

Without his help I would be in a poorer position. And the rent money was vital.

12

We were fortunate to buy tickets for the sea crossing to Larne, given that it was a holiday weekend and all the ferries were very busy. Ronnie was driving, at least on the first leg to Cairnryan. I had wanted to call in on Jodie when we were passing by Ayr, but time did not permit, the A77 south of Ayr was slow at the best of times, and time was tight. Jodie had had her operation and was recovering. A success the vet had declared, but it would be a while before she recovered fully.

As we waited in our car lane to drive onto the ferry, Ronnie pointed out that the ferry terminal was built on part of the site of the former Cairnryan Military Port No 2. From this military port, in 1944, the *Empire Constellation* had departed on its ill-fated journey, with its cargo of gold, over seventy years ago. Its sinking, by an enemy U-boat, had changed my life, an unforeseen consequence of enemy action, that had rippled down through time. The gold salvaged by the Robinsons from the ship had corrupted them, led them into crime which had ultimately produced the chain of events which had led to Catherine's death and the search for my son.

The journey lasted over two hours, as the ferry edged slowly across the Irish Channel, also taking a long time to dock at Larne in Northern Ireland and unload its cargo of cars and trucks. It was nearly seven o'clock before we eventually departed Larne, on an elevated section of roadway perched above the small town, dominated by a large power station, starting the journey south, the initial part through Northern Ireland.

We bypassed Belfast and headed down the motorway towards Dublin, crossing the border, into the Republic, where Ronnie's foresight paid off as he had signed up for a toll tag account to enable us to avoid having to stop to pay tolls on the republic's toll roads.

This was my first excursion out of my own country even if in many ways Ireland didn't seem a foreign country because you could often see, from Islay, the northern coast of Ireland, stretching all the way from Rathlin Island to Donegal. Indeed, it seemed strange to be on the other side of the North Channel, the stretch of water that separated Islay from Ireland. We skirted Dublin to reach the N7 motorway, and continued driving, for a further hour, until we reached Kildare where Ronnie had booked accommodation for the night.

The next morning was cloudy, eventually becoming sweeping rain which seemed to dampen our spirits with our conversation more sporadic, less animated than the night before, when we were busy talking about Guinness and all things Irish, including films produced in the country, like John Wayne's, *The Quiet Man*. Ronnie's knowledge was as usual encyclopaedic.

By mid-morning we stopped at a little town, called Adare, and had a coffee break. It lay to the south west of Limerick, where Desmond McGrory's drug empire had originated. I switched on the radio just to blank out the negative thoughts I was having about the drug baron as we passed near his home town.

The roads were slower after Adare and trucks often held us back, difficult to pass. It was early afternoon before we were driving along the southern edge of the Dingle peninsula, one of several peninsulas in the south west of Ireland stretching out into the Atlantic, like the tentacles of a jellyfish. The sun was now out and we could begin to appreciate the beauty of the countryside looking south over Dingle Bay to the area known as the Ring of Kerry, green hills stretching out in the distance. By late afternoon we had reached Dingle, a small fishing port, and stopped for fish and chips in one of the many cafes and took a quick look around to stretch our legs.

Dunquin was now only half-an-hour away. The road by Slea Head to Dunquin was both spectacular and narrow, sometimes perched on the very edge of steep cliffs which tumbled down to what was a frothing turbulent sea. Large waves crashed against the cliffs as they had done for many millennia. This was where the Atlantic Ocean met Europe. We passed the roadside shrine of the white marble statue of the crucified Christ with statues of three women bowing at his feet.

'Prayer,' Ronnie muttered, 'you need that on this road,' as tired and exhausted after a long journey, we finally approached Dunquin. Out to sea were the Blasket islands, a group of now uninhabited islands reached by boats from Dunquin harbour or from Dingle, the dying sun highlighted their silhouette of craggy rocks, the sky turning red burning up the sea. The view was stunning, which temporarily dulled the tension I felt as we reached our destination.

'Do you recognise the view?' asked Ronnie, not waiting for my reply, 'it forms the backdrop to one of my favourite films, *Ryan's Daughter*. You didn't think I came here just to keep you company,' and he laughed, displaying his usual good spirits.

The village consisted of houses scattered across the lower slopes of the surrounding hills, with more houses nearer to the sea and surprisingly to us, a low long heritage centre to commemorate the lives and heritage of the Blasket islanders.

We quickly found our bed and breakfast accommodation, a bungalow at the end of a rough track, run by an elderly couple, Dan and Kayna Maguire, who made us welcome and gave us tea and soda bread spread with homemade jam. Dan worked for a local fisherman and was a retired fire fighter, keen to share his knowledge of the local area and its history.

We chatted some time, telling them about Scotland, Islay and, of course, whisky, but I was wound up and soon brought the conversation around to the O'Hallorans, fishing for any nuggets of information.

'Quinn's farm,' said the husband, 'not many go there. Keep themselves to themselves. Both must be eighty now,' and he looked to his wife for confirmation and she agreed.

'What takes you there?'

'We are sightseeing, but an old aunt suggested we look him up while we were here. I think that she was an old flame, wanting to know what happened to him,' I smiled, hoping that my reason did not sound too feeble.

'That must have been a long time ago. They live their own life and don't bother anyone, refuse help in running the farm, even at their age they are fiercely independent. We see them occasionally at market, but I've never really spoken to them,' replied the wife, 'your aunt must have been some woman to appeal to Quinn.'

No mention of a young boy staying there then, which was disappointing. It didn't look promising for our visit to the farm the next day.

Ronnie soon moved the conversation on and was talking to them about the film, *Ryan's Daughter*, delighted to find Kayna had met Robert Mitchum the male lead, and had been star struck by him and been used as an extra, one of the pupils in Mitchum's class. Ronnie was impressed, even more so when Kayna went to the sideboard and pulled a signed photograph of the star from a drawer and another of herself and a group of pupils dressed up for a scene, in period clothes, taken on rocks beside the schoolhouse used in the film.

Not many Hollywood heroes arrived in the area. The film had transformed the economy of what was then a really poor area and was still attracting visitors. Mitchum played the role of a middle-aged school teacher who married a young Sarah Miles, who was soon bored with him and had started an affair with an English officer, which led to tragedy. The film company had even built a school house, which featured in many scenes, and still survived. There was little left of the other local locations, like the village built for the film or the army camp. They described the location of the schoolhouse set and I presumed at some point we would be visiting it; Ronnie's interested aroused. Many cast members had enjoyed parties at the local bar Kruger's, with the locals, swilling back pints of the black stuff. I also guessed correctly that Ronnie would want to visit the bar. It would do no harm and a couple of pints would help relax us after the long drive.

. . .

So a little later we walked to Kruger's Bar, up the hill past the Blasket Centre. Kruger's had the added distinction of being the most westerly bar in Europe and where the committee for the Campaign for Real Ale had been formed, many years previously. We ordered pints of Guinness, what else, and sat by the window overlooking the sea. Ronnie took a few sips and then pint in hand was up examining the many framed pictures, hanging on the wall, of scenes and characters from *Ryan's Daughter* and another film called *Far and Away*, also set in the area, starring Tom Cruise and Nicole Kidman.

Quite a number of locals were arriving, by the sound of their accents and the bar soon started to fill up. Many seemed to know each other and soon there was a healthy noise of laughter and voices competing with each other, many speaking in Gaelic, this area was still a stronghold of the ancient language. A late arrival, overdue by the welcome and banter he received on his arrival, took a fiddle out of a case and soon started to play, accompanied by clapping and some singing.

About twenty minutes after, I noticed a man arriving on his own, with shoulder length hair, wearing a dark grey shirt and denims. No one acknowledged him and he stood with his back to the bar, elbow resting on the bar counter nursing a pint of Guinness, surveying the scene. After a few minutes, he slowly wandered across to my table, where there were still a few spare seats. As he approached I saw that his long hair was turning grey, especially at the temples, his face lined, his chin pointed, his hair hanging over his body like a mop head over the pole. His head lowered avoiding eye contact.

He pointed to one of the seats and I nodded, not bothered that he was joining us. Ronnie eventually came back, his pint half finished and sat down smiling briefly at the man, before turning to me full of enthusiasm about what he discovered about the films shot on location near here.

We eventually started talking, guardedly, about our visit to Quinn's farm not mentioning any names. You could never be too careful, I had discovered.

I was aware that the man had started to study the two of us and was going to change the conversation back to films, when he said: 'Are you here to look for Jason by any chance?' Both of us looked startled, my stomach flipped, my mouth opened searching for words but before I could say anything, he went on, 'Come on, Peter, you haven't come here for the scenery or old film locations, have you?' Then he turned to Ronnie. 'Maybe you have,' his manner clipped, not over friendly.

Before we could say anything or react in anyway, he took out his phone and began to text someone and a minute later sent it. My phone pinged - message from Alan Siviter and he leant across and showed me the text he had sent to confirm the connection.

'Lucky, I am a friend,' he stated, 'you two are very careless, heading for trouble. Let me introduce myself, I'm Steve, I spoke to you last week. Surprised you don't recognise my voice. I have followed you from Cairnryan on your quest for your lost son. You didn't know did you?' and he shook his head, his long hair swishing across his face, like a curtain. 'Spent the night in Kildare, had coffee in Adare, ate fish and chips in Dingle and you Ronnie were looking at the bronze statue of Fungie, the resident Dingle dolphin, outside the tourist board office while you were eating a fish supper.'

'I work for Nick, if you haven't already guessed, who is now very worried about the both of you. Wanted me to keep an eye on you.'

'Because of Cumnock?'

'Yeah, that was stupid, but our intelligence suggests that McGrory had already taken a big interest in you and your son, Jason - he only found out that you had a son with Catherine, shortly before Catherine revisited Islay. He was obsessed with her but what shall we say, he doesn't like to share. Exclusive type. You spoiled that, didn't you, Peter? People have to pay when they cross him. You won't be the first!'

I was stunned, turning to Ronnie for his reaction but he was silent, his face fixed, looking shocked, but no doubt like me trying to absorb what he had just been told.

Steve went on: 'This is his backyard, for goodness sake. He has a large house just up the road, near Ballyferriter just north of Dunquin, which he uses for weekend parties. He's not in the country at present but he has many eyes and ears around here.

See the group by the table at the door. Don't all turn and look at once,' he said, exasperated. The guy with the leather jacket and fiddling with his earring - O'Brien is his name. He works for McGrory. Not a nice piece of work.'

'So why would Catherine hide Jason here, if it is so dangerous?'

'Didn't have any other relations, so no choice. She thought that her son, sorry also your son, was safe here. But, as you know, events on Islay when she saved you, alerted McGrory. She had crossed him - that's why he had her killed by her brother, no less. Until then Jason probably was safe, hidden from sight, not that he lives here now, I think, on a regular basis. But it would be the last place that McGrory, would think of searching,' and Steve had ensured that his voice was low, couldn't be overheard. 'Now, your penchant for creating mayhem, has been noted - Islay first, being tricked into going to the Robinson's farm by the Americans, turning up at Linda's care home. The talk is that he wants to meet you, something that I would strongly advise against.'

I sipped my pint, a reaction to buy time, while I worked out how to react to what Steve had said, and a second later Ronnie did the same, finishing his pint in a few deep gulps.

'You are a long way from home,' Steve added ominously, 'and if you are discovered, you might never return.'

I felt an even bigger guilt trip. My actions had not only put me at risk but also those of Jenny, Ben and now Jason. Ronnie and Maria were also in danger. Life has consequences as the Rev Walker was fond of saying and it seemed that Desmond McGrory was not in the forgiving business.

I stared out of the window, the night had now fallen, and saw my reflection in the window. I looked as if I had seen a ghost, the crowd of people behind me, also reflected in the glass appeared like a gang of ghouls discussing my fate.

Steve stood up to leave a few minutes later. 'Having come this far,' he said, 'I know that you will still want to try and see Jason - you are a determined type, but don't hang around a moment longer than you have to. Over here you are very isolated and we don't have as many good contacts with the local police and the app only worked because I was close to you,' he added.

'Where are you going?' I asked, alarmed that he was leaving.

'To sleep, it has been a hell of a long drive. You are not my only case, but certainly the hardest work and I have to be elsewhere tomorrow,' and he paused, as if he was going to say something more, eventually adding, 'take care,' and with that parting shot he was gone.

...

We left Kruger's bar, not long after Steve, and walked back. Neither of us talked until we were clear of the bar.

'I'm sorry that I have got you into such trouble,' I said, apologetically.

Ronnie shrugged: 'Quite a chain of events. Not much you could have done about it. We'll just have to deal with it.' The sentences stumbling out disjointed, staccato like. 'Hopefully, we can leave here soon, I feel quite uncomfortable,' he added.

'Me too,' but then I was here by choice, Ronnie was putting himself at risk because of his loyalty to me.

The rest of the walk was made in silence as we made our way back to our beds, not that I would imagine that either of us would sleep. O'Brien had given us a cold stare as we left, but he probably did that to all newcomers, I hoped.

13

It was with some trepidation that we turned off the road, the next morning, and headed up the dirt track towards Quinn's farm. The track was potholed, with a high central strip of grass, all of which slowed us down, the Mondeo's exhaust scraping the ground. High bushes of red fuchsia lined each side until we reached the end where the track widened into a small farmyard. Several old ploughs covered in moss and slime were seemingly abandoned in one corner, at the side of a ramshackle barn. In front of the barn was a battered, rusting pick-up, with a cracked windscreen. At right angles to the barn was a small farmhouse, once white, now tarnished by age and peeling paint. The main door was at one end, part of a small porch, with three windows facing the farmyard. As Ronnie stopped the car I saw one of the curtains move and as we got out a man, presumably Quinn appeared, his shirt sleeves rolled up, wearing a flat cap on top of unkempt white hair. He was clean shaven but had bushy eyebrows, a mixture of grey and white, giving him a fierce look.

'Is it Mr O'Halloran? I enquired, deciding to be formal.

There was no reaction, just a stare which focussed on me as he took time to assess the situation.

'Who are you?' he said eventually, but his penetrating gaze, made me think that he had already worked it out. The similarities between Jason and myself were obvious from the mop of brown hair to the shape of the face.

'Peter Meldrum,' I replied, holding out my hand, which was ignored.

'You took a long time.'

'No,' I answered firmly, 'I came as soon as I found out, which was a week ago.'

'What do you want?'

'I want to meet my son, get to know him.'

'He's attends some fancy boarding school in England,' which was a statement not a denial; he could be around.

It was Ronnie who broke the silence.

'We have come a long way, at short notice. Peter is very anxious to meet Jason, who he believed was dead. Jason's middle name is Quinn, where else would we go.'

Quinn turned away and started towards the farmhouse, but he turned slightly, 'Follow me,' he said gruffly.

We entered what was the kitchen, an old dog lying on a rug by a paraffin heater. There was a kitchen range by the outside wall, with a kettle and a pot sitting on it, beside a Belfast sink, which was cracked and dirty. There was a wooden door on the far wall which was slightly ajar and led into a living room, a pair of binoculars hanging from a hook on the door.

The dark varnished sideboard was ancient, stained, chipped. It was obvious that they had little money or were beyond caring about the state of the house.

Quinn's wife, a small woman, with thinning white hair, very slight, wearing a floral apron, said nothing, as Quinn pointed to a few wooden chairs, beside the fire, and we sat down.

'Would this help?' I asked producing the copy of Jason's birth certificate and the class photograph. I had also brought old photographs of Catherine and I dating from our school days.

Quinn briefly glanced at them and then at me.

'I believe you. Catherine knew that you would turn up, if anything happened to her.'

Catherine had a lot of faith in me, it seemed, but here I was, within a week, hundreds of miles away searching for my son. Quinn's response indicated that he knew that Catherine was dead. So many questions tumbled about in my mind.

'Can we meet, Jason?'

'Not possible at the moment. Can you wait?'

'Maybe a couple of days, but after that we would have to go back. But, as Ronnie explained we have come a long way.'

Ronnie moved in his seat and I saw that he was trying to see into the other room and I tried to follow his line of vision, aware of a slight creaking noise. Was someone behind the door - could it be Jason lurking there, listening in?

'With it being a holiday weekend, I hoped that Jason might be here, home from boarding school.'

'He might not want to see you. I'll ask him when he returns.'

I had a strong feeling that he was here, possibly behind the door.

'Come back tomorrow,' Quinn said, 'same time. Catherine gave me a letter to hand to you, was confident that you would appear here someday. I'll look it out for you.'

I wondered what it would say.

'That would be good of you.'

Ronnie interrupted.

'Is the old school house set used in *Ryan's Daughter* on your land.

Quinn shook his head. 'A neighbours.'

'If we have to wait until tomorrow, then we will visit the schoolhouse this afternoon, once we have had lunch, to put in time. I'm keen on old movies, it would be interesting to visit a place where they shot the film.'

It was a strange digression and then I understood that Ronnie was dropping a hint about our whereabouts. If it was Jason next door, he would know where we were going to be.

As we drove away I thanked Ronnie.

'That was clever. If Jason is curious then he can outwit Quinn and at least he can have a better look at us. Strange to believe that I might have been that close to my son and yet I have never met him. Quinn's an odd one,' I continued, 'very deep, suspicious, but then he must have known the Robinsons well.'

'I don't think that he expected our visit. We took him by surprise and he is not the sort of person that can be pushed about.'

'The house was very dilapidated, I can't believe that Catherine would have been happy with the arrangement. She must have been desperate to hide him here but she did also send him to a boarding school, which would be expensive.'

'She lost me when she left Islay and then she had to lose her son to hide him from McGrory. How terrible.' Then I realised what Catherine had meant in her message to me, hidden on my mobile. She had lost me when she left Islay and she had lost Jason by having to send him away.

We drove on in silence, I was pondering what a cruel hand life had dealt Catherine. The only thing I could do was to find Jason and create a new life for him.

'I wonder what his accent will be like. I want to meet him. No, I want him to be with me,' I added emphatically, 'I've already missed out on the first ten years.'

Ronnie didn't reply, kept his head down. I knew what he was thinking: would Jenny be able to accept him, especially when she wanted another baby. Lurking behind the increasingly complex scenario was also the McGrory factor - what would he do to us, if given the chance.

14

We had a few hours to fill before we went to the old film set, so we decided to visit Dunquin harbour, a local landmark. The harbour was reached by a steep twisting concrete path which eventually led down to the small harbour, protected from a precipitous drop on each side by low walls. Two jagged stacks rose out of the sea to the west and between the harbour and the Blasket Islands there were more rocky pinnacles breaking the surface. Dangerous waters, which could be navigated only with local knowledge and in calm seas. The hardy islanders must have often been marooned in bad weather. As it descended the path veered away from the cliff edge, creating at the bottom a space between the path and the cliffs, where boats were stored, bottoms up - some of them traditional Irish currachs, animal skin stretched over a wooden frame.

'Do you want to go out the Blasket's, lads,' asked a man sitting on a lobster creel, repairing it with a large needle and twine. Hidden by the wall he surprised us, as we hadn't seen him, and we both jumped, making us realise how nervy we were. Steve's message had got through to us, be alert, trust no one.

'Not today, thanks,' I answered, recovering my poise.

'The swell is not too bad and I have an outboard motor.' I

shook my head.

'Where are you from? You sound Scottish.'

'Aberdeenshire,' replied Ronnie, now learning to hide any information that would alert others.

'I know a few crew who work the boats out of Peterhead.'

'That's just up the coast but I am more of a land lover.'

We breathed in the fresh salt air and headed back up, my calf muscles aching, with the steep climb, by the time we reached the car.

'We'll head to the Blasket Centre for lunch, while we are waiting,' I suggested, time hanging heavily on us. We paid for tickets, looked at the exhibits, read about the struggles of the islanders to survive. We learned about the literary heritage of the islands, but barely took anything in and finished with a plate of soup in the restaurant.

'Let's go,' Ronnie exclaimed, as it reached two o'clock. 'If Jason was behind the door and heard our message and understood it, he'll turn up I'm sure. If not there is always tomorrow.' I sensed Ronnie's spirits were sagging and that he was very worried about the consequences if we were discovered by McGrory's men. Both of us wanted to get away as soon as possible. I appreciated his support - others might simply have left.

We parked the car by the side of the road, a short distance out of the village, and walked along a track, past another house and there it was perched perilously close to the top of ninety foot cliffs. Just as the Maguire's had described - the old schoolhouse built for the film, its stone walls intact. Most of the roof had collapsed, leaving just a few tiles and the wooden trusses. A low stone playground wall surrounded the building, with separate playgrounds for boys and girls and separate entrances to a large classroom. The private quarters to the rear had not been so substantially built and all that remained was a rusting metal frame supporting the roof.

On the sea facing wall of the schoolhouse was a small plaque of crumbling concrete - Kirrary National School, 1893.

Inside was crumbling plaster exposing the breeze blocks used in the construction of the set. The chimneys were only for decoration, the insides capped off. The pupils would have been fascinated by the view, over to the Blasket Islands, if it had been a real school classroom, watching storms approach.

It was a strange building, built to convince those watching the film into believing that it was genuine, but it was a facade, a shell designed to make filming easier. For someone unaware of its purpose it would be a puzzling building to encounter but then that was what films did, create an illusion to spin a story.

Ronnie wandered around, his interest aroused and I watched him photographing different parts of the set. Behind the school was a grassy slope topped by a rocky outcrop. On the far side, a short distance away was Quinn's farm.

I sat on the low wall, glancing at my phone, it was now after two. If, and at the moment it seemed a big if, Jason had been there, had heard and was able to come, then he might appear. We had to wait. Ronnie came over and sat astride the low wall which increased his line of vision as he could easily look to either side.

He smiled at me, a look of sympathy on his face: 'We are a long way from Islay.'

In every way, I mused.

The weather was dry, but there was a stiff breeze, so eventually I huddled behind the low playground wall, my knees hunched up at my chin. Ronnie appeared motionless but I could see that he was taking in the scene in all directions. An hour past, then two, our spirits now ebbing.

Ronnie got up and stretched and then quietly, he muttered, 'There is someone looking at us from the rocky outcrop at the top of the hill. Don't move. He or she, I can't tell has been watching us for about ten minutes.'

It was an effort not to move. A few minutes later, it seemed longer, I enquired: 'Is he still there?' I said, making a hopeful assumption.

'Yes. Hold on. He's moving among the rocks. He's studying us through binoculars. So it was a boy - Jason? If we look at him, he will probably run. Stand up, Peter, so that he can see your face.'

I obliged, letting the observer see my side profile and then slowly I turned, keeping my eyes, with great difficulty, averted from the rocks and looking towards the film set. If it was Jason, I was sure that he would recognise me as the person who was at the farmhouse this morning. We were two peas in a pod.

There was a stone lined path, which led from the school gate towards the cliff edge. Ronnie indicated that we both walk down it, a short distance and look out to sea.

More minutes past and then I heard a sound from the school building, like someone stumbling. We froze.

'Give him time, Peter.' It was Ronnie who had the cool head, my emotions were blocking my thoughts, my head buzzing. Ronnie knelt down, picked up a stone and threw it over the cliff edge, which enabled him to glance behind him, as he bent down to pick it up.

'He's in the building. I caught a glimpse of a face at one of the windows. It's a young boy.'

Ronnie issued his instructions: 'I'll walk along the track, further along the cliff, and appear to be interested in looking out to sea. I'll hop over the wall some distance along and run back to the rear of the building, cutting him off. You jump the wall at the front and call out his name.'

My heart was thumping, breaths shallow and fast. I forced myself to keep staring out to sea until Ronnie was some distance away. Then I turned slowly, trying to conceal my intentions, and walked back, sitting on the wall for a moment, as if I was taking a rest, and then flipped my legs over the low playground wall, as if I was adjusting my position.

I saw Ronnie sprinting across the hillside to the rear of the building. It was time, my heart was thumping.

'Jason, I am your Dad. Come out, I want to meet you.' Words I never expected to say echoing off the film set, carried by the wind.

I waited a minute.

'Jason,' I repeated, 'I'm your Dad. Mum would have wanted us to meet.' Maybe, just not on a windswept hillside in Ireland and in these circumstances.

I saw him briefly peer out at me and then disappear, but he emerged from the left of the two doors at the front of the building - the former boy's entrance.

He stood hesitant, his brown hair tousled by the wind, his eyes wide staring at me. I held out my arms and he lowered his head and then rushed towards me, burying his head in my chest. Tears ran down my face and he looked up, seeing my emotion, he flung his arms around me.

'Mum's dead,' he said, between sobs, 'she always said that you would come for me - save me.'

'I will,' I replied, and then words became meaningless and we held each other. Ronnie emerged from the schoolhouse, out of breath, but smiling.

'This is Jason,' I said, 'my son,' I added, as Ronnie reached us. I am sure he knew that, but I felt had to say something, announce the fact to the world. I pulled back from Jason and examined him. He wasn't that tall, lean, his slightly upturned nose reminded me of Catherine's and when he smiled, his eyes blinking, it was Catherine. Life can be emotional. I led him to the low wall and we

116

sat side-by-side facing the sea, my arm around him.

'Have you come to collect me, father.' His voice was refined, with a surprisingly English accent and quite formal. I hadn't expected that but it was no doubt a product of his English boarding school.

I ruffled his hair.

'I would like that,' but not sure of how long that might take and not wanting to raise false hopes, I added, 'I'll talk to Quinn tomorrow.'

'I heard Granda and Nana talking. They believe that you are my father. They are wondering what to do. I believe that they want me to return to school after mid-term. I want to go with you.'

'That might take time,' I cautioned, 'but I will take you back to Scotland when I can.'

Ronnie broke in: 'Quinn's standing up there watching us.'

I looked up to the rocks at the top of the hill. Quinn was standing there, still wearing his flat cap, looking down on us.

I waved to him but didn't expect to get a response, but I wanted him to know that I had met Jason.

'I think that you should go to your Granda. I don't want to worry him.'

Jason looked up at me: 'Of course, father. I look forward to seeing you tomorrow,' and he slightly bowed his head, retreated a step and then turned and ran up the hillside towards Quinn. He stopped after a few yards and smiled: 'Goodbye father.'

Ronnie came across: 'We'll soon get him talking like us - just give me time.'

I was lost in my thoughts, as I watched him reach Quinn, look back and then he gave me a wave, before the two of them walked over the hill.

'How are you feeling, Peter?'

'I can't begin to explain,' I replied, 'let's get back to the car.'

The Maguire's made us most welcome with tea and this time a lemon sponge, dusted with icing sugar. They insisted we have a meal with them. An enticing Irish stew and a few drams of Irish whiskey helped the evening to pass but my thoughts kept returning to Jason, my son.

15

My dream started to change, something impinging on it rousing me, dragging me from my dream state, and as I became semi-conscious I became aware of the telephone ringing in the house and eventually Dan's voice answering. He did little talking and then he went to the front door, the outside lighting came on illuminating our room. He was outside for a few minutes and then he returned to the phone, speaking quickly and I couldn't make out what he was saying. I heard Dan moving about and then the front door shutting, pulled softly behind him and then his car started. The outside lights went off and I turned over and went back to sleep.

The next morning Dan wasn't at the breakfast table and Kayna was quieter than usual but no explanation was offered for his absence. We paid Kayna for our stay and were packing the car when Dan returned, looking tired, his face white and drawn, pausing at the door.

'You better come in,' he said, and as we followed him we noticed a strong smell of smoke from his anorak.

'Can you get me a cup of tea, Kayna?' and his wife looked worried. As he took off his anorak I saw black patches of soot on his sweatshirt and realised that there must have been a fire, locally.

'Dingle fire station phoned me last night. They were already fighting a fire near Ventry,' a village that I remembered that we had driven through on the road to Dunquin from Dingle, 'and wanted me to check on reports of a fire at Quinn's farm,' he paused so that we could absorb that information. 'I could see the flames from the house here and phoned them back. Since they were busy they sent a unit from Tralee, over the Connor Pass. I went to Quinn's farm,' and he shook his head, Kayna quickly moving to his side putting her arm around him, 'and the farmhouse was well ablaze,' his voice cracking with emotion, as he shook his head, reliving in his mind the images he had seen. 'I couldn't do anything. The flames even engulfed the barn. It was a bloody inferno. They had no chance. I'm sorry.'

He hung his head. I was horrified, bad enough what had happened to Quinn and his wife but what had happened to Jason, did he escape and how could I ask - I had never mentioned Jason to them.

Ronnie spoke: 'Quinn and his wife?' reading my thoughts.

'We found their bodies and that of the dog. We think that it was a paraffin heater that exploded, that started the blaze.'

'No other bodies?'

Dan looked puzzled: 'No, why would there be, and we did a careful search. You always do,' he added.

'Of course,' replied Ronnie.

'Daniel is more used to dealing with fires than you boys. You both look shocked, I'll get the kettle on,' and she busied herself as I am sure that she had done on similar occasions.

The good news was that they hadn't found the body of a wee boy. So Jason must have escaped the fire but where was he? Why didn't he show himself to the police? Had it been an accident or was McGrory somehow involved. My heart lurched: Had he been kidnapped?

'I'm sorry about Quinn,' Kayna said.

The last image of him standing on the hillside was etched on my mind.

'I didn't really know him, didn't after meeting him either,' I reflected. 'But it is still a shock, and his wife. He didn't even introduce her.'

'So it was an accident,' asked Ronnie, 'probably that old paraffin heater.'

'They think so, certainly looked that way, but the fire investigators and police will check it out.'

'You need a shower and a good sleep, Dan,' said his wife, and we took our cue.

'We'll be on our way. A sad end to a pleasant trip. Thanks for your hospitality.'

In the distance I could see wisps of smoke arising from what remained of Quinn's farm. As soon as we got in the car I said, 'We have got to find Jason and there is only one place I can think to look.' I was shaking, head buzzing, desperate to find out what had happened to Jason.

'We'll be there in a couple of minutes,' and Ronnie drove away from the house.

'It would have been a big complication if we had mentioned Jason,' he went on to say, 'but if we find him what are we going to do.'

'He is my son, no one around here knows about him. I'll take him back with me.'

Ronnie didn't comment, leaving me time to reflect on my proposed course of action.

We retraced our footsteps from yesterday and soon arrived at the former school house.

There seemed to be no one there. My heart sank and I called out his name: 'Jason,' I repeated his name, only louder, 'Jason.'

I vaulted the low playground wall and raced into the old classroom area and there he was, huddled in a corner looked frozen and terrified. I ran to him, alerting Ronnie, and sat down beside him. Jason was trembling, mute and ashen white.

'It's okay,' I said, 'You're with me now. I'll look after you, I promise.'

Ronnie produced a Mars bar: 'Eat this, Jason,' he ordered, 'it will help.'

'It's all I have got,' he explained, 'but he needs some sugar. I'll get a blanket from the car,' and he left.

It wasn't the time for questions but knowing that Jason was safe was one thing. Now my mind turned to how the fire was started. The paraffin heater was certainly old but was it too much of a coincidence that the fire had burnt down while we were here? Was it an accident or had McGrory's men found out? Had word got out about our visit? I reckoned that we just had to get away. The police weren't expecting to find any more victims. There certainly would be questions to ask if they did discover that Jason had been in the house. Life was complicated.

On Ronnie's return I took him aside.

'Do you think that he needs medical attention? Might be better to let the authorities know,' I suggested.

'He looks uninjured, just shocked. If we alert the authorities then McGrory will find out, if not from contacts with the local police, then from press and television reports. We would never get out of Ireland.'

That was the confirmation I wanted. There was no easy answer, no correct solution. It was like being back at High Coullabus farm with the Americans that night in Islay. If I made the wrong decision there would be consequences - could be big consequences. I thought of using the app on my phone but Steve had said that the app wouldn't work around here. However, I decided to check and I took out my phone and rang the 'Alan Siviter' number and waited while the number rang out, eventually it cut out. No one available, we were on our own.

I went back to Jason: 'Feeling any better?'

He nodded. The Mars bar had helped and he had stopped trembling, a little more colour in his face. There was little smell of smoke from him and he was fully dressed, which seemed surprising. I would ask questions later: now was not the time, but that was puzzling.

'I think that we should just go. Stop soon, get Jason a cup of tea.'

'Okay,' replied Ronnie, adding nothing, his thoughts hard to decipher.

Jason hadn't said a word, his eyes the only insight to his thinking and he avoided meeting my gaze. This had to be traumatic for him. We would need help but not here on the far extremity of Ireland. We need to get him back home quickly. With that thought, my mind was made up.

Ronnie drove on up the road passing Quinn's farm. By the side of the road were several Garda police cars and a fire support vehicle. Jason started to hyperventilate and Ronnie quickly found a passing place, beyond the farm, and turned the car around, taking an alternative inland route to Dingle. There we found a cafe and got Jason a mug of tea and he nodded when I mentioned a bacon roll. It seemed to help him. I went into a shop with him and bought a jacket, a jumper and a few tee-shirts. Jenny probably wouldn't agree with my choice of colours but it did what was required.

We then drove over the Connor Pass which was just as dramatic as the last stretch of the road to Dunquin from Dingle; a low wall separating cars from a precipitous drop to the valley floor far below and with limited room for passing.

We reached Tralee, then Adare and bypassed Limerick. The more distance between us and Quinn's farm, the better I felt. I kept turning around to check on Jason. Approaching Kildare, Jason suddenly shouted: 'Stop,' and we just had time to pull over before he was sick by the roadside. I cleaned him up and Ronnie suggested stopping in Kildare but at a different place.

We found a bed and breakfast house on the outskirts. It appeared to be a woman who lived on her own and she made us welcome. I bathed Jason and dried him. He sat on my knee wrapped in a big bath towel and leant against me. He still didn't say anything which worried me. Again I was torn, tortured, wondering whether I had made the right decision. Time would tell.

A little later we took him to a local cafe that the landlady recommended and got him some food. While Jason was eating Ronnie nipped out and was gone for about half-an-hour. When he came back he said that he had been on the phone to Maria and had alerted her.

He gave me his phone saying, 'I don't like that app on your phone. Maybe they can listen in. Phone Jenny on my phone, we need to prepare her.'

I accepted the phone. It wasn't an easy conversation but Jenny appeared to understand and despite, I am sure many reservations, she promised a warm welcome for Jason.

The news about Jodie was not so good. The leg was taking time to heal, the vet not sure that the operation had been a success after all. Life was not just difficult, it was becoming a juggling act and I couldn't afford to drop any of the balls.

That night Jason slept beside me and several times during the night appeared to be having nightmares.

The next day we headed north crossing the border about midday and got an early evening ferry back to Cairnryan. An hour and a half later we reached Ayr.

16

Jenny was perfect; immediately putting her arms around Jason, and making him feel welcome. Jodie tried to give me a welcome but I could see that she was limping badly, her injured leg bandaged and taped and she flopped down on her dog bed by the kitchen door, obviously uncomfortable. The others, like Jenny, were welcoming. Thinking that in the presence of so many adults Jason might be overwhelmed, Ronnie and Maria left the room and went for a walk along the beach. No doubt they had much catching up to do.

Mandy was soon busy in the kitchen making tea, coffee and sandwiches. We had eaten on the ferry but we were tired and hospitality and support was what we needed. When I sat down, Ben who had been a little hesitant and not his usual bouncy self, came and sat on my lap, draping his arms around me. With the arrival of Jason we mustn't forget him.

Jason was wide eyed, tense and hesitant, almost mute. He was only ten, a very vulnerable age and the trauma had really affected him. Jenny eased him onto a seat and stayed beside him, a protective arm around him. I could see Jason looking around, wondering about his new surroundings and all the people.

When I went through to the kitchen for a top-up of coffee, Colin followed.

'I am not going to mention that I am his uncle or half-uncle or whatever. I'll leave it to later,' and that seemed a wise step but only a small part, I sensed, of what he wanted to discuss.

'Yeah, I think that he could be overwhelmed; is overwhelmed. There is a lot for him to take in. We'll also need to keep an eye on Ben as he will feel the loss of status.'

'So you are going to make him part of the family?' The question was blunt. Was he concerned for Jenny or upset by Jason's connection to the Robinsons?

'I'll need to discuss what happens with Jenny, but what choice do I have. Everyone else in his family are dead or in prison. What a bunch!'

Colin's manner softened: 'Sorry,' he said, 'it's all confusing, brings back memories. We'll support you whatever you both decide to do.'

I knew he was worried about what the arrival of Jason would mean for Jenny but she almost seemed energised by Jason's arrival.

'Was the fire deliberate?' he asked.

'Most likely, but I hope to find out more when Jason opens up and can talk about it. So far he said nothing, worryingly quiet. Thanks so much for taking care of Jodie. I hope that she makes progress soon,' I added, trying to change the subject.

'We have a further appointment with the vet tomorrow, but it will take time. She's settled here, so we are happy to look after her and remember we will cover the costs,' he reminded me.

I was grateful and thanked him again, it was one less worry.

Ronnie and Maria had now returned, Maria collecting her bags to pack in the car, when I came back to the room.

'We're heading off,' Ronnie said, travelling to stay with Tim and Elizabeth, at Loch Sween, for a few days before we travel back to Jura.'

'Thanks,' I said, 'for everything,' words of gratitude seeming inadequate. 'I'll get you a good bottle of single malt, but that's just a gesture.'

'Just one,' and Ronnie laughed, but he read the emotion in my face and knew that I was grateful.

. . .

Fortunately not knowing how long my trip to Ireland would take I had taken almost a week off work. I was not due back until the Thursday. Life was busy when we got home, ensuring that Jason could settle in the spare room and trying to make him comfortable. Ben even offered some toys and Jenny chided me for not getting pants and socks for Jason - 'typical man,' she said, 'to forget something as basic.'

Jenny was incredible, really busy, motherly to Jason but not ignoring Ben and I let her know how much I appreciated her support. I made sure that I spent time with both of the boys.

I knew that Jason was due back from mid-term at the beginning of next week and I asked for the name of the school to contact them. For the first time, since Ireland, Jason was vocal, tearful and adamant. He didn't want to go back.

'Father, I hate the school,' still speaking very formally and after a few seconds, 'the boys make fun of my accent. I'm not posh enough. I hate the food,' was the final statement. There was a lot of emotion bubbling up. At least we could ease these concerns.

I eventually got the school's name and Googled it. I spoke to the head teacher, guarded in what I said, and explained that I was his father and was now caring for him since the death of his mother and that he would not be returning. He immediately expressed sympathy. I also asked him not to give out any personal details to anyone who contacted him and he agreed to note that on his record. I requested that all his personal possessions be packed up and sent to us. When I told Jason, he brightened up, giving a big smile, even when I told him that he would have to go Ben's primary. I thought that we could leave enrolment to the next week.

Jenny, despite all the extra chaos, was somehow still trying to finish paintings for the exhibition in Aberfoyle and was going to travel up on Saturday with Ben to deliver some of them. We agreed that it would give me a chance to have a day with Jason and Malcolm was coming over.

We tried to settle into a routine getting the boys to bed early, making sure that we read Ben his bedtime story and that we spent time with Jason.

The evening before I went back to work, the boys settled, I poured us both a generous glass of red wine and we slumped together on the couch. With my arm around Jenny, I took the opportunity to thank her and tell her how much I loved her. How I wanted another baby. She snuggled in and we sat in silence enjoying each other's company and the peace.

I was starting to doze, the effects of the wine, when I heard Jason crying, then screaming. Both of us jumped and I ran upstairs. Jason was sitting bolt upright in bed, crying, bathed in sweat. I had expected more nightmares at some point and it seemed that they had started. Jenny looked in and went to the bathroom and got a cloth soaked in hot water and mopped his brow. I held his hand and spoke reassuringly. Jason appeared lost, his mind far away and it was a few minutes before his eyes refocused and he looked at me.

'What was it, Jason, a bad dream?'

'The man was back.'

'Which man?

'The man who was at Granda's house.'

I tried not to react, to put him off his revelation.

'When?'

'The fire...'

I waited, glancing across at Jenny. Jason's breathing became laboured again and his eyes widened. He was going to scream. I gripped his hand trying to give reassurance.

'Tell me what happened on that night,' I said quietly.

Jenny offered him some water. In a few minutes he had calmed down.

'Granda didn't want me to go with you.'

'That would upset you?'

'I cried. He sent me to my bedroom. Nana was very quiet.'

Quietly, he sobbed.

'It's okay,' said Jenny softly, 'you are safe with us.'

'Mum said that I would be.'

Again that certainty that Catherine had instilled in him.

'Go on, Jason, tell me about the man.'

He sat up and sucked in his breath.

'He came to the window and tapped it. I thought it might be you and I pulled back the curtain,' and he turned away, eyes brimming.

'It wasn't you.'

'Tell me about him.'

'It was dark.'

'Murphy started to bark and Granda got up. He came through to my room - saw the man and ran out to get him. I put on my clothes and went to the kitchen to help Granda.'

'He was out. I heard shouting. They were fighting. Granda told me to get Nana. Granda fell and the man tried to grab me. I ran away.'

Jenny spoke softly: 'You did the right thing, Jason. That's what Granda would have wanted.'

'I ran up the hill. I waited. I saw fire.'

Word must have got out. Someone had tried to kidnap Jason.

'Are they dead?'

'Yes, but you did all you could. You did the right thing.'

At some point he would need professional help, but at the moment he needed to know that we were there for him, that I loved him.

17

I made an effort to be in earlier than usual for work on my return. It enabled me to miss the heavy traffic and I was at the security gate before eight. The security guard, who I was beginning to recognise and even have the occasional short chat with appeared sullen, glancing at his security screen and frowned before turning and operating the security gate As I drove past I saw him twist his head and speak into his radio.

It was easy to find a parking place at this time and I parked just outside my communal office, which was on the ground floor, separated from the parking area by a strip of bushes. I saw Pence's car a few spaces away, so he was also having an early start probably having travelled from Islay the night before.

I grabbed my briefcase and headed in through the foyer, attempting to swipe my pass through the security system reader. It wouldn't work despite repeated attempts. I held the pass up to the assistant, behind the desk, and shook my head.

'Wait a minute,' she said, and attempted to allow me in from her office, before coming out and releasing the mechanism manually. She looked flustered:

'You're persona non grata,' she stated, 'but that can't be correct, the system can be temperamental,' and with that I was through and heading for my office, which was deserted, though

I could see Hector's coat, so he was also having an early start. My problems didn't end there because the computer wouldn't boot up. I hoped that it wasn't going to be one of those days. I pulled open my drawer to put my packed lunch in it and found it empty. My diary, pens and a few other belongings were missing and then I realised that the photograph of Jenny and Ben was also gone. I was still mulling over what all this meant when Hector appeared.

'You're early,' he stated, but the usual warmth was missing. My heart sank - something had definitely changed.

'Keen to be back,' I replied, trying to sound perky but there was no response.

'Come with me,' he said, and it was a command not a request.

'Is there something wrong?' but he blanked me. I followed him along the corridor and realised that we were heading towards the human resources department. I was now tense, wondering what was happening. I couldn't imagine why they wanted to speak with me. A door opened and I saw Pence Gifford about to step out until he saw me and then the door was quickly shut. His expression - grim, devoid of any recognition, increased the anxiety that I was now feeling.

The head of human resources was a Ms Palmer, a lady who had warmly welcomed me on my first day, steered me though my induction day and had offered me all her support. I reached her office and was shown into her small anteroom. Hector pointed to one of the seats and I sat down as he strode past me and entered her office. I caught a glimpse of Ms Palmer and another person, a man, who I didn't recognise with an open attaché case on his lap, pouring over some sheets of paper.

Okay, I was in trouble, that seemed obvious, but I didn't know why. And no small complaint would have elicited this response. My heart sank. I think that I had arrived for work before they were fully ready for me.

A few minutes passed and I took a paper cup, from a blue plastic tube, and filled it with water from the water cooler in the corner and sat back down. I was aware of talking but the voices were low, deliberately so that I could not overhear them. I crushed the paper cup and put it in the bin and took out my phone, alerting Jenny by text and put it away quickly as the door opened and Hector stood there filling the frame.

'Come in, please,' he asked, his face showing maybe a hint of emotion, but no warmth, maybe just relief that they were ready - but for what? Ms Palmer stood up from behind her desk, a small woman, usually vibrant with energy, with a strong personality but today she appeared shrunken, her energy switch muted.

'Mr Meldrum, please come in,' and she pointed to an empty chair. In the corner I noticed a clear plastic bag with my possessions in it.

'Can I ask what all this is about?' I enquired, trying to sound calm, but I was aware that my voice revealed tension. The words lacked conviction, dissipating quickly in the room.

Ms Palmer sounded business like: 'Mr McAlpine, you know, is your line manager and this is Mr Porteous, a lawyer from our legal department. During an upgrade of computers in your department, we discovered numerous illegal searches of the internet, which showed extreme child pornography. Images that were very distressing to the technician who stumbled on them and to each person who has subsequently viewed them.'

I think my face showed my surprise, but the others ignored my reaction.

'Impossible,' I said, 'I have never searched for, viewed or been interested in pornography of any type. No doubt, if I searched on the internet I could find pornography, I believe that it is very common but I have never tried. Check my computer at home, you'll find nothing. You said child pornography,' I questioned, disbelieving,' that is horrible. I have got a young child of my own.'

The three of them sat mute, like vultures waiting to pounce, rip their prey apart.

'Do you not believe me?' but they didn't need to answer my question by saying anything, their expressions told me.

'Show me some of this pornography,' I demanded, aware now that my armpits were damp, my body hot, face flushed. I felt like screaming: 'It's because I'm upset, not because I'm guilty.'

Ms Palmer swivelled her computer screen and nodded at Mr Porteous, as if seeking permission. She called up a file and opened, what appeared to be a collection of images and clicked on the first one. A picture of a small boy, Ben's age, appeared with a man. I turned away.

'That's disgusting, unbelievable, awful. Close it down,' I demanded, my anger rising.

Mr Porteous spoke: 'Your computer shows numerous searches for similar material, during company time, ever since you arrived. This is not just an isolated occurrence.'

'No,' and I was shouting now, 'impossible. Would others not have noticed?'

'Images could be downloaded without opening and transferred to a pen drive.'

'How did they get through your security filters? Ms Palmer said, at my induction, that there were filters to restrict downloads.'

'It can be done, it seems. The technician identified a buried programme that would circumvent our safety protocols on your computer.'

'You seem to have made up your mind that I am guilty, already. I am innocent.'

Now I was getting angry.

'We are deciding whether we should call in the police. I believe that pornography like this will lead to a custodial sentence.

134

Do you wish that?'

The question lingered in the air and suddenly I saw their end game, where this was leading. They didn't want to call in the police, it would be bad for their business image.

My phone pinged. I took it out of my pocket. It was a message from Jenny: 'What is going on?'

How could I begin to tell her. Surely, she would believe me. I groaned. The others looked unmoved.

'I have no idea how these images got on the computer. You can check my pen drive, my lap top at home. I am a happily married man.'

There was a silence, none of them apparently wanting to take the initiative, outline the next steps - the end game.

'I am innocent,' I stated again, with a pleading tone.

Mr Porteous coughed, clearing his throat. 'None of this is easy. We are disappointed to have discovered pornography on an employee's computer but we are sure of our facts. The evidence is there and experts have checked everything. There is no doubt; you have repeatedly downloaded images of a criminal nature. Obscene and repulsive,' and the emotion, the repugnance was apparent, as he spat out these words and Hector nodded slowly in agreement, his mouth hanging open, in disbelief, at what was going on.

'You are, of course, entitled to a lawyer or representation, would suggest that you strongly consider that course of action. It is your right, but we would then need to go to the police. We are offering you a way out. Resign now, voluntarily. We will provide two months' salary and allow you to remain in the company house for the same period of time. Do you wish time to consider our proposal?'

'I will fight this. Someone has planted these images on my computer. Which company did the upgrade? It could have been that technician - that woman.'

'They are a respected company. She was very distressed by what she found. Indeed, she may take the matter to the police herself.'

'I am innocent,' I repeated, more stridently, but their faces remained impassive, Hector's almost hostile, the others blank. I'm going home to talk with my wife and consider my options.'

'They are very limited and we will involve the police,' said Palmer, with an edge to his voice, a menacing tone.

I stood up, shaken, disbelieving. Already my mind was pondering who would do this. It didn't take long to work out. McGrory would have the means and the motive.

I stood up and my eye saw the plastic bag the picture of Jenny and Ben exposed. I thought of them and all that had happened because of my actions. Then I got angry: 'You think that you are doing the right thing by the company and therefore what happens to me doesn't matter.'

Ms Palmer rose to that: 'That's not true.'

I cut her off: 'Yes, it is, your words, when you first spoke to me, were just those words, meant to spin an image of a benevolent company, caring for its employees. No one interviewed me, about these accusations, took time to look at my history. Mr Gifford knew that I had inadvertently crossed a drug gang, and my actions helped a big drug bust. They are set on revenge. They have made my life hell. You knew Mr McAlpine was never to give out my personal details, now you know why. You took a phone call from a care home in Cumnock, a couple of weeks ago, where I had gone looking for a son, I believed had died, a son I didn't know that I had until a few months ago. The manager had noted my work number and yes I did phone during work hours. Tell me was the upgrade planned before that call was made to Mr McAlpine or after? Was my department the only one upgraded? I want to know the name of the company, also the woman who did the upgrade? She didn't appear upset when she packed up - she just said that the computers would run faster. I want to know how you checked out her findings. You are good at making your mind up, but not at answering my questions.'

They sat impassive, looking away, the lawyer ruffling through his papers.

'This isn't good enough, you are all too quick to damn me, get rid of me. I mustn't interfere with the company image,' I added sarcastically, and I scowled at Ms Palmer. 'Go ahead contact the police. I'll fight these accusations; I owe my family that much and myself.'

'You are suspended until further notice,' Mr Porteous stated, looking up, appearing relieved to finally announce his verdict.

'Fine, no doubt we will meet in court,' and I stood up, grabbed the plastic bag containing my belongings and walked out marching down the corridor. I reached the security desk and demanded that I be allowed through. I got in the car, noticing that Pence Gifford's car had gone, and drove to the security barrier. The security guard was talking on his radio as I arrived but quickly raised the barrier. The hardest part for me was that Pence Gifford had believed them.

18

Malcolm sat looking pensive, a pen resting on a small notebook, where he had made careful notes, both balanced on his knees. Jenny looked across at him anxious, the emotion and lack of sleep of the last twenty-four hours evident on her face which devoid of makeup appeared drawn with no colour.

'I know you well, Peter,' he started, 'I don't believe that you are downloading porn from the internet. I will, with your permission, take your laptop, pass it to an expert, a friend of mine, who will examine it. I don't expect to find anything. You also need to employ a lawyer, I know a good one. I can talk to him if you wish.'

'Please,' I replied.

'The call from the care home and the upgrade may be coincidental. It is critical, however, that we try and link these events. I have heard of similar incidents where a company has used an upgrade to place incriminating evidence on someone's computer, but it is difficult to prove. It is a pity that you don't know the name of the computer company, but, of course, you had no idea that it would be so significant. The technician, did she have a company uniform, or a logo, something to identify the company?'

He looked across at me, sympathetically, 'Try and remember.'

I had been trying, so hard. 'She wore a blue sweatshirt and there was a badge and a symbol and a name above it. The badge was red, but...'

'I'll check out websites. Companies often show pictures of their employees at work. I'll try and show you some examples. We might be lucky. Then I can run some background checks. I do that sort of thing all the time. It is not much but it is a start. Keep believing,' and with that he finished off his coffee, which must have been cold given that he had been here for nearly two hours, and stood up.

'I'll get back to you when I discover anything.'

I thanked Malcolm, so did Jenny, who asked after Alison's pregnancy as he left.

...

'He was very helpful, we can just wait to see if he turns up anything,' said Jenny, when Malcolm had departed.

Up to yesterday I had felt reactive, responding to events. Being chased by thugs, bringing home a son who I thought was dead, were not normal events. Being accused of stashing porn felt like a personal attack on my character and my family. I had to fight. Jenny felt the same way. Importantly, she believed me, never doubted, but knew the challenge I now faced and wanted to fight alongside me. If anything we were more determined and stronger as a couple. What didn't break you, made you stronger.

The letter, recorded delivery from the company, had arrived the next morning. I had expected it. I was suspended on full pay but would be called to another meeting shortly. I could bring along someone to represent me.

I collected the empty coffee cups and took them through to the kitchen, rinsing them under the tap.

'I'm going to the garage to sort out my paintings for the trip tomorrow,' said Jenny, who had followed me through to the kitchen. 'Somehow I have managed to get there - all ready. Life is not meant to be easy, just not this difficult,' she looked at me trying to hide the exhaustion on her face, attempting a smile.

I hugged her tight. 'Without you,' I said, 'I would not cope. I need you and know how fortunate I am to have you.'

'I love you to,' she replied, 'but we better finish this conversation tomorrow,' and she wiped away a tear, 'or I won't be ready for the trip. Now, I really have to sell paintings, to pay my husband's lawyer's bills,' softening the last statement with a smile.

An hour later she returned, washing her hands at the sink and coming through to the lounge, where I sat, the company letter in front of me, trying to recollect any details about the woman who had upgraded my computer. I was convinced that her visit was no coincidence, but of course I could be wrong.

'I can only imagine what you are thinking,' asked Jenny.

'The letter is so cold, so impersonal, not what I expected.'

'It has to be, it's a legal process, especially when their plan to get rid of you backfired. Good on you to stand up to them and Malcolm's right; we'll get a lawyer. We'll fight them.'

As she spoke Jenny lifted up the rest of today's mail, which was unopened, our focus earlier had been on opening the latter from my employer.

'Usual junk,' said Jenny, inspecting the envelopes. 'A cruise offer. Oh, that is to the previous tenants. An offer from a wine club and a letter addressed to me, redirected from Islay,' and she discarded the other letters and ripped open the A4 sized white envelope and extracted several sheets. Jenny read the first page and then quickly, and with interest, glanced at the others. My own interest was aroused.

Jenny looked across at me a smile on her face: 'This is from the Shona Tyler Trust, money left from the said Shona Tyler to advance and encourage the work of emerging artists. It seems my work has come to the committee's attention and they think that I am a fitting beneficiary for an award.'

'Let me just check this out again,' and she reread the letter and handed the top sheet to me. I quickly scanned the contents with rising excitement.

'I want to be convinced.' I took out my smart phone and Googled the trust. It was genuine, had been established, in England, six months ago, two years after the death of Shona Tyler. I Googled her, she was a rich widow, who wanted to leave some of her money to help budding young artists - art had been her passion. The committee met twice a year and made awards to artists. Artists could apply or the committee could approach. Someone had put in a good word for Jenny - good news at last.

'What's the deal?' I asked.

'This is wonderful,' and I could see Jenny's eyes filling up again, but this time with joy.

'A month in Mull, they supply a house where we can live and I can paint seascapes again. They also pay a gallery to display my works - it is on Iona, where you dad lives.' That was a bonus. 'I travel across to Iona once a week and spend the day meeting people, talking about my work. All expenses, including travelling to and from Mull included. Wow!'

I took the award sheet and read over the details.

'This is just what we need. The boys can go the local primary. I don't need to go to work. It's perfect.'

'It's too good to be true,' Jenny suddenly cautioned.

'We'll double check everything, run it past a few people.'

'But,' and I held up the award sheet, 'it appears that we can go in the next couple of weeks. We need to reply quickly, the award was made two weeks ago and we have only got this now.'

The mood had changed, the seed planted by the award had acted like yeast, raising our spirits, infusing us with hope.

141

19

Aberfoyle

Jenny was quite cheerful. While the situation with my job seemed so much worse, the injustice, the unfairness and the anger, generated by what she was sure were false claims had brought us closer together. She had rarely seen me so motivated. Then the unexpected funding to allow her to paint in Mull for a month was just out of the blue and was just what she needed to regain her painting mojo. Seascapes were her thing and a month painting by the sea would restore her. And I also wanted another baby, which so pleased her. Jason was a nice kid, polite, well-spoken and so wanted a family. In other circumstances, I'm sure, she would have preferred not to have someone else's child as part of our family, but this was different and I appreciated her acceptance of Jason. For today, hopefully, she could put the threat of McGrory and his lot to the back of her mind. Ever mindful, however, she had checked that Ben had his mobile with him and we had even bought one for Jason and installed the app. They would be eternally vigilant and hope that McGrory would forget about them. Be positive, make today different. I heard Jenny humming to herself, something she hadn't done for a long time.

Jenny and Ben left the house after nine, in her campervan, the first stop a gallery in Blanefield, a village twenty minutes from their house. If things were looking up she would try to place some of her work at other galleries in the area. She saw immediately that the gallery in Blanefield was small, space at a premium. The owner knew of her upcoming exhibition at the Fairy Dell Gallery, in Aberfoyle, and had seen her work. 'Come back, in a few weeks, when the tourist trade picks up for the spring and I'll think again,' he said. So not a 'no' but a 'maybe'. That fitted today's mood.

Buoyed by that she moved further north to Killearn and another gallery and adjoining tearoom. They also were just opening for the season but were willing to take some unframed prints. Jenny negotiated a price and promised to return with the prints later.

This was what life was like for artists. You didn't just need talent you had to work hard: be prepared to sell yourself, something that many artists weren't comfortable with.

From Killearn, Jenny continued along the A81, crossing the A811 road to Buchlyvie and followed the road north to Aberfoyle. Now she was in the Trossachs a popular tourist area, accessible for those living in Glasgow and for the many bus loads of visitors drawn by the romantic image of the area, created by Sir Walter Scott and his writings. Think of the poem: *Lady of the Lake*, and stories about Rob Roy. Loch Lomond lay to the west, another magnet for visitors. This was an area that she felt could promote her work.

The road wound north, getting busier, few straight stretches to overtake and she was aware of some vehicles behind and allowed, where possible, for them to overtake her, since the campervan couldn't be pushed these days. Not all were in a hurry she noted.

Ben was in good form, pointing out a path for walkers, as they bypassed Gartmore village, created from an old railway, which he proudly announced that he had walked with his dad and Malcolm. Malcolm was so enthusiastic about walking these disused lines. Everyone had different interests, each to his own. I had enjoyed the walk and so had Ben though he had fallen asleep at the dinner table, his head slumped over his food, and I had had to carry him up to his bed still in his clothes.

These memories continued to warm her, adding to her positive mood. She was pleased that Ben was very cheery; pleased to be out and about with his mum. It was a good age for a kid, she thought, growing, becoming more independent but still needing you. And that made her think of Jason, poor kid, losing his Mum and the rest of his mother's family. He had been through a lot.

It was now the last stretch to Aberfoyle, Jenny having turned left at a road junction, the looming hills forcing the road to detour. The approach road to Aberfoyle was narrow, lined with a mixture of old and new housing, some cafes and shops. It was a community which depended largely on tourists and the harvest from the many trees which had been planted on the area's hilly slopes by the Forestry Commission. The art gallery was located in the village close to the road junction for the Duke's Pass, a steep winding road which took you towards Loch Katrine, Glasgow's water supply, and the heart of the Trossachs.

Time for coffee and an opportunity to clear her head, decide on her final pitch to the gallery owner. You still had to promote your paintings, even if he was keen on them, agree on profit margins, convince him that he was getting a good deal.

At the tourist office, before the art gallery, Jenny turned left and looked for a parking space near the Scottish Wool Centre, a modern building created as a tourist venue, built on the site of the old railway station and sidings. She was getting as bad as Malcolm, she thought, smiling to herself. Jenny drove beyond the wool centre where there was shade offered by trees. She didn't want the sun damaging any of her work, however unlikely that was.

'Ben, can you see a good place?' Jenny always liked to involve him.

He sat up pleased to be involved.

'How about beside the black van.'

'Which one, love' she said, and Ben pointed to a black van with a yellow panel on the side showing a company name and a dripping tap, parked in the shade of the trees.

'The plumber's van?' and Ben nodded. She had noted it travelling behind her for the last few miles, not willing to overtake and then passing her once she was in the car park, although the driver had already disappeared. Jenny parked in a bay near the van and they got out, Ben releasing his safety belt and jumping down, turning to his Mum with a big smile.

'Ice cream.'

'At this time,' she exclaimed, but he knew from her expression that he would get some; because she was in a good mood. There was still an hour before her appointment with Mr Scott, at the gallery, subconsciously she straightened her dress, glanced in the rear view mirror, checked her make-up before leaving the campervan, a ritual.

Jenny took Ben's hand and they wandered around to the front of the centre. There was a pen there with different breeds of sheep and another with ducks. Ben was immediately drawn to them and a young assistant, her long red hair tied back was pleased to talk to him. Jenny joined in the conversation for a minute but the morning sun was surprisingly hot and she wanted her coffee so she dragged Ben away with a promise that they would return later.

Jenny sat with her coffee, pondering about what to say to Mr Scott. Ben beside her eating his vanilla ice, topped with raspberry sauce.

A local Church of Scotland minister, Robert Kirk, who lived

in the seventeenth century, and claimed to be in touch with the fairies had created many myths about them in the area. He had died on the slopes of a nearby fairy dell, spirited away by the fairies, some claimed. The connection was well-promoted and hence the name of the art gallery. Jenny had tried to interpret the story, using it as inspiration, incorporating it in some of her paintings; it hadn't proved easy. The local slate quarries, now no longer being worked, had proven easier to paint; the abandoned quarries, fractured rock faces, old workings had been more productive. The gallery owner had been encouraging and now he would see the final paintings. This wasn't what she usually did, hence she was tense.

Ben finishing his ice cream, wanted to return to the sheep pen. Jenny gave the usual warnings and checked he hadn't left his mobile in the campervan, and that the assistant was still around, and let him go outside. She could still see him from where she sat. Having finished her coffee, checked on Ben, she went to the toilet, adjusted her makeup for a final time and then wandered outside, blinking in the strong sun. Ben was still talking to the assistant. 'Good,' she thought, that he had the confidence to chat to adults.

Ben turned when he saw her, his face shining; the assistant smiled at her.

'I need the toilet,' he said suddenly, and Jenny replied, 'be quick, we don't have much time.'

Ben ran inside to go to the toilet and Jenny wandered around to the campervan.

. . .

Jenny was glad to have left the campervan in the shade, feeling the heat from the sun, as she crossed the car park. The campervan was old enough that it needed a key to open the door. As she took out the key, she heard a voice from the other side of the campervan. 'Can you help me please?'

She unlocked the door of the campervan and walked round to the other side.

It was the plumber's van and she saw a man's back turned to her searching in the back of his van, which was empty apart from a single cardboard box, some pipes, an old toilet and some cables.

She stopped: 'Did you call me?'

The man turned and she saw the handgun immediately. Her first thought was of Ben, glad that he wasn't there. At that point, startled, she couldn't have given a description of him, her mind blank.

'Do what I say. Don't try anything! I'll use the gun. Reach slowly into your handbag and get your phone.'

This was Jenny's worst nightmare. She pulled out her phone. 'Throw it into the trees.' After a pause, she obeyed.

'Good, clever girl. Come here,' and Jenny stepped forward, he grabbed her, pulling her hands behind her, slipping on handcuffs. Roughly, he pushed her into the van, kneeling on her back, while he produced tape from the box and taped her mouth.

'Don't resist, darling,' he said, as Jenny struggled. He was strong and easily pushed her further into the van, reaching for a cable which he slipped between her arms and fastened to a clip at the side. He jumped up, slammed the doors shut and seconds later the engine started and he pulled away.

Ben was crossing the car park, when the van sped past him, not knowing that his Mum was in the back.

20

Ben was confused. The campervan door was unlocked but Mum was not around. He walked around it, she was not there. He waited a minute, then walked into the wood, maybe she had gone to look at the flowers, which he knew she liked. Ben had been told often enough; be careful. He stepped into the cool of the woods, sunlight shafting through the branches. And then he saw a mobile phone and recognised it as his Mum's and picked it up.

'Phone Dad,' the words echoed in his mind. Ben took out his phone and called me.

I answered the phone, 'What is it Ben?' he was probably too young to pick up my concern.

'Mum's gone.'

'What do you mean?'

'I got back to the van. She's gone. I found her phone in the woods.'

'Where are you?'

I recognised the location from the walk with Malcolm a few weeks ago.

'Malcolm's with me and Jason, we'll be there soon. Go to the shop, say that you are lost. Tell them your dad's coming soon. Be careful. Love you, Ben. Show them how to phone me, if they want.'

I quickly explained to Malcolm and picked up my phone, ringing the Alan Siviter number. After a few minutes Steve answered.

I swiftly described the situation.

'I'll phone the police. I have more clout. I am in Glasgow. I'll get there as soon as possible. Stay calm.'

By now we were all in my Golf and ready to go. I felt strangely calm; having prepared for this moment for so long.

Meanwhile, Ben wandered back across the car park to the sheep pen where the assistant was and told her. 'Mum's gone. My Dad said I should speak to someone.'

The assistant looked at the wee boy in front of her, his face now worried, a change from a few minutes ago. 'I'm Di,' she said, 'let's walk over to her car. I am sure she will turn up soon,' the expression on the boy's face, however, showed how worried he was. Ben took her hand and they wandered over, Ben pointing out the campervan. Di looked around, peered inside and walked over to the woods.

'What's your mum's name?'

'Jenny.'

Di called out: 'Jenny,' several times, walked into the woods, repeating her call. There was no reply.

'Come with me,' she said, taking Ben's hand again and they walked back, Ben looking around anxious. Di took him into the Centre and spoke to the manager.

'Probably nothing, but keep him with you. If the mum doesn't turn up, then we'll call the police.' Di was of a mind to do that anyway and led Ben outside. As she got outside a police car arrived in the car park, stopping on an empty disabled bay outside the Centre. Two police officers got out, a man and a woman, the man spotted the campervan and headed towards it, the female officer hesitated and Di ran forward with Ben, explaining who they were. The three of them then headed to the officer who was now by the campervan.

The female officer questioned Ben gently, kneeling down beside him, as she did. The other officer was on the radio. Di was fidgeting, anxious, still holding Ben's hand, but overhearing some parts of the radio conversation: this was a kidnap situation.

Ben was holding up, just!

'Were there any other cars nearby when you arrived?' enquired the policewoman, who identified herself as Val, who was crouched down smiling trying to be reassuring.

'A plumber's van.'

'How do you know it was a plumber?'

Ben described it and Val smiled, immediately passing on the information by her radio. Ten minutes later a second police car arrived and a police sergeant got out with another constable.

'I've just come from Loch Katrine direction, no such van passed us,' and he looked at the constable for confirmation.

'The van could have gone up Loch Ard direction,' the constable suggested.

'He'll be trapping himself if he did, it's a dead end.'

'This is a major alert,' and the sergeant turned away from Cathy and Ben.

'Intelligence services involved,' he stated, quietly to the other police officers, 'high priority and every second vital.'

He turned towards Ben: 'We'll soon have your Mum back. Don't worry, son,' but as he walked back to his car the grim expression on his face told a different story. The first few minutes would be vital, they needed a quick breakthrough.

. . .

I arrived and parked near one of the police cars. The area, around the campervan had now been taped off. My heart sank and I rushed towards Ben, hugging him.

An inspector, a young looking man, with not a hint of grey but with a quiet air of authority, was now in charge and updated me, and Malcolm who had joined us, was now holding Jason's hand.

'What about the other vehicle?' I asked.

'Your son gave a description of a plumber's van, that's all.'

The inspector saw the startled look on my face and I pulled out my mobile, searching through it.

'Ben, was this the van?'

Ben looked.

'Yes.'

The inspector took the phone,

'Are you sure, Ben?' the inspector enquired.

'Yes.'

I filled the inspector in and remembered the later photo taken on the ferry.

'There's your suspect.'

Good work,' and I turned to spot Steve, who had just arrived, getting out of his car, pulling on a jacket, his long hair untidy, flapping around his pointed face. I thought he appeared tense, and reacted immediately when shown the photo of the suspect.

'I know that man - he's called Connor Brown. An associate of McGrory,' he continued, almost as an aside to me, 'but not been used much by him recently. Peter, you know his brother Roy Brown who is on remand for his drug activities on Islay.'

It was Steve's turn to get busy on his mobile and the inspector also turned to his radio.

. . .

They hadn't driven that far, maybe twenty minutes, before the van turned off the tarmacked road and bumped along a rougher track, Jenny getting thrown about, trying not to be sick, which she knew with her mouth taped, would mean her choking. The van stopped and she heard the man moving away from the van, but he returned after a few minutes and opened the doors.

Jenny immediately saw that she was in a wooded area - fir trees all around. The man, thickset, short cut hair, grabbed her arms and unclipped her and dragged her towards a small wooden house; to a door, with a wooden frame beside it, containing a gas cylinder. Stumbling, her clothes now muddy, Jenny was pushed inside and was thrown on the floor of the kitchen. The man didn't pause, dragging a chair with side arms over to her, he hauled her up and pushed her onto it, threatening her if she struggled. Ripping tape with his teeth, he bound her legs to the chair legs and then he released her hands from the handcuffs and bound them with more tape to the arms of the chair.

Jenny found herself in a small kitchen, a sink by the window, some old Formica topped units and a small round table. There was one another chair in the kitchen and a door, to another room, which was shut.

The man pulled the kitchen window curtains shut and turned around to face Jenny.

'I'm going to hide the van. I'll be back. Then we can talk.' He was out of breath, sweating, and quickly turned away, shutting and then locking the door behind him. A minute later she heard the van drive off.

Jenny wanted to cry but forced herself to take deep breathes through her nose, trying to calm down.

. . .

The area of the car park behind the Scottish Wool Centre was now blocked off and an incident trailer was on its way.

'I have an address for Connor Brown,' Steve proclaimed,

and the inspector got on the radio, declaring a few minutes later, 'a team is on its way.'

'He couldn't have made it to his house in the time frame. He must be nearby, he will have set this up in advance,' suggested Steve.

Officers were now mingling with the visitors to the Scottish Wool Centre and asking if anyone had seen a plumber's van on their journey to the centre. One young boy said: 'I saw one, with a dripping tap on its side,' and the boy's father agreed.

'The van was spotted travelling south towards Glasgow on the A81,' the father stated. They told me minutes later.

The police had checked with the DVLA and now had the registration of Connor Brown's car - a blue Vauxhall Insignia.

Malcolm was following the developing story intently and had messaged his paper. He was on the inside for what could be a massive story for him, although he knew that in deference to his friend he might not be able to write it up.

The inspector was good at keeping them informed and minutes later, he gave me the thumbs up. 'They're in,' and there was a frustrating long time before he reported further.

'Brown wasn't there, nor was his car. We didn't expect him to be. It was a small terraced house. Pretty untidy. There was an old ferry ticket wallet on his bedside table - CalMac. That supports your story. The officers are searching the house thoroughly.'

I could only pace about, Malcolm was by now keeping Ben and Jason occupied and watching Steve on his phone, the inspector and Steve were talking and then the inspector was called back to one of the cars. He came over towards me after a few minutes.

'They have found pictures of you and Jenny, at the house, taken on a beach, presumably Islay. He has been stalking you. We suspect that he is not far away. Officers are out searching for the van.

My stomach turned wondering what could be happening to Jenny.

. . .

The man had returned, after an hour, and locked and bolted the door behind him, disappearing through the other door and then Jenny heard the toilet flushing. He returned drying his hands.

'The van's well hidden and wiped clean of fingerprints.' He paused: 'Well then, Jenny, what are we going to do now,' almost as if it was a surprise that she was here. His eyebrows arched, his forehead wrinkling, a hint of a smile. 'I'll be out of here soon, walk to Buchlyvie, along the cycle track, across Flanders Moss, pick up my car and I'm away.' His smile deepened, 'All planned, eh,' and he seemed proud of himself.

Then he became more serious, the smile vanished he lent forward over Jenny, she now becoming aware of his breath, which was sour, bitter.

'My brother is in prison, will be for a long time, due to your husband. I want my revenge - you're the victim. You're the nearest I can get to punishing your husband - collateral damage.' He let the last two words linger, as if he was proud of them. 'Sad for you isn't it?'

Jenny could only squirm, the bile in her own mouth bitter, the need to go to the toilet desperate, her mouth dry and she was also very thirsty.

'Mr McGrory has a way of dealing with those who cross him. I'll keep to his standards - it ensures that people are wary of him.' Jenny watched in horror as he pulled what looked like a bullet from his pocket and a pair of pliers.

'Metal bar,' he stated, as if reading her thoughts, 'needs to be heated' and he turned towards the small cooker and turned

154

on the gas, lighting it. Jenny could hear the hiss of the flame. He placed the pliers beside the cooker on the Formica top.

. . .

'We've found drugs, personal use, and a small handgun, no bullets as yet. They are examining note pads etc.'

The incident trailer had now been towed in and was in place and more staff had appeared, computers now up and running. Two forensic officers were pulling on white overalls.

A support liaison officer, Linda, she called herself, had joined us and the others offering hot drinks and chatting - beside the trailer. Time hung heavily. I was now praying, hoping for divine intervention. The inspector came down the steps of the incident trailer and looked for me.

When he reached me he said: 'the search is ongoing but we found a notepad under his bed. We have made out the imprint of names on the notepad - mean anything?' and he showed Malcolm and me, the names that they had found, which he had written down - 'Bac Mor' and 'Drumfechan'.

'I can tell you,' said Malcolm, and attention focussed on him.

'Bac Mor doesn't mean anything, sounds Gaelic, but Gartmore station was renamed Drumfechan when it was used in the making of a film - *Geordie*, I think it was called. Where is Ronnie when you need him,' he said to me and the inspector looked puzzled but he quickly went on 'There could be a house with that name near the former station site and it is on the road towards Glasgow.' I remembered the name, confirmed what Malcolm had said.

The inspector called out and Steve and a sergeant appeared, Steve putting away his mobile quickly.

'It might be nothing, it's the nature of investigations,' he cautioned me Meanwhile, Malcolm had looked up the National

Library for Scotland website and found an old map of the station site and used one of the site's features to link it side-by-side with a present day satellite image. 'There are several houses in the vicinity,' and he gave general map coordinates.

'Take a car and go to Gartmore station site and look for a house named Drumfechan. I'll radio more info as I get it,' ordered the inspector.

Steve asked to go with them and jumped in the back of the police car, which sped off.

. . .

Jenny watched in horror as the metal bar glowed red, wondering how he was going to use it on her. Her control over her bodily functions had all but gone. The man turned sniffing the air and smiled at her.

'You won't be dead when I leave you,' the man explained, 'but you will wish that you were.' Jenny swore to herself, the sadist was enjoying the power he had over her, her eyes drawn to the red hot metal.

He took out a packet of wipes and began wiping door handles, taps anything that he could have touched and when satisfied, he packed his small bag and put it by the door, ready to leave.

'Well let's do this,' he said, matter of fact, no emotion in his voice, as if he was a dentist about to extract a tooth.

. . .

With flashing lights, the police car sped towards the site of Gartmore station, about twenty minutes south of Aberfoyle, and about a mile from Gartmore village and now due to road alignment was on the right of the road as you travelled south. The site was muddy, only the former station master's house remaining, the area filled with logs from felled trees, waiting for transport.

As the police car stopped one of the policemen jumped out and rapped on the door of the former station master's house, which stood in a clearing beside a forestry track . An old woman appeared at the door startled by the arrival of police.

She hadn't seen any van but there were some wooden houses on the other side of the road, in the woods. 'Drumfechan' - yes, but couldn't remember which one, looking puzzled as they sprinted away from her.

They ran under the road bridge searching, spotting two small wooden houses, in clearings amongst the trees. Steve took control and quickly headed towards one and ordered the officers to check the other. There was no van to be seen but Steve saw recent tyre marks outside the house as he ran towards it.

The man ripped the tape from Jenny's mouth and grabbed her hair pulling her head back using tape to position her head so that her mouth was kept open. Jenny started to scream but he slapped her.

'Once the hot bar is down your throat, you will feel pain like never before, not be able to breathe,' and he seemed pleased, enjoying Jenny's reaction, the look of fear in her bulging eyes, ignoring her pleas for mercy.

Steve heard the scream and ran quicker towards the house. He smashed the kitchen window with a gun which had been concealed in his jacket, pulling the curtain aside, in time to see Connor Brown poised with the glowing metal bar above Jenny's mouth.

Brown turned surprised and went to mouth something when Steve fired and Connor's head disappeared, a cloud of crimson and brains momentarily spreading out. Clambering onto the window sill Steve jumped in and reached Jenny hacking at the tape with a knife, he quickly found in a drawer. Once released Jenny ran through the door to the bathroom and he heard her being sick.

There was a banging at the door and he unlocked and unbolted it, letting the officers in. One gagged as he saw the headless body, the other got on his radio and Steve went to check on Jenny.

21

I was watching the inspector talking on his radio and saw the expression on his face. He seemed pleased, then he frowned. My emotions surged and dipped. This guy held my future in his next few utterances.

'Jenny is safe and is unharmed,' he explained, turning to me with a mixture of compassion and authority, which suggested a bright future in his profession. 'She is being taken to hospital in Glasgow to be checked over. An officer will drive you there in your car. You have been through too much to drive yourself,' he added.

'What happened?

'Connor Brown is dead,' and I understood the cause of his frown. This made life complicated. Deaths always meant endless investigations. He could say nothing more but a lot must have happened. Malcolm absorbed the information, his journalistic instincts must have forged a thousand questions, but loyally he supported me and kept quiet. The scoop was for later.

'Mum is safe and well' I said to Ben, who was looking anxiously up at me.

'And we are going to see her now. It's good news,' and I lifted him up and hugged him, tears running down my face. Jason hung back but as I put Ben down, I called him over and we all clung together for a moment. It was a good outcome, for everyone but the kidnapper.

It was Linda, the police liaison officer, who drove us. Malcolm sat with the boys in the back. We left Aberfoyle and soon after passed near the crime scene, as we crossed a bridge over the former railway track, and saw below us several parked police cars, lights flashing and an ambulance. We couldn't see the house where Jenny had been held prisoner, from the road.

We reached Glasgow, wound through streets to reach the motorway and shortly after reached the Royal Infirmary. We parked outside the Accident and Emergency entrance and quickly walked in. Linda identified herself and a nurse took us along a corridor to a screened off cubicle, a policeman sitting outside it.

A consultant came out as we approached and stopped us: 'Are you Jenny's husband?' he asked, when I said yes, he went on, 'I've sedated her and she will be very sleepy. She must rest. Just spend a few minutes with her - reassure her.'

'Take your sons in with you. Jenny wants to see you but no questions just let her know that you are there. Apart from the trauma of the situation, she has no physical injuries. She'll be here for observation for a few days.'

I pulled back the curtain and there was Jenny, propped up on pillows, having heard our voices, she tried to smile but the sedatives were taking effect and she looked very drowsy. Ben rushed before me and clutched his Mum.

'Ben was a hero,' I said, 'phoned me right away - did everything as we told him to. Jason was also a great support,' and I pulled Jason over towards me. I glanced at the monitors, all seem normal, the blips on the screen suggested that she was calm, recovering. It could all have been so different and it was now that the impact of what had happened hit me: as my own adrenaline started to dip.

The consultant was waiting outside the cubicle. 'We'll move her to a single room when we are satisfied that she is okay and the drugs are working. Come back this evening - and get some rest yourself.'

He was right, I could feel the emotion inside me, with the tension off I was all over the place. I knew that my relief about Jenny would soon turn to anger. Linda escorted us along the corridor and outside to our car. Once home Linda said that she would stay and deal with any phone calls, press intrusion, and she smiled at Malcolm.

'Alison is coming to pick me up at the end of her shift, in an hour,' he said, going into the kitchen offering to make everyone coffee.

. . .

Linda, the police liaison officer suggested that I went up to my bed, while she kept an eye on the boys, but, of course, I couldn't easily sleep - my mind racing. Ben opened the bedroom door a few minutes later, dinosaur in one hand, and stood looking at me and when I smiled rushed across and climbed in beside me. He slept.

I must have eventually dozed, waking when I heard the doorbell ring. I got up leaving Ben and went downstairs. It was Alison, looking ashen, disbelieving at the turn of events. I had to get used to that, what happened was horrific.

. . .

Later, in the evening, Linda took us back to the hospital and escorted us up to Jenny's ward. At the far end a police officer sat, standing up as we approached.

'Just wait a minute,' she said, 'officers are with her. It shouldn't be long.'

We were shown into a small anteroom and a few minutes later we heard voices and I recognised one of them and quickly went to the door.

Nick was wearing jeans and a grey sweatshirt, which highlighted his sallow complexion. He was smaller than I remembered him, but that was probably just in contrast to the chief inspector, who was very tall and immaculately turned out in his uniform. There was tension between them as they left Jenny's room. I caught the end of a terse exchange.

'We need to know what was discovered using the cyber kiosk,' demanded Nick, but any conversation was curtailed by my appearance, although always alert, Nick knew that I had overhead them.

'Nick,' I said, 'it is not a surprise to see you here .

'I'm pleased that Jenny is safe, he replied, 'I'm told that she will be fine in a few days.' The chief inspector said nothing but I saw him giving an annoyed glare at his officer who stood behind me, probably for letting me out of the anteroom.

'I'll come and see you tomorrow, Peter,' and he turned away heading up the ward, beside the chief inspector, barely level with his shoulder.

When I went in Jenny was sitting up still obviously feeling the effect of the sedatives. 'Oh, thank God that you are okay.' I leant over and kissed her and sat down beside her, holding her hand.

'Is Ben okay?'

'Yes,' I replied, 'he was wonderful, did everything right,' and I quickly filled Jenny in on what I knew. She had forgotten our earlier visit.

She was speaking very softly, her mouth dry, even after I gave her a sip of water.

'He tried to kill me. The guy you know as Steve shot him, just in time. I don't think that the police are pleased with him.'

Maybe not, but I didn't care, as far as I was concerned Brown had given up all rights to life when he kidnapped Jenny.

The boys then joined us, Jason hanging back, but Ben very clingy with his Mum. Later Linda took us home and another officer arrived to take her place.

. . .

Next morning, not long after I had phoned the hospital for an update on Jenny, two detectives arrived and took a statement from me and a specially trained officer spoke with Ben. They were pleased that I could identify Brown. While the photo on the ferry was not so clear, the picture they showed me from their files was sharper. There was no doubt, it was definitely him.

The replacement liaison officer came in with coffee for us, Jason helping with the biscuits. The detectives were very thorough, quizzing me about the events on Islay. There was no doubt about a motive.

Shortly after they left Nick arrived. Unshaven, wearing a patterned blue shirt. The pressure on Nick and his colleagues to get results must be immense, but I still couldn't warm to him, empathise with his pressures.

He accepted a coffee. 'You did well yesterday, so did Ben. But we were still very lucky. We can't rely on another moment of inspiration that your friend, Malcolm had. I have no doubt that Brown would have killed Jenny but Steve in shooting him saved the day. My police colleagues would have liked him alive,' and I knew that he was alluding to the tension between the police and him.

'Brown was low life, just like his brother but not as bright. I fear that his motive was personal - revenge - and the kidnapping was not instigated by McGrory. The police concur. They found

Brown's car, parked a couple of miles away and a laptop in the boot and using a device called a cyber kiosk, it enabled them to override passwords and any protections; they got a full data analysis,' he explained. I think that Nick was disappointed that the police were analysing the laptop first. 'We don't know if they found anything yet,' and annoyed that the police were restricting access to the information found on it.

He then quizzed me about my visit to the care home and to Ireland.

'I'm afraid that you will have to remain vigilant, especially now you have Jason. Desmond McGrory, is psychopathic, however you want to define that - he's a heidbanger, as you might say in Scotland. He takes irrational grudges against people, gets fixated on women, obsessed by them. I believe that he was obsessed with Catherine. Catherine didn't send Jason to Ireland for a holiday or to a boarding a school for an education - he was being hidden, which suggests that McGrory was unhappy when he discovered that she had a child. And you are the father and also screwed up a profitable smuggling route. So the spotlight is on you.'

I mentioned the invite to Mull. He appeared very thoughtful, his expression difficult to read.

'Could be good for the two of you, get away. Probably, help with Jason - integrate him. But you have to make up your own mind about that. Let me know what you decide.'

I told him about the accusations made about me downloading porn.

'Can't be sure about your office machine but the rest are clean. We've checked, routine. I'll make enquiries. Let me know if you find out anything that could help us. Planting porn on someone's computer is frighteningly easy,' and he made a note of the little information I had given him.

I was very tired and didn't see Nick out but remained sitting on the couch, lost in my thoughts.

'Dad,' and I felt a tug at my sleeve.

'Yes, Ben,' but then I realised it was Jason and opened my eyes and smiled. Progress, the first time he had called me dad and not father.

'When I brought in the biscuits for the police, I noticed a photo on the table. I saw him before.'

Now I was alert: 'Where, Jason?'

'He was the man outside my bedroom window the night of the fire.'

'Are you sure?'

'Yes.'

So Brown had been following us around, even to Ireland. He had tried to kidnap Jason. Somehow that didn't fit in; if it was personal why go for Jason? He hadn't been responsible for Brown's brother being imprisoned.

In the afternoon I visited Jenny again, pleased to see that she was more herself, although knowing that the sedatives were largely responsible. We talked about Mull and decided to go.

Later I got a text from Ronnie.

'Heard from Malcolm about Jenny, Glad all are safe. Send her our love. We are thinking about you all. We are now back home. Our house was burgled while we were away. Trashed. Phone you soon. Love Ronnie and Maria.'

Was the burglary a coincidence? I found that difficult to believe. The thug who chased me out of the care home must have made a note of the car registration and the number was linked to Ronnie. They were tenacious which worried me. With the focus on recovering Jenny I had also missed the opportunity to ask Steve where he had disappeared to in Ireland after he had spoken to us in the pub.

22

Jura

Gil's home was about a mile further out of Craighouse than Ronnie's house. As usual for a short distance Ronnie chose to walk to reach the house, which was one of three small terraced single bedroom cottages originally built by the estate, set back from the road and for Jura unusually there was a small scrub oak wood to the rear. Facing east the rough hewn stone was catching the morning sunlight. Ronnie vaguely remembered being at a party in one of them, many years ago, but was not sure now which one. In front of each cottage there was a small garden, the first one was neat and tidy; it was planted with roses. The garden in front of Gil's house was also neatly planted with shrubs. The third house appeared empty, the grass had not been cut since the previous winter; the grass long and unkempt like a poor haircut.

Ronnie walked up the narrow path, knocked on the wooden door, its red paint peeling, and waited. He knocked again, began to suspect that Gil wasn't in, his trip wasted. He wanted to talk about the final arrangements and payments for taking Gil's first survivalist group by boat to the west coast of the island. Gil had said that the people were arriving in a week, a group of four, a couple from the continent, Holland he believed and two Americans. After the third time of rapping on the door, he was certain that Gil was out, but just to be sure he turned the handle

- few people on Jura locked their doors. Even after the trashing of his own house, Ronnie still didn't lock up on leaving. What was the point, the burglars would have got in anyway; the policeman had as much as admitted it.

He edged the door open and peered inside. There was an open coal fire on the rear wall, the fire had been reset, with paper and wood, with two easy chairs by it, facing each other, and a table with a floral plastic cover spread over it underneath the front window. On top of the table was a free standing wooden cross, the sunlight streaming through the window casting its shadow at an angle over the cover. Ronnie hadn't expected that, never thought of Gil as religious. The bedroom door was partially open and he could see a rolled up sleeping bag on a bare mattress. Gil was certainly not one for luxurious living. Military life often made one get by with little, he assumed. Confirming that he was not in Ronnie pulled the door shut and turned surprised to see the Rev Walker walking up the path.

'Hello, Mr Walker, I mean, Rev Walker,' he said caught off-guard.

'Is he not in, Ronnie?'

'Seems not. I hadn't arranged a particular time but hoped to catch him. Business,' Ronnie added.

The minister smiled: 'I had arranged to see him,' and he glanced at his watch. 'Usually, he is very punctual. I'll wait a few minutes and see if he turns up.'

'I'll come back later. If you see him please let him know that I was here,' and Ronnie walked down the path back towards the road, passing the minister's parked car.

Having only gone a few hundred yards in the direction of Craighouse a battered Land Rover came down the road and Ronnie turned hoping that it might be Gil. It wasn't Gil but Torquil, the factor, who stopped and wound down his window.

'Looking for Gil? He caught the Oban ferry from Port Askaig. I ran him along this morning. Something cropped up unexpectedly. Luckily, it was Wednesday the day the ferry goes there. I don't know when he will be back. He never says very much, does he? Do you want a lift?'

'Thanks but I better let the minister know that Gil is away, he's waiting for him.'

'Okay, I'll wait.' The minster informed, Ronnie climbed into the Land Rover.

'Terrible what happened to you,' Torquil said, as he drove off, 'how's Maria coping?'

'Taking it well, although we lost her laptop and the house was trashed. Cups, plates smashed, television knocked over, drawers opened and emptied. They even ripped the bedding off the bed and slashed the mattress. You could say that they did a thorough job.'

Torquil looked sympathetic: 'They can't be from Jura, we would know. It so unusual for people to come to the island and do this - vindictive. And they weren't spotted. No one saw anything. What did the police say?'

'They sent a car across from Islay, took a statement, spoke to neighbours. I don't suspect that they will discover the culprits.'

'Sadly,' Torquil concurred.

By now the Land Rover had reached Ronnie's house and Torquil stopped, leaving the engine idling.

'We have tidied most things up and replaced the smashed items. Maria is annoyed about the laptop - contained pictures of her missing sister.'

'Yeah that's a pity, she'll take that hard,' and Ronnie agreed as he opened the vehicle door.

'I was surprised to see the minister at Gil's house again,' said Torquil.

Ronnie thought of the cross on the table but decided to say nothing. Gil was private, if he wanted to tell people then he could do so himself.

Ronnie thanked Torquil for the lift and got out. Maria looked edgy when the door was suddenly opened, not expecting Ronnie back so soon, a legacy of the burglary. Nothing seemed as safe, their private space violated.

'You're back early.'

'He wasn't in,' said Ronnie, and went through to the kitchen putting water in the kettle and switching it on to make a cup of coffee.

'According to Torquil, who gave me a lift back, Gil left early to catch the ferry to Oban. Unexpected.'

Maria looked surprised and Ronnie also told her about the minister.

'And there was a wooden cross on the table.'

'Gil's a deep one - seems a lonely type.'

'Maybe few friends on the island but he's in touch with some people; there were quite a few postcards on the table.'

Ronnie added coffee granules to a mug and poured boiling water into it, adding sugar before he stirred it.

'It's a nice day, I'm going out to the decking,' he added, opening the sliding patio doors. He sat on the wooden bench next to the open door and sipped the coffee, enjoying the peace, listening to the bird song. Spring was a good time of year although he noticed a few jobs needing done: the grass tidied, the vegetable patch needing dug over. 'They could wait,' he thought, settling back.

The door bell sounded, its chime dying away and he heard Maria talking and a familiar voice: Joan the post woman. Another day he might have gone and talked with her, asked how her partner, Bill's job at the distillery was going but he was enjoying sipping the coffee wondering why Gil had gone away so abruptly.

Then he heard a loud scream, his peace shattered, he hurriedly put down the mug of coffee and ran inside. Maria was standing, in shock, her face ashen, holding what looked like a photograph. Her mouth opening and shutting, wordlessly. Ronnie snatched the photograph from her and looked at the photo, searching for confirmation, but all he got was another piercing scream as Maria stood tears running down her face.

Part Two

Snare

23

Administrators from the Shona Tyler Trust had contacted us and arranged for Jenny's paintings and materials to be uplifted, which was a help because the police had not yet released her campervan with investigations ongoing; Connor Brown's death still causing ructions. The work involved in preparing the paintings for transport had taken up a lot of Jenny's time, given her a new focus. The trust had chosen a gallery about to be opened on Iona - the Nunnery View Gallery to display her paintings. The gallery was located not far from the ferry slipway and close to the medieval Nunnery, one of several historic buildings on the island. Dad had often spoken of Iona and its history, so we were particularly looking forward to our visit and also catching up with him. The removal company were also delivering Jenny's painting materials and some of our possessions to our rented house in Kintra, on the mainland of Mull, opposite Iona. Everything was being made as easy as possible.

Because we had been so busy, we hadn't had time to visit Jodie, in Ayr, who was recovering slowly, her leg improving. We missed her but knew she was in good hands - Colin and Mandy had already formed a strong attachment to her - it was difficult not to.

Still trusting in my Golf we packed the car and set off. Jason

175

was settling in well forming a close bond with Ben and Jenny. Part of it, I believe, was relief that he was not being asked to return to the boarding school. We were not, however, a normal family setting off. We always checked our phones and reminded the boys to have their phones on them at all times, the shadow of McGrory was ever present.

We headed out of Glasgow, up by Loch Lomond, bypassing Crianlarich and stopped at the Green Welly in Tyndrum for coffee and a break. I could see Jenny glancing at the wing mirror several times checking on the traffic behind us. I did the same as we could never let our guard down, Aberfoyle had ensured that.

Leaving Tyndrum we took the A85 road to Oban passing through more dramatic landscapes, cheek-by-jowl with the railway to Oban, space for both often at a premium as hills and lochs crowded in. Patches of snow remained on the highest peaks or slopes sheltered from the sun. Loch Awe sparkled in the sunshine and then Loch Etive, bridged at its narrows by the spectacular Connel cantilever bridge. Shortly after, the road turned south-west passing Dunbeg before we reached Oban, our first destination. The road descended steeply into Oban, the streets narrow and busy with the first tourists of the season. We found it difficult to park so we headed straight to the ferry terminal and booked in. So far so good. A quick walk along the promenade pointing out to the boys McCaig's folly, a round tower on the hill overlooking Oban Bay, a famous landmark, with its many arches. Nearer was the red brick chimney of the Oban distillery, which interested me, but we didn't have time to visit.

The ferry sailed out of Oban Bay, slipping passed Kerrera Island heading across the Firth of Lorne to the Island of Mull, impressive hills in all directions and as we neared Mull we passed Duart Castle perched on a headland. The boys were excited, stretching our knowledge of the many hills and islands we passed with their questions. The fifty minute crossing was a lot quicker than the two hour crossing to Islay. Islay and Mull had similar populations, indented coastlines and coastal cliffs but Mull was far larger with more offshore islands, like historic Iona, Ulva, Staffa and the Treshnish Isles on the west coast.

Once off the ferry at Craignure, it was a simple choice either right to reach Tobermory, the largest settlement on the island or left to start the journey towards Iona, nearly thirty five miles away. We turned left, the road, quickly became single track with passing places. Progress was slow as we wound through the glens, campervans, in particular, slowing us down. Like Islay I realised that you had to adjust your clock, slow to island time and appreciate the rugged beauty of your surroundings.

The road descended to a junction at the head of Loch Scridain but we stayed on the road, passing through the village of Pennyghael, travelling on the southern edge of Loch Scridain, steep cliffs and hills over the loch to our right. As the road hugged the contours of the land we were afforded glimpses of the glimmering open sea ahead and the small islands further west.

We had reached the Ross of Mull, a long peninsula which stuck out south-west from the rest of Mull. We travelled though the village of Bunessan, the largest village in the area, passing the primary school that the boys would attend while they were here. The road climbed as we left the bay where the village nestled. Jenny sat entranced, her artist's eye assessing the scenery with delight, turning looking back over to the mountain core of Mull, with its highest peak, Ben More. The rocks were changing, the island's turbulent geological past dictating their nature. Basalt was giving way to white and red granite, the latter particularly reflective in the sunlight. Jenny had been looking forward to viewing the red granite for herself , having done her homework, she saw potential for her paintings, as had many artists before her, and was not disappointed on this sunny morning. Mull had scenery on a grander scale than Islay but some of the outcrops of rocks connected by areas of moorland and machir, were familiar to me from Islay; the machir alive, at this time of year, with spectacular displays of small flowers.

This was a landscape which would reward exploration; a landscape which had inspired artists for generations. Thanks to Shona Tyler, Jenny was going to be able to make her contribution.

Shortly after passing a filling station, we reached a small loch, with a church perched between it and the road. Just ahead was Fionnphort, the ferry terminal for Iona. I glanced at Jenny wondering if we should make a quick visit to it, but we were all tired. We would leave the final mile to Fionnphort until tomorrow. I spotted the sign for Kintra and turned right. The boys became more alert, the twisting road had quietened them, the journey seeming endless to them, now they knew that they were getting closer to their destination.

The road was windy, crossing moorland, with, at one point, a farm straddling the road, with sheep jostling for space on the warm tarmac of the road. I saw Jenny checking her wing mirror again relieved that no one was behind us. The countryside was dotted with large granite blocks, rounded and craggy, puncturing the moorland, grass clinging, in places, to the surface of them with an occasional bold sheep munching tufts of grass near the top of the crags.

After a mile the road emerged from between granite rocks to be rewarded with a spectacular view over the sea to Staffa, with its world famous Fingal's Cave and beyond that Ulva. Further west was a ribbon of small islands: the Treshnish Islands. To the east on Mull were spectacular cliffs, narrow waterfalls tumbling from their steep slopes, like ribbons of tears, with Ben More standing aloof behind the cliffs, master of all it surveyed. To our left was our first glimpse of Iona. Even the boys, now alert, sensing that the journey was ending, were impressed.

'The sea, the big sky, oh this is stunning,' Jenny was enthusing, breathing deeply, hungry to fill her lungs with the fresh air. 'What scenery, what potential,' and Jenny exhaled a second later as if she was trying to release the tension in her body.

The road took several more sharp turns before descending to a small tidal bay with a row of houses along the inner edge - Kintra, with a small island in the bay. Black faced sheep, many with lambs, were scattered over the hills, a few stranded on the small island, which looked tidal. There was a small car park next to a bridge over a small stream. I crossed the bridge found the white two storey house, opening a wooden gate and parked the car at the side of the house and using the key forwarded to us, let myself in through a small porch at the front.

With the boy's help we unpacked the car and soon we were settled in. Ben and Jason had chosen to share a room, which we thought was a good idea and we took the bedroom upstairs overlooking the bay.

I checked the mobile signal - there was none, but there was a landline, so we weren't completely out of touch. The phone was too high up on the wall for Ben but I pointed out a small stool which he could use. All this was becoming second nature.

I knew that Jenny was still taking some tablets to help her nerves but I could see a difference already, the strain was slipping from her face, which had more colour. The trip had invigorated her.

I went out to the back garden which was long, rising towards the rear, fenced off from marauding sheep, which were munching the grass in the neighbouring fields. In the distance, on a stunted hillock was a small wind turbine, whirling, its low hum audible. At the top of the rise was a garden hut, fronted with glass, which we had been told about - perfect for Jenny to paint. I walked to it with the boys and admired the view over the small bay looking out to sea and the north end of Iona. My mind naturally drifted to Dad, looking forward to seeing him tomorrow. He was always so positive but it had been many months since I had last seen him and I thought he had looked tired on that occasion.

My thoughts were interrupted by a loud piercing scream and I saw Ben running towards me.

'Snakes,' screamed Ben and I shouted at Jason who I saw gazing intently at something in the long grass at the back of the garden. I recognised the black zigzag markings, the scaly brown skin and saw that there were, in fact, two adders entwined.

I tried to calm Ben down clutching him, feeling his heart thumping in his chest.

'Come here, Jason,' I called, but he didn't move and instead turned to me: 'They're coiled up together, being very friendly,' and his cheeks blushed.

Jenny had now reached Ben, taking in what had happened.

'It's like Islay,' I said to Ben, trying to sound calm, 'you have seen them there and they are also very common on Mull. You are more likely to see them, especially when they are mating in the spring. Let's go in and not disturb them: anyway you are not meant to harm them.'

Jason walked past: 'They're making babies,' he commented casually.

I hadn't got used to ten year old boys, yet.

'At night, when the matron had gone, we used to talk about how babies were made,' he explained, wandering back towards the house.

'How do they do that?' asked Ben.

'Just by being very friendly to each other,' said Jenny, hoping more detailed explanations could wait for another day, life was complicated enough. I walked back towards the house but when I glanced back at where the adders had been they had slithered away.

Later we left the house. It didn't take long to explore the area. We wandered past the row of houses, all of different styles, but mostly single storey, like former fishermen's cottages, but on the whole holiday houses, it seemed, as most were unoccupied. At the far end of the bay there was a large granite crag which towered over a small cottage and a path led by it, in front of the cottage, which we took to reach a headland. We climbed to the top of the headland and were again rewarded with wonderful views. The boys were soon chasing each other up and down grassy slopes ignoring Jenny's warnings to be careful. We so needed moments like this, I felt, as Jenny and I stood absorbing the view, taking in the restless sea. We stood side-by-side arms around each other, breathing as one, our synchronicity enhancing the moment.

On our return we walked past our house, over the bridge and walked up the steep road to some houses at the top of the hill and then back down, as if we were marking our territory.

A lady, probably in her fifties, hair grey, cut with a fringe, came out of a two storey house with a garage, two houses away from our house, as we crossed the bridge from the car park and spoke briefly, very friendly.

'I'm Cathy,' she said, a smartly turned out woman, in jeans and a warm purple coloured woollen sweater, wearing large dangling silver earrings, 'I have been expecting you. I had to direct the couriers when they had arrived searching for your house.' Her husband, Jim, she added, would be pleased to take us out on his small boat if we wanted. 'He likes company, especially when fishing,' and we readily agree to her welcoming gesture. This was like the welcome I would expect on Islay, so already I felt at home.

That night we put the boys to bed. Both seemed tired and were soon asleep. Jenny and I got a bottle of wine and opened it up in the bedroom watching the sun go down, trying to identify an island that we could just glimpse out to sea, but which had been much clearer from the headland. It was low lying, with a hill in the centre, with wide stretches of low land to each side and cliffs where the land met the sea. I checked out the tourist information map.

'It's the Dutchman's Cap,' I said, after a minute, 'I wondered what it was called. Small peak, wide brim and turned up at the edge. One of the Treshnish Islands.'

'Such a dramatic landscape, geology has certainly worked hard,' replied Jenny, cuddling into me again but I sensed that she had other things on her mind. 'This is so much what we need,' and her hand stroked my hair. I reached out kissing it. 'What did Jason mean by the adders being very friendly?' she asked, innocently with a smile, looking up at me coquettishly.

Later, we weren't ready for sleep and we sat again by the window savouring the dregs of the wine bottle. The light had gone, the incoming tide had circled the rocky grassland in the bay, creating an island with several sheep stranded on it, unconcerned chewing the grass.

'Jason is settling in very well. He never leaves your side, always wanting reassurance, not surprisingly.' I had noticed his attentiveness but I was pleased to hear that Jenny thought he was settling in. I agreed, thanking her for making such an effort.

'He looks very like you: the smile, the hair, that certain look.'

'Catherine's nose,' and Jenny laughed.

'Yes, but he's part of you, reminds me of you when you were younger and he desperately needs love. I know that Catherine loved him but that family...'

'They could be challenging,' I agreed, interrupting.

'But how could a mother send him away?' queried Jenny.

'The alternative must have been worse and that doesn't bear thinking about.'

As we sat, the silences grew longer as the wine relaxed us, each of us comfortable. I spotted out to sea, the lights of a boat emerging from the south, its shape gradually becoming clearer as it drifted passed the end of the bay. It was a sailing boat, quite large, tall masts, its sails billowing, catching the wind. I pointed it out to Jenny who was half asleep.

'Our own pirate ship,' said Jenny, dreamily, 'Ben will be pleased.'

24

Both boys appeared happy as the head teacher took Ben and Jason away from the reception area to meet their new teachers. I noticed with satisfaction that Ben had reached out and taken Jason's hand as they left him. If the sea views from their temporary primary school were any measure of a school then they would enjoy an enriching experience.

It was a cloudy day with a strong breeze and so I hurried back to the car, stopping briefly in Bunessan to collect some shopping that Jenny wanted and further on at the filling station to put some diesel in the tank. Everyone had time for me, service slow but friendly and efficient: again it reminded me strongly of Islay.

Jenny was waiting for me on my return, coming out to the car, waving to Cathy, who was returning from a walk before we drove the short distance to Fionnphort. The village consisted of a line of houses mainly to the left of the road leading down to the ferry slipway. From the general store and post office down to the sea there was ample parking on both sides of the road, mostly empty at this time, the first visitors of the day having not yet reached this remote part of the island. There were parking charges so we turned around and parked for free beside the Columba Centre, a derelict building a short distance away down a side road on the road to a place called Fidden. We grabbed our small backpacks and headed to the ticket office to buy our tickets for the journey and then made our way to the slipway, watching the small ferry coming over from Iona, being tossed about by the waves, on the first of many trips it would make that day. At last the weather was improving; the sun breaking through the clouds.

Iona appeared very close, only a mile away across the Sound of Iona, with a cluster of buildings near the ferry ramp on the island and then going north, Iona Abbey and then Dun-I the highest hill on the island. Although of modest height Dad had described the views from Dun-I as unbeatable. He was keen to climb it with us but the plan for today was to explore the Abbey and catch up with each other.

To the right of the ferry terminal was a small beach, with a single large boulder cleaved in two, in the centre, which intrigued me and then a hillside with much evidence of the now distinctive red granite. I noticed Jenny casting her artist's eye over the scene, judging proportions, checking the light and shade; composing a painting in her head. As the ferry, the *Loch Buie*, one of the smaller members of the CalMac fleet reached us, its bow door descended until it hit the concrete slipway, making a grinding noise, our view of Iona was now partially obscured. We gave over our tickets and went to the small passenger lounge as it was still too cold to sit outside. Given that we would spend a lot of time on Iona, the scene would soon become very familiar. We settled down for the short ten minute crossing.

On the other side we again waited as the ramp went down, only one vehicle, a builder's van was on our crossing, leaving first before the passengers were allowed to disembark. Few vehicles, namely only those who lived or had work on the island, were permitted to cross in their vehicles.

I caught my first glimpse of Dad at the top of the concrete slipway and waved.

A minute later we reached him, both of us hugging him. Immediately, I could see that he was older, thinner, his complexion pale. I pulled back a little my arms still around his shoulders and studied his face. He was very pleased to see us but there was a haunted look on his face.

'Are you okay, Dad?' it was blunt but said out of concern.

'Yes,' but I sensed a hesitancy and felt guilty that I hadn't managed to see him for so long, since he settled on the island since Mum's death. He had aged, maybe that was it. Having not seen him for a while I would notice the difference but I could see Jenny also quietly assessing him, the slightly awkward silence broken when he declared: 'Let's go to the Martyr's Bay Restaurant for a cup of tea,' and he pointed to a modern building just beyond the public toilets.

Dad filled us in on his life on the island. His work at the Abbey which meant that he met many people from all sorts of backgrounds and countries. The tradition at the Abbey was ecumenical, so embraced people from all strands of the Christian faith, drawn by the island's unique location and history. Here St Columba arrived from Ireland to spread the Gospel. Many myths surrounded his ministry and the island had a long history, more recently the Abbey, which was a ruin for many years, was rebuilt under the direction of George McLeod, a charismatic minister from the Church of Scotland, who formed the Iona Community.

Dad talked about his involvement in the life of the Abbey, spoke of Mum, who like me, he still missed a lot and wanted to know how we were doing. That was a difficult conversation, with Jenny and I having agreed in advance what to say. He knew about Jason and was keen to meet him and see Ben again. We had just felt that we didn't want to overwhelm him on our first trip. In that regard we had been wise. We didn't mention the allegations about me having porn found on my work computer and he was also unaware of what had happened recently to Jenny.

From the restaurant we wandered back towards the slipway and then headed up the gently sloping road past shops until we reached the Nunnery View Gallery. Jenny was keen to see it although we knew that it wasn't opening until the next day. A sneak look in the window could tell a lot about the owner's preferences; inform how Jenny would pitch her work. The building had been constructed recently, standing opposite the Nunnery, the extensive ruins of a convent, originally built around 1200AD. Beautiful gardens surrounded the ruins. To get permission to build an art gallery so close to the ruins was impressive.

I noticed that Dad was glad to stop, which worried me, sitting down on a bench outside the gallery. Jenny peered in the window studying the paintings displayed on easels in the window display and looking further into the gallery at paintings hung on the gallery walls. They consisted of recent work by local artists and prints of more famous artists, like Cadell and Peploe, who were part of a group known as the Scottish Colourists. The two artists were close friends, the only two members of that group to use Iona for inspiration in their paintings. Both of us had studied their paintings before coming here. Jenny preferred Peploe who worked only using oils, Jenny's preferred medium. I liked Cadell mainly because he included people or signs of human activity, like a boat sailing by. I was pleased that I could identify each artists work correctly.

Jenny then studied the notices on the door, which gave opening times, advertised events at the Abbey and a bring and buy sale at the local primary. She appeared concerned and it only took me a minute to understand why - there was no mention of her work and none of her paintings were on display.

Jenny looked at me puzzled: 'I would have expected, at least, some mention of my work, after all I am to be the artist in residence one day a week.' I noticed Dad lost in thought, in a

187

world of his own, unaware of our discussion, as I expressed my own surprise.

'We will be across first thing tomorrow and speak to the owner then - Dougie Paterson, isn't it?' I knew little of him, only a picture on the website, a balding middle-aged man, with a fringe of greying hair, with a heavy moustache and a ruddy complexion.

I called on Dad, and we wandered through the ruins of the Nunnery and along a winding road, past the St Columba hotel and opposite it an unusual building with a very low door, which most people would have to duck down to get through.

Eventually, we reached the gates of the Abbey. The views in all directions were stunning. The Abbey, was so impressive, built of red granite of local origin, with its tower and sense of history with a high free standing cross in front of it. Behind the abbey was the spectacular backdrop of Mull, with the Ross of Mull in the foreground and then the sea cliffs and hills of Mull beyond, the view was breathtaking. There was something special about Iona, experienced as soon as you stepped off the ferry, its isolation encouraging a different way of life. Vikings raided, on one occasion slaughtering monks at what became known as Martyr's Bay. Kings were buried in the grounds, the historic book of Kells, beautifully illuminated Gospels were crafted here, by the monks, many believed, before being removed for safety to Ireland. Columba set off from here to bring Christianity to the rest of Scotland. Pilgrims still visited to pay homage, to seek answers to eternal questions, to contemplate deep mysteries, to live lives of frugality, humbling themselves before God. Iona was steeped in spirituality and most visitors could sense that even today.

Dad led us through the gate, waving at the people who worked in the ticket booth, who knew him, and we walked by the 'street of the dead', the path used by those bringing bodies to the Abbey for burial. We had a personalised tour, through the west door of the church leading to the nave of the church where services were held each day. From the nave a door led into the cloisters, where it was possible to close your eyes and imagine hooded monks in procession chanting in Latin, although the present cloisters were rebuilt in the last century, after the war. There were also museums, with their partially reconstructed crosses. We were touched by the imagination of men and women who had dedicated their lives to a higher being, whose lives could inspire others in their search for meaning.

I could see Dad was getting tired and I suggested that we walk back to the hotel that we had passed earlier for lunch, pleased when he agreed. I suppose that our lack of recent face-to-face meetings had built some barriers, so we had to take time to rebuild trust and to relax in each other's company. I decided not to probe Dad about his health. If there was a problem, and I was sure now that there was, I would leave it to another day.

After lunch we parted, Dad returning to the Abbey, looking forward to our return visit tomorrow, the two of us walking back to the ferry slipway. As we waited at the slipway for the ferry: the colours of the rocks, many covered in lichen or encrusted with shells, the seaweed, the sandy beaches, the turquoise sea were all entrancing Jenny and me. Colours meant so much to her and on Iona they appeared so vibrant. I could sense her mind at work assessing, planning, new canvasses taking shape in her mind. She watched a woman perched on a rock knitting, marvelling at how the colours she knitted tied in with the surroundings, the pink of her wool matched by pink seaweed. On Iona you had peace to knit while waiting for the ferry.

We couldn't stay on the island too long, needing to get back to collect the boys. The ferry took a slightly longer route, which it did at low tide, to avoid a sand bar in the middle of the Sound of Iona but the journey took the same length of time. We walked up to the car passing about ten single decker buses lined up that had brought visitors here from Craignure, most to visit Iona, some to take a boat trip to Staffa and others to cram in both destinations.

Time was tight to get to the school before the end of the school day. We headed away from Fionnphort reaching the loch just outside the village catching up on a black Mercedes saloon, travelling slowly. I edged up behind it and as we drew level with the church, which sat on the bank of the loch, it pulled over into a passing place. I flashed my lights to thank them and as we drew level I saw the rear tinted window going down and had only the briefest glance of someone sitting in the back seat, a man, leaning forward saying something to his driver.

We sped on having to stop a few times to allow traffic to pass before we reached the hill that led down to Bunessan. This was the kind of driving I was used to, having lived on Islay. Jenny turned around a few times, always vigilant eventually commenting that the Mercedes was keeping up with us. Once through the village we reached the primary school with minutes to spare before the end of the day. We parked and Jenny got out to wait for the boys when they emerged. Five minutes later the bell sounded and the pupils appeared, the two boys some of the first out, Ben looking around for Jason before they came towards us Jenny and I could see the smiles on their faces, happy smiles. They both came into the car, excited talking about their day, comparing teachers. Jenny handed them both juice and I started the car turning it around in the now almost empty car park. Jenny's hand suddenly gripped my thigh and I followed her direction of gaze. In a passing place a short distance away, the black Mercedes saloon sat, the rear window down and someone was staring in our direction. When he saw that we had spotted him, the window rose and the car moved forward slowly. Why was it that even on good days, happy days, there had to be something unsettling?

25

I had dropped the boys off at school and was returning for Jenny who I could sense was anxious; puzzled by the lack of publicity and absence of her paintings at the art gallery on Iona. The gallery would be opening today for the season, so we would get some answers. I was also aware as I drove back to Kintra, that the Golf was misfiring, sounding unhappy. I was no mechanic and I couldn't remember the last time I looked under the bonnet, but hoped that it was nothing serious.

As I parked the car at the small parking area, beside the bridge, in Kintra, the engine ran on even after I turned the engine off, finally shuddering to a stop. Cathy and her husband were standing outside their house, the only other people staying in Kintra, at present, it seemed. He looked across at me alerted by the sound and then kissed his wife on her cheek before getting into a Post Office van and driving over the small bridge, giving me a wave as he passed.

Jenny was waiting outside the front door of our house, our backpacks on the ground beside her. She picked them up and walked across the bridge: 'Doesn't sound too happy,' she stated, looking at the car.

'I know, I know' I replied, 'I'll look at it later,' but given my mechanical skills, I was unlikely to resolve anything. However, it did restart, after Jenny got in, creating a cloud of diesel fumes.

The weather bright, we sat outside on the exposed red plastic seats on the upper deck of the ferry, *Loch Buie*, for the short crossing. The sea was a deep azure colour. The Abbey, which could often appear hidden in the lee of the hill behind it especially if it was cloudy, stood out, its red granite catching the sun. Iona looked very alluring, very inviting this morning.

On arrival on Iona a BBC Alba truck, the Scottish Gaelic television service, trundled off the ferry followed by a couple of cars and then along with about twenty other passengers we followed, ready to explore the charms of the island.

Jenny and I headed up the road passing the newly opened ferry passenger shelter and past the general store and a craft shop, to reach the gallery just in time for its opening.

Inside we both quickly scanned the walls for evidence of Jenny's paintings and our suspicions were confirmed - there were none on display.

I recognised Dougie Paterson from his picture on the website, appearing even more rotund in the flesh. He was the only person in the shop, wearing a bright patterned shirt which was struggling to stay in his trousers, working at the back, sorting some prints in a rack. He turned towards us giving a big welcoming smile: 'Please feel free to look around,' he said, waving his arms, 'just opened, I think that you will be surprised at the range of stock that we have,' he added confidently.

'I'm Jenny McDougall,' Jenny stated, holding out her hand.

For a second the smile flickered on the owner's face, but quickly returned as he limply shook her hand.

'Pleased to meet you. I was expecting you sometime this week.'

'That's good, I know that the Shona Tyler Trust has been in touch arranging the exhibition of my paintings.'

There was an awkward impasse.

'Yes , they have been very insistent, very fair and I got a delivery of your paintings last week.' He appeared hesitant his smile appearing more forced, as he tried to continue, but Jenny interrupted: 'I can help you set things up; you must be very busy, with you just opening.'

'That's true, luv,' he replied, 'but I'll be honest, they forced your exhibition on me. Your paintings are too abstract, not the Iona style. Not what I'm looking for. Tourists want the traditional prints also some contemporary takes on them. Scenes they can identify from their visit to the island. Your paintings require interpretation.'

That was no doubt true, although loyalty to Jenny precluded any comment from me, but they were also highly regarded and why hadn't he realised that they weren't suitable before accepting the grant money.

'Why did you accept the exhibition then?' I enquired, adding, 'oh by the way. I am Peter, Jenny's husband.' There was no handshake.

Paterson seemed almost pleased to switch his attention to me.

'You'll understand, I have just started, the money was very good, upfront.'

His expression, was one seeking understanding.

'It's good that you have been paid,' I said, 'but surely that means you are obligated to meet their conditions. Jenny is a well-known artist, she will attract those interested in her work, if they hear about the exhibition.'

'Look, this is awkward. I am sure that your wife's work is good,' and I could see Jenny becoming annoyed as she was being ignored, 'but I am sorry her work is not for me,' his cheeks becoming tinged with pink, more like his photo. 'You're getting a month's holiday, all paid. You can produce more paintings when you are here. I get start-up money. Can we not leave it like that?'

He stared beyond Jenny as two potential customers entered the shop, the smile returning.

'Excuse me,' he said, 'I must deal with my customers.'

I saw that look on Jenny's face as she stepped in front of him blocking his way. He stopped in an exaggerated way as if Jenny had pushed him: 'Apart from being dishonest, something the Shona Tyler Trust will discover, you didn't even have the courtesy to phone me, talk to me. We arrived expecting to see my paintings on display. I know that you have received them and I was also to be artist-in-residence once a week. We had planned our trip around that - now you are dismissing me. Don't you think that...'

'Listen luv, you are making things awkward. Take your good fortune and go. I won't tell anyone. I have got customers. I need to make a living.' The heavy moustache was flexing on his upper lip, his anger mounting.

'Look luv,' the repeated use of luv did grind with me, but being sexist was only one of his unattractive traits, 'they have even paid me to return to you your unsold paintings. If you are so good, you'll have no problem selling them elsewhere. Now, I must attend to my customers,' and he pushed past us, the welcoming smile returning as he addressed the two customers: 'Can I help you, ladies?' he enquired, of the two women who were examining some prints.

Jenny's eyes brimmed with tears; this was a setback too many.

'I'll be back to discuss this another day,' I said, trying to propel Jenny towards the shop door.

Any attempt at politeness gone, Paterson retorted firmly: 'And you'll get no further forward. I don't want your work. I'll post your paintings back later today.'

Jenny shrugged and turned towards the door and I followed.

'Greed and poor customer relationships will finish your business and it can't happen too soon,' I blurted out, it wasn't my most articulate retort, but my anger got the better of me.

'Get out,' he shouted at me, 'and don't return.'

The two ladies looked startled, sensing the atmosphere and edged towards the door.

'They are just going,' Paterson explained to them, but they appeared embarrassed and heads lowered left quickly.

We walked across the road, entering the Nunnery ruins and gardens and flopped on an empty bench. I could feel the blood pumping around my body, heart rate high.

'He was so rude, is it because I am a woman?'

'Sexist,' I replied, but I was also puzzling over what had happened. The Shona Tyler Trust had provided funds, but did not seek sufficient guarantees - amateurish. It was all a mess and had enabled Paterson to exploit an opportunity to profit, to subsidise his business start-up.

'Hey,' I said, trying to sound cheery, ' we are now free to explore the area and you'll have more time to paint. We've done our bit, the Shona Tyler Trust won't want their money back.'

Jenny leant into me, her tears making my shirt damp. She didn't deserve this latest setback, not after missing out on the launch at Aberfoyle. I was worried; there was only so much that someone could take.

'We still have time before we meet Dad, so let's go and have some coffee.'

There was a coffee shop next to the Iona Heritage Centre and we took our coffee outside sitting in the shade of trees.

'What is it they say: what doesn't kill you makes you stronger.'

'That was Nietzsche, if I remember my lectures, but he wasn't exactly a ball of fun,' and she smiled, 'let's make this a family holiday. Paterson is a sexist pig.'

'He is also ignorant, doesn't recognise talent and wants to make a quick buck.'

Jenny smiled: 'Someday, he'll regret how he treated me,' and I nodded agreeing.

After finishing our coffees we wandered up towards the Abbey watching out for Dad. The BBC Alba van was parked to the side of the road, its back doors open, a technician crouched listening through headphones watching dials on a sound deck. As we got near he took the headphones off, got up and walked through a gate into the Abbey grounds and we saw that he was talking to Dad, who must have just been interviewed. Naturally we followed and Dad smiled as we approached.

'My one and only television interview,' he said proudly, 'my fifteen minutes of fame.'

Standing beside him was a face I recognised but couldn't quite name.

'I'm Fergus,' the man said, and I could instantly link him to a documentary on BBC Alba that I had recently watched, something about emigration from Uist to the Americas, I think.

'Hello Fergus,' I replied, thinking that the guy was a lot shorter than I imagined, which was rich coming from me.

'You must be, Peter,' he stated with confidence, ' and you must be Jenny, the well-known landscape artist. I've seen your work - very impressive. I hope that you are here to capture scenes on Iona.'

Fergus certainly was good with words and I could see confidence flowing back into Jenny.

'I was telling him about you two,' Dad said, slightly spoiling the moment.

'What were you being interviewed about?'

'The changes to the Abbey, the accommodation areas are being upgraded. No one else was available,' and Fergus laughed.

'Your Dad did very well. I even got him to talk about the family name and how he lived on Islay for most of his life. It will be on An La`, the Gaelic news programme tomorrow.'

Part of me wondered if that was wise.

Fergus checked his watch: 'We better be going. Nice to have met you, Tom,' and he shook his hand. No one ever called Dad, Tom, only Thomas, but there was Dad smiling, looking better than yesterday, I thought.

As the television crew packed up Dad suggested, given the weather, that we climb Dun I, the highest hill on Iona, but still of modest height. Jenny was keen and so we continued on passing the Iona Community shop, Dad pointing out the George McLeod Centre to the left and eventually we left the road, crossed a stile and headed towards the hill.

I reached the top first and stood marvelling at the panorama, the ever present wind tugging at me. To the west were the islands of Tiree and further north Coll, both low lying, and closer the line of rocky islands that formed the Treshnish Islands, with the Dutchman's Cap, now easily recognised, with I could now see a smaller island to the south almost attached to it. From this vantage point the low cliffs that surrounded the Dutchman's Cap, that formed the brim of the cap, obvious. The small hill, in the centre appearing slightly pinched at one side. Shifting my position, I could see Staffa and the entrance to the bay at Kintra, Ulva, another island, and behind the hills of Mull again resplendent in the sun.

Then I heard Jenny shouting: 'Peter, Dad's not well,' and instantly I spun round to see Dad being helped to sit on the ground by Jenny.

'I'll be okay,' he said, as I reached him, 'it's just my heart, not a heart attack. It's my atrial fibrillation.'

He had taken a pill out of his pocket: 'PIP, pill in pocket,

197

any water?' and Jenny reached into her backpack and produced a bottle of water, which he drank a little of to swallow the pill.

'I'll sit for a while until my heart calms down, the AF makes me dizzy. I climbed the hill too quickly.'

'And you had the excitement of the TV interview,' added Jenny.

'What is AF,' I asked, 'and how long have you had it,' I wanted to know, determined now to broach the subject of Dad's health.

'Atrial fibrillation, my heart does funny things - goes too fast sometimes, the rhythm goes all wrong, the signalling is wonky. I take pills for it, they don't cure it but they control the heart rate, mostly, but it is unpredictable. It can be okay for weeks then it suddenly reoccurs. I think Mum's death was the original trigger, not sure.'

'You should have told me. I want you to see the doctor. Is there one on the island?'

'No but the local GP practice visit the island regularly. I have an appointment to see him this afternoon anyway.'

'That's good news. Were you feeling bad yesterday?'

'A bit.'

'Why didn't you say?'

'I didn't want to spoil anything. It usually settles with tablets and rest.'

I took my jacket off and put it around Dad and sat down beside him, my arm around him. Words could wait until later.

It was chilly at the top of the hill, very exposed to the prevailing wind. After some time I felt Dad's pulse, it was beating more regularly.

'Let's get you down,' I said, and encouraged him to get up. I kept a grip on him as we descended the grassy slope, Jenny ahead searching for the best footfalls. We waited with him until he saw the doctor, who felt his pulse and did an ECG, declaring that the trace looked normal.

Jenny was looking at her watch and I knew we had to leave to pick up the boys. I gave him my phone number for the house and we left.

'What a day,' I declared, as we headed to the ferry. The Golf, hiccupped but eventually started and we headed to Bunessan, my thoughts split between concern for Dad and the feeling that Paterson wouldn't have blanked us if we were dealing with a reputable trust. Maybe another question for Malcolm to check.

We brought the boys home, keeping an eye open for the black Mercedes but we didn't see it. I was annoyed I hadn't noted its registration. So much to learn about the ways of the world.

26

Glasgow

Malcolm was waiting as Alison came out of the Royal Infirmary emerging onto Wishart Street that ran between the hospital and the Necropolis, one of Glasgow's oldest cemeteries. Watching in his wing mirror he saw Alison spotting the car and heading towards him.

'You look tired,' he said, as she sat in the car.

'I am, it was a long shift and I'm sure that I felt the baby kick,' she replied, touching her stomach tenderly.

'You'll have to be careful to take care of yourself and the baby.' It was a familiar conversation - but home-work balance was a tricky topic for a dedicated journalist. Without further comment, Malcolm started the car and pulled out into the road.

'Are you sure that you still want to go ahead with this?' enquired Alison, and Malcolm didn't miss the brief look of concern.

'Yes, I need to do this for Peter's sake and because it is just wrong, an injustice, what has happened to him.'

Alison sensed her partner's determination - he always stood up for what he believed to be right; it was one of the reasons that she loved him.

The Necropolis, a large Glasgow cemetery with many burial tombs was on the hillside to the left, fringed by trees beside the road, and on the right was now the rear of Glasgow Cathedral. They drove under a single arch bridge that linked these two city landmarks and arrived at a junction, keeping left until they reached Duke Street. They passed under a railway bridge and soon after reached the bottom of Whitehill Street. Malcolm searched for a parking place and pulled in.

They both got out: 'Wait for me in the cafe, I shouldn't be long, that's if she is in.'

Alison leant up and kissed Malcolm softly on the cheek: 'Be careful,' was all she said, everything else had been discussed the previous evening.

Malcolm waited, watching Alison enter the cafe, taking a seat by the door and started up Whitehill Street, which gradually rose in height as it left Duke Street behind. The street was typical of many in this part of Glasgow, a mixture of older four storey tenements mingled with more modern flats. He still wasn't sure of how to proceed but trusted his instincts, after all no military plan survived first contact with the enemy, and this was his equivalent.

He arrived at the security door of the tenement block he was looking for and took off his glasses and cleaned them with a hankie. Vision clear, a few seconds taken to summon courage, he examined the list of names and finding the name he pressed the button beside the name. The light flashed and he waited.

A tinny voice responded several seconds later: 'Hello, who is it?'

'I'm Malcolm Baxter from the *Strathclyde Evening Echo*,' he paused, 'I would like to talk to you about a story we are going to run. Your name was given to me. I was hoping that you could help me.' The dye was cast.

'What is it about?' the voice sounded curious, as he hoped.

'TGG, the company you work for.'

'What have they done?' and the voice sounded innocent, not

defensive. Maybe she was a good liar.

'That's what I would like to speak to you about. Can I come in, it would be easier?'

There was no further question and he heard the door unlock. He entered climbing the stairs towards the second floor, aware that someone was leaning over the banister watching him. He glanced up, his heart racing, sure that she matched the description. Early twenties, blonde hair cut short, not dressed in her company outfit but in leggings and a loose fitting blue top.

'I'm Malcolm,' he said, as he reached her extending his hand. The handshake was limp, her hand slightly damp - was that a sign of nerves? He couldn't be certain.

'Can I come in?' and she pushed the door open, revealing a large hall with a high ceiling.

'My colleague is sitting out in the car. We thought that a visit from two men might be too much,' and he smiled. 'I think it better that we talk in confidence,' but she now knew that he wasn't alone.

'What's this about?' and there was an edge to her voice as she directed him into a lounge, with a bay window overlooking the street, a large television in the corner and a green three piece suite which had seen better days. Malcolm was now aware of a strong smell of tobacco and something sweeter. He had smelt nothing like that off Kirsty but someone else who lived here liked pot.

'Can I sit down, Kirsty, if I may call you that?' and she nodded, but Malcolm sensed that she was anxious. She sat perched on the arm of the couch, legs crossed defensively, arms folded loosely across her chest.

'It has been brought to our paper's attention that TGG have issues. Our contacts suggest that the police are curious about their operations,' he paused to let that sink in, but also to draw breath, Malcolm was now on shaky ground: he was acting alone.

'It's their backers, where is the money is coming from to develop the business.'

Kirsty cut right in: 'I am just an IT technician straight out of university, that has nothing to do with me.'

'Maybe not, but these backers can make demands, ask you to do things, put pressure on you.'

Kirsty's lips narrowed: 'So?'

'The paper could be running an expose.' Now he was definitely in uncharted waters.

'Tell me about the Islay Distillery work that you did recently at their Glasgow headquarters.'

Bull's Eye. Kirsty almost physically recoiled, almost doubling up, her arms suddenly wrapped tight around her, leaning forward.

'Upgrades,' and Malcolm let the word hang in the air.

'I install upgrades. I don't know what they contain.'

'Kirsty,' and he was about to continue when he heard a key turn in the door of the flat. A man entered the room taking in the scenario, his neck heavily tattooed with a dark rose, wearing a tracksuit: 'Who's this?' he snarled, his accent heavy, his manner instantly confrontational.

'I'm from the evening paper. We are doing a feature on Kirsty's company. We wanted to add depth, interview some of the workforce.' Kirsty seemed pleased that Malcolm had quickly explained his presence; she wasn't as quick thinking.

'In their own homes - are you a joker? Who is this guy, Kirsty?'

Belligerence shone from Kirsty's partner as he leant towards Malcolm, the smell of alcohol and stale tobacco strong on his breath.

'He was just going,' stated Kirsty, standing up, almost pleading with her eyes for Malcolm to get up and go.

'Yes I am,' said Malcolm standing up, 'the company would

appreciate your support; they mentioned you as a valued member of staff. I hope that I can interview you at some point.'

Even Kirsty knew that was a lie, but she also knew that Malcolm was on to her.

Kirsty walked quickly to the front door hoping that Malcolm would be drawn in her slipstream, sucked out the flat. Malcolm obliged. Outside the door was an electricity meter cabinet and checking that her partner couldn't see him, he placed his business card face down on the top of it.

'Thank you,' he said, as he started down the stairs. So near, now he would have to hope that she contacted him.

27

Jura

The *Casablanca* was being tossed about by the churning waves, pitching and rolling. Ronnie held tightly to the wheel absorbing its every judder. Ahead the sea foamed, the water rose and fell, the boat dipping and rising, shaking, groaning at its treatment.

'Look to starboard, Gil,' he shouted above the roar of the waves, and the whirlpool, the water twisting and turning, creating a gaping vortex. 'Tell them to take a good look because I am going to pull away.' Gil turned slowly bracing himself and shouted back at the three men and one woman crouching under the awning at the back, splattered by the waves, soaked, water running down their lifejackets, their faces white, attached by safety rope to rings in the side of the boat. Tied securely, in the rear of the boat, were five yellow kayaks.

'This is as close as we can get,' he shouted, 'we're turning away now. The Corryvreckan can be worse than this,' but no one seemed to be listening as they watched the maelstrom, fascinated, hypnotised by its sheer power. Gil had promised them an experience, not an easy ride. They were here to be tested, learn about themselves, experiencing the power of the surging tides was only a taster. There was one couple from Holland and two Americans in the party. Ronnie had met them at the hotel in Craighouse where they stayed for the first two nights, getting basic instruction from Gil. He had observed them as they ate and drank together, assessing them. One of the Americans was carrying excess weight Gil had declared on first inspection of the group, unimpressed, although Ronnie had thought he was just burly. Probably Gil had identified something in the American that he saw as weakness, an instinct forged in the conflict of war, where weaknesses could cost lives.

The slightly burly American threw up, the sickness holding in the air momentarily, then descending and splattering those around him. It started a chain reaction and the others also started to retch. Gil studied them, watching how they reacted: how they coped.

As they passed Eilean Mor, off the north coast of Jura, the tidal race, created by the flood tide, was carrying the boat forward but the turbulence was easing. Gil left the cabin and joined the group at the rear.

'Ronnie is going to take us down the coast, where we will get out and paddle to the shore. Just remember what I told you and stay calm.'

In the harbour at Craighouse Gil had put the team through basic kayak training, teaching them what to do if the kayak flipped. The harbour, however, was tranquil, protected, a safe space. It made his life easier that everyone had some experience of kayaking but he still drilled them until they were tired, responded automatically, not relenting until they had met his standards.

Ronnie edged the boat out of the tidal race, his destination the relative calm of Loch Tarbet, the sea loch, which almost split Jura in two from the west, where the water was more sheltered.

'We are going to paddle up the coast in the direction we have just come from. I have selected a sheltered cove where we can go ashore,' he explained, the message reassuring after what they had been through. 'We'll secure the kayaks and return to them in a few days when Ronnie comes back for us. Any questions?' Ronnie judged that they just wanted to be on firm ground, their white faces told a story, at the moment maybe one of regret for signing up.

He had got to know Gil better or had he? Gil disclosed what he wanted to, when he wanted to, and to work with him he had to accept that. There was no explanation of his sudden departure from Jura a few days ago, it was really none of Ronnie's business, but he had seemed even more impassive on his return. However, now and again Ronnie noticed the hands trembling, how Gil used deep breathing to force control over his body, which at times, Ronnie sensed, wanted to rebel against his iron self-discipline.

They had spent time together planning the wilderness experience, so Ronnie knew what the first participants were going to endure. Several trips on the *Casablanca*, around the coast of Jura, had been required while Gil moved equipment, disappearing once on shore, hauling gear into position, hiding it at the rear of some of the many caves found on the west coast. Ronnie spent his time waiting for Gil's return, either fishing or observing the bird life.

Conversation was always at a premium, although he sensed that Gil liked him and Maria, who he had now met on several occasions, having visited their house for a meal. After the meal and a glass of wine or whisky, he seemed more relaxed, even smiling. He was compassionate, a guy who Ronnie imagined would never desert his colleagues whatever trouble they were in, but Gil coped by keeping a lid on his emotions, staying cool.

Watching as the participants put on safety helmets, edged into their seats on the kayak, while Gil held their kayak close to the boat for each of them in turn, they fastened their spray decks around them and over the cockpit, bobbling about on the waves, gripping their paddles. As the group left under the careful eye of Gil, the kayaks drifted apart, Gil shouting detailed instructions, encouraging them to stay together, reminding them of basic points. As the kayaks were paddled away from the boat, Ronnie powered up the outboard and swung the *Casablanca* around. No one in the party seemed to notice as they concentrated on their task of reaching the shore.

28

I stood beside Jenny at the bedroom window, her arms folded, while she watched Ben and Jason playing at the front of the house. The tide was out, the small island in the bay accessible. A couple of sheep had scarpered as the boys explored the rock pools left behind by the receding tide searching for squat starfish and scuttling crabs. We were pleased that the boys had forged a friendship, the gap in years not appearing significant as they played. Ben enjoyed having an older brother, Jason desperate to fit in with us. It must have been difficult living in the Robinson's home, then sent away to boarding school and then Dingle during holidays, never it seemed to be allowed to return home, contact with his mother restricted. Jason must have felt unloved, unwanted. I still couldn't imagine how Catherine could have done that unless... circumstances must have been dire to send your own kid away like that, I kept reminding myself and Catherine would have been a great mother.

It was the weekend and we intended to spend it together. A visit to Dad was a priority, to check on his health, introduce him to Jason and let him see how much Ben had changed. Exploring the coast around Kintra would be fun, the many small coves, ruined cottages, working out exactly what we were seeing out to sea.

Jim, Cathy's husband had offered us a fishing trip on his small boat and we had invited them along this evening to have a drink, get to know them better. Jim was a part-time postman, filling in his time working at a local garage. Multi-tasking was often an essential part of island life, as I knew from Islay. He had also promised to have a look at the Golf, work out why the engine was running rough. I was a bit embarrassed, knowing that the cause was lack of maintenance.

'Go out to be with the boys,' Jenny asked, 'I'm going to be busy in the kitchen and I don't want them left alone.' As always that touch of apprehension, a cloud on the horizon of a clear blue sky.

I sat on the edge of the bed, lacing up my walking boots, getting ready. Jenny came over, sat beside me giving me a cuddle and kiss. That was more like the Jenny I knew.

'Better go,' I said, kissing her gently in return, 'all we are missing is Jodie.'

'Not for long. I got a call from Colin last night, when you were out with the boys, meant to tell you about it. The vet is a lot happier with her leg - almost healed. The trouble will be prising her away from Colin and Mandy.'

I stood outside the house, blinking in the strong sunlight, glad for my anorak, due to a stiff sea breeze. At the far end of the hamlet, I noticed another house occupied, the door open; people here for the weekend. I shouted on the boys and walked over the marshy ground at the edge of the water before reaching them.

The rest of the morning was spent exploring rock pools, working our way to the far end of the bay and then up to the headland. The sea looked choppy, the trip sealed for the boys when we saw some dolphins offshore. We were hungry by the time we returned.

'Your Dad phoned, while you were out, we're going across

for lunch,' Jenny informed us. The aroma of scones being baked permeating the kitchen, made me want lunch sooner rather than later.

The ferry crossing was choppy, the boys excited to be on board, to be visiting Iona. Dad was waiting, looking chirpy, broad smile on his face, when he saw the boys. He treated us to lunch in the Argyll Hotel, eating outside at a picnic bench overlooking the beach by the ferry slipway. We didn't go near the art gallery, although I did see Paterson in the distance talking to someone.

After lunch Dad announced that he wanted a rest, the medication for his atrial fibrillation tiring him. 'Nothing to worry about,' he explained, but he enjoyed a short nap in the afternoon. However, he encouraged us to go on one of the chartered cruises out to Staffa. 'Well worth it, a couple of hours well spent.'

The charter boat was busy heading at speed out past the entrance to the bay at Kintra, all of us going quieter as we experienced the choppy seas. The island's world famous columnar basalt cliffs and cave reminded me of the rib cage of a dead whale from this direction. Formed by early lava flows cooling and contracting, their hexagonal shape naturally forming, like a honeycomb. It was too rough to land on the island but we passed the entrance to Fingal's cave and on our return, dolphins followed the boat making it a memorable day. I looked for Dad when the boat returned to Iona, but he wasn't there.

We left on one of the last ferries, tired but content and while the Golf stuttered again we made it back to Kintra. As we returned, Jim, wearing an oil stained boiler suit and a baseball cap which was protecting his balding head from the sun, was putting rubbish in one of the bins near the bridge.

'I'll have to check that engine tomorrow,' he suggested, as the engine again ran on after I had switched off the engine. 'I'll take it along to my workshop and garage. It probably just needs a service, some tinkering.'

'That's great, we are looking forward to seeing you and Cathy later.'

. . .

Ben was so tired that he hardly managed to finish his meal, even Jason was yawning. I set the wood burner and looked out the whisky and wine. Just after eight there was a knock on the door and our guests arrived. Both spruced up for the evening, bearing wine and some chocolates.

It turned out that they were from Glasgow where Jim had worked for one of the big car firms as a mechanic and Cathy as a secretary in an insurance brokers. Fed up living in Glasgow Jim had yearned for the island life, to get out of the rat race. He was also keen on painting, dabbling in water colours, so he and Jenny got on well.

They could both answer any questions that we had about the area. I was curious about the sailing boat that we often saw sailing past the mouth of the bay.

'The *Kerry Star*, has been around these parts a lot this last year. Registered in the Republic of Ireland, giving rich people the experience of life under canvas. I got a close up from the shore once when she was moored in the anchorage at the Bull Hole, quite modern - lots of electronic gizmos to make life easier. Not really life under canvas when you have diesel engines. I couldn't see inside the cabins but I imagine that they are quite plush. I know that they have a chef onboard, an Irish guy, met him in the Keel Row, you know the pub and restaurant in Fionnphort, one night. Didn't say much but he was making a good living, must be rich people who own it. The boat is often found off the west coast of Erraid, near the Tinker's Hole, a safe mooring, not too far from the Torran Rocks.'

I must have looked puzzled and Jim needed little encouragement to explain further: 'The Torran Rocks lie to the south of Erraid, hazardous to boats, if you are not careful. It's where David Balfour's boat, you know, the hero in Robert Louis Stevenson's book *Kidnapped*, sank and he was shipwrecked on Erraid. If they can sink fictional boats the rocks must be dangerous,' he added with a smile. 'The beach is now named after him, very white sand, very attractive. It's also known by its Gaelic name: Traigh Gheal, the white beach. I like the Gaelic names; they are more romantic sounding.'

'Now Jenny,' he said, 'you must visit Balfour's Beach; you'll find true inspiration there, I'm sure, for your paintings.' He finished his whisky and put down his glass: 'Good stuff this, Peter,' and I refilled his glass, not for the first time, Cathy was amused, knowing that Jim liked to talk, tell a story.

'The island was the source of the granite used to construct a lighthouse Dubh Artach, on a treacherous outcrop of rock, about fifteen miles to the south. There is an old quarry on the island where they quarried the stone. The lighthouse like many around our coasts were built by the Stevenson family who were famous for constructing lighthouses. Robert Louis Stevenson's father, Thomas, built Dubh Artach and the family spent time locally, hence Robert using the area in his book. Balfour was his mother's maiden name.'

Cathy rolled her eyes: 'Too much information,' but Jim continued unperturbed, his enthusiasm fuelled by the whisky.

'The lighthouse was some feat of engineering. The granite rocks had to be cut very precisely leaving no gaps that the water could penetrate as it not unknown to get ninety foot waves crashing onto the lighthouse. It must have been very lonely out at sea and scary, but they also built an observatory on Erraid so that the lighthouse men could signal the shore. The observatory is now disused, the lighthouse long automated, but the building is worth visiting.'

'Erraid is a interesting island, New Age community live there, have for a few years, using the old lighthouse keeper's cottages. They are very welcoming; offer week long courses, getting back to nature, exploring your inner self, that sort of thing. With the Spring Solstice coming up they will be holding festivals.'

Jim was now in full flow, espousing the history of the area. Cathy, I noticed glancing at her watch, as the evening progressed.

'I really think that you should both visit Erraid; it's a tidal island you can walk across at low tide best from Knockvologan, beyond the campsite at Fidden, where you can park the car and walk down a rough track to the beach.' Turning to Jenny he continued, 'wonderful angles for painting. Return when the sea is rough, you'll be inspired. It is also the route David Balfour took to get off the island. You'll also notice something, which I am sure you will want to incorporate in a painting, Jenny.'

Jenny was enjoying this, leaning forward listening to every word.

'There are two metal hooks sticking out of the sand. Also the wooden prow and stern of a sunken lifeboat but the sands shift all of the time, and you can't always see them, but the heavy metal suspension hooks are always visible. The lifeboat was found floating off shore and was dragged in. The lifeboat was from the *Arandora Star*, a requisitioned liner taking German and Italian internees along with some German POWs across the Atlantic. Unfortunately, it was sunk by a U-boat off Ireland, in 1940, and while hundreds were saved by a passing Canadian destroyer, eight hundred drowned. I always wondered why was the lifeboat was empty? Were the occupants of the lifeboat rescued or drowned? No one knows. Now its remains are buried under the sandy beach.'

Jenny was alert absorbing the story, her face flushed with a combination of the heat from the log burner and the wine.

'We'll have to visit the beach,' she proclaimed.

'That's Monday taken care of, Peter,' said Cathy with a mischievous smile.

'We must be going before Jim finishes all your whisky, but there is one small thing. Has Jim mentioned that he spoke with Jason yesterday?'

'No,' I said, puzzled.

'Oh, it's just that Jim stopped Jason burning rubbish at that old ruined cottage in the next cove. There was a tramp living there for a while, using the ruins as home, but he hasn't been seen for a while, has he, Jim?' she said, looking to Jim for confirmation.

'It was just that Jason was using some of the wood that Tommy stored. No malice, just didn't think that it was safe, so I stopped him.'

'That's okay, Jim, we would want to be told,' Jenny said, 'thanks. We'll speak to him. It sounds dangerous and is a bad example for Ben.'

Jim got up a little unsteadily: 'I used to store some things there, lobster creels and some rope, but when Tommy arrived, I removed them. He arrived from nowhere, a bit of a drink problem according to the people in the Fionnphort stores. You would see him walking about everywhere, must be difficult to put in your days. Anyway he must have returned home or moved on. No one has seen him for almost a couple of weeks.'

'I know the ruin that you mean,' said Jenny, ' the one with the well near it, which is covered with corrugated metal and weighed down by stones. That alone is dangerous. We'll keep the boys away, if I am not with them. I might do some sketches there, the ruin has potential with the outcrops of red granite around it.'

29

Jim knocked on the door early the next morning, unshaven, looking rough, slightly hung over, asking for the car keys, thanking us for an enjoyable evening. Shortly after, making now familiar backfiring noises the car was driven over the bridge, to Jim's wooden garage and workshop, by the side of his house. The boys were up early soon out playing in the garden whilst Jenny retreated to the hut at the back of the garden, that look on her face suggesting she had ideas for paintings that she wished to develop. I tidied up around the house, reset the wood burner and eventually took a cup of coffee outside sitting on the low stone wall surrounding the barbeque area to enjoy the bright morning, keeping an eye on the boys.

I remembered what Jim had said about Jason setting fire to drift wood at the ruined cottage. Jenny and I had talked about it after he and Cathy had left. Fire always fascinated boys, but it was dangerous and so we would talk to him when we found an appropriate moment.

Close by I heard the sound of my car being revved. Late morning the couple who had arrived for the weekend drove past the house, leaving the hamlet with only two families again.

Near lunchtime I spoke to Jenny and slipped away walking up the headland to enjoy the vista, passing Jim whose head was buried deep in the engine well of the Golf. The views, the fresh air, quickly removed any lingering traces of a hangover for me.

As I returned from the headland Jim was waiting for me, wiping his hand on an oily rag. 'Good news and bad news,' he stated, and I waited.

'The car hasn't been serviced in a very, very long time.' That was a statement of fact, 'and so It needs new filters. I thought I had some, but I don't. I'll collect them on Monday but I'm afraid that you can't drive until then. I've also adjusted the handbrake and cleaned the brakes, but you need new brake pads all round,' he added for emphasis. 'I can get them at a good price.'

'Listen, 'I replied, 'I'm embarrassed at the state of the car and appreciate what you are doing. Just give me a price and include your labour.'

'I'll just charge you for the parts,' he insisted, ignoring my protestations.

'Cathy thinks that you both have had a tough time recently, so we hope the change here does you good.'

He didn't smile but his eyes conveyed sympathy. I wondered whether Jenny had said something to Cathy.

'Thanks,' I replied, simply.

'Could you help me?'

'Of course.'

'With Tommy gone, I want to tidy up the ruined cottage, return my creels. I didn't mention last night, but when I was over at the ruin, the time I spoke to Jason, there was an unpleasant smell from the well. Could you help me remove the boulders holding down the corrugated metal, there's more than usual, which is strange. There might be a dead animal underneath and if there is, I want to remove it and clean up the water supply. I used to use it to clean the creels and other gear. We could go after lunch.' I agreed. 'Maybe change into old clothes; it could be messy,' he suggested.

I did wonder how an animal could have got trapped underneath, however, I was only too pleased to do a favour in return for Jim working on the car.

. . .

Jenny stayed with the boys and Jim and I wandered from my house along the south side of the bay trying to avoid the boggy patches which impeded our progress, picking our way slowly from clump of grass to rock and so on. As we climbed, the view to the sea opened out and I asked Jim about the Dutchman's Cap, now clearly visible.

'The Dutchman's Cap is one of the Treshnish Islands. There are eight of them - strung out over nearly seven miles - they are really important now as a place for grey seals to breed and lots of different seabirds - guillemot, razorbill, fulmar and of course, puffins, nesting on them. They have been uninhabited for,' and he stopped for a minute. 'I think that the last people left Lunga nearly two hundred years ago. Without people the wild life can flourish and they are protected now - a site of Special Scientific Interest.' Jim was only too pleased, as usual, to share his local knowledge, it seemed.

'The Dutchman's Cap is probably the most distinctive island in the Treshnish Islands, with its hump, an old volcano, the low lying ground around a glassy lava field. Pretty inaccessible because of the cliffs. To the south west of the Dutchman's Cap you have Bac Beag, its smaller sister, the two almost connected by rocky outcrops. Beag means small in Gaelic.

Of course, the Dutchman's Cap is also known in Gaelic as Bac Mor, Mor meaning big. Bac can mean bank or obstacle; some dispute over its exact meaning.' Jim's enthusiastic knowledge was again on display and it took me a few seconds to absorb what he just said: Bac Mor - that was the name left as an imprint on Connor Brown's notepad. Was that just coincidence? Then I walked on a few steps before another thought occurred to me. I remembered what Mary had said at Beattie's funeral, the message that Jimmy the taxi driver had passed on. Jimmy had overhead two men talking in the back of his car when he was taking them to the airport. They mentioned my name and Barry More. Jimmy was concerned, didn't feel that it sounded good. Did they mean Bac Mor? Mary could easily have been confused - probably was. What was the connection between me and Bac Mor and who were the men?

Jim looked uncomfortable: 'Am I rambling on?'

'No,' I replied, 'you just set off a chain of thoughts. It would take too long to explain and is maybe nothing anyway,' I added, trying to convince myself more than Jim.

'It doesn't sound like a good chain,' replied Jim, shrewdly.

'Let's get to the cottage,' he said, to fill my awkward silence, my mind still racing.

We clambered down from the hillock we had just climbed; the ruined cottage ahead. I wandered into it. The red granite stone walls of the roofless cottage still looked as if they could defy Atlantic storms for hundreds of years to come. Inside were two stone partitions, separating a central area from a room at each end. A stone hearth in one suggested that's where the human inhabitants lived and the other end was used as a small byre for animals. In between the two stone partitions, someone, presumably Tommy had fixed a tarpaulin as a roof, which had now fallen down. This was where Jason had built a fire and aimlessly I probed the ashes with my foot. There were a few half-burnt postcards, bizarrely they looked as if they were Italian scenes, grand cathedrals. I wondered outside, now becoming aware of a stench from the area of the well - a rotten smell, unpleasant.

I sniffed the air: 'There is a smell, we better investigate.'

Some of the rocks were very heavy, taking the two of us to drag them off the rusting corrugated metal, scrapping the surface, leaving lines where the rust was scratched away. After the last stone was removed, we paused to catch breath. We lifted the corrugated metal with some difficulty, peeling it away from the ground underneath, until one corner was raised. The stench which had been partially trapped under the corrugated metal was now fully released and was awful. I retched, letting the metal slip. We both jumped back as the metal again sealed whatever was underneath. I just caught a glimpse of black water and a few bubbles.

'Sorry,' I said, 'the smell got to me.'

Jim agreed: 'Definitely, something not right in there. Try again, maybe try to use a stone to prop up one side, so we can see what's below.'

Without talking, we rolled a stone towards one of the corners and tried lifting the metal sheet again, Jim pushing the stone with his foot under the sheet as we managed to prise one corner up and then we dropped it onto the stone which Jim had manoeuvred into position. By now we were both sweating, stepping back as the stench intensified.

'Now that we have prised up one end, let's try and pull the sheet off the hole,' Jim suggested, and again we worked in tandem, pulling the sheet a few inches off what I now saw was a wooden frame. Encouraged and not trying to breathe too deeply, we managed to expose half the hole.

Jim suddenly screamed: 'No,' and I looked in the mouth of the well.

'It's Tommy,' he gasped, and I saw a man floating on the surface, the body swollen, his eyes bloodied and bulging, mouth taped, white and shrivelled skin, some small creature slithering across his lifeless face. His hands looked misshapen, fingers at an odd angle. We both turned away, Jim dropping to his knees overcome with shock. I retched again and again, retreating from the hole, the smell permeating my very soul.

30

It took us both some time to recover. Jim crouched on the ground, wiping his mouth, eyes glazed. He knew the victim and was stunned by what must have been an horrific death. I couldn't get rid of the image of the victim's bloodied bulging eyes, blood vessels ruptured by terror, pain or something worse that I could not imagine. It was like after you had peered at a bright light, the afterimage remained etched on your retina, haunting you. I didn't know Tommy, so I was a little more detached, but I had seen death. Charles Robinson's lifeless body lying on the beach at Machir Bay, was an image that had kept playing out in my mind for many months afterwards.

I turned to Jim: 'Are you okay?' a silly pointless question but it was the best I could come up with.

'Give me a minute,' and he stayed huddled, his arms now wrapped around him tightly, rocking back and forwards.

'I knew that something was not right but I didn't expect that. Poor soul. Who could do that to another human being?'

Sadly, I could think of someone more than capable of such savagery and was just hoping that he wasn't involved but my gut instinct was telling me that he probably was. And I still hadn't worked out why the name Bac Mor was found imprinted on Connor Brown's notepad. There had to be a link - it was too much of a coincidence.

Eventually, I helped Jim to his feet, not sure if I was any better, but like the survivors of any trauma it was important to do something.

'Let's get back to your house, inform the police.'

'I'm sorry that I brought you along. This is terrible.'

'Listen, it's not your fault.'

Jim, who must have been in his late fifties, suddenly looked his age. Together we made our way back to Kintra, our feet getting soaked as we stumbled taking no care where we placed our feet, just desperate to get away from what we had discovered. We reached the small car park and passed the house: glad that the boys were at the back of the garden. Cathy immediately grasped that something terrible had happened, listening incredulously, as I explained what we had found. She held the dishcloth that she was holding over her mouth trying to suppress an anguished cry.

Cathy got her husband to sit down and switched on the kettle.

'I'll call the police,' I said, and Cathy pointed to the phone, which was in the hallway.

Police Scotland's call centres are centralised and it took the operator sometime to locate Kintra. When I described what we had found I am sure supervisors and others were immediately alerted. 'A police car is on its way,' she stated, 'try and remain calm. We'll be there soon.' If the nearest police car was in Tobermory or Craignure, or even Bunessan, that could take some time.

I declined the offer of a cup of tea and headed back to our house to alert Jenny. I would have preferred that Jenny and the boys had gone away somewhere else for a short time, before the police arrived but with no car that wasn't an option. Ben and Jason were kicking a ball about as I passed them, finding Jenny in the hut sketching on a pad. She was lost in her thoughts, smiling as I opened the door of the hut, instantly abandoning her sketching as she saw my face.

Her reaction was muted, not always a good sign, anxiously glancing outside checking on the boys and then focussing on me. I left out many details, didn't mention Bac Mor, kept it simple.

'What do we do,' she said.

'Wait for the police. Nothing that we can do for poor Tommy.'

. . .

The police car arrived within the hour, two uniformed officers getting out, looking a little anxious and I went across identifying myself. I offered to lead them to the ruined cottage and they accepted, one of them, the older one, asking questions as we scrambled across the rough ground.

I pointed out the well and the older one shone a torch into the gap between the corrugated metal cover still resting on the boulder and the surface of the water. He gasped and handed his torch to the other one whose reaction was the same.

. . .

Another couple of hours and the place was swarming with police, the small car park full with more vehicles parked at the top of the hill which led down to Kintra. Cathy was busy making tea, handing out biscuits for the officers, keeping an eye on Jim, whose colour had returned but still had the appearance of one who had seen a ghost, which in a sense he had. The first officers had sealed off the area with blue tape, spoken at length on their radio and had taken a brief statement from Jim and me, before asking us to remain in our houses.

With the victim dead there was no rush to remove the body before a careful examination of the crime scene had been completed. Eventually the Senior Investigating Officer, a detective inspector, is how he identified himself, came across to our house, introduced himself and spoke with me. He introduced two CID officers who remained with me and started taking a detailed statement. Not being a suspect they treated me with sympathy. At some point their records must have linked my name with recent events in Aberfoyle and Islay because after a short break their attitude changed. Their curiosity then intensified, their questions more probing.

I tried to remain calm for Jenny's sake, deciding that we had to get off the island as soon as possible. Cathy popped in early evening, letting us know that she was still worried about Jim; the local GP coming out to see him. She apologised that Jim had involved me and for any stress that it had caused. If she only knew; we had known worse.

The next morning we were informed that the body had been removed.

Later Cathy returned, to let us know that she was going to the shop in Fionnphort.

'Do you need anything?' There were a few things and I suggested that I went with her, partly interested in seeing what was happening up the hill, as we had been trapped in Kintra since the day before.

We headed off passing several police cars, parked in a farmer's field. A tent had been set up, the flap on one side open, and we saw several officers standing, next to a metal urn, holding cups and eating sandwiches.

The store in Fionnphort was quite busy but by the time we had collected our shopping we were the only two left.

'Poor Cathy, it must be a nightmare for you,' said the woman behind the counter.

'A real shock for Jim and Peter here, they both found his body,' Cathy replied, and the assistant smiled understandingly at me.

'So he was tortured. Poor Tommy, such a nice man, who would think of ramming a metal bar down someone's throat.'

'How do you know that Linda?' Cathy enquired, aghast.

'I overhead two policemen talking about it outside the shop when I was putting out the newspapers.'

This was no coincidence. Whoever had killed Tommy had used the same technique as Connor Brown. McGrory must be behind it, which made our presence in Mull no coincidence.

Cathy drove home, a car in front of us, which turned into the field that the police were using. As we passed the rear door of the car was opened and Nick got out, studying the scene, no doubt searching for the SIO. His face was drawn, worried, but then he probably had good reason. I wondered if he would call in on me. Once again I had many questions to ask him.

31

Cathy and Jim knocked on our door early next morning.

'Come in,' I said, pleased to see that Jim looked more himself.

'I'll take my wellingtons off, they're a bit muddy' replied Cathy, 'I was just taking some hot drinks up to the two policeman guarding the crime scene. They have erected a tent over the murder scene. It's cold and lonely up there. Not so many police around this morning unlike yesterday when they must have been about a dozen, combing the area.'

'Did they say anything about the murder?' I enquired.

'No, just that they wouldn't be around much longer and they will seal off the well, but they didn't say when.'

'I wouldn't be wanting to wash my fishing gear there again. Oh Peter, that was horrible,' Jim said, 'who could do that?'

'There are people like that around - probably drug related. Maybe Tommy was hiding and they found him. Maybe he owed a lot of money, I don't know.' I was vague not wanting to get drawn further in our conversation pleased that Jenny had come downstairs, her hair still wet from washing it, rubbing it dry with a towel.

'Morning, how are you, Jim?' she asked.

'Better than yesterday,' but the expression on Cathy's face suggested that she was not convinced.

'Not good for his blood pressure,' she said, 'but the doctor gave him some valium and he slept well. Not keen on it though, it makes him sleep too deeply and he snored. Kept me awake. Anyway we just want to say sorry for putting you through an ordeal. It is not usually like this, there are not many murders in Kintra,' and Cathy smiled.

'We are going to head home,' I said, 'with the art gallery not wanting Jenny there is no need for us to stay and it will be good to get the boys back to their regular school.'

Cathy looked down at the floor but Jim spoke up.

'I understand, I'll get the car parts that you need, but they won't arrive until tomorrow at the earliest.'

'I'll take the boys to school and pick them up: I'm going that way anyway,' Cathy stated.

'And I'll want you to visit Erraid after everything I told you about it. Take your mind off what's happened. I have to pick up some parcels and then I'll collect you and take you over to Knockvologan, a small farmstead, in my van and from there you can walk across to the island, as it will be low tide. It'll do you both good and it's a lovely day, you'll see the island at its best. Our way of saying sorry for what happened.'

I turned to Jenny and she seemed to brighten up, 'Yes,' she said, 'that would be lovely,' and I concurred, it would cheer us up.

We were waiting for Jim as he drove down the hill, later in the morning, and parked, grabbing our backpacks and locking the door.

'The place is buzzing about poor Tommy,' Jim said, as I got into the front beside him. 'People are angry, they liked him. He minded his own business and no one deserved to die like he did.'

I wanted to change the subject before Jenny, who was checking her backpack, climbed into the van beside me.

'Did you manage to order the parts for the car?'

228

'Oh yeah,' he replied, 'might be a couple of days.'

As we passed the field that yesterday had been busy with police vehicles and personnel I noted that there was only one vehicle and a handful of policemen standing around. There was also no sign of Nick, which was good, as I didn't want Jenny seeing him.

We reached Fionnphort and took the single track road to Fidden, crossing moorland with the usual outcropping of granite, approaching a camp site and farmhouse. Jim stopped and took some parcels from the back into the farmhouse, chatting for a few minutes at the door. Everyone knew him, it seemed, and I had no doubt what the topic of conversation was today.

'Right one more delivery,' and we headed along a twisting road past a few houses before turning off at what appeared to be a fresh track leading around a hillock. We emerged at a new house built beside an old quarry, the house surrounded by the steep sides of the quarry walls. There were high ornate black metal gates across the road and a high stone wall to each side of it.

'They like their privacy,' Jim muttered, with what I detected was a hint of contempt, unusual for him, as he got out of the van and spoke into an intercom attached to a gate post.

The gates swung inward and Jim drove into a wide parking area in front of a two storey house. The house certainly was new, the grounds unfinished with a large garage to one side, which was open and empty. Next to the garage two black quad bikes were parked.

Jim fetched some packages from the rear of the van and some letters, taking them to the front door. As he waited I looked around again noticing several security cameras. The door was eventually opened and Jim handed his deliveries over not engaging in any small talk, turning away quickly.

'Don't like them,' he declared, as he turned his van around, 'never any time for you. Anyway, we are on Mull, who needs security gates or security cameras.'

I saw Jenny who had been checking her camera raise her head and look in the rear view mirror. The gates swung shut behind us and we drove back towards the road.

'I'll take you down to Knockvologan now, it's just a mile from here.'

We reached the road and my heart sank as the black Mercedes saloon, which had followed us the other day drove up from the Knockvologan direction, pulling over into a passing place. Instinctively, I put my head down, covering my head with my hands nudging Jenny who quickly did the same. Jim stopped and then after a few seconds proclaimed, 'Oh surprise, surprise they are letting me through, usually they demand right of way,' as if this wasn't the first time that he had encountered the Mercedes. He swung his van onto the road. Peering through my fingers I saw a hand reach from the back of the saloon car, touching the driver's shoulder and he responded immediately pulling out onto the road.

'Sod them, can't make up their minds,' and Jim accelerated onto the grassy verge and drove past, glaring at the driver who was forced to pull over. 'No manners, arrogant, unfriendly swine.'

Had they seen us? I wondered, and I glanced at Jenny, who had gone white staring at the floor of the van.

'Okay?' said Jim,' looking across to us, 'sorry about that, didn't mean to give you a fright.'

'Coming from Islay, I know all about single track roads,' I replied, making light of it.

Five minutes later we reached a farm house with a field next to it enclosed by a low stone wall, an abandoned vehicle rusting away in one corner. Opposite were some outhouses. Hens were running around pecking the ground, a Border Collie emerging from one of the outhouses, starting to bark.

'This is your destination folks - Knockvologan. Take the rough track straight ahead, which winds down to the beach. Remember to look for the metal hooks in the sand, Jenny.'

I didn't fancy going back up the road. They could be waiting for us.

'Jim, I have a big favour to ask. Is there a pier on Erraid?'

'Yes, built when the lighthouse was being constructed,' he reminded me.

'Could you pick us up from there in a few hours in your boat?'

'Well, yes, of course,' he replied, slightly surprised by my request.

'That would be great. It's just Jenny was saying last night that she hadn't seen the coast. It might give her more ideas for her next paintings.'

Jenny immediately picked up: 'Jim could you? That would be wonderful.'

'Aye okay, I did promise you a trip in the boat. Might be rough.'

'A whisky at the end will settle her stomach and yours.'

'Right, you are on,' and he paused, before continuing, 'two this afternoon would probably best suit the tide.'

'Jim, thanks. We better get started. Thank Cathy for picking up the boys.' I didn't want him to forget.

Clutching our backpacks, we started down the rough track heading round a bend as quickly as we could, while Jim took a package into the house

'That was the same car that followed us the other day.' It was a statement from Jenny, not a question.

'Yes,' and I think they saw me. If we leave the island by boat, we don't need to go back up the road.'

'I realised that, but what if they follow us down here.'

'Then we need to get across to Erraid quickly.'

'Do you think it's McGrory?'

'I don't know, it would be an unbelievable coincidence if it was.'

'Like a dead body being discovered next to our house.'

We were almost trotting along the rough track, descending towards the beach.

'I didn't tell you,' said Jenny, 'but I checked out the Shona Tyler Trust again. Phoned a friend who had access to the internet'

'And?'

'The website has been removed. She tried phoning them as we did, but the number was not just engaged, as it was with us, now it was unobtainable. It was a bogus trust. Probably set up to lure us here. I was suckered, my pride made me want to believe it.'

'No it was desperation, Jenny. We thought our luck was changing.'

'Am I just being paranoid ?'

'Let's hope so,' I replied, but deep inside I knew she wasn't.

We passed a boat house and reached the beach. The metal hooks were there, protruding from the sand on the shore, as Jim had described, their story, maybe one of failure to escape, very relevant to us. We hurried on scrambling over rocks to reach a stretch of wet sand that separated Mull from Erraid. The tide, as predicted, was out.

32

In the distance, I suddenly heard, the throaty roar of a quad bike, possibly more than one. We both picked up speed, splashing through the wet sand, aware that our footprints would remain visible for some time, an easy trail to follow. It was only a few hundred yards but it seemed longer before we reached the shore of Erraid. Next to the shore the sand dipped leaving deep pools of water. Without saying anything we both plunged in up to our knees, the water cold, catching our breath. Jenny stumbled but I caught her and then reaching out for a bush, pulling myself up onto the dry ground. Twisting, I grabbed Jenny and pulled her up beside me.

The hillside in front was covered with heather, bushes and patches of exposed rock. Urging Jenny on, I helped her along the shore line, keeping low behind bushes, until I saw an outcrop of rock that we could hide behind.

'Not far,' I said, trying to be encouraging but it was unnecessary, Jenny was keeping up with me. We both flopped behind the rock, out of breath, but I grabbed my backpack, taking out my binoculars focussing on the rocky shore opposite. In seconds two quad bikes emerged, like angry hornets, their engine roaring, stopping briefly searching for a navigable route through the outcrops of rock on the far shore.

Quickly, the driver of the lead quad turned his handlebars and the engine noise increased as he steered a course through the rocky outcrop and onto the sand, the other following behind. Our footprints were dispersing, the water erasing the pattern in the sand, but the route taken by us was still visible. The quad bikes, picked up speed, racing across the tidal beach, their tyres spitting out sand and water behind them.

The lead quad reached the shoreline on our side. The driver braked as he reached the deep pool on the shore line, cutting the engine, knowing that he couldn't use the quad bike to get onto the island at this point.

Dressed in jeans and a black sweatshirt, wearing sunglasses, muscular with cropped hair, he appeared every inch somebody I didn't want to meet. He jumped off the bike, waiting for the other bike to stop, which it did seconds later, its engine noise petering out. The driver of the second quad bike remained on his quad, while the first driver spoke to him, pointing away from us along the shoreline, and the second quad took off racing along the sand, looking for a place to make landfall.

Meanwhile the first driver pulled up the seat squab and pulled out what looked like a handgun, thrusting it down behind a belt. He scrutinised the hillside, whilst walking along the shoreline.

Suddenly he shouted, 'Come out Meldrum, make it easy. Bring your wife. Come out with your hands up,' his accent sounded Irish, another link with McGrory.

Jenny was hugging the ground, her foot subconsciously moving back and forwards, scrapping the ground behind her, preparing to bolt.

'He can't see us or he would have pointed the gun at us. Keep calm,' I whispered, but I was really also trying to reassure myself.

'If I shoot you, it's your own fault,' and with a quick glance around the rock I saw him waving the gun above his head. 'Make

234

it easy,' he repeated.

I heard a splash as he dipped into a pool of water by the shoreline and I grabbed Jenny. Both of us crouching low, we left the security of the rock and wormed our way through bushes, working our way up the hillside.

I heard a loud crack and we both flattened ourselves to the ground. It was a warning shot nowhere near us. As we crawled along the ground we reached a path, a sheep trail, tufts of wool caught on the jaggy yellow gorse bushes, which lined it. There were bushes on both sides and we used the path to run further away from our assailant.

The trail suddenly opened out and we dived to the ground landing on a cliff edge above the sea. Floating on the water between Erraid and the mainland was a rubber dingy, two men in it, one sitting holding paddles, the other scanning the hillside with binoculars.

'We need to go back. They haven't seen us.' There were beads of sweat on Jenny's forehead and as I spoke she wiped them away with her arm, her voice croaking: 'How many are there?'

I shrugged, and pulled her gently back along the path we had come, noticing a gap in the bushes and directing us both through it for several yards. Just in time as the man who had followed us onto the island ran past along the path we had just left, feet pounding on the ground, the vibration finding an echo in our trembling. I dared to glance up and saw him waving to the people in the boat and then retrace his steps, stopping, sniffing the air like a dog, head moving from side to side.

'You'll suffer for this,' he shouted, and I clung tighter to Jenny. 'Come out,' he shouted, now sounding angrier. Then he spoke into a radio, a message that I couldn't make out. He then swore before I heard him running back along the path.

We were still close to the cliff edge and when I glanced down the two men were rowing away heading towards the tidal strip of sand between Erraid and the mainland, no doubt to join the search team on the island. I grabbed Jenny's arm and we headed in the other direction, clambering up the hillside, trying not to disturb the bushes.

There was another crack and I saw a sheep startled running, bleating. About fifty yards away I saw our chaser and was also aware now of the whining sound of a quad bike approaching.

We reached a rocky outcrop with little cover and realised that we could see the other side of the island. A distance to our right was a white sandy cove, David Balfour's beach, I presumed, and further out to sea was the *Kerry Star*. In the distance across the sea, to the east, I could see the Paps of Jura, Islay and Colonsay - anyone of them would seem a safe haven at the moment. Almost crawling we reached a gully between two rock faces and paused.

I signalled for Jenny to wait and as I edged away she began to tremble, gasping, drawing deep breathes.

'I want to study the boat,' I said, 'I'm not leaving you,' and I quickly reached a vantage point, using the binoculars, from my backpack, to examine the boat, its sails being raised as I looked. It was too much of a coincidence that the boat was there. I was sure that there had been no dingy on the shore at Knockvologan and so the dingy must have come from the *Kerry Star*. I returned for my camera and took photos as I watched several crew preparing the boat, attempting to raise the anchor as it was preparing to leave. Then I noticed a man standing by one of the sails scanning the hillside through binoculars. He was holding what looked like a radio in his hand and speaking into it - that was the clincher for me, he was directing the search for us.

I returned to Jenny and listened out for any movement near us, then we used the gully to get around to the back of the island.

This was desperate, my mind racing trying to think how we

could get off the island. The sun now high above us, I glanced at my watch - midday. Two hours until Jim returned. We had to be waiting for him.

Nearing a path we stopped, hearing the sound of an approaching quad bike - it soon hurtled past us heading down to Balfour's Bay. Looking round I saw bushes moving about a hundred yards away near the gully we had just left and our chaser emerged. We had to keep going.

We were working our way around the island approaching the west coast, Iona now coming into view. Ahead I saw a small white circular, metal building recognising it as the disused observatory Jim had told me about. We kept away from it and edged around the lip of an old quarry. We were now above the former lighthouse keepers' cottages, near a path that led down by a reservoir. I could see the pier and my hopes receded when I saw a quad bike parked near it, guarding access. Our escape route blocked.

We started to scramble down reaching a ledge, pausing to determine our next steps, when a voice spoke quietly to us: 'I'm Seth, you are both in trouble it seems.' We jumped turning in the direction of the voice, my chest heaving, aware of the blood pumping around my body. Seth was sitting in the lotus position, legs crossed and feet placed on the opposite thigh, but they unfolded effortlessly as he stood up. A dramatic tattoo of a bird of prey covered one half of his face, a long earring hung from the opposite ear. He was bald apart from a pony tail protruding from the back of his head. His appearance as startling as it was unexpected.

'We don't like people spoiling the sanctuary of our island, it upsets us, brings discord. I also realise that you are the victims and we must help you. We know if they find you worse will happen and our peace, harmonious link between us and nature will be disrupted. Follow me,' and he started quickly down a path. Neither of us demurred, glad that someone else was taking responsibility, making decisions and we followed him. Seth must have been in his thirties, I judged, as he sprightly crossed the ground. Our efforts, taxed by our journey so far, were more laboured. We passed the small reservoir and reached a wall at the rear of the row of cottages. Seth opened a gate to a garden, vegetables growing in neat rows. He opened the back door of the cottage and ushered us in looking back up the hill as he did.

Satisfied that we hadn't been spotted, he shut the door, led us through a small kitchen and into a lounge, which looked on to the road that led past the front of the cottages. Checking outside, he pulled some heavy floral curtains across blocking the light.

The room was almost empty, a large circular rug, partly covering a stone floor, a wood burner with a stack of wood beside, a music centre in one corner, three wicker chairs and some large candles in ornate brass candle stick holders were near the wood burner.

'Welcome,' he said, his smile revealing several missing teeth, 'you are safe here for the moment, but the men chasing you, I sense, are very angry and determined; they will not give up.'

He looked at both of us intensely, seeming to absorb our feelings. After a minute he said: 'You are both very troubled, anxious. We will help you.'

I wondered who he meant but was grateful of any support and expressed our thanks. I explained about Jim but he seemed lost in thought.

'Please sit down. I'll infuse herbal tea for you and then I'll go and speak to some of my friends, see what I can do.'

Seth went into the kitchen, put water in the kettle, lit the gas ring underneath it and prepared the herbal tea. His actions, slow and measured, began to calm us. I was aware that we hadn't said much, but he didn't appear concerned. Handing us each a mug of herbal tea, he said: 'I'll be back. Wait here and don't look out of the window. They are looking in windows, knocking on doors, upsetting many,' and with that he was gone out the front door.

Jenny and I just looked at each other, words hard to find, but aware that hope had been restored, if only temporarily. We were covered in mud, our clothes wet and my jacket ripped but that was the least of our concerns.

We waited in the darkness of the room, the dark comforting, becoming aware of the smell of wood smoke and incense which hung over us. Until Seth returned we were unable to discuss next steps; our future rested with him.

Twenty minutes later, he returned, using the back door accompanied by two men and a woman in her forties, proud of her long greying hair which was tied back, her blue dress long and flowing.

'I'm Avalina, leader of our commune. We are aware that men from the house across the beach are chasing you. They have disrupted our community life several times recently, especially with their quad bikes disturbing our sanctuary. Our values will not allow them to do you harm, be assured.' Avalina had a presence, a spirituality which you could draw energy from. I saw Jenny's face relax, her mouth almost forming a smile, making a connection with the woman. The other men stood around waiting on her next words.

She wasn't hurried, focussed on us, reassuring but I sensed that her mind was working out how to proceed.

'Seth, alert the commune, tell them to prepare for a festival, white robes. Bring some for our guests. Joe use the empty bag for carting wood, put their backpacks and jackets in it and take it to the pier. Keep their possessions concealed.' The men left quickly.

Avalina smiled at us, her face serene: ' We will watch for your friend and let you know as he approaches. I sense that you have been through great anguish. Maybe when all this is over you will return to the island and learn more about yourselves and restore peace to your souls. We welcome all who are sincere.'

I was aware how little I had spoken and Jenny was also quiet: 'Thank you,' I said, simply, but with meaning, picking up my half-finished mug of herbal tea, which was now cold, but still refreshing, my mouth still dry, the fear of the last few hours lingering, but now much reduced.

'You can wash at the sink, if you wish to freshen up and there is a composting toilet out the back but check first, they may be around.'

I glanced at my watch, which Avalina noticed: 'Don't worry we have time,' and with that she left.

...

Within the hour members of the commune started arriving, dressed in flowing white robes, the women with garlands of flowers resting on their heads. Two women took Jenny aside, dressing her and pleating her hair, adding colour to her cheeks. Seth gave me white robes, held by a rope around the waist, adding stripes of blue and red to my cheeks.

He smiled at my reaction: 'We are acting up, but it will also disguise you.'

Avalina returned looking with satisfaction at our transformation. 'Jenny you link arms with the girls and do what they do. Peter, you keep your head down and stay in the middle of the group you are with.'

We formed up: men and women separated. Seth reappeared, I hadn't noticed him going, announcing: 'Your friend is approaching.'

The room quietened, conversations ceased, everyone appeared composed.

'Let's go,' said Avalina, and the front door was opened. I

blinked in the sun. Across the road was another low granite wall and more vegetable gardens. We turned left, the women in front holding hands forming a ring, moving around in a circle heading towards the pier, which I now saw. The men followed more serious, our heads bowed, me in their midst.

I saw one of McGrory's men sitting astride a quad bike, bemused by what he saw approaching him, a sneer on his face. The women danced past him, one offering him a daffodil, which after a second, he accepted. 'Maybe stuff it down your gun,' I mused, spotting the barely concealed weapon stuck in his trousers. Due to his sunglasses I couldn't see who he was looking at, an old trick used by bodyguards.

The procession slowly passed him, me desperately trying to maintain their steady slow pace, trying to control myself by breathing deeply, and eventually we turned down towards the pier passing several stone buildings. It seemed to take ages to reach the pier, built many years ago to take the stone hewn at the quarry out to the lighthouse offshore, the sides of the pier built from the same granite.

I heard the sound of an approaching boat and looked up spotting Jim, at the rear of his boat guiding it towards the pier. Goodness knows what he thought when he saw us all. Avalina motioned us forward, some of the men blocking the narrow entrance to the pier, beside the building. Jenny hugged her and I gave her a kiss on the cheek. 'Take care,' she said. We stripped off our outfits and as Jim stopped the boat by the pier, our gear was taken down stone steps, to Jim and then we, in turn, walked down the steps and into his boat.

Jim's expression was unreadable. 'Please let's get away, quick, I'll explain later,' and we thanked the community members. Jim started up the engine, the noise of the outboard motor increasing as he swung round and headed out towards the Sound of Iona. I looked back and waved, noticing a commotion by the entrance to the pier and the quad bike driver racing down the pier brandishing a handgun. Then he was caught up with the women dancing, blocking him and he briefly disappeared from view, emerging after a struggle, at the edge of the pier. He lifted his weapon but the next second it was thrown up in the air landing with a splash in the sea.

'Nice flowers, Jenny, and what's with the war paint,' Jim said, jerking his head back in surprise when he saw the state of us. 'You must have some story to tell,' he added.

'Over a whisky tonight, Jim,' I promised.

33

The sea was flat calm, the phut-phut sound of the outboard motor echoed off the granite rocks on the shore. We made serene progress up the Sound of Iona, thankfully no sign of the *Kerry Star*, Jim sitting at the back of his small boat steering. Jenny and I sat recovering, the tension of the last few hours etched in our faces, masked only slightly by the coloured strips on our cheeks. Jim must have been desperate to ask more questions but he remained silent, thoughtful, observing us.

We passed Fionnphort and the ferry ramp and then the old mine workings at Torr Mor, the granite quarry workings on the far side of the hill that overlooked the ferry terminal, rose coloured in the afternoon sun. Jim had explained something of their history. Despite a recent attempt in the 1990s to revive the quarry, the workings had been finished by the end of the First World War, due to cheap imports. Jim pointed out, as we passed, the uneven steps known as Jacob's Ladder, which extended from the quarry workings down to the small quarry pier. There were piles of discarded granite, all slowly being reclaimed by nature - bracken and brambles spreading slowly across the granite softening the hard angular edges of the cut rock. Jim had told us before how the granite was used for bridges in Glasgow, the docks in Liverpool and places abroad. His information drifted through our minds without connecting, but had a soothing effect nonetheless.

We passed through the Bull Hole, the narrow but deep anchorage between the mainland and a small offshore island where the Iona ferry resided overnight and eventually reached the entrance to the bay at Kintra. The tide was fully in and we beached on the shore just short of the road in front of the house. Jason and Ben rushed out to meet us from Jim and Cathy's house, Cathy not far behind them.

I thanked Jim as I stepped out of the boat whilst helping Jenny ashore and invited him and Cathy around later. Jim immediately accepted. 'I would love an explanation of what was going on,' and I saw Cathy peering at the fading coloured strips on our face, which even washing with sea water hadn't totally removed, her own curiosity aroused. The two boys were also intrigued, Ben rubbing my cheek but too shy to say anything.

. . .

'I don't need any whisky, a cup of tea would be nice,' Jim said, as he sat down and Cathy added a similar request. There was a pause as I got the tea and we all looked at one another, not sure how to begin.

Jim spoke first: 'The crowd at Quarry House are not very nice. Lots of talk about them locally. The people on Erraid have had problems with them - being disturbed when they use their quad bikes to race around the island. They don't have much respect for people, the locals notice things like that.'

'They were up to their tricks today,' I replied.

'Chasing you?'

'Yes.'

'I knew they were angry, the way that the driver of the Mercedes swung his car across the road. On my return they were waiting for me, asking questions about you. There have been lots of rumours since they took over the house a few months ago. It was a new build but the original owners, a couple from London, divorced and it was empty until the Dowd's bought it, built the wall and gates and installed security cameras. There's been some coming and going and lots of parcels delivered. There is also a link with the *Kerry Star* - guests of theirs use it.'

'They're from Ireland,' stated Jenny.

Jim nodded, 'Mr Dowd is driven around in the Mercedes, rarely seen. I heard someone call him Desmond, this morning. He was in the backseat of the Mercedes but elusive behind the tinted windows, like a ghost.'

Jenny blanched and Cathy reacted instinctively leant across touching her arm, trying to provide comfort. I felt that familiar tension in my stomach; my heart rate racing,

'You know him?' she asked.

'We know him as Desmond McGrory, must be the same guy. He's a drug dealer from Ireland. Unlikely that he would use his own name. The authorities would like to get their hands on him.'

I turned to Jenny for confirmation that she wanted me to explain more and she said: 'Tell them what happened.'

Both Jim and Cathy were by now leaning forward in their seats, Jim putting down his mug of tea.

'We ran into them last year in Islay,' I began, and told them the story.

They both heard me out in silence, Cathy turning away and covering her mouth when I described what happened on Machir Bay, Jim sitting back in his seat, eyes focussed on me, listening intently.

I brought them up to date with recent events, leaving out the allegations of porn being found on my work computer, because they weren't true.

'It sounds as if someone wants you here. You are being drawn into a trap - used as a snare. But who would go to such lengths to set up a trust just to entice you?'

'Desmond McGrory would. I inadvertently damaged his operations, exposed the Islay drug route and he won't forget or forgive. It seems also that he had a crush on Catherine and when he discovered my relationship and about Jason it upset him. He's a bit obsessive.'

'He's a psycho,' stated Cathy, with anger, her voice more shrill, 'a control freak. He needs to be stopped.'

'I'm sure that the authorities have tried,' said Jim, his voice simmering with just as much emotion as his wife's, but his tone deeper. 'What worries me is that you're experience in Aberfoyle sounds similar to Tommy's.'

'That's correct. Remember what the woman in the shop said, Peter,' added Cathy.

Jenny twisted her head, 'You didn't tell me that,' she said, an irritated edge in her voice.

I held up my hands: 'No, I didn't,' I replied, 'I didn't think it would help.'

'Of course, it wouldn't,' said Cathy quickly, realising how Jenny was reacting, 'I wouldn't have wanted Jim telling me.'

'Tell me more about what happened when you drove back up the road this morning?' I asked Jim, trying to steer the conversation onto different ground.

'They were waiting for me, blocking the road, quad bikes revving. The Mercedes was still there. They demanded your names. I said I didn't know you, had just picked you up - often act as an unofficial taxi. One of them, a tall guy, was quite menacing, aggressive, leaning into the open window in the van, inches away from my face, as if he was going to haul me out of the van and hit me. His breath stank of garlic. I blanked him, but I have to admit

I was worried.'

Cathy was fidgeting in her seat, adjusting her top, alarmed by what she heard.

'Where did they go?' he demanded.

'You know the area - down the road. After that who knows - maybe walking along the coastline,' I explained.

'The guy backed off when he saw that I wasn't going to help him and someone jumped out of the back seat of the Mercedes, it wasn't McGrory, because he issued instructions and ended by saying: 'you know what the boss wants - now go get them.'

'Anything else?' I asked.

'The tall guy said: 'Get Steve to launch a dingy, search the coast line. He'll be able to recognise them.

'Say that again,' I asked.

'They said that the guy called Steve would be able to recognise you,' he repeated.

'I wonder if that is the same Steve that I met in Ireland and Aberfoyle, even though he saved Jenny in Aberfoyle, he could be working for McGrory.' Jenny drew a sharp breath, then blew out her cheeks, 'like a double agent,' she queried.

Jim went on: 'One of the quad drivers said: We'll cut across the beach to the island and find them if they are there.' Then they were gone racing down towards the beach on their quad bikes and I drove past the Mercedes. I knew you were in trouble. You looked frightened when I left you and you were keen that I picked you up by boat, which I thought was odd but then I realised that you didn't want to bump into them, probably knew them. I realised that you were in some sort of danger from them but had no idea why until now.'

'We were,' and I told them what happened next.

'So it was a gun, I saw fall in the water?'

'Yes.'

247

'They are good people on Erraid, maybe they look at the world differently, but they don't cause harm. It says a lot that they helped you,' Jim stated.

'You are both in a lot of trouble,' Cathy added.

'We were lured here,' I said, 'but I was thinking that the discovery of Tommy wasn't in their plans. The police presence is protecting us. Maybe they saw an opportunity when Jim took us right into their den. They will be even angrier now that we evaded them and are aware of them, know where they live. We have exposed them and they don't know what we will do next.'

'When I took the two policemen guarding the well, a hot drink, this evening,' Cathy said, 'they told me that they expected to be away tomorrow or the day after. Their investigations are almost complete for the moment.'

'We need to get away,' I said.

'I'll fix the car tomorrow, have it ready for the next day.'

'That would be wonderful.'

'That's the day we are going to Glasgow, isn't it, Cathy?'

'We are going to visit my daughter, she's expecting a baby in a few months.'

'We'll travel in convoy,' Jim added, 'you'll be safe if you are with someone.'

That seemed a good idea. Troubled and concerned they left shortly after.

. . .

I showed them both out and returned to the lounge. 'I understand why you didn't tell me how Tommy died. What a horrible way to go,' and she lowered her head, closing her eyes, probably trying to blank out the thoughts that his death conjured, especially for her.

I sat down beside her on the settee putting my arm around

her drawing her close to me. At least we had each other.

'You didn't tell them about Nick. I think that was wise.'

'No, I don't know how he fits in. He didn't discourage us from coming here although he made it clear it was our choice. I wonder if 'Bac Mor' is a code word for a surveillance operation they're running. They would be desperate to trace McGrory and the experience of how they acted on Islay is that they choose their time to pounce. I don't believe that they would set up the Shona Tyler Trust, that must be McGrory. So they were happy for us to be the bait in the trap, use us as a snare to draw McGrory out and not discourage us from coming here. Nice work, Nick,' I added, with a touch of sarcasm.

'Have you tried to use the app to contact him?'

'I tried on the landline earlier when you were feeding the boys.'

'And?'

'Number unobtainable. Once the police go we are on our own.'

Jenny buried her head in my chest again, they were no tears, just despair. I also felt despairing, a sense of helplessness, a pawn in a bigger game and no one cared what happened to us.

I had, somehow, to pick myself up and run through what had happened today, especially what Jim had told us. I had a thought, and I got up and fetched the camera from the bedroom, where I had left it. I sat on the edge of the bed switching on playback, going through the images of the *Kerry Star* that I had taken earlier today, annoyed that I hadn't taken the telephoto lens with me on our trip. The bridge was to the rear overlooking a short expanse of deck, with stairs leading down below deck, in the centre. The boat was upmarket, the fittings gleaming brass, everything with a touch of luxury as Jim had suggested. The pictures were sharp but from a distance. I could make out people on the deck and saw the guy with the binoculars and radio. Unfortunately the binoculars blocked his face, although his hair seemed long - that would most likely be Steve. The camera allowed me to zoom in on pictures but the images quickly lost sharpness. I played around with the pictures, zooming in and out trying to catch the face of the man with the binoculars. I studied the best close up of him intently until my eyes were blinking. I couldn't be certain but he looked very like the man, certainly in size and maybe even the way he stood, that I had met in Dingle and Aberfoyle. If so then Steve was working for McGrory and not Nick. I wonder if Nick knew.

Did that explain why he phoned me after the incident at the nursing home. Wondering what I was doing there? Jason had identified Connor Brown as the man whose face he had seen at the window in Quinn's farm. Could they have been working together? They were both in the same area at the same time - coincidence? But then why did he shoot Brown, who was probably working for McGrory? Was he frightened that Brown would implicate him? My head was buzzing - too many thoughts not fitting together, the jigsaw pieces remained scrambled.

34

The next morning I was waiting outside the house with the boys as Cathy got into her car and drove the short distance until she was level with me. I opened the door, the boys jumping in with their school bags and packed lunches already for another day at school.

I let Cathy know that I had given Jason a letter for the teachers, to let them know that this was their last day. She assured me that she would make sure that the teachers got the letter. She and Jim had obviously spent some time discussing what we had told them as she emphasised that she would be there to pick up the boys. A night's reflection had heightened their horror at what we had endured.

'Jim said that he would pick up the car parts when he finishes about eleven,' was her last comment as she released the handbrake and drove off. Again I thanked them.

I returned to the house and Jenny and I got busy packing for our departure. The morning went quickly, Jim returning with the parts for the car and got into his overalls ready to start work. I asked if I could use his van to get to Fionnphort and he handed me the keys even before I explained that I needed to say farewell to Dad. Jenny decided to stay behind and I knew Jim would keep an eye on her. As I drove up the road I noticed that there was still a police car parked in the field - that offered some protection, but once they had gone, what then.

It was going to be hard to say goodbye when I didn't know when I would see Dad again. I was also worried about his health. So my emotions were fully in play as I took the short ferry crossing to Iona, the journey let me draw breath and be grateful for the handiwork of nature: the restless heaving sea, the rocky granite landscape, so stark in the sunlight, the hills of all shapes and sizes, the plethora of small islands from isolated rocky crags to sun kissed strips of green and, of course, the expansive sky. How could a spiritual heaven such as Iona and Mull, where people came to search for answers to big questions, coexist, with the soulless greed of McGrory and his henchmen, determined to exploit others for their own selfish profit, damming their victims to a lifetime of misery and squalor. How could good and evil coexist so closely, only a few miles apart? Maybe it was closer than that - a decision of the mind. My musings were only disturbed as I heard the ferry ramp being lowered on our arrival at Iona.

I had alerted Dad, so he was waiting for me. His face was maybe more pinched, the eyes surrounded by more fret work, than I remembered from Islay days but a lot had happened since then. He was, however, still resolutely upbeat, content within himself, his faith a source of strength. Dad had no doubt that when he crossed over, as he put it, he would be meeting up with Mum and his Saviour. I admired him for that: my own faith several notches below his, not as thought out, dragged into action only when things were dire.

We went to the Argyll Hotel, its brightly painted purple window frames standing out from the red granite facade of the hotel. Close to the pier, it was ideal only a short distance to walk. We sat outside on a warm spring morning, with coffee and shortbread, chatted, talked about the past, about Mum and laughed at some of the memories only we shared, as if we didn't have a care. A rare interlude of calm in a churning world.

After an hour I noticed dad's concentration wavering, touching his tea spoon several times, moving it about the saucer, then sweeping the shortbread crumbs with his fingers from the bench much to the interest of the many small birds who darted in to feed. Dad began to sag, look weary, his eyes tired squinting more in the sunlight. I became aware of his breathing, the rise and fall of his chest, slightly laboured, as if he was trying to control the intake of air.

'Are you okay?'

'I'm alright, Peter,' he replied firmly, trying to make light of my concern, 'it's just my heart rate, a bit erratic. A mind of its own, but as long as I have the tablets, it will be okay.'

He stopped and gave me that look that I remembered from my youth - I'm in charge, everything will be fine, a benevolent look from a loving father. Except it wasn't, the roles were beginning to change, more fluid.

'I'm alright, Peter,' he declared again, but the repetition was revealing, 'you get back to Jenny and the boys.' The exuberance was still there but I was now aware of a shadow slowly encroaching, enveloping his soul, his vitality, restricted and frustrating him.

'I was so pleased to catch up. Jenny's a wonderful lass. Ben is growing fast. Jason's also a fine lad. I can see a hint of Catherine in him and that's no bad thing.' It was a final statement, rapidly delivered, a summation of what he wanted to convey. Such statements were becoming more important to him as time slipped by.

We rose and put our arms around each other, and I went to pay. He waited outside, stooped, no longer the immovable rock of my youth, now less confident, more aware of his frailties. He accompanied me back to the ferry, trying to keep up the pretence that he was alright and watched as the ferry left. My last glimpse was of him sitting down on a bench a little too quickly. It wasn't comforting, quite sad, especially because I couldn't linger. I had to deal with my responsibilities to the next generation which were threatened by the force of evil, an evil which had invaded all parts of my life and of those I loved.

I was back with Jenny by early afternoon, thoughtful, trying to prepare for what lay ahead, putting to one side all the concerns about Dad, because I had to focus on the challenges that lay ahead.

35

Glasgow

The cafe was nearly empty; business slack. Most people came in for cigarettes or bottles of coke, some for the ice-cream for which the cafe was famous, but its glory days were behind it. Times had moved on, supermarkets pinching most of its casual business. Malcolm sat alone to the rear of the cafe, avoiding the glare of the hanging lamps, clutching a cup of coffee, a copy of the late edition of the *Strathclyde Evening Echo* in front of him, trying to complete the Sudoku. His concentration was divided between the Sudoku and the door. The phone call had been brief, the instructions, however, precise and so here he was and she was already half-an-hour late. The young assistant behind the counter was sitting on a stool, looking bored busy texting on her phone and only looked up at the last minute as he approached the counter, with its display of various flavoured ice-creams in plastic tubs, behind a curved glass screen, with a request for another cup of coffee.

'I'll bring it over,' the assistant replied, her boredom temporarily lifted.

Outside the traffic in the road was sporadic, pedestrians few, the heavy rain further driving away casual custom. It was going to be a long evening for the assistant and him, he mused. A quiet corner: a perfect place to meet but she hadn't turned up. Change

255

of minds, last minute nerves, Malcolm could only speculate.

The assistant brought over the coffee and placed it down.

'Waiting for someone?' it was a brave attempt at conversation from one he judged to be about sixteen, probably still at school.

Malcolm was about to reply when the door of the cafe was pushed open and there she was, not instantly recognisable, the blonde hair now dyed black and streaked with red, face heavy with makeup, wearing ripped jeans and a shapeless black top sparkling with tiny gems under an anorak which was dripping wet and which she unzipped as she came in, shaking off the rainwater. Kirsty walked over, not making eye contact and pulled back the chair opposite and sat down, quickly glancing at the assistant, who seemed surprised, trying to work out the relationship, intrigued.

'Coffee?' enquired Malcolm, and Kirsty nodded adding, 'black, no sugar.'

Both remained silent, waiting for the coffee to be brought across, tacitly accepting that they didn't want anyone listening in on their conversation. Kirsty took off her wet anorak, the water dripping from it wetting the floor, puddles forming behind her. Kirsty's head was lowered, not wanting to engage with Malcolm, and it was only when the assistant brought across the coffee, and Kirsty briefly lifted her head, that he spotted that Kirsty's heavy makeup was attempting to mask a hint of a bruise.

'Thanks for getting in touch. I appreciate it,' said Malcolm, discreetly touching his jacket lapel.

'Am I in trouble?'

Malcolm kept his voice low: 'Kirsty it's a crime to be in possession of porn of that nature and to distribute it, also causing an innocent person to lose their job and livelihood.' He had decided to be blunt.

'I was following orders, didn't know what the upgrade contained.'

'You didn't check it?' his mouth opened in surprise at her statement, his expression stern.

Kirsty looked towards the shop counter, her head lowered further.

'Who runs TGG?'

'Joe is my boss but he is not the director. I have only ever seen the director, only spoken a few words.'

'His name?'

'Mr MacArthur.'

'He's listed as a director at Company House.'

'Why did you ask then?' her tone edgy, immediately becoming defensive.

'I need to check details, it's part of my job, an important part,' he added.

'This is not the first time, is it?'

Kirsty looked down.

'Kirsty how often have you done upgrades like that?' he asked again, insistent.

'Not often. Look I need my job, it's paying the rent.'

Was that your boyfriend I met at the flat?'

Kirsty swiped at her eye blinking.

'Did he hit you?'

'Not your business.'

'Of course. I just don't like seeing someone with potential going wrong. Give me more details about the upgrade. I want to be clear about what you did and how.'

Malcolm took out a small notepad and a pen. After twenty minutes he was satisfied and pushed the notepad across the table: 'Read it, sign it and date it,' he said quickly. Kirsty took the pen and signed the page and pushed it back. Malcolm felt relief, picking up his coffee cup, the coffee cold but welcome, his mouth dry.

'Thanks, I will do all I can to help you,' he said, standing up, pushing back his chair, the sound of the legs scrapping on the floor echoing around the cafe, alerting the assistant who stopped playing with her phone.

Malcolm settled the tab and Kirsty and he walked to the door, standing together, in the entrance, the rain having eased off. Both ready to depart heading in the same direction. Malcolm ran his hand through his hair as if he was wiping off raindrops and walked away from the cafe. From the other side of the street he heard a car door shut. He was passing the entrance to a narrow lane, bins standing ready to be emptied the next morning, when a hand grabbed him pulling him into the lane, spinning him around flattening him against a brick wall. He was aware of the stench of tobacco and alcohol as he was pinned against the wall with force, catching his breath. Profanities echoed along the lane, uttered inches from his face, repeatedly with venom. Kirsty's boyfriend held a knife to Malcolm's throat: 'I knew you were up to something, trying to steal her.'

'No,' screamed Kirsty, 'leave him be, Wayne.'

Wayne's face contorted, inflamed by a cocktail of drink and drugs, the knife point hard against Malcolm's throat. Suddenly there was a scuffle and the knife was yanked away, two men hauling Wayne to the ground his hands being pinned behind his back, handcuffs slipped on.

One man knelt on Wayne's back, the other asked as he stood up: 'Are you okay, Malcolm?'

'Yes thanks, just in time,' replied Malcolm, his hands sweeping over his body as if he was trying to get rid of any trace of his attacker, then feeling his throat.

'Almost missed your signal, half asleep waiting for you to come out.' The other officer had searched Wayne's pockets producing a bag of white powder.

'What's this Wayne? Come on, let's take you away, your

time's up.'

Malcolm discreetly touched his lapel again, switching off his recording device.

Kirsty stood shaking: 'How did you know about him?'

'I have my contacts, they told me about Wayne.' Breathing deeply, his throat still sore, he thanked the two policemen.

He felt sorry for Kirsty, despite her wrong choices: 'If you are lucky you won't hear from me again,' he said, his expression softening. Kirsty leant against the brick wall next to her, searching his face for confirmation of what he had just said, a smile slowly spreading across her face.

36

Iona

Thomas Meldrum had been delayed; guests arriving by a later ferry than expected. By the time he had made them comfortable, explained the house rules, he was late for his rendezvous with his friend. He left the Abbey, passed the St Columba hotel and reached the grounds of the Nunnery. The island was quiet now the day tourists had returned to Mull. He passed only one couple who were out for a walk, the rain having stopped, the puddles starting to dry. The bird song was beautiful and he stopped to breathe in the moment, looking over to Mull, the red granite outcrops adding a sense of warmth to what was still a cool spring evening.

As he approached the Nunnery ruins he passed a woman, who he vaguely recognised, with her dog on a lead, smiling, as most people did on Iona. As he entered the Nunnery he noticed two men sitting on one of the benches, the nearer sprouting a bushy red beard, and he had the fleeting thought that their backsides would be getting wet from the damp seat.

He had reached the other side of the Nunnery emerging onto the road opposite the Nunnery View Art Gallery, when he felt a hand touch him. He turned surprised expecting a friend but instead saw the two men who had been sitting on the bench a moment before, now behind him.

'Did I not see you on BBC Alba the other night?' the bearded man enquired smiling.

'Yes, I spoke briefly about the changes at the Abbey,' Thomas replied, quite taken that the man could recognise him.

'So you are Mr Meldrum?' Thomas smiled acknowledging the question, 'Peter's dad?' the man added.

'Yes,' but something had changed, the expressions on the men's face freezing. The other man quickly grabbed his arm tightly, Thomas responded trying to push him away. The bearded man then clutched Thomas's other arm.

'You are coming with us,' he said, glancing around checking no one was witnessing what they had done. The men were young, strong, their grip firm and Thomas was dragged, almost carried, along the path out of the Nunnery gardens, turning away from the direction of the slipway. He could feel his heart thumping, fast then slow and then there was no rhythm, just discordant beats and he stopped trying to resist, feeling dizzy. Thomas quickly prayed, a natural instinct for him. He needed help.

Islay

Pence Gifford looked out from his lounge window, across Loch Indaal, the waters choppy this evening, spotting the distillery at Bruichladdich, wondering for a brief moment what their next release would be. Distillers found it hard to switch off. Tastes, trends were always changing, difficult to keep up, especially when your stocks took years to mature. But that was the alchemy, mixing and matching, using your skill to create fresh expressions. Lost in thought, he was startled when the phone rang.

'Mr Gifford?'

'Yes,' he replied, still lost partly in his thoughts.

'I am paying a visit to Islay this weekend. I was wondering if I could speak with you.'

37

The next morning brought rain, lots of it, driven by strong south-westerly winds. Anything further out than the small island in the bay was obliterated by the driving rain, the headland only glimpsed between squalls. The sheep huddled together next to the house, lying against the wall, for some protection and warmth.

Thankfully Jim had finished working on the car the previous evening. A short trip to test the brakes had been successful and the car was also running smoothly again, like a new car. He would still accept nothing for his labour.

This morning Jim was out the front loading his car, not seemingly bothered by the rain, the front of his car facing the wind and rain, the rear hatchback compartment protected to some degree.

In contrast the gusts of rain made loading my car, parked by the side of the house, facing the other way, difficult. Anything loose flapping about, an empty plastic bag caught by the wind billowing, before being sucked into the air, rising high, before disappearing into the distance.

By ten we were ready; the cars packed. We had booked on the lunchtime ferry from Craignure and we wanted to give ourselves time to get there. When Jim dropped in he suggested leaving a little earlier due to the conditions.

'Not the best of mornings, I heard that the Iona ferry is off, still stranded in the Bull Hole. 'He saw the expression on my face. 'Don't worry, the Oban ferry will sail the weather is not so bad up there, at the moment, and the forecast is improving. Oh, I meant to tell you,' he added, 'when Cathy went to take hot drinks to the police this morning they had gone.' I suppose that wasn't a surprise, and given the weather the police would have only been too pleased to leave the crime scene.

Both boys were dressed for the weather, wellington boots with elasticated tops and waterproofs. Jim had struck up a good rapport with them and was joking with them about the weather. Ben was playing with a toy tractor running it along the arm of the settee and Jason was drawing with a pencil on a sketch pad, a habit he had picked up from Jenny.

Jenny was looking tired, a poor night, the return of the nightmares, anxious to get away.

As I made Jim a coffee, the phone rang. Apart from Colin, Jenny's brother, this was our only call. I picked it up.

'Is that Peter Meldrum?'

'Who is asking?' I answered cautiously, not recognising the voice.

'Hi, my name is Stewart McIntosh, I'm a friend of your father, Thomas,' the voice sounded friendly, non-alarmist, but my chest still went tight something telling me that this was bad news, the slight pause before he went on stretched.

'He was taken ill this morning, at a friend's house, fortunately the doctor was staying on the island visiting a friend, so was able to help him.'

'What's wrong,' I said, and Jenny was immediately alert.

'It's his heart - bad turn, the doctor has increased the medication.'

After yesterday, I had half expected this but the timing was lousy. Jenny was now talking quietly to Jim, who was glancing back and forwards between the two of us trying to assess our reaction, especially mine, to the news I was receiving.

'He wants to see you.' Now that was not like Dad, who never made a fuss, so it had to be serious.

'How bad is he?'

'Heart rate very high and not going down.'

'Are they going to move him to the hospital?'

'Not sure, they can't anyway until the ferry is running again.'

'Will you come across when the ferry resumes?'

'Of course.' Jenny was trying to second guess the conversation while Jim knowing that something was wrong was distracting the boys who had stopped playing, both watching me warily.

'Can I speak to the GP?'

'He's away seeing someone else, a visitor has had an accident, broken arm, tripped in the Abbey cloisters.'

'Can I phone you back?'

'Not for the next few hours, because I am going out.'

'Do you have a number for the place where Dad was staying?'

'Sorry. If you can't get across phone me this evening or if I hear anything more I'll phone you back. Stay around the house.'

'Send him my love,' and he agreed hanging up. I noted the number. Outside the rain continued to batter the window, so there was little prospect of getting across in the next few hours.

'Dad's had a bad turn - his heart. He's asked to see me.'

Jenny was biting her lip, trying to work out the implications of what I had said.

I thought for a minute but really there was only one decision I could make.

'I can't leave. I have to see him.' By now Jason had stopped sketching still holding the pencil, but turning it quickly between his fingers nervously.

'I want you all to leave as planned and hopefully I can follow on tomorrow.'

'I don't want us to split up,' said Jenny.

'I understand but we are all packed and ready and it is better that you are off the island.'

Jenny was twisting her hair around her fingers, an old habit returned, unsure.

'If it helps,' said Jim, we can accompany Jenny and the boys to your house. You can use my van, when you leave, and park it at Craignure. Put the key on top of the rear wheel. I'll pick it up on my return.'

Jenny crossed her arms, uncertain, her mouth narrowed.

'This is difficult but I need to be with Dad. You know how I felt after yesterday.'

'You're right,' said Jenny suddenly making up her mind, 'you stay and with Cathy and Jim driving in the car behind I'll be fine, but promise me you will take care.'

I was so relieved. I wanted her safely off the island but I couldn't leave Dad so unwell.

'No,' shouted Jason unexpectedly, snapping his pencil and jumping up, 'I'm staying with Dad.'

We were both shocked with the emotion in his voice. 'I'm not leaving,' he shouted again.

'Jason you have to go,' I stated, not raising my voice, keeping it calm.

'I'm staying,' and he thumped the coffee table with his fist and darted past my outreached arm, as I tried to block him, and out the back door into the rain. I followed a second later to see him racing up the garden ignoring my calls to return. I grabbed my anorak and sprinted after him. By the time I reached the hut at the back he had clambered over the fence and was running away across the field.

I turned around towards Jenny and Jim who were both now standing by the door, raising my arms in despair, yelling in frustration. I was sure, however, that he would return, but not sure when. I checked my watch; they had to leave in twenty minutes. I trudged back to the house the rain blasting me, my face soaked, my clothes dripping, my mind made up. Jenny and Jim were waiting inside.

'He's still unsettled, needs me more than I imagined. I doubt that he will return until he sees the cars leaving. A little bit of a Robinson in him,' I added, mainly for Jenny's benefit.

She grimaced, acknowledging my last comment. 'In a sense I'm glad that you will have company but promise me that you will return as soon as you can. I hope Dad is okay, send him my love.'

'Of course.'

'And make sure that he has a shower and that you dry his clothes.'

'Yes, yes,' I replied, and Jim smiled adding, 'We'll take care of them, Peter. See them safely home but I doubt that you will get across to Iona today.'

I thanked him. A short time later I held the wooden gate open despite the wind to let our car out. Minutes later the two cars drove off up the hill leaving Kintra behind, and I went back into the house quickly to get out of the rain. I waited. Ten minutes later the back door opened and Jason ran in and over to me. His eyes wide, tears adding to the rivulets of rain on his face, his body trembling, a mixture of cold and anxiety. He knew that he had done something wrong, reacted inappropriately, but he was still learning to be part of our family.

'That wasn't clever, Jason,' I said, handing him a towel, but drawing him close. His tears flowed, 'sorry,' was uttered quietly through the sobs. He really wasn't a Robinson: he was my son.

38

The weather never improved, the Ross of Mull continued to be buffeted by strong winds and driving rain, with no hope of the Iona ferry leaving its shelter in the Bull Hole. I found myself pacing the lounge worrying about Dad, anxious that Jenny and Ben would get home safely. I phoned CalMac relieved that the ferry to Oban had left on time, but there was a warning that later sailings to Oban could be disrupted. At least they had got across to Oban. I asked about the Iona ferry to discover that it was cancelled for the rest of the day. I wasn't surprised.

I tried to phone the friend's house where Dad had been staying, but there was no reply, Stewart McIntosh's number ringing out. I then tried the office at the Abbey and the George McLeod Centre and no one could give me more than sympathy when they heard that he was taken ill. It turned out that it was his day off and no one had heard that he was unwell. I tried the doctor's surgery in Bunessan but the receptionist was not able to disclose any information and suggested that I tried contacting Dad again.

I watched, with frustration, the rain running down the window panes, the stream of water cascading off the overflowing gutters onto the ground in a steady stream, an incessant drumming sound, irregular and irritating, making me feel trapped. Jason was quiet watching television, curled up on the settee, tired out by his tantrum. By the late afternoon, I put on the wood burner to take the chill off the air and then the phone rang. Jenny was home safely and I gave out a big sigh letting them know that Jason had turned up shortly after they left. At least one problem was solved and soon after Jason found a board game in a cupboard and we set it up and played Monopoly for an hour.

After that I tried all the numbers on Iona, again with no change - either no one to answer or no news until one lady, Barbara, sensing my torment offered to go around to his room and check if he was there after she finished work. I gave her my number and waited.

Two hours later, Barbara phoned back. Dad was not in his room at the Centre and hadn't been seen all day. She had then phoned her friend, a nurse, who lived on Mull. She was told that the Doctor had not been on the island today. I gripped the phone tighter, breathing more deeply. So McIntosh was lying. Who was he? He had sounded local by his accent. The nurse had then phoned the doctor's surgery in Bunessan to discover that there was no record of Dad being unwell this morning. Now I was really worried - where had he gone? I then tried Stewart McIntosh's number again and it kept ringing out. After repeated calls to the number the phone was picked up and a breathless voice answered, having just got into the house. The person sounded confused when I called him Stewart. 'No one of that name lives here,' he said, puzzled. I checked the number, it was the correct number that I had been dialling.

'I never lock my door, few do around here,' he explained, and after checking back through the previous calls, he confirmed that someone had phoned my number from his house. Alarm bells rang: someone had phoned to stop me leaving. Why? And where was Dad?

I sat down on the settee to consider my options, aware that Jason was staring at me wondering what was going on.

I decided to phone the police to report a missing person and ended up talking to someone who knew little of Mull but took details and asked me to phone back if he was still missing in the morning. Hopefully, Dad would turn up but their response was anaemic. If I reported my other problems they would likely have dismissed them and more important on an island like this they did not have the resources to respond quickly.

Now I was convinced, more than ever, that we had to cope on our own and was just very relieved that Jenny and Ben had got home safely. I looked at Jason, regretting that he had chosen to stay, hoping that I could protect him from harm, determined to try. McGrory knew where I lived. Should I abandon the house? I could use Jim's van but they knew it and I would be vulnerable on the road and anyway where would I go? They could be waiting up the hill.

'Jason,' I said, as I put down the phone, 'I want to talk to you.' I didn't try to frighten him but suggested that someone had tried to keep us back on the island, stop us leaving. We had to beware that we might be visited by bad people, so we had to stay alert, be ready. Jason appeared to take it in, picking up a poker by the fire and I tempered his fervour but did mentally note where he put it down.

For the first time I mentioned McGrory's name. Jason's face showed recognition, his mouth falling open, then he screwed up his face.

'Tell me more,' I asked, curious. We had been guarded in what we told Jason, hadn't used McGrory's name in front of him.

'He visited our house a few months before Mum left. I didn't like him, neither did Mum. They argued a lot. The last time he was angry at Mum and the next day I was sent to Granda and Nana.

Then Mum came over and took me to that school in England.'

'Did you ever see Mr McGrory?'

'I peeked out from behind a door when he was arguing with Mum.'

'What was he like?'

'Small, little hair, not nice, nasty face. I didn't like him or the men who sat outside in a car waiting for him.' I did wonder what a nasty face was like but I think I got the gist.

'What were he and your Mum arguing about?'

Jason went quiet, his face reddening, his head lowered.

'Okay,' I said, 'something that you didn't like' and Jason nodded and I noticed that his eyes were filled with tears. I probed no further and just put my arm protectively around him.

'Jason,' I said, ' 'I think we should be ready. Men like them may come tonight.'

The wind had been dropping in speed, the rain easing off but a sudden further gust of wind hit the window shaking the frame, spooking me. I looked out, the tide which had gone out was starting to come in again, water lapping around what would shortly become an island again. By the time it would be fully in, it would be dark.

39

I got Jason prepared for bed but made him keep his clothes on and his wellington boots and outdoor jacket by the bed. We both had torches handy. I gave him clear instructions and made him repeat them back to me. His eyes grew bigger as he listened but I sensed that all he wanted was to be beside me, regardless of what might happen. There was already a strong bond forming between us. I locked the doors put out the light and sat by the bedroom window staring into the gloom. Sleep would be impossible. I had to stay awake, alert, ready for action, prepared for a long night.

The rain had stopped by midnight, the heavy mist starting to lift, the land in the bay an island again, a refuge for a few sheep.

I didn't feel tired, the flask of coffee by my side frequently raided, caffeine adding an edginess, making me restless. Downstairs the phone rang, jolting me. I ran downstairs, in darkness, but didn't answer; the number unknown. Were they checking to see if I was in?

I ran back upstairs to resume the vigil, glad to see that Jason was now sleeping. I peered out the bedroom window, eyes straining, watching. Suddenly the sheep turned and ran through the water towards the shore, bleating. Through the mist I glimpsed a brief flash of light. Then nothing. Then a shape pushing towards the shore, a blur in all the gloom, then the shadow sharpened - a boat.

'Jason,' I shouted, 'get up. We've got to go, now.' I ran to the bed shaking him. He was drowsy then alert. 'Boots on,' and I helped him prepare.

'Let's go,' a final glance showed the boat almost at the shore, figures ready to jump out.

We ran downstairs, I picked up the poker and we ran to the back door, unlocking it. The cold damp night air, made us both gasp, or was it nerves. I heard the scraping sound of a boat being dragged on land and saw movement just across the road. A torch beam cut through the darkness, illuminating the fence between us and our neighbour. I pushed Jason's head down and propelled him around the corner. We reached the barbeque area just in time to see someone attempting to climb the fence. Instinctively, I lashed out with the poker, hitting him hard. There was a groan and he slumped.

'Run,' I said, with passion driven by fear, but keeping my voice low. We sprinted up the back garden and reached the hut, dropping down behind it. Several torch lights criss- crossed the back garden, one showing up the man I had hit getting up feeling his shoulder, then rubbing his head. I could hear him swearing. I could also see the sodden imprint of our footsteps, something which I hadn't thought about, our escape route signposted, easy to follow.

We had little time. Using the shadow to the rear of the hut we ran together to the fence at the back and I helped Jason over, jumping after him. A torch beam illuminated the fence, a few yards away to our right. Now crouching we ran along the back of the houses, searching for the gate that led from Jim's house onto the field, grateful that Jim never locked anything. I undid the latch and pushed Jason through, following him quickly. Our breath was visible in the cold night air as we paused temporarily protected by a conifer hedge.

Jason's eyes were bulging, tears not far away, his body trembling. I pointed to the house and we ran down, trying to make no noise, reaching the back door. I was counting on something that Jim had said - that he left instructions for deliveries to be put inside the back door - it was always unlocked, something as a native of Islay, I understood. I turned the door knob and pushed, the door creaked, the noise sounding loud, but it opened. Now I saw a torch beam out at the front of Jim's house and was glad that we were inside. I pushed the door shut feeling for the lock and turned the key.

'Inside the house,' I whispered, and crouching we moved across the kitchen floor. At the last moment I saw a torch beam moving up the side of the house and pushed Jason under the kitchen table. We lurked there and saw a face peering in the window, a torch beam shining in. We hardly dared to breathe as the beam traversed the kitchen, briefly restoring colour to the surfaces and appliances, passing over the kitchen table. We forced ourselves against the rear wall, hoping that the overhanging plastic table cloth would conceal us. The beam lingered. I watched it with hypnotic fascination, like one waiting for a snake to strike. The beam dropped onto the floor and edged back towards us. I tried to pull my foot back further. Then the beam was gone, the intrusion cut short by a shout. We waited, our breathing sounding very loud, Jason gulping down air, on the edge of hysteria.

'We'll go upstairs,' I whispered, and urged Jason, who was paralysed with fright, towards the door. Then I saw a torch beam brighten the window again and I pushed Jason back under the table, leaving myself exposed, until I crammed myself in a tight space by the door, hidden by the end of a row of kitchen units, my knee protruding. I held by breath as the light, once again, played around the kitchen. Cooker, work surface, mug tree and mugs, 'I love Mull', in bold letters on the side of one. Time frozen, every detail absorbed. The beam flicked back then continuing its journey - fridge, red toaster, red kettle, empty toast rack, salt and pepper set disguised as two hens, chopping board. Closer still, my body contorting, shrinking and then the beam stopped. I drew breath, the window smashed and a shout went up: 'He's in here.' I grabbed the poker and lashed out at the figure attempting to push into the kitchen, drawing blood: rage and more oaths.

I grabbed Jason, wordlessly hauling him towards the door and shutting it. I faced the intruder, his face bloodied, twisted and dazed. Behind him another face appeared hauling back the injured man and lunging at the space left, his foot on the frame of the broken window, poised to jump in. Again the poker hit its target, unbalancing him and I rushed forward pushing him out, spotting a third man arriving and then hearing someone battering on the back door, the door shaking.

I left the kitchen, pushing a chair under the door handle and ran upstairs. Time was short - had they seen Jason? Jason was lying on the landing, huddled up, in a foetal position. I grabbed him, pulled him into a bedroom, looking around frantically for a hiding place. I yanked back a sliding door and pushed him in, telling him to stay in the corner behind a row of dresses and pulled the sliding door shut.

By now the door into the hall was being kicked, the chair being pushed back, and with a crash a body came hurtling through, falling then picking himself up, programmed by instinct to search his surroundings. The lounge door was thrown open, its hinges groaning, a torch beam scanning the interior. With a grunt the bathroom downstairs got the same treatment and then I heard him pause at the bottom of the stairs. There were more shouts and the front door was opened, a pack of salivating hunt dogs was forming. I had to distract them, not sure if they knew that Jason was still with me.

I opened the bedroom door slowly, temporarily blinded as the hall light was switched on. I roared, lifted my poker and raced down the stairs, lashing out, making impact with one body, using the poker as a makeshift sword, jabbing at another and broke through to the outside, past grasping hands. I reached the road in front of the house, pausing, my breath clear in the night air, deciding which way to go and started to race towards the headland, hoping to draw them after me.

By now someone was giving chase, I heard the heavy laboured breathing, and footsteps drawing closer, my chaser cursing as he called my name through gasping breaths. My lungs were heaving, the acid contents of my stomach in my mouth, my legs becoming heavier, adrenaline fading. I spotted a gap between two houses and changed direction aiming for it, scattering wheelie bins as I ran past, their contents spilling out. I had forgotten that there was a gate at the end and steeled myself to climb it, as hands reached out, holding me back as I tried to vault it. Unbalanced I fell back and fists and feet pounded me until I lay quiet, the oaths of my chasers echoing in the narrow gap between the houses, gradually dying out as they themselves recovered composure.

I was dragged to my feet, bloodied, a hint of satisfaction when I saw the state of some of my attackers. Surprisingly little that was coherent was said as I struggled, until one man, his face cut and bruised stepped forward: 'You bastard,' he said, as he punched me hard in the gut, all the air driven out of my lungs, my stomach retching, I doubled up. Strong hands gripped me and dragged me out onto the road, where my hands were bound tightly behind my back with a black plastic tie and I was roughly dragged towards the rowing boat drawn up on the narrow shore.

'Search the houses,' I heard someone shout and I prayed that Jason would not be found. I was dumped in the back of the boat, a man remaining with me, whilst the others started their hunt. Some time past, my hopes rising, that they wouldn't discover Jason. The cold air was making me cough and splutter, the metallic taste of blood strong in my mouth. I tried to maintain focus, but maybe as a sedative to my soul my mind drifted, full consciousness elusive.

Then I heard the news that I didn't want to hear: 'We've got the boy,' and shortly after Jason was brought out of Jim and Cathy's house, his arms bound behind him, shouting and squirming, his face tear stained and wet.

'Don't hurt him,' I found the energy to shout, the words sounding feeble, carried away by the breeze, ignored with contempt by our attackers with one muttering, 'We'll leave that to Mr McGrory.'

Jason was dumped beside me, my attackers pushing the boat out, their feet gouging the sand, the boat bobbling as they jumped in. The outboard was started as someone yanked the cord. The boat was turned around and headed out of the bay. The air was noticeably colder, the water choppy. I retched again. I could barely lift my throbbing head, my wrists hurting where the plastic tie dug in. When I did raise my head I saw Jason looking at me anxiously. I attempted a smile, which was greeted with a laugh by the man steering the boat but I was pleased to see Jason attempt a smile in return. When I looked up next I saw the *Kerry Star* not far away, its navigation lights glittering in the dark, steps being lowered down the side. Hands gripped me and Jason again, a roll of tape was produced, one of the men biting off strips from the roll, which were then roughly fixed over our mouths.

40

Our boat butted against the side of the *Kerry Star*, the swell almost tipping the boat over as one of the men grabbed the steps that had been lowered down at the side of the larger boat, quickly tying a rope to the metal safety rail on the outside of the steps. I was kicked in the back and then pushed forward onto the steps. Jason followed behind and we were led up to the deck. A deckhand, in a red shirt with an image of sailing boat emblazoned on the chest, with smart blue, bell bottom slacks, appeared maybe expecting a guest but turned away quickly not wanting to know what was happening. On the deck one of our captors pointed down the stairway I had seen from Erraid a few days previously, leading into the bowels of the boat. Glass doors slid open automatically as we approached the stairway. At the bottom of the steps was a glass partition leading to a small dining room which was deserted, no lights on, but there was a lingering smell of spicy food. I was pushed to the left and saw that on each side of the stairs were cabins, three to each side of the boat. The area gave an impression of luxury - a deep pile dark blue carpet, polished wood surfaces, ornate light fittings, framed pictures of nautical scenes hung on the walls between the cabins. We were given little time to absorb the surroundings as we were propelled past the cabins each of us firmly held by two men.

I heard laughing from one cabin, it sounded as if people were drinking, having a party, enjoying themselves. I could understand that they would not like us to be seen, not the usual guests. One cabin door was slightly ajar and I got a brief glance of a girl lying on a four poster bed, wearing a flimsy negligee, eyes open, but glazed, as if she was on drugs. We reached the last cabin on the port side, if my nautical knowledge was sound, and the door was opened and we were pushed inside. The cabin was similar to the one I had seen inside already with a four poster bed, bedside units with lamps on top, a dressing table and in the corner an ensuite toilet. Two men remained with us, the second man producing lengths of rope and we were bound to separate posts of the four poster bed, the rope tied round our waists. Jason struggled as they tied the rope, making a lot of noise, despite his mouth being taped. The man tying him to the bedpost raised his hand and Jason went quiet but continued to wriggle. And I couldn't help him. I was helpless. This was the first time I could see any of my abductors in light and there was little to distinguish between them - all seemed to wear dark sweatshirts and dark denims and showed little expression, dealing with us with grim robotic efficiency.

One of the men left immediately and the other stood studying us for a moment, his face almost expressionless, his mouth narrowing as he said without much emotion:

'You'll stay here until he arrives. He wants to deal with you himself. If it was me you would be suffering now, but he is better at it,' the mouth twisting slightly in a sneer. He did a final check on the plastic ties around our wrists and left shutting the door behind him. I heard the door being locked.

I looked across at Jason, unable to speak, only able to make a gurgling sound due to the tape across my mouth, and ended up raising my eyebrows to convey some emotion, solidarity with him. He tried to express a response, his eyes wide, moving his body from side to side. How I regretted that he was in this position, wishing that he had left with Jenny and Ben. The pain in my head made concentrating difficult, my vision blurred, the pain inflicted by the blows difficult to deal with, especially since I couldn't move, cramp settling in, threatening to overwhelm me. I closed my eyes trying to clear my mind - struggling to think of a way to escape.

Jason suddenly kicked me on my leg jolting me and I opened my eyes to see him straining twisting his body round until he was side onto the bed. He was attempting to raise his hands away from his back and bring them down hard. Slowly, he was able to raise his hands further, increasing the force with which he brought his hands down. I could see what he was trying to do, nodding in encouragement and then the plastic ties snapped and his hands were free. He ripped the duct tape off his mouth, smiling proudly at me, and worked on the knotted rope around his waist, picking at it, loosening the rope and then it slackened and he was free to help me. Immediately, he pulled the tape off my mouth and before I could say anything he bit at the plastic tie binding me, breaking it. I brought my hands around rubbing them, trying to bring them back to life, as Jason undid the knot on the rope binding me to the bed. We hugged each other both in tears of pain and elation.

'How did you know how to do that?' I asked.

'Sam taught me,' he replied, enigmatically. I looked puzzled.

'Sam was in my dorm,' he explained, 'and we often tied each other up, trying to escape, when the matrons had gone at night, otherwise it was boring. I saw that technique on a SAS video.' Jason told me how he clenched his hands together making them big, and screamed a lot, when they tied his hands as if the plastic tie was hurting him. Being a boy he reckoned that they went easy and the plastic tie was left loose giving him wriggle room.

'Remind me to thank, Sam, if we ever meet.'

'You won't, he was sent home for attempting to set fire to the school.' Even in my befuddled state I now realised why Jason was good at setting light to things - he had been well trained.

'Did they discover it,' I asked, suddenly remembering.

Jason shook his head and took off his right wellington boot, exposing a syringe taped to his leg. Pulling off the tape, he handed me the syringe, a cap on the needle. I had counted on them not searching Jason as thoroughly.

'Well done,' I said, and he smiled, as I added, 'this should help us.' It certainly was effective when used in the nursing home and I was glad that I had kept it.

'When someone comes in I'll wait behind the door and jab him. But we will need a diversion to escape.'

Jason looked around and went into the ensuite bathroom, coming back out with an aerosol spray. He rummaged through the drawer in the bedside table, producing condoms, which he held up to me and then threw away when I shook my head. This was no time for explanations. Then he produced cigars and finally a lighter, which when he picked up and flicked it, producing a small steady flame. I knew what he wanted to do.

'Sam was a good teacher,' I said.

'Sam wasn't his real name,' adding, 'we called him Sam after Fireman Sam.'

I almost laughed, then I covered my mouth. We had to remain quiet. A fire would provide a good diversion.

We put the rope loosely around Jason and he kept his hands behind his back - someone entering would think he was still tied up and I would pounce with the syringe.

From somewhere in the boat I became aware of loud music, the bass notes providing a steady beat. We waited. Someone walked past and we froze until we heard giggling - they weren't looking for us. We were both cold and hungry. My body ached but all I could provide it with was a glass of water from the basin in the ensuite.

Then we heard the sound of someone approaching, hoping that the liquid had lost none of its effectiveness and tried to remember not to use all of it on the first person. Whoever it was had stopped outside our room and I heard the door being unlocked. Jason was in position, so was I.

The door swung open and it was the man who had been the last to leave the cabin who entered, holding a tray with some food and water. He saw Jason taking a second to realise that I wasn't there. It was long enough for me to plunge the syringe into his back. The response was instant - he collapsed, at the doorway, falling into the cabin, dropping the tray, but behind him was a second man and he reacted quickly pulling out a gun as he entered. With all the force I could summon I slammed the door against him, trapping his arm and handgun in the room. Quickly using the syringe again, I stabbed his hand emptying the remaining contents into his hand.

After a second he went limp dropping the gun. Jason immediately grabbed it and I pulled the body inside. A quick glance showed that no one else was in the corridor and I shut the door quietly. We pulled the two men away from the door, leaving them dumped on the floor.

We edged out the door, checking again that the passageway was clear, Jason holding the lighter and aerosol, me the handgun. We could see a cupboard ahead built into the rear of the stairwell. I turned the handle on the cupboard door and opened it. Inside was a bin and cleaning materials. Jason saw several bundles of paper towels and I nodded. He pressed the nozzle on the aerosol and lit the spray with the lighter producing a roaring flame, a homemade flame thrower. Quickly the paper towels caught fire and we retreated shutting the door.

We edged along the corridor and froze as a door opened but the occupant was far gone, eyes glazed, empty champagne bottle in one hand.

'More champers,' he stated his voice slurred, holding up an empty bottle, rocking back and forwards.

'In a minute, sir,' I replied, trying to remain calm, pretending to be a crew member.

'Whose having the boy?' he muttered, and I lost it punching him hard and pushing inside his cabin forcibly, angry at his suggestion, shutting the door. We reached the bottom of the stairs and anxiously glanced up. No one there.

As we walked up the steps I saw a security camera, red light blinking, the lens moving, focussing on us.

'Run, Jason,' and we raced to the top of the stairs, watching in horror as the door slide shut in front of us. Trapped. I heard footsteps running along the corridor. Should I use the handgun? But what if it was an innocent passenger. Unlikely, I thought, but I couldn't just shoot people. Time stopped, probably no more than a couple of seconds, then the fire alarm sounded and the door slid open automatically. The sudden drop in temperature, inrush of cold air, revived us, spurred us on and we ran out onto the deck. 'Which way? ' I questioned, Jason, disorientated, starting to panic. Jason dragged me towards the starboard side and I saw the gate in the deck railing. A voice shouted out to stop and I turned pointing the handgun at a deckhand who dived for cover behind a lifeboat. I noticed that wisps of smoke were now swirling out from below decks.

Jason grabbed me and we swung over the gate, relieved to see the boat still moored at the bottom of the steps. We edged down the steps to the boat, holding onto the railing.

Jason was leading me down the steps and he jumped into the boat working on the rope which tied the boat to the *Kerry Star*. Above us sirens were sounding, we could hear people running about, shouting, someone emerging from below decks naked. I pulled the cord on the outboard and nothing happened. Jason leant forward and turned a switch. I tried again and the motor roared. We pulled away and as I looked up a man appeared pointing a rifle at me. I pointed the handgun unsteadily at him and pulled the trigger. There was a flash and the recoil pushed me back into the boat, the bullet hitting the side off the *Kerry Star* and ricocheting of the steps, but the man disappeared.

In a short time we were some distance from the *Kerry Star*, patches of swirling mist masking our escape. The *Kerry Star* was all lit up smoke was billowing. On the deck I could see a lot of activity, people running about, a lifeboat being prepared to be slung over the side. If McGrory wasn't angry before, he would be now.

I looked at the boy sitting opposite me, head lowered, but his eyes fixed on me, my heart swelling with pride and love. Catherine would have been so proud of her son; as his father, so was I. I held out my hand towards him and we hi-fived and then he grabbed my hand, moving over to my side, bonding complete.

41

I was lost, not sure which direction to go in, scanning the horizon for landmarks, but it was pitch black, no stars with the cloud obscuring any lights that might have helped me but also making pursuit more difficult. In the distance, however, I could see the *Kerry Star* lit up and wanted to be as far away as possible. It had been not far from the entrance to the bay at Kintra, so I didn't want to go near there. The wind was usually from the south west, it had been earlier. I turned the boat until I was facing into the wind, believing that direction would take me down the Sound of Iona. Beside me Jason was also busy searching, finally nudging me.

'The Iona ferry,' and I saw the navigation lights. Knowing that it anchored in the Bull Hole overnight and I steered the boat towards the lights. As we drew nearer I could see the dark outline of the ferry. Jason gripped my arm again, alerting me to the sound of an outboard motor, picking up speed, approaching from the south, but, as yet, I couldn't see any boat.

I cut back our speed, waiting at the stern of the ferry, positioned to go either side. Was the boat friend or foe? I shivered, the night air chilling me, my clothes clinging to my body still soaked in sweat. Suddenly, a searchlight cut across the surface, picking out the side of the ferry, searching, and then revealing us, its brightness quickly playing across the boat and us, blinding us. A voice shouted out: 'Your safe, Meldrum, wait until we reach you.' Jason gripped my hand firmly as the boat approached, pulling alongside. As my eyes adjusted I could identify a rigid inflatable with several dark shapes aboard. I was relieved to see that there were no weapons pointing in our direction. Soon someone was holding the two boats together and another person clambered on board.

The spotlight shone briefly on his face revealing a man, possibly younger than me, clean shaven, hair tousled by the wind, but smiling: 'You both okay? I'm Alex.' We nodded, neither of us capable of saying anything, as he studied our faces, taking in the cuts and bruises on mine.

'We'll soon have you back at the ferry slipway and get you a hot drink and patched up,' and then he turned to me, a slight smirk on his face, 'but first Nick probably has a few questions.' He moved over taking the helm, as we moved to the side, and throttled back the engine. We passed the silent ferry and a few minutes later, reached the ferry slipway at Fionnphort.

Our boat nudged up the slipway and stopped, Alex cutting the engine before jumping out and pulling the boat further up the concrete slipway and we got out. The RIB grounded beside us and its occupants also got out. Nick was standing a few feet away, beside the waiting room for the ferry, a radio in his hand, which was by his side. I could hear the crackle of the static and then a message confirming that no distress call had gone out from the *Kerry Star*.

'Was McGrory on board?' Nick demanded, desperate to find out.

'We didn't see him. I think that he still had to arrive. Good to see you too,' I added with a touch of sarcasm.

'Damn,' and he put the radio to his cheek, 'suspend 'Bac Mor',

I repeat, suspend 'Bac Mor'." He waited for a response, confirming his instruction before turning back to us. So 'Bac Mor' was the name of the operation to capture McGrory and it was organised by Nick.

Alex nudged us closer to Nick who was standing in a pool of light from an LED streetlamp. Nick's face was drawn and white, with more than a trace of stubble, the eyes tired as he observed us, his shoulders hunched against the wind but also indicating a weariness, which I had last seen in a police cell in Ayr.

'You did well to get off the *Kerry Star*,' which was unexpected praise from him. 'We'll debrief you later today,' which made me glance at my watch - we were in the early hours. The realisation made me feel tired, the adrenaline of the last few hours leaving little reserve.

'Jason needs rest. We are both very cold.'

'Alex will look after your needs and guard you.'

'So you missed him, again.'

Nick didn't like failure, I knew, but the flicker of annoyance that briefly crossed his face disappeared to be replaced by a cold determination.

'He's up to something but you don't get to his position without a sixth sense of danger. We raided his house tonight but he had gone, along with everyone else. We'll get him,' he added, but I sensed that was more bluster than confidence.

'Tipped off by someone?'

Nick paused, rubbing the stubby antenna of his radio slowly up the side of his face as if he was pondering my comment.

'Do you trust Steve?' I said, before he could reply, almost surprising myself, not sure where the thought had sprung from. 'I thought that I saw him on the *Kerry Star* the other day.'

He looked surprised but quickly replied, 'with my life.' That killed that strand of conversation.

Then I remembered my dad. 'My dad is missing...' but Nick cut me short again.

'He's safe. We stopped him walking into a trap the other evening and we are keeping him away from McGrory. He has his medication,' he added, anticipating my next question, 'but like you Meldrum, he is naive.'

'Someone said that he had taken ill,' and I searched my brain, which was increasingly befuddled by exhaustion, 'Stewart McIntosh was the name of the guy.'

'You probably heard the voice of McGrory, he's a great mimic. They wanted you to remain behind, isolate you. McGrory likes to play a part in the chase. You know why. We'll bring your dad across tomorrow, let you see him,' he added.

I felt relief then a surge of anger. 'Why didn't you tell me before?'

'The important thing is that your dad was safe. If we had told you they might have found out about our operation and that would have screwed things up. You should be appreciative that we stopped his abduction. I saved your father from sharing the fate planned for the both of you.'

Alex, sensing the tension and recognising that Nick, at the moment, was only interested in the whereabouts of McGrory, pointed the way to a car parked on the slipway, indicating that it was time to go. Nick must have signalled to him that the conversation was over but I didn't pick up on it. I was so tired and suddenly aware that Jason was shivering, clinging to me for support. As Nick turned away attention focussed back on his radio, another thought was dragged out of me.

'The app no longer works,' and Nick turned back to me, a scowl on his face and then I realised that he had used us as bait, a snare to catch McGrory, leaving me alone with Jason to face McGrory's thugs.

'You let us come here, knowing that McGrory was luring us here, hoping to catch him.' I wanted to hit him, my hands clenching, forming fists but Alex read my intentions, even before I could move and grabbed me. 'Enough action for one night, Peter,' he said firmly, as he steered me away towards the car.

'You chose to come. It was your decision and if the app doesn't always work blame budget cuts,' were Nick's final words, sharply delivered, as I was bundled into the car.

'But I didn't know all the facts. You did,' I shouted, wanting to continue but the car door was shut and Alex started the engine turning the car around and off the slipway. Nick was already on his radio, my presence forgotten.

42

When we got back to the house in Kintra Alex asked us to wait in the car while he checked out the house and then he called us in. He had a hot shower already running for us, the steam filling the bathroom. We stripped off immersing ourselves in the hot water - my wounds stinging, bruises nipping. By the time we had towelled and dried Alex had hot drinks ready.

'Nick has a lot on his mind, he put a lot of effort and resources in trying to stop McGrory,' he said, as we sat in the kitchen, sipping hot chocolate, maybe hinting at Nick's curt demeanour and its impact on people. 'For him McGrory is also personal, we have lost good people due to McGrory's activities,' though he wouldn't elaborate, I was sure that he was referring to Tommy. 'I'll stay here, you better both get some sleep, you must be very tired,' and so I found myself back in the bedroom looking over the bay, in very different circumstances to those of a few hours ago, the tide now receding, dawn streaking the sky. I checked that the *Kerry Star* had gone before I drew the blinds and lay down. Jason was already asleep on the bed, pale and exhausted. I felt that surge of paternal love; how well he had done and how I had developed a relationship so quickly with him. My mind was still racing over everything that had happened until sleep overwhelmed me.

Somewhere in my dreams I heard a phone ringing, but it quickly stopped.

It was after eleven before I awoke, Jason still sleeping, so I quietly got up and went downstairs. Alex had been joined by a colleague, a woman, probably in her thirties, auburn hair cut in a page boy style, with deep set eyes and a face covered in freckles. They smiled as I entered the room and welcomed me, the woman calling herself, Jackie. Both were sipping coffee and immediately put the kettle on and made me a cup. Jackie picked up her radio and updated someone that I was now awake.

'Your wife was on the phone, she's coming back when we told her something of what had taken place. Malcolm is bringing her,' and I explained who he was. Ben was now staying with Jenny's brother in Ayr.

...

Nick arrived late afternoon, his face grey with exhaustion - had he slept at all? He spoke with my two minders and then came into to see me. I know that he had a difficult job but I just didn't take to him. Jackie joined him and they quizzed me about what had happened. They were particularly interested in the *Kerry Star* and what I had seen whilst on board.

'Sounds like a floating brothel,' was Jackie's comment and Nick did not disagree. 'He's entertaining friends, sailing back and forward, almost wanting to attract attention to himself. That's not like McGrory. He's up to something,' and Nick looked exasperated, frustrated unable to work out what it was.

We were interrupted by a car arriving, coming down the hill into the bay, and Jenny and Malcolm got out. Nick shrugged and left. I don't think that I had been of much use to him. Jenny came in hugging me her hands tenderly feeling the bruises on my face, studying my face, assessing how I was. It was so good to see her. Jason, interrupted us, keen to explain how he had helped me escape and Jenny gave him a lot of attention, grateful for his actions. Who would have guessed that boarding school could provide such practical life lessons.

I couldn't give an answer when the inevitable question about McGrory came up -had we escaped his clutches for ever? McGrory was persistent and I kept upsetting him, so I felt it best not to answer directly. Anyway she knew the answer - we both did. I found Malcolm in the kitchen talking to Jackie gently probing, ever the journalist searching for the next story. He smiled as I entered, looking curiously satisfied with himself.

'I have some news for you but I'll catch you later.' I assumed that it was about Alison's pregnancy and muttered something about, 'looking forward to that.'

Next to arrive was Dad brought along by another of Nick's team. He looked tired but perky, our conversation mostly about his health, seemingly unaware of what had been going on with me. I decided not to alarm him. We were making a meal and asked him to stay but he refused wanting to catch the last ferry back to Iona. He left quite soon after, driven back to the ferry not wanting to make a fuss, Jackie reassuring me that someone was keeping an eye on him.

We were eating, I had managed to rustle up some cheese and macaroni, when the phone rang. Alex got up and answered and immediately looked across at me.

'More friends arriving, you're very popular. Ronnie and Maria are on their way in their boat from Jura. They will be here later this evening. I can put them off if you are too tired.'

I shook my head. 'Pleased to see them,' although I was surprised that they had chosen this moment to visit us, not sure what they knew of recent events.

. . .

292

As dusk set, I spotted the *Casablanca* as it moored some distance out in the bay, bobbing about in the choppy sea, gleaming white, the awning extended from the cabin to the stern. We all walked out to the shoreline and watched his dingy approaching, Maria perched at the front, waving to us. As the dingy grounded Ronnie cut the engine and they both clambered out.

Ronnie seemed surprised to see Malcolm, but pleased. Maria seemed almost nervous, not giving her usual warm greeting, hesitant, rubbing her hands down over her hips as she stood. Maybe she was chilled by the cold breeze.

'It was a good excuse for a trip', Ronnie explained, 'try out the engine after its service and catch up, it's a bonus that you are here, Malcolm. How's Alison?' It all came out a little too fast, and I saw that Jenny had picked up on their unease.

'Come on in, you don't need an excuse and I am sure that Peter has some whisky,' and she put her arm around Maria saying, after a second, 'it must be cold out at sea.'

'We're staying on the *Casablanca*, trying out its facilities,' said Maria, 'we didn't want to impose on you.' Maybe they had changed or improved them. I didn't really care.

They had a further surprise when they met Alex and Jackie in the kitchen but were quickly shown through to the lounge where the wood burner was on. Maria found a seat on the settee beside Malcolm, Ronnie grabbed a cushion and sat on the floor beside me.

'What's been going on, why the spooks?'

'Just watching over us. I had another run in with McGrory last night.

'You okay?'

I pointed to the bruise under my left eye. 'Mostly.'

'Where are they now?'

'That's a good question, he seems to have disappeared.'

'Good, all clear, at the moment. All you need now is a holiday.'

'A job would be my first priority.'

'I can help there,' said Malcolm. Jenny and I both switched our attention, eager for any update.

'I managed to trace the IT technician, Kirsty, is her name. She admits that she loaded your computer with the images.'

Jenny blew a sigh of relief.

'And?' the word sounding impatient, tense, lacking grace for what he had achieved.

'I have recorded her confession and taken it to Pence. He was very happy - seems you can have your old job back,' and he looked expectantly at me.

'If I want it. My trust has been shattered, they offered no support. They assumed that I was guilty.'

'I understand, but the images were damming.'

'They believed that I was capable, that's the point,' I replied, trying to hide my bitterness.

'Take your time, Peter, don't rush anything.'

'I won't. Jenny and I will talk it over. But thanks, you did a great job. I owe you a big favour.'

'That's what friends are for.'

The evening was subdued, not the usual relaxed affair, with whisky lubricating the proceedings. Maybe we were all tired, I don't know, but soon Ronnie and Maria excused themselves. I watched them walking back to the dingy, Ronnie leading the way. Jenny slipped her arm around me. 'I wonder what is wrong between them,' she said, quietly in my ear. 'There's tension between them, they're unhappy. As the dingy headed back to the *Casablanca*, Ronnie turned and waved but Maria stared straight ahead. It summed up their evening.

As I went in I apologised to Malcolm for not showing greater appreciation for all his efforts and learnt more about what he had done. Maybe it was the warmth in the room but after a few minutes I fell asleep on the settee.

43

Jenny was remorseful the next morning, after discovering the ordeal that Jason and I had been through, feeling that she had abandoned me by going home. I reassured her that it wasn't her fault, no one could have foreseen that we would be kidnapped. With our guardians still at the house talking with Malcolm over breakfast and Jason still asleep, we wanted some personal space and decided to go for a walk up to the headland near the ruined cottage. It was the first time I had been back since discovering the body. Apart from a few bits of police tape fluttering in the wind and signs that the grass had been trampled, little remained to indicate what had taken place. The work to fill in the well had not been started, the corrugated metal cover still pinned down by red granite boulders. The sheep, spread out over the grassy slopes, some with lambs munching the grass.

The cottage was once again abandoned or so I thought but as we approached it I heard a noise, what sounded like a voice speaking softly, and slightly spooked, I told Jenny to wait while I investigated. I crept up to the cottage and peered inside.

Beside the hearth I saw a bald headed man crouching, wearing shorts and a scruffy tee shirt, his hands held high, speaking - praying. He was unaware of my presence until he stood up - it was Gil. He didn't seem too pleased to see me; interrupting his private devotions. As he stood up I saw that he had left flowers and a simple cross, made from drift wood held in shape by blue twine, on the hearth.

Wordlessly, he acknowledged my presence and I called on Jenny, 'It's okay, its Gil, and she stepped into the ruin.

'A bit far from your usual haunts,' I said, not trying to sound unfriendly, just curious. 'How did you get here?'

'Ronnie and Maria brought me, of course,' he replied, as if I should have known. Indeed, it was surprising that they hadn't mentioned that Gil was with them.

'I came to pay my respects. I served in Afghanistan with Harry for many years. He would say that he saved my life and I would argue that I had saved his,' a rueful smile played on his lips and I wondered what mental images were going through his mind. 'I think that we were both correct. We were very close, saw a lot of action together.'

'Do you mean, Tommy?'

'Oh yes, but that was just his last cover name.'

'Did he work for Nick?' I enquired.

'I recommended him, feel sort of responsible for what happened. We kept in touch, sent each other postcards, hi tech eh?' and as he stared blankly at me I saw the sadness, the emptiness in his eyes. 'The postcards stopped coming. I knew something was wrong. Tried to find him, a few weeks ago.'

'How do you know Nick?' I asked.

'Very well,' as if he had misheard my question. 'he is my brother after all or more correctly my step-brother. Our father married a few times, quite common in the upper classes, his name was Lord Drescoet.'

I was taken aback; fancy Nick and Gil the sons of a Lord.

He lowered his head again, his eyes closed, lost to us, for a moment, then he opened his eyes again: 'Do you believe in grace?'

he seemed to be pleading but it took me a minute to realise what he was asking.

'The forgiveness of sins by the sacrifice of Christ on the Cross,' he elaborated when he saw the mystified look on my face.

'I've heard the Rev Walker explaining grace,' Jenny said. 'if you seek forgiveness from Christ, you will receive it - whatever you've done.'

For a second Gil's eyes lit up, hoping, before the brightness dimmed.

'The minister has been a help to me but I have a lot to seek forgiveness for. I did a lot of things in Afghanistan that were cruel, but necessary to survive. I also exposed a lot of people to danger and let them down.'

'I'm sure that you were just obeying orders,' but Gil didn't look reassured by my comment.

'Is that why you moved to Jura, to find space, peace to allow you to recover,' it was Jenny now, gently probing.

'It takes time,' not a direct answer, but an acceptance that the journey he was on was not an easy one. 'My father knows the local laird - old school mates.'

'We wish you well,' said Jenny.

'Pray for me, he replied, with an expression of despair on his face, the death of Tommy had affected him deeply, bringing to the surface buried memories, his eyes empty, but pleading for support. 'I'll look out for you,' he added, which didn't make too much sense.

Always tactile Jenny put her arms around him, but his body didn't respond, the guilt that consumed him refusing to yield, his body stiff. With a final look around at the ruined cottage and the covered well, his mind tormented by the thoughts of what had occurred here, Gil then turned away walking back to the shore.

'A troubled man,' I said, when he was some distance away,

descending into a sandy cove towards a dingy drawn up on the shore.

'What did he mean by 'I'll look out for you.'

'I don't know, but he meant it in a supportive way, I am sure. So he is Nick's step-brother and they are titled, the sons of a Lord. You wouldn't think it of either of them.'

My thoughts went back to the day that I saw Nick arriving when the body had been found. He had looked troubled, having lost someone. The chain of command ensured that he carried the burden, was ultimately responsible. How could he explain what had happened to Tommy's family. Nick would have to examine himself and the decisions that led to Tommy's death. Could it have been avoided? We continued our walk in silence.

Ronnie and Maria arrived back on shore, in their dingy, just before midday, Ronnie walking up the shore ahead of Maria, who strangely hung back; picking at what looked like a broken fingernail but appearing hesitant to join us, something on her mind. They joined us for lunch, Jackie having gone to get some bread and tins of soup from the shop in Fionnphort earlier in the day.

Alex was on the phone when we came into the kitchen, taking orders it seemed in a one-sided conversation.

I could see Malcolm's bag sitting in the kitchen, packed, and knew he had to return. I wasn't sure what we would do. If we wanted a lift then we had to return with Malcolm.

Alex eventually hung up the phone as the tomato soup was being served. 'Nick is pulling us out,' and he addressed the comment to Jackie, who seemed to expect it.

'The *Kerry Star* has sailed south, nearing Northern Ireland now, McGrory has gone to ground, so the operation over here is complete. Jackie and I are needed elsewhere.'

'And I need to return,' Malcolm added, 'an important

interview to carry out tomorrow.'

'So do we,' said Jenny, catching my eye and I knew she was anxious to get away, too many bad memories, be reunited with Ben.

'Why not sail back with us,' said Ronnie, and Maria became more animated agreeing.

'A good idea. Nice cruise, weather conditions set fair. Relax a bit and you can stay with us tonight and we will drive you to Glasgow tomorrow. We have the Islay ferry booked, we were going to Glasgow anyway, so you are not putting us out.'

'That's nice...' Jenny began, but Ronnie was insistent.

'We could do a spot of fishing on the way. It was on our mind to propose it but when we found out what had happened we were reluctant to suggest it. We haven't had a chat since Ireland,' reminding me of what he had done for me, deliberately or not. 'Jason will enjoy it, won't you,' he said, turning to Jason who nodded vigorously. 'Well that's settled. If we leave within the hour we'll make it back to Jura tonight and still have time for a spot of fishing on the way. Maybe you'll catch a shark, Jason.'

Jenny still looked unsure.

'I can take your baggage back,' suggested Malcolm. 'Wish I could join you.'

'Sounds better than what Nick will have lined up for us,' added Jackie.

'Ronnie, give me details of your route,' asked Alex, 'I am sure Nick would expect us to ask that.'

Neither of us particularly wanted to travel back by the *Casablanca*, but we were unable to find a good enough reason to decline the offer.

'Okay,' I said, not wanting to glance at Jenny, feeling trapped into accepting the invitation, 'we better get ready.'

'That's super,' replied Maria, brighter than she had been on her arrival but Ronnie looked down at his soup and pushed it to one side. Something was bothering him.

Part Three

Retribution

44

I took a last look at the hamlet of Kintra as the *Casablanca*
engine started up, the boat pulling away from the mouth of the
bay, towing a small rubber dingy behind it. As the boat swung
around I also saw the Dutchman's Cap or Bac Mor out to sea, now
forever associated in my mind with a surveillance operation. We
sailed down the Sound of Iona, passing the Bull Hole and then the
Abbey to our right and the cluster of houses around the slipway
on Iona. The terrain was now familiar each landmark etched with
memories, probably very different from those of other visitors.
The ferry was just leaving the slipway at Fionnphort, the sea
churned up as it manoeuvred.

Ronnie was in the cabin alongside Gil, who remained almost
mute, having barely acknowledged us as we clambered on board.
Jason was watching what they were doing, perched behind them,
but there was little small talk, no bantering with him, his questions
answered briefly. We sat in the back with the awning having been
folded away, Maria was leaning back, eyes closed, occasionally I
could see her mouth moving wordlessly, lost in dreams, lost in
thought. Jenny kept looking across at me, but didn't seem to want
to break the silence, her eyes darting back and forth, restless,
taking in everything but focussing on little. It didn't take much
to realise that she was impatient, the journey, a detour that she

didn't want but felt obliged to accept.

I knew of the sand bar in the Sound of Iona that the ferry had to avoid and assumed that navigation was complicated in this area, hence Ronnie and Gil's concentration. Most of all I didn't want to think, just let my face bask in the sun as I lay back, wanting nothing more than to rest, to purge my mind of the last few days, rebuild a mental stasis that allowed me to recover. Every time that I opened my eyes, however, the passing scenery evoked more memories. Erraid, its small white observatory perched on the hillside and as we swung around the island the sparkling white sands of Balfour's Bay. At least Stevenson's main character was fictional, he hadn't really suffered and he escaped in the end.

We passed through the gap between Mull and the Torran Rocks, cruising along the south of the Ross of Mull. Jenny seemed more relaxed or was it resigned and she shifted over beside me snuggling in. I put a protective arm around her, enjoying the warmth of her body, the familiar contours that always pleased me. I saw Maria briefly open her eyes, take in the movement and then close them again. As the *Casablanca* edged away from Mull's shoreline and edged out to sea, towards the island of Colonsay, with Jura and Islay in the distance, beyond, I fell asleep.

Two things woke me, one was I realised a change in the tone of the engine, it was slowing down and secondly Jenny moved, sitting up. I blinked, aware that my face was burning after its exposure to sun and salt air, and sat up. Colonsay was a lot closer. It was an island that I had only visited once and then just for a day. I picked up some binoculars which were lying on the seat nearby and used them to scan the coastline, wondering if I could recognise any landmarks. Eventually I spotted the golden sands of Kiloran Bay, evoking memories of a picnic there with Mum and Dad, many years ago, paddling in the sea and exploring some caves.

'Saving fuel, Ronnie?' Jenny enquired, as the *Casablanca* slowed down.

'We are ahead of schedule and not in a hurry and we have used more than I expected. I want to maintain a reserve.' Jenny didn't comment. Jason came back to join us and I could see that he was becoming bored. I handed the binoculars to him and told him to look for dolphins.

Maria was also now awake and suggested that she put on the kettle for coffee and that certainly perked me up. Maybe, after all, the journey was doing us good, providing respite, some rest. The water was soon boiling and we were handed cups of coffee. Somehow coffee always tasted different, better, out at sea.

'Dad, there's another boat,' and Jason pointed towards Colonsay, which we had now almost passed. I could just see a cabin cruiser, not unlike our own, leaving the shelter of the island, white froth to the rear, rising and falling as it crashed through the waves. It was in a hurry, unlike us, wherever it was going.

'It's not saving fuel,' muttered Jenny, and I smiled. Maria was now standing up looking in its direction, a hand over her mouth.

'Give me the binoculars, Jason,' and I took them focussing on the approaching boat. It wasn't close enough for me to make out too many details but appeared to be heading towards us. For a second I felt unsettled, then I dismissed my fears. Why would it be heading for us? More probably its occupants were going fishing.

In the cabin Ronnie and Gil were deep in conversation, talking quietly, heads together. If anything they were steering towards the other boat.

'Do you know them, Ronnie?' I asked, repeating my question, when I got no answer. I focussed on the boat again, aware that we were slowing to a stop, now aware that this was no coincidence.

'Ronnie,' I said, getting up, 'what's going on?'

'I'll explain in a minute.'

'Why not now?' and he turned briefly towards me, his face ashen.

Maria spoke, 'Everything is under control,' and Jenny immediately latched onto her comment.

'What is under control?'

I saw Gil take over the control of the boat and Ronnie came back to join us, crouching down in front of us, looking at the deck, avoiding eye contact.

'Everything will be fine, I promise. I couldn't tell you before,' and I felt my stomach churn and Jenny grasp my hand tightly, gasping.

'Remember that our house was burgled,' and I nodded, wanting to speed up what he was about to reveal, noting that the other boat was closing fast.

'It was McGrory's men. As well as wrecking the house they stole the laptop and examined it. Discovered that Maria had been searching for her missing sister, Hanna.'

'They had her, Peter,' Maria declared, her voice sounding excited, as if we would understand.

'Threatened to kill her and us if we didn't hand you over.'

'So you are going to have us killed,' shouted Jenny, her anger like mine erupting, 'because that is what they will do to Peter, probably me and Jason as well, if they get a hold of us. Slowly, painfully. I don't believe you. I sensed that there was something strange going on when you two turned up. Should have trusted my instincts. Some friends you are.'

'It's my sister, you must understand and anyway we had no choice.'

'Sacrifice us. Can you live with that Ronnie?' and I stood up, hands balling into fists.

Gil had now reduced the boat to an idle and joined us.

'I said that I would look out for you and I will. Follow my

instructions and we will all be safe.'

'I hope so,' said Jenny, but she sounded no calmer, her voice cracking, shaking her head in disbelief.

By now the other boat was only twenty yards away and I could see two men, one very tall with a muscular physique watching us, the other squatter, both wearing short sleeved tee shirts and shorts. More importantly, I spotted, they appeared to have handguns. Between them stood a waif like creature, thin and barely managing to stand, shivering in a white dress, which clung to her body, outlining her skeletal contours.

Maria screamed, 'It's Hanna,' and she became hysterical, her body trembling, her hands clutching her face. Ronnie told her sharply to sit down and get a grip.

Gil was absorbing the scene hanging by the entrance to the cabin a hand on the frame of the cabin.

The yards between us closed until the boats were nearly touching. The tall man, who I could see was unshaven, his nose had obviously been broken, bent to the right, grabbed Hanna and raised his handgun to her head. She seemed unaware, drugged. I now realised that there was a third man who was steering the boat.

'Right, Ronnie,' said the shorter of the two men, who had long blond hair and his familiarity of his comment gave another twist to my gut.

'Everyone throw their mobiles phones in the sea. Hurry,' he demanded, and reluctantly we obeyed. He then jumped onto the *Casablanca* and fired a shot into the cabin hitting the radio.

'We have Hanna, we want Meldrum and his son,' demanded the man holding Hanna. Fair swap.' Jenny swore repeatedly, a stream of oaths, but both the men just laughed at her, increasing her frustration.

'You must be Jenny. You are not on our list but it can be

extended and you're Gil,' and he spat in Gil's direction, the spittle landing on the cabin window, running down the window slowly, whilst forcing the gun harder into Hanna's face until even in her drugged state she reacted, moaning. It was a clear warning.

'Come on Meldrum, hop on, we don't have much time and the blond haired man remained on the *Casablanca* grasping a safety rail on the cabin for support, his handgun moving back and forwards as he surveyed the scene, keeping watch.

I looked in disgust at Ronnie and then in despair at Jenny, bringing her close, hugging her, muttering in her ear that I loved her. Jason joined us, starting to hyperventilate, gasping for breath.

'Look at them,' said the man who had remained on their boat and he laughed, distracting the other man, who turned away for a second, and Gil erupted into action, sensing that their attention had wavered shouting out loudly, 'This is for Harry,' repeatedly, which had the effect of disorientating everyone.

His hand darted into the cabin and immediately produced a handgun firing it at the man who held Hanna, his knee exploded, blood splashing out, splattering Hanna's dress with red spots. The man screamed releasing his grip on Hanna, clutching at his knee. But Gil wasn't finished, he turned to the man closer to him and fired point blank. He clutched his stomach and bent double. Another shot hit his chest and he toppled over into the water. It was over in seconds.

As the other boat revved up for a quick escape, Ronnie jumped forward snatching Hanna, as she swayed, tottering, about to fall into the sea pulling her into our boat. Gil fired some shots at the other boat, shattering the windscreen as it pulled away. The tall man on board was roaring in pain, but he still managed to produce what appeared to be a sub machine gun and fired, raking the back of the *Casablanca* as we dived for cover, but causing no obvious damage. Ronnie jumped grabbing the wheel and revved up the *Casablanca's* engine. In seconds the other boat was turning away, Gil fired another shot through the side of the other boat and we heard a scream.

There was silence, the sea quickly dispersing the blood stains, the blond haired man floating face down, his body limp, his blond hair fanned out, wafted up and down by the rippling waves. Jenny was screaming, out of control. Jason was mute, looking like he was going to be sick. Maria was holding Hanna tightly whispering in her ear that she was safe. Frankly, Hanna appeared totally spaced out, beyond redemption, an empty shell. A lined face aged before her time, hair dyed blonde, with black roots showing and cut as if with a pair of shears. Her arms told the full picture, pockmarked where she had injected or been injected. The beautiful sister that Maria had described no longer existed.

Ronnie ceded control of the Casablanca to Gil and came towards me hand held out, a gesture of reconciliation. I pushed it away angrily.

'How dare you,' I screamed, 'putting my family at risk.'

His nostrils flared as he breathed heavily, 'Well maybe I am sick of getting you out of trouble. You owed me one and we are okay, we survived. I knew Gil could pull it off.'

We stood facing up to each other until I turned and was sick over the side of the boat, the latest episode catching up with me. Then I flopped on the bench seat, shaking, my mind all over the place. Ronnie touched my shoulder, 'Sorry,' was all he said and I saw him turn away shoulders slumped.

Gil sat on the bench opposite, drained by his efforts, gripping the wrist of the hand that had fired the handgun with his other hand, but it didn't conceal the fact that his hands were shaking. He saw me looking at him.

'The family motto is to attack first. It helps in war - suddenly being aggressive can turn the battle your way. But you can see that the strategy has had its impact on me. Now what do we do, Peter? We have just declared war on one of the biggest drug dealers. They will be after us in no time. Your family are not coping, you have lost trust in your friends, there is an unpredictable druggie on board and I don't know how much longer I can be relied on.'

'Gil, I know that we can rely on you. Thank you for what you did just there.' I wanted to reassure him, knew that we might need him.

He stood up, looking at me carefully, as if he was running a check on my words for sincerity, and without saying anything he went into the cabin where Ronnie joined him. They huddled together in animated conversation until I shouted: 'You know that they are other people on board. Shouldn't we know - no more secrets.'

Gil took the lead: 'Discussing options.'

'We would all like to hear them.'

Jenny stirred raising her head, the after effects of the latest nightmare etched on her tear stained face, Jason huddling under her arm.

'They were expecting us to go to Islay,' started Ronnie.

'I won't ask you how they would know that,' and he tried to ignore the comment but it made him pause and then talk faster, as if trying to cover up his hesitancy.

'We head to Jura travel along the west coast, to avoid the worse of the tidal race from the Gulf of Corryvreckan. We can manage the Gulf in our boat, despite the conditions being bad at this time. Then we cut across to Crinan, on the mainland, I don't think that they would expect that, and contact Nick, the police and get help.'

I said nothing but Gil spoke.

'I understand what has just occurred has changed relationships, maybe forever, but if we are to survive we must put aside our differences and work together. To be clear Ronnie is in charge of his boat, we do what he says. They will come after us but the plan gives us a chance.

I moved between Jenny and Jason, not having a clue what to do next, putting my arms around both of them. Maria was still talking to Hanna, in her native language. She wasn't getting much of a response. Others had risked a lot for very little return and they hadn't even asked me if I had wanted to be involved.

45

There was silence on board as we cruised towards the coast of Jura. Everyone lost in their own thoughts, recent tensions discouraging conversations apart from Hanna, who was groaning and shouting out as the drugs began to work out of her system. Maria was trying to help, holding her close and using a towel to wipe her face as she was sweating and trembling. I had little sympathy, which was bad of me, I think, and Jenny appeared irritated as the shouting stopped her from concentrating on her own thoughts, of which, I was sure there would be many. Ronnie was grim faced looking ahead, while Gil sat to the stern scanning the horizon towards Colonsay with binoculars, which was unsettling. He expected trouble and he was the expert.

We reached Jura, at a point just north of Loch Tarbert, the loch which almost splits the island in two. To the south the Paps of Jura were dominating with their quartz strewn surfaces sparkling in the afternoon sun, some powder puff clouds hanging around their peaks, but we quickly turned away from them heading north along the west coast towards the Gulf of Corryvreckan. Even from a few miles away I could hear the roar created by the maelstrom and could only imagine the turbulence as the waters surged, at pace, through the Gulf from the east, creating vortexes of fast flowing waters. I had been through the Gulf in similar circumstances with Ronnie, so I wasn't too worried. His plan seemed sound to me. Indeed, it was probably about the only thing that he and I could agree on at the moment. My disappointment with him and Maria mounting by the minute, as my initial shock at the recent turn of events diminished and my emotional reaction kicked in.

The west coast of Jura is one of the last great wilderness spaces in Europe, empty, uninhabited, hardly touched by man, few tracks. Herds of deer and feral goats roam free, creating by their grazing the only paths. Being surefooted they know how to pick out a route to new pastures through boggy ground and bracken covered hillsides, which is a help to walkers. Outcrops of layered rocks, broken and fragmented by exposure to the strong south westerly gales dominate the coastline. There are several caves along the coast some of which I had explored with Ronnie, from his boat, their floor mostly covered in deep layers of goat dung and the occasional decaying dead goat. However, I had never gone far inland. Apart from those who enjoyed trampling through such terrain, seeking solitude surrounded only by nature, the only other intruders were shooting parties keen to cull deer, organised by the large estates, which own most of the land on the island.

We maintained a distance several hundred yards offshore, the sound of the engine echoing off the rocky cliffs. Soon I could feel the waves of exhaustion and my eyes were drooping. Soldiers in wartime talked of exhaustion after spells of action, the adrenaline surging highs replaced by a numbness as exhaustion and memories set in. In my mind I could vividly see Gil firing his gun, blood splashing, a bony knee exposed, a body tumbling into the sea, his face frozen in surprise, and a frail half-crazed woman being grabbed and pulled on board.

I don't know how long I had dozed when suddenly I was awake and alert, aware of a change but not sure initially what it was. I had been here before, an hour ago. Then I realised that the engine was slowing. I saw Gil peering over the stern of the boat and turning back to Ronnie. From the expression on Ronnie's face, I knew that he was expecting bad news and I sat up, carefully moving Jenny's head from my side and letting it rest gently on the bench beside me.

Gill shook his head and I could see Ronnie grimace, his mouth twisting, biting his lower lip. Whatever it was he blanked me, didn't want me involved, knew what my reaction would be.

'It must have been the bullets from the sub machine gun,' Gil explained, and said almost as an aside to me, 'we have been losing fuel.'

Ronnie covered his face with his hands, absorbing the information, wanting to be somewhere else, cutting the engine, as he pondered what to do next.

'I can't risk the Gulf,' he stated, one of his hands now rubbing his chin.

You needed power to get through the Gulf in the present conditions. It wasn't as if our boat would be spun round and eventually sucked down the vortex of the whirlpool but without power we could be capsized by the standing waves, the turbulence, the vicious currents.

'We can land on Jura and get help. I know the area well,' and it was Gil now adapting to the changed circumstances, suggesting a solution. 'Near the top of that valley, about a mile back, I built a shelter for one of my survival expeditions. Very basic but we could use that, stay there, until we work out what to do,' and he cast an eye around the motley crew, few of whom were up to a long trek.

'Jura has only the one road so at some point they would be

waiting for us, so we avoid it. If we hide for a bit then we can find an alternative route for someone to seek help.'

Ronnie didn't disagree with Gil and despite not knowing if I was part of the discussion I added, 'sounds like the best option.' Jenny by now was stirring, 'What's going on, Peter?' she demanded, her voice dry and sounding shrill. My explanation did not improve her mood and she pulled Jason closer to her and glared across at Maria, who had a blank, undecipherable expression on her face as she held Hanna tight to her, oblivious.

'Let's strip the boat of anything useful and get ashore using the dingy. Once ashore we get to the shelter.'

'You're certain that they will be after us?'

'Yes, Peter. Drug dealers have a lot of resources and a thirst for retribution,' and the conviction in Gil's voice left no doubt.

Jenny shivered, inside I felt my stomach twist. Ronnie turned away as Hanna shouted out again and then started sobbing. I wasn't sure if she even understood the conversation or if she was just suffering cold turkey, but she sounded like a ghost from a Shakespeare play proclaiming doom, not what we needed.

. . .

We quickly packed what we could and I pulled in the dingy and clambered down to it. The swell made it difficult, but Gil handed Jason down and then Jenny followed. Using the oars I rowed the short distance to the shore. The sea was breaking over the rocks, which were covered in green slime and I struggled to get ashore, eventually just jumping into the cold water which reached up to my waist, jolted by the temperature. However, I was able to hold the boat against the rock long enough until Jason and Jenny scrambled ashore. I pointed out a shallow cave which they could use for temporary shelter.

I clambered back onto the dingy and rowed back out to the

Casablanca. Gil pulled me on board and this time he went down to the dingy and helped Hanna and Maria on to it. With the two of them deposited onshore he returned and we packed our few possessions, our backpacks and a few items from the boat - the first aid box, some food and fresh water. Gil rowed me back and then returned to the boat. One final trip was required to bring Ronnie back. From the shore I noticed Gil using the binoculars and then pointing out something to Ronnie. Hastily it seemed they both got into the dingy and rowed quickly to the shore.

'There's a boat approaching rapidly. Looks like we have some company. Let's get away from here.' Gil urged us to get moving and soon we were working our way up a rock strewn slope, Gil leading and me bringing up the rear. We made it to the top of the slope and Gil urged us to stay low and used his binoculars to study the horizon, frowning as he did.

'The boat is moving fast,' and he handed me the binoculars. I could see the direction of travel - heading for us. They must have spotted our boat. I could just making out some figures leaning over the top of the cabin. 'They're coming, aren't they,' said Jenny, and I nodded not wanting to alarm Jason.

The ground was boggy at the top of the slope and we had to pick our way jumping from rock to rock, which slowed us down. Out to sea, the boat was getting ever closer and I saw a flash of light, shuddering as I realised that someone was probably scanning the shoreline with binoculars searching for us. Instinctively, I crouched down as Gil led us along the cliff top and then down into a narrow gully and up the other side, crossing a narrow burn, which ran down to the sea. And then we were losing height, as we entered a valley which narrowed towards the sea. We made our way down a broad slope, the ground opening out, a bracken covered hillside ahead, with several outcrops of rock, on the other side of a burn and to the right the sea, now glimpsed through a vee shaped gap in the hills.

Gil knew where he was going and we squelched our way across the terrain, Maria hanging back encouraging Hanna, Ronnie now taking up the rear. Jason was tiring so I grabbed him and hoisted him on my shoulders. We crossed the stream and we paused but Gil shouted for us to hurry up. 'They'll use drones,' he explained, 'we need to find cover.' Looking around, there was little to find, no trees and only a few stubby bushes.

Lungs bursting, mouths dry, limbs aching we reached a rocky slope, where Gil stopped. He paused to check his bearings and then led us up the slope stopping to the rear of an outcrop of rock and pulling aside a camouflage sheet, which I hadn't noticed. He held up his hand for us to stop and quickly using a torch he looked inside.

'Checking for adders. They like spots like this, bask on the rocks in the sun. Gave a couple on the last trip a real fright.' Then a few seconds later, 'Okay, let's go in.' As we stooped under the sheet, I glanced out to sea, the boat was almost at the coast.

We flopped inside, out of breath. The shelter was low the sheeting spread over rocks and a couple of pieces of drift wood propped up the sheeting. It was claustrophobic, cramped with a trickle of water running down one side, beside a rock.

'Good,' said Gil, 'well done. However, nobody must go outside unless I say so, whatever the need. Understand,' and he met each of our eyes in turn, emphasising his point by adding, 'You don't want to be caught.' Jenny turned to me and we shared a worried look, we both knew what that would mean.

46

'Look,' and Gil handed me the binoculars, 'above the hill we clambered down. Raise the binoculars,' and he pushed them up for me, 'do you see it?'

I searched for a minute and Gil leant forward raising the binoculars slightly higher. Then I saw it, a drone, high in the sky, a black blob at this distance, certainly not a bird.

'It will have a high resolution lens scanning the ground and probably a heat seeking camera, which will be more useful at night when the temperature is cooler. The Taliban used them a lot. The inside of the camouflage sheet is heat reflecting, so we should be okay at the moment.'

'Pray for cloud and rain,' he said, 'then we can escape when the visibility is poor.'

'No one go outside,' Gil reminded us turning to address everyone, 'there are sealable plastic bags you can use if you need the toilet and I am collecting that trickle of water,' and he pointed to a steady drip of water which was being collected in a plastic container. 'We'll survive until darkness. They are searching for us but they know that soon others will realise that we are missing, hopefully Nick. Stay positive.' That was an effort given the rising temperature inside the cramped claustrophobic shelter, the lack of water and food and the presence of numerous flies buzzing about.

After an hour I lifted the camouflage sheet again a little at the edge, picking up the binoculars again. I could still see the drone but also at the top of the hill I now saw two men, with what appeared to be rifles.

. . .

It was now late evening, dusk, the sky to the west fading as the sun dipped below the horizon. I could hear the noise of birds settling down for the night - the dusk chorus, and I lowered the edge of the camouflaged sheet. Gil sat motionless, conserving his energy, ignoring the flies and now the midges. Flies could be swatted: midges just descended in Biblical multitudes making life miserable. Hanna had gone quiet, deep in sleep or what passed for it with her, and Ronnie and Maria sat holding hands, stony faced. Jason was curled in Jenny's arms asleep. It was my turn to watch for developments outside. The men had disappeared after a few minutes, hours ago, and had not reappeared and I could no longer spot the drone. Survival was the priority. Keep going minute by minute until help came, as surely it would. I lifted the sheet again watching as a herd of deer came down the valley towards the stream, lulled in by their activity, as two young stags squared up. Autumn was the time for rutting, this was more a squabble, a play fight, practise for the real thing.

Suddenly the herd got spooked and moved away startled by something or someone. As the deer fled I could now see several men, with rifles, spread out, approaching the burn below us. I now counted four. Alerted I nudged, Gil, who took the binoculars.

'They're extending their search in this direction but they won't want to be caught out in the dark. They know my reputation,' he added with a thin smile, 'and they don't know what weapons we have. They'll play safe. More a show of strength.'

Eventually one of them blew a whistle and they turned back.

'Be careful,' said Gil, 'they have left someone behind that low ridge to study the hillside, to see if we reveal ourselves thinking that they have gone. Usually they are ex-army types wanting fast money, not knowing what they are getting drawn into but they are dangerous none the less.'

. . .

With the lack of cloud cover there was a distinct chill and the midges and flies continued to torment us, however hard we tried to ignore them. Gil was studying the terrain in front of us, eventually handing Ronnie the binoculars. He spoke softly but everyone listened intently: 'We need to get help. Keep watching,' he reminded Ronnie, as he saw Ronnie turning to listen, 'do you remember where I left the kayaks that you brought round for me?' Ronnie grunted.

'Good, I will take you Maria and Hanna over there, it is about a mile south. There is also a cave with a narrow entrance close to the boats. I suggest that we make Maria and Hanna comfortable there and you paddle to Loch Tarbet and get help.'

'I don't want to leave them.'

'Of course but Hanna wouldn't manage to use a kayak in her present state,' and then even Gil gave in swatting midges from his arm. 'I'll stay with them for a while until they are settled. By morning you should have raised help. Gil continued as if that was decided, 'then I want to discover what we are facing and I am going to pay a visit to our friends. But I'll come back for you, Peter. However, if I am not back by 5 am, just before dawn, then you must start to make your own way south. Climb the slope and descend on the other side to a path. You can't miss it, it's the only one, used by stalkers. Head east fast and keep your eyes open. There is so little cover.'

Nobody was happy but Gil dismissed alternatives.

'Peter, what is your favourite whisky?

'Islay, of course but my tastes are changing,' I replied, thinking about recent events.

'How about Springbank?' mentioning the famous Campbeltown malt whisky.

'I like...' but he cut me short with a laugh, 'please use it as a password. If someone says Islay as they approach then get the handgun out. Hopefully, I will be back by five.'

A few minutes later Ronnie and the girls were ready to leave with Gil, Hanna's eyes staring but unfocused and anxious, with Maria keeping a firm grip on her arm.

'Gil handed me over his handgun. There are three bullets left, use them wisely and keep the last for yourself. You do not want to be caught,' and with that they left.

47

The hours dragged past, each of us trying to sleep, only Jason managing. We said little knowing that voices carried far in the night air. The star lit night would have been spectacular in other circumstances but tonight it depressed me as I wanted cloud, even rain to provide cover for our escape. We had used almost all the water which had been collected and almost finished the chocolate bar that Gil had left. We were thirsty, hungry and cold, our spirits sagging. At one point I heard a rifle shot and wondered why the gun had been fired. Had Ronnie or Gil been spotted?

By half four Gil had not returned and both Jenny and I were becoming concerned not wanting to leave on our own. We huddled together for warmth, the handgun by my side, Gil's final words of advice haunting me. If any of them had been caught they could reveal our position, so we had to move before they came for us.

By five he still had not returned so we wakened Jason, a hand over his mouth so that he wouldn't scream out and alert others. He gradually became more awake. Jenny gave him a little water that had collected and I gave him the last of the chocolate.

'Okay,' I said, 'time to go,' and I had a last look down towards the stream. Everything seemed quiet but someone could be hiding, waiting, looking for us. We pulled back the camouflage sheet and crept out heading up the hillside, the cold air clawing at us, reminding us that we were not prepared for our trek. We crouched as we climbed, darting between rocks, increasing speed as we saw the first light of the new day to the east. Having reached the top we didn't pause but headed down, only able to see a few yards in front of us. Despite trying to avoid boggy patches my feet were soon wet and muddy and I could hear Jason struggling. I stopped and picked him up and put him on my back which made me more aware how tired I was, how heavy he felt, but his needs were greater. He hung his arms around my neck and gripped me tightly with his legs. We struggled on, the morning light lifting shadows, the landscape becoming clearer and with that the danger of being spotted also increased. Down below I saw the path that Gil had mentioned, in reality a very rough track. I stopped, swiping away some flies and wiped my brow, trying not to let Jenny see how exhausted I was.

By the side of the track was a stream, running parallel for a few hundred yards, and a little further on there were a few large boulders and a solitary bush between the rocks, which we could use to rest and hide beside. As we approached the stream, I stumbled into a patch of bog, the muddy water reaching my knees. With an effort I extricated myself having to put Jason down, the squelching mud dragging at my legs as I did so. I then flung myself down by the stream, glancing around and not seeing anyone I cupped my hands and drank deeply. Jenny and Jason followed my example. It helped but the water just made me more aware of how hungry I was. Jenny's face was etched with exhaustion and splattered with mud that she was too tired to wipe away.

'We must keep going,' I said, the words spoken to encourage myself as much as Jenny but I don't think that either of us believed them.

'What happened to Gil?'

'Who knows. I think that we are now on our own. Hopefully, Ronnie can get help,' but in my heart I sensed that was unlikely.

Then we heard the sound of a vehicle approaching and hid behind one of the large boulders, crouching down. The noise drew closer and I glanced along the path spotting an all-terrain vehicle cresting a small hill to the east. Beside the driver sat a man with a rifle across his knees, scanning the landscape, both enclosed within a roll over cage. I gripped the handgun tightly and waited. The vehicle drew level without any change in the engine noise and passed us by. They had to be searching for us, the hunt had begun early.

Should we risk using the track? It would be quicker; use less energy. Jenny looked at me and I could see that she had also reached the end, the limits of her energy. We huddled together for mutual support, Jason sitting on the ground, equally exhausted.

We spent a few minutes like this until I heard the sound of the vehicle returning. 'Desperate times,' I whispered in Jenny's ear, 'desperate measures.' She listened to my plan and agreed. Crouching behind the boulders we waited until the vehicle was nearly level and I jumped out in front of it gun pointing at them. Both men were startled by my sudden appearance and immediately spotted the gun, the driver braking, the guy in the passenger lifting his rifle, but I ran pointing the gun at him remembering Gil's maxim of taking the initiative: 'Throw away the rifle,' I yelled, and after a brief pause he dropped it onto the ground. Jenny ran out and grabbed it. 'Get out,' I was waving the gun in front of them holding it in both hands.

'Okay,' said the driver, 'you must be Peter, be reasonable,' and he started to step down.

'Lie down, flat on the ground,' and he obeyed. The passenger got out but stood his ground. Jenny was pointing the rifle at the two of them, eyes shifting from one to the other. I walked along the side of their vehicle and looked in the back. There was rope which I grabbed and Jason now joined in using it to tie the driver's hands behind his back and finding a knife in the front of the quad bike to cut the rope. He also bound his feet. The passenger seemed more headstrong, smiling as if we wouldn't manage to tie him up, almost taunting us. I brought the handgun closer but he just continued smiling. I lost it with him smashing the handgun across his face and Jenny stuck the rifle in his back. 'Get down,' I screamed, and he did slowly wiping the trickle of blood from his face but fixing me with a thunderous frown. Jason tied his hands behind him and was about to tie his feet when he kicked out, catching me on the thigh unbalancing me, but Jenny screamed: 'Stop,' and she fired just missing him. Both Jenny and the man looked startled, Jenny shaking. He dropped to the ground quickly and Jason hurriedly tied his feet. I was rubbing my thigh as I climbed into the driver's seat, the engine still running.

'Come on,' I shouted, and in a few seconds we were heading away and in the rear view mirror I could see both men writhing about trying to wriggle free. I tossed away the small hand held radio I found lying on the dashboard.

We drove for about ten minutes, the track twisting and turning, crossing a stream and then climbing a steeper hill and as we reached the top we saw the east coast.

'Not far now,' I said, my hopes rising, as we rounded a corner, but she just touched my leg alerting me and groaned. Ahead stood two men with rifles pointing towards us and as I thought about how to react a third man emerged from behind and reached in switching off the engine. 'All out,' he ordered.

Parked just around the next corner I could see another all-terrain vehicle with a man getting out. He quickly walked over to us.

'I'm Tim O'Brien,' he said, smiling at us, 'I know someone who is very keen to see you all.' I think that it was also relief that showed on his unshaven face. His tone changed, 'Tie them up and put them in the back of the vehicle. Mr McGrory will, I am sure, give us all a large bonus.'

My resistance was almost gone. I sagged, slumping in the back and looking up at the blue sky. A sea eagle was hovering above a distant hill, it was free; I was captured, it could protect its brood; I had failed, it had a future; I knew mine was bleak and probably very time limited.

48

The journey seemed to last forever. The three of us kept bumping together as we crossed rough ground, the plastic ties biting into my wrists and ankles. Even Jason had not resisted their attempts to bind his limbs, the game was over. I knew what my fate would be and tried to blank it out as you did prior to a visit to the dentist but this time the pain would be more searing, more prolonged. I would plead for Jenny and Jason to be dealt with more humanely.

We stopped and I opened my eyes. As far as I could see we were in the middle of a peat bog. Jenny twisted around and then leant over giving me a kiss. I tried to respond but hands roughly grabbed me and the opportunity was lost. I mouthed, 'I love you,' before I was dragged out and I could see we were by the coast, the sea not too far away, a cool breeze on my face. The ties on our legs were cut and the three of us were marched along a narrow path and rounding a hillside I saw a small bay below, the sea a beautiful turquoise blue, which seemed at odds with my mood. There was a speed boat anchored in the bay, a dingy drawn up on the beach. To one side of the bay was a small cottage, with a red metal roof, pierced by a metal pipe, white walls and a small window to each side of a wooden door. In front of the cottage were a few lobster creels positioned around the ashes of a fire. I recognised the cottage as one of the few bothies in the area where people could sleep overnight. The path became steeper as it twisted down towards the cottage but firm hands ensured that we did not stumble.

The door was opened, the wood rotted, barely attached to the frame, which was in an equally bad state and we were thrown inside. The earthen floor was streaked by a shaft of light, from a window, which reached to a metal wood burner with a pile of logs stacked beside it and a small metal box. Empty crushed cans of beer, wine bottles, remains of a barbeque, half eaten rolls, and small crushed gas canisters littered the floor, showing how visitors had used and abused the bothy. There were two metal chairs with faded red plastic seats and back supports, one against a wall and the other lying on its back.

It took me a minute to realise that huddled In one corner covered in blood was Gil, who looked up slowly when we entered, peering through half closed eyes, his face swollen and cut. 'Sorry,' he said, so softly, with a strange whistling tone, that I could hardly make it out, the effort obviously hurting him, his mouth bloodied, with blood seeping down his face. Several teeth lay on the ground near him. In comparison we had been treated lightly but then I knew why - I was being saved for the boss.

The door was pulled shut and we were left alone. I broke the silence. 'We tried to get away, almost made the east coast, commandeered a vehicle, a bit like Steve McQueen in the *Great Escape*,' and Gil smiled weakly at my description: 'You did well, it's never over.' I am sure that statement was quoted from some military manual intended to gee up the morale of prisoners.

I crossed over to Gil, but he shook his head, 'leave me, I can cope better like this.' I realised that his hands were bound behind his back.

I then went to Jenny and gave her a kiss, 'I thought I had missed my opportunity,' I said, adding, 'I will always love you,' I said, leaning forward restricted with my hands tied behind me.

Her eyes swam with tears, 'Quite a journey,' her voice full of emotion, 'not what I expected but apart from the last few months I wouldn't change anything,' and she attempted a smile.

'Jason, you are the bravest boy that I ever met,' I said turning to him, 'I'm so proud that you are my son.' I meant very word, he had been a revelation, but he sat mutely, exhausted but his eyes were glistening.

'And don't forget Ben.' How could I. It was too painful to talk about him; we were both missing him so much. I was just glad that he was spared all this, hoping that Colin and Mandy could look after him and, of course, Jodie.

Our introspection was interrupted by more voices approaching outside. The door was opened and there stood Steve, his long hair dirty, his angular pointed face seemed more pronounced as he partially blocked the light from outside, his narrow chin thrust forward.

'Visitors,' he sneered, and Ronnie, Maria and Hanna were bustled inside, hands tied behind their backs. 'Party complete and Mr McGrory is on his way,' he added, briefly glancing over at Gil before he left quickly. Nick wasn't a great judge of character, I mused.

'None of us are very good at this,' I said, and maybe Ronnie detected a hint of reconciliation in what I said because he muttered, 'We've had some good adventures together.'

'I didn't get the kayak far from the shore, before they spotted me. They picked up the girls easily,' and I saw the cuts and bruises on his body. He had put up a fight.

Maria wouldn't meet my gaze but Hanna seemed more alert and she smiled towards us, but it was a smile of someone who didn't know what was happening, eyes vacant and she went over to the back wall and sat down, lost in her own world.

I heard the sound of a helicopter approaching the bay, the noise increasing, as it hovered, the pilot selecting a place to land, the breeze generated by the downdraft spilling into the bothy under the door. As the sound of the whirling blades ceased, there was brief silence then I heard shouting. I waited for the door to open. I was finally going to meet Mr McGrory, the pleasure was all his.

49

The door was pushed open and two men entered, one whose arms were heavily tattooed, the other almost as wide as he was tall, with a shaven head. Both had to duck their heads to avoid the low door lintel, and then took up their position to each side of the door, assessing us for any sign of resistance, their faces inscrutable. They were wasting their time, we were all done. They were followed by McGrory who easily made it through the door, despite wearing a Panama hat. He was also wearing a white linen jacket draped over his shoulders, a pale pink shirt buttoned down at the collar and tailored pale blue denims. Quite immaculate; unlike the rest of us. He stood still demanding attention, his gaze sweeping the room, pausing for a second only when he saw Gil hunched in the corner, giving a brief smile: 'Nick will be upset,' he commented as he took off his hat. His hair once red was thinning, the face thin, cheeks pinched, a narrow nose, the nostrils splayed, lips pale with a small purple spot on the lower lip - probably in his mid-forties. Not a strong face, certainly not attractive and the wane smile was ineffective, but then he held all the cards, he didn't have to try. Desmond McGrory was enjoying the moment, milking it.

'So good to see you again, Hanna, so soon, you can't keep away from me,' the sarcasm lost on her in her present state, but his attention had already switched, 'and you must be Maria, not so pretty as your sister once was.' Maria spat on the floor, just missing his highly polished black shoes, 'Oh dear, but just as feisty, it seems.'

'And Ronnie, torn between love and friendship and losing both.' Ronnie twitched and the bald thick-set heavy, moved to respond. 'Don't worry, Aiden, they're beyond fighting, just a spasm of a dying body.'

'And now the Meldrums. Wow, Peter, I'm impressed, no I really mean that, you have put up a great fight. Jason, welcome, my boy, you're mum was quite a naughty girl, you know. And Jenny, artiste extraordinaire, susceptible to pride - Shona Tyler, I was disappointed, a touch gullible. However, I am going to buy one of your seascapes as a memoir of this occasion, let your estate benefit.'

The show was almost over, the display of power complete, he was savouring the moment.

He shouted, 'Steve,' and Steve trooped in obediently, head lowered, hair like a curtain masking his face. 'you were worth the transfer fee, Steve, for this alone. Now it is time to pay some of it back. 'Take them outside, except Peter, of course, and line them up on the beach, kneeling towards the sea. Aiden, you help.'

Steve produced a handgun, which had been tucked in his belt, and started to usher people to the door. Jenny turned to me, her face full of emotion. I smiled, but she couldn't respond, tears running down her face and she was roughly pulled away by Aiden. It probably was easier for both of us that the parting was not prolonged. Jason followed, starting to cry. I had to fight to hang onto my sanity, angry for what was happening to the others, but feeling faint, distraught, scared. The two girls were led out with Ronnie behind them. He was a good friend who had made a devastatingly wrong decision, in truth, I was still fond of him, and we both smiled fleetingly, a brief moment of contrition.

Steve and Aiden returned to lift up Gil and he was dragged between the two of them out the door, moaning, crying out in pain. McGrory stood to one side of the door observing everything. 'Trust no one,' he muttered as Gil left, 'it only brings disappointment and failure. He thought that Steve was still on Nick's side,' he added.

'Brian tie Peter to the chair,' and I was grabbed and roughly pushed onto the chair. He produced plastic ties and each leg was fixed to a different chair leg. Effortlessly, he broke the tie around my wrists, before tying each arm individually to the chair. He then picked up the chair that was lying on its back, lifted it and dusted it down offering it to McGrory. He examined the seat for a moment, decided it was clean enough and then sat down.

'Thank you, Brian. Take my jacket and hat, then get Steve again.' Brian went to take the jacket but McGrory, stopped him, 'Almost forgot,' he said, and he took a small plastic container from a side pocket, after which he allowed Brian to take lift the jacket of his shoulders, take his hat and go out. He placed the small plastic container on the ground, watching my eyes as he did so, but offered no explanation - he didn't need to.

Steve came in, looking anxious. 'I don't see the primus stove.' Steve looked down avoiding his gaze. 'Look at me,' and he waited until Steve raised his face, which he quickly turned to the side trying to avoid meeting McGrory's eyes. 'It is not good enough, I expect everything as I require it, when I require it.'

'Sorry, Sir,' Steve replied meekly.

'I gave you the instruction only yesterday,' not letting go, holding Steve's gaze, making his point, leaving Steve to squirm.

'I know, I'm sorry.' McGrory let the silence linger, Steve became more and more uncomfortable.

'Light the wood burner, I suppose that we have the time,'

turning to me he added, 'you're not going anywhere are you, Peter?'

Whilst Steve prepared the fire, producing firelighters and matches from the small metal box, lying by the wood burner, I tried to blank my mind, aware that McGrory's attention was now focussed on me, studying me, his eyes, which were like black orbs watching me, probably waiting for any sign of weakness, ready to take advantage. They say that your eyes are windows into your soul, but I couldn't discern any in him, a total lack of empathy, of humanity.

I smelt the stirrings of the fire, the sulphur flush of the spent match, saw wisps of smoke rising, then a small flame taking hold. McGrory didn't even look at Steve. 'Come back in ten minutes, I'll need you then.' Now I had a timescale, what remained in my stomach churned, my bowels were loosening - I was fighting for control of my body.

In a sudden movement McGrory grabbed my chair and twisted it around, settling down on his chair a foot away, in front of the wood burner, pulling up my chin and forcing me to look at him.

'Almost there. Now we can talk. It has been a good spring. I've enjoyed it.'

I don't think he expected me to reply because he went quickly on: 'I've kept Nick busy, wasting his time and resources on his operation 'Bac Mor'. He was so curious wondering what I was doing turning up in Mull. Was I setting up a new supply route for drug smuggling or switching to people smuggling? Who knows? Each time the *Kerry Star* sailed he followed, back and forward we went, mesmerising him, Nick wondering what I was doing, sniffing around. In truth I was enjoying myself, having a break, sharing it with my friends. My hospitality is wonderful as you might have noticed whilst you were on board, everything is available. Operation 'Bac Mor', what a waste of resources,' his mouth twisted in contempt. 'He was even willing to let you come, to draw me out, use you as a snare. That was not playing fair, was it, Peter? I wouldn't recommend him as a friend. Nor could he even save his brother, or is it step-brother? Relationships in aristocratic families are always so fascinating, so complex, aren't they? Even his lieutenant, his right hand man, Steve, was persuaded to switch. Nick is fighting a losing battle. A million pounds is nothing to me, but it is much more than Nick's annual budget. How can you stop drug smuggling with that sort of budget. But when you are struggling with a family and a mortgage, a million pounds is very tempting. Steve does not need to work again, although through loyalty to me he'll keep helping out. He just doesn't realise it yet, soon will.'

'Of course Nick can't be professional with me, with him it is also personal after what I did to Becky, one of his team, and lover, although don't tell Amelia, his wife. I don't think he will ever forgive me,' and he looked at me, 'so painful running into me, burning inside, unable to breathe.'

He examined the ground, pushing a half eaten roll, which was lying on the ground, to one side with his foot before his attention returned to me.

'Steve has been useful, letting me know what you were up to at the care home, followed you to Dunquin. He was also keeping an eye on Connor, not the brightest. Connor screwed things up, he was just meant to kidnap Jason, but he got into a fight with Quinn and the farmhouse burnt down. He was unreliable kidnapping Jenny, wanting revenge for his brother's imprisonment. I didn't sanction that. I had Steve kill him, told him where to find him, before he became a liability. I saved Jenny, you know. Are you grateful, you have had more time with her. I hope you used the time wisely,' and he winked at me.

'Let them both go,' I asked, trying not to sound if I was pleading, which I am sure is what he wanted.

'Not possible now, Peter,' and he said it not in an aggressive way, more matter of fact as if we were discussing selling a couple of horses. 'They will all be shot and their bodies dumped at sea.'

'However, back to my spring activities. All the time I was distracting Nick I was elsewhere in the country establishing new routes and he wasn't even aware. Come on say something, Peter.'

A small fly landed on his thigh. His gaze was diverted as he flicked it away, carefully examining that it had not left a mark on his denims. He reached into his trouser pocket producing a small tube of anti-bacterial gel and carefully cleaned his hands. Then his attention switched back to me. 'Say something, Peter,' the emphasis on the second word, now much stronger.

'You must have planned everything very carefully.'

He seemed pleased with my response.

'Yes, including the insertion of porn on your work computer. You had to be punished for what you did at the care home. It also made you desperate enough to believe that Jenny had got funding for Mull and Iona ' He chuckled and added: 'You don't get to where I am without planning, determination and ruthlessness.' This time he lengthened the last word to emphasis it.

'And of course Maria. When Ronnie helped you out at the care home, we decided to follow that up, give him a clear warning, wreck his house. We hit gold dirt. Maria had been waging an on-line campaign searching for her sister and Maria turned out to be Ronnie's wife. Maria has caused a bit of trouble, as people took up the campaign, almost had Hanna killed, so her body could be found and the campaign ended. We would have made it look like suicide or a lover's tiff. We had to stop importing women for a few months. But when we discovered the connection I saw an opportunity. Wasn't sure if I was going to use it, held it back in reserve, but it worked out fine. You always need options.'

'Which brings me to Catherine. She was a wonderful young woman; I am sure that you would agree. Talented, a very good operative. I craved her but she repeatedly said that she didn't mix personal and professional, was more interested in a career. I respected that since she was making me large profits; I bided my time. Then my accountant pointed out some anomalies in her accounting. She was putting money aside for herself. No one does that to me,' he added, giving a slow disbelieving shake of his head.

'I had others investigate and then I paid a surprise visit to her house to confront her. She wasn't there but Jason was. Catherine had had a relationship, had a child and wasn't interested in me. I couldn't accept that, you understand. I found out about you and devised a small test. The Islay connection was unravelling, Nick was getting close, a rare success for him. It was time to get out. I ordered Catherine to kill you, a test of loyalty. Of course, she failed - she didn't kill you only drugged you and tried to protect you. Jason had also disappeared, hidden by her. Lessons had to be seen to be learnt, unfortunately for you. You and your son have to be killed, to purge the stain of your relationship with Catherine.'

'I arrived on the island to confront Catherine for not killing you and to find out where my money had gone. She was brave and wouldn't talk. I satisfied my passion for her and then ordered her brother, Donald to kill her. As you know he slit her throat, so scared that I would do worse to him. He deserves to rot in jail.'

I was horrified, poor Catherine. I burned with hate for McGrory who looked back with a hint of contempt and then amusement, a smile growing, his tongue flicking against the purple spot on his lower lip, enjoying my reaction. He checked the fire now burning in the wood burner and lifted the plastic container, opening it. Inside was a small metal cylinder pointed at one end which he didn't touch, just left it on display.

'Steve,' he shouted, 'bring me the tongs,' and Steve who must have been lurking at the door, came in with a pair of metal tongs, wrapped in silk.

'Thank-you. Stoke the fire, it is not hot enough, yet.'

Steve busied himself, blocking our sight of the wood burner, as he added more wood, leaving the door almost shut but not quite closed, as he left.

McGrory's mood suddenly changed. He jumped at me stopping an inch from my face, anger distorting his face, his spittle spraying me as he bellowed, 'Where is my money?'

I rocked back in the chair from his onslaught. 'You are going to tell me,' and he used the tongs to place the metal cylinder in the wood burner, watching it as it slowly turned red, letting me sweat.

'I'll ask you once again, Peter. Where is the money?'

'I don't know. I hadn't spoken to Catherine in years, didn't even know that she had borne me a son.'

'You expect me to believe that?'

'It is the truth.'

'Come on, Peter. Tell me and I'll make it quick.'

He deliberately checked the fire again, teasing me, stretching out with the tongs and then stopping, turning to me, smiling.

'Peter, tell me. It's a matter of honour, you understand. No one can cheat me.'

I was sweating, starting to tremble, not able to contain my fear. McGrory shook his head.

'So be it, Peter. I am sorry, truly sorry.'

'No you're not. You're just a mad bastard.'

He stiffened, enraged, his face muscles tensing, his tongue rapidly interrogating the purple spot on his lip as he plunged the tongs into the fire, using them to grasp the metal cylinder, which was now glowing red hot, bringing it to my face. I could feel the heat. Perspiration was running down my face, my clothes damp, as I flexed my muscles trying to break the ties which bound me.

'Steve, it's time' he shouted, but Steve didn't appear. 'Steve,' he shouted again, louder, impatient. He leaned back on his chair, in line with the wood burner, annoyed that Steve had not appeared.

McGrory twisted on his chair. Suddenly, there was an explosion, a deafening roar, the door of the wood burner blew open, rocking on its metal legs , the door banging on the side of the wood burner; sheets of flame and searing heat shot out. McGrory's hair caught fire, his face seared, his clothes catching fire as the force of the explosion blew him off his chair, smashing him against the bothy door, which gave way under the explosive force. Waves of fiery heat spread out, the explosive force knocking me back, my chair tipping over. I could smell burning flesh. Outside I heard gunshots, rapid firing, shouts, screams and my body sagged, passing out.

Then I felt hands breaking the plastic ties, pulling me outside - it was Ronnie. I swayed, as he held me, still deafened by the roar of the explosion, disorientated. I saw McGrory's smouldering body, what remained of his clothes blackened, with the metal cylinder embedded in his neck, saw him squirming, his face distorted with pain, grimacing. I kicked him hard, my pent-up anger no longer containable. I staggered about, saw Jenny and Jason, Jenny screaming but I couldn't hear what she said, only her mouth opening and shutting. I watched, as if from a distance, as Steve and Gil were firing. Then Ronnie suddenly pushed me to the ground and I saw him staggering, warm blood splattered on me, as he fell on top of me.

I looked up at the sky saw figures standing on the cliff top, appearing like Indians do in a Western, silhouetted on the skyline ready to confront the cowboys. Indians to the rescue or was it cavalry, but my mind was going. I was told later that I shouted, 'Indians,' but my consciousness was fading as Jenny grabbed me kissing me, cradling my head in her arms.

50

I slowly drifted in and out of consciousness, aware that there were people about, that I was in a room where it was cool with the whir of machines a constant background noise. At one point I heard a woman's voice, soft, warm, reassuring me but then I drifted away again. Finally, I awoke, saw that I was in a room, whose walls were pale green, with a roller blind reducing the external light. I moved and groaned, aware of machines beeping, a heart trace crossing a screen, fluids finding their way into my body, from a bag, through a cannula on the back of my hand. As memories flitted back, I felt tense, the heart rate responding until I felt a hand softly grip mine. I knew that touch and my eyes opened and my head slowly swivelled and there was Jenny, gently stroking my hand. She was also wearing a hospital gown, her hair tied back, smiling, an anxious look on her face, which softened, as my eyes focussed.

'We're safe, Peter, McGrory is dead. Jason and I are fine.' The words seemed distant, but precious and only by repeating them a few times could I absorb the significance of Jenny's words. I felt lost In a strange almost out-of-body experience, my lips moving but words wouldn't emerge: my mouth too dry. I lost consciousness again.

By the afternoon I was stronger, sitting up for a short time, able to smile and acknowledge those around me, but everything was an effort, my ears buzzing, as if there was a series of mighty ocean waves crashing over me: speech distorted through a cauldron of noise. A doctor had been in to see me, checking me out, and she issued instructions to a nurse who was sitting beside me but I couldn't make too much sense of them. I flitted in and out of consciousness; brief moments of lucidity, followed by a descent into a fog and what passed for sleep.

The next morning they made a determined effort to rouse me, wash me, tidy up the bed. The morning round followed and a consultant, I presume, asked questions, which the nurse answered and then the consultant leant close to me.

'You are in the Queen Elizabeth Hospital, in Glasgow. You were brought by helicopter here from Jura. You're on the mend, Mr Meldrum,' she said, 'however, you need to rest.'

Later in the morning Jenny reappeared, still dressed in a hospital gown, and sat beside me, holding my hand again. I slept mostly. Later Ben appeared, with Jenny and he ran towards me to hug me, but Jenny stopped him, allowing him just to hold my hand. Everyone appeared happier.

'Where's Jason?'

'He's downstairs. I've been with him,' said Jenny. 'He's fine, very resilient, they say, just some bruising. The consultant didn't want you to see too many people, too quickly - you need to rest.'

It took a few days, for me to be sitting up eating and drinking. A nurse produced a mirror, which showed my face red, as if deeply sunburnt, my eyebrows and hair singed. Memories of the explosion came back; of McGrory being blown out of the bothy, burning, screaming, his words, his threats forever lost, swallowed up in the ether. By now Jenny and Jason were constant companions, the roaring in my ears diminishing, allowing me to hold a conversation.

Nick's men, it seems, had arrived to find the situation largely under control. They were the cavalry I had seen on the hilltop, not Indians, thankfully. The fire fight which followed the explosion had been brief but intense. Having grabbed the initiative Steve and Gil had soon wounded or killed several of McGrory's men, the others fleeing. The pilot of the helicopter had surrendered. The speedboat had attempted to leave but had been stopped by a police boat. Only one man had attempted to continue the fight and after firing at me he had been shot. Poor Ronnie had saved me by jumping in front of me and pushing me aside, taking the bullet intended for me.

'He's recovering in an adjoining room,' Jenny explained, 'wants to see you, when you are able. He saved your life.' I detected a softness in Jenny's tone, she had forgiven him.

Eventually my mind sharpened, understanding and taking in what I had learnt. 'I thought that Steve was a traitor?' I blurted out.

'No, he had been working for Nick all along. Knew Gil well from the past, another former soldier from Afghanistan. Gil had spotted him near the bothy, when he was reconnoitring, after he had left Ronnie and the girls. Gil got Steve's attention and they planned between them what to do, after they heard, by radio, that we had been captured.'

'But Gil was badly beaten up?'

'No, Steve had claimed to have found him, brought him in at gun point and then pretended to beat him up in the bothy, not letting others in. In reality some teeth were extracted from a goat, shot by McGrory's men earlier, and I remembered the shot that had been fired that night, and smearing Gil with some of its blood, had convinced everyone that he was in a bad state. Steve had given him a small gun and ensured that the plastic ties could break easily. Once outside they had waited for the explosion and then attacked McGrory's men.'

'Yes, the explosion. What caused it?'

'The last time that Steve had checked the fire he had put a full gas canister in the back, a small canister that was intended for use with a primus stove, that he had hidden beside the wood burning stove. That's why he didn't respond to McGrory shouting for him to return, he was anticipating the explosion. It was an anxious moment, then the explosion blew McGrory outside. He suffered terrible burns and fragments of burning wood were driven into his body along with the metal cylinder intended for you - poetic justice. He writhed around in agony while the fire fight ensued, screaming, begging for help.' I had kicked him at one point, I recollected, as I staggered around outside, before being pushed to the ground by Ronnie. 'Someone eventually put a bullet in him, to give us peace. No one saw who did it,' and Jenny smiled. Some secrets were best kept that way.

Then another sequence of events came to my mind from the past, words came tumbling out. 'Catherine had been ordered to kill me that night at Machir Bay. It was no accidental meeting on the beach. McGrory had pursued Catherine but she had rejected him claiming that she didn't want to mix business and pleasure. McGrory was furious after he discovered she had a child. McGrory had wanted Catherine to kill me, a test of loyalty to him. Catherine only drugged me, paid for that with her life.' More was coming back to me. 'McGrory had found that Catherine was fleecing him.'

'You know what all this means, Peter, and I studied her face not sure, 'it wouldn't have mattered if you had gone to the Robinson's farm that night or not they would still have come after you. It wasn't your fault.'

That made a difference to both of us as we sat in silence.

. . .

Was it the third or fourth day of my hospital stay, I wasn't sure, that Ronnie was wheeled into the room in a wheel chair, his left arm heavily bandaged, held at an awkward angle to his body. He appeared drawn, the effort of meeting me tiring in itself and he sat mute beside the bed. I broke the tension stretching out my hand to grab his good arm, a smile reinforcing my feeling.

'I owe you my life. Thanks.'

Ronnie bit his lip, trying to suppress his emotion.

'I got you into a lot of trouble, you, Jenny and Jason could have been killed.'

'McGrory is dead, nothing else matters.'

'Maria was obsessed with finding her sister, Hanna. She had set up an internet campaign to find her.' I nodded, somehow I knew, then I remembered that McGrory had told me.

'After the care home incident, they found out, presumably, from the car registration, where I lived and wrecked our house, stole the laptop. We received an envelope, with pictures of Hanna, informing us she would be killed if we didn't follow their instructions and deliver you. It...'

'was an impossible dilemma,' I replied, completing his sentence, 'you had to obey their instructions. I understand, friend. I don't think that I could have acted differently.'

Relief shone from Ronnie's face, dipping his head, exhaling hard, changing his posture, as he shuffled his body in the wheelchair. I didn't embarrass him by looking at him, I understood his emotion, shared it, and felt my own eyes moistening.

'Gil came in one day, and saw Maria upset, just after he had arrived back from a visit to Oban. He wanted to help, now I know why as his friend Harry had just been brutally murdered by McGrory. A lot of Nick's team were recruited from Gil's platoon in Afghanistan. Nick had also worked there in intelligence. The brotherly connection proving useful. Gil made us promise not to tell Nick, didn't want him to know. I suspect that Nick would have interfered and we wouldn't have got Hanna back. His mission was personal, rescue Hanna, but also revenge for what happened to Harry.'

All this was interesting but I wanted him to know: 'Without you, I would never have found Jason.'

We sat in silence, a kindly auxiliary came in with a tea trolley and afterwards we both supped our coffee.

'How is Hanna?'

Ronnie shook his head. 'It will be a long recovery. Her parents have arrived from Romania and they met up last night, it seems. They will take her home, but she has been through a lot, so it will take time.'

'And Maria?'

'She has changed. This has been such an ordeal but,' and he looked at me without hope or despair, 'we will work it out, somehow.'

. . .

I had expected a visit from Nick, but he didn't appear. Eventually the consultant allowed the police in to talk with me, deeming me sufficiently recovered, and they took a statement, but since they had already interviewed most of the others the conversation did not last long.

51

We sat in silence as the ferry ramp was raised and the ferry started its short journey across to Jura, from Port Askaig, in Islay, heading at an angle, against the tide, towards the opposite shore, allowing the fast flowing water to bring it to the ferry slipway opposite at Feolin, on Jura's south west coast, overlooked by the Paps of Jura. We both felt strange being back on Jura. There were two other cars on the ferry and I noticed like us they were sombrely dressed. I guessed that they were going to the same funeral - Gil's.

We had just returned home to Glasgow when Malcolm phoned. He had heard that Gil had committed suicide, using a shotgun that he had borrowed. There were, as the police often report, no suspicious circumstances. His funeral was being held in the small parish church in Jura, just through Craighouse. It was his wish to be buried on the island. The Rev Walker was taking the service having struck up a close friendship with Gil and someone who Gil trusted and could speak to about his time in Afghanistan.

As we arrived and parked several people were already entering the modest white harled building, through the small porch at the southern end. The interior was bright, the sun streaming through the side windows and the stained glass window at the far end. As I entered I noticed the family members, at the front, beside the raised pulpit. I recognised Nick with a dark haired woman by his side, presumably his wife. Next to Nick, standing talking to a woman, was a tall white haired man, wearing a kilt and tweed jacket, who looked to be in his seventies. To his side was a younger woman, maybe in her fifties with dyed blonde hair. I took them to be Lord Drescoet and his wife.

We sat towards the rear just behind Ronnie and Maria, who were sitting with other friends. They both turned, Ronnie only managing a half turn and both acknowledged us, Maria who had just returned from Romania, particularly warm, more like her former self.

As the coffin was brought into the church, draped in a Union flag, the Rev Walker leading the way, we all stood. The service was emotional, Nick's father, Lord Drescoet, paid a moving tribute to his son, and talked about the family tradition of military service and the cost to the family over the generations.

The Rev Walker picked up on that point, describing some of the conversations that he had with Gil or Gilbey as he called him, that he could share, many were confidential. How he was a person of great personal integrity, who had led his platoon, in Helmand Province in Afghanistan. He and his platoon had held a dusty fort in a fiercely hot summer, absorbing daily attacks by the Taliban. To begin with the locals had turned their backs on the British troops, a gesture of rudeness, the village elders fearing that their presence would just bring the wrath of the Taliban on their community. Gil and his men built positive relationships, which took time and effort, and were gradually accepted. However, a decision taken by commanders based some distance away, at Camp Bastion, led to the withdrawal of the troops, a decision Gil knew would place the villagers in peril. So it turned out and when they had cause to return they found that many in the village had been killed, young women raped and many tortured. Gil found that difficult to live with, felt responsible, and later resigned his commission. The war in Afghanistan left Gil deeply traumatised, struggling and requiring years of therapy. 'This is the true cost of war,' the minister added.

'Gil's personal faith had helped him and he was beginning to recognise the offer of forgiveness through faith in Jesus Christ. This sustained him as did the relationships he had built with fellow soldiers who could understand his trauma. Gil found life on Jura wonderful, the pace of life, the people, the wilderness areas all soothed his soul. He had recently felt strong enough to start a business, offering survival courses; wilderness experiences for small groups.'

'The recent sad loss of a friend, a particularly close former colleague, triggered a response, unsettling him. Gil offered to help some new friends and did successfully, but the old memories returned to haunt him and he took his life. He meant no guilt to attach itself to anyone as it was memories from the dusty plains of Afghanistan which reached out to invade the tranquillity of Jura, and ultimately overwhelm him, not the events here.'

We watched as the coffin was lowered into the freshly dug grave and then wandered back to the car. Jenny nudged me: 'Nick is coming over.'

He joined us, appearing for once very smart in a blue suit wearing a black tie. 'I am sorry that I have not been able to update you but recent events have taken a lot of my time,' and we knew he was referring to Gil. We gave our condolences.

'We have all been greatly affected by Gil's death,' an admission of vulnerability that I hadn't expected to ever hear from Nick. 'His last action along with yourselves and my team, have brought significant success. Apart from McGrory's death, which no one mourns, we found his mobile phone and laptop with a list of contacts. We are aggressively pursuing individuals, learning more about the organisation he ran, with contacts spreading throughout Europe and beyond. Someone will attempt to take over but the supply lines have been severed, at least temporarily, and much human misery avoided.'

'And we no longer have McGrory chasing us,' stated Jenny.

'And Becky has been avenged,' I added, and Nick's eyes narrowed and his expression froze for a minute.

'You can go about your lives in peace, enjoy your family. I believe that for you all, the nightmare is over,' but his words were grudging after my revelation about Becky.

'Amelia is waiting, you better go,' and he turned sharply walking towards her.

I could see Jenny wanting to say more, how Nick had needlessly exposed us to more danger by letting us go to Mull, but I put my arm around her, drawing her closer. It was time to let go.

52

I had forgotten what a normal Saturday evening could be. We were enjoying a pizza, delivered to the house, talking about the football results, although Jenny had less enthusiasm for that than the boys. Jodie was lying watching, waiting for any crumbs, titbits that would come her way. Life was returning to normal. Jenny glanced across at me, lifting her eyes from watching Jason and Ben feasting on the pizza and smiled, the weariness, the tension had largely gone, her hair glistened with health, her eyes sparkled. This was how it should be.

The doorbell rang and I went to open it, not concerned or anxious but as people normally do. Mrs Johnstone, our nearest neighbour was standing, a large box, wrapped in brown paper at her feet.

'Sorry to trouble you, Mr Meldrum, but this arrived after you left for Mull,' and she pointed to the parcel. 'We have just come back from a cruise and I had forgotten about it. Sorry,' she repeated.

'Thank-you for handing it in. I wasn't expecting a parcel,' and I looked at the label. It was for me and I lifted it, searching for the sender. It was from Jason's boarding school and I realised that it was the return of his possessions, which we had asked to be sent on. I quickly explained a little of that to Mrs Johnstone and then after shutting the door, brought in the parcel, setting it down on the floor beside the now empty pizza container.

'Who took the last slice,' I said smiling, and I saw Ben looking guilty.

'I think these are your possessions from the boarding school, Jason,' and he moved over to the parcel.

'Can I open it, Dad,'

'Of course,' and he started unravelling the string bound around the parcel and then ripping the brown paper off exposing a cardboard box and Jason pulled off the lid. Inside neatly folded was his uniform, sports gear and trainers. He hauled them all out and as he lifted a pair of trainers an envelope flitted to the ground. He looked at it and handed it to me. I was expecting a final invoice but then I recognised the handwriting. It was from Catherine.

Inquisitive I ripped the envelope open. Inside was a single sheet. Jenny was now curious, waiting for me to read out what it said. I glanced at the writing and immediately folded it up, handing it over to Jenny, who unfolded it and read, her eyes growing bigger and eventually, having read it for a second time, she handed it back, blowing hard through her mouth, that was also my reaction.

We played with the boys for half-an-hour, a game of snakes and ladders and then got them ready for bed. Jenny eventually managing to settle them. Ben then wanted a story, Jason listening in.

When Jenny came downstairs I was already on the laptop as she picked up the sheet of paper again.

Peter - the letter from Catherine began - if you are reading this, you know all about Jason, a wonderful boy. It probably means that I am no longer around. I hope that you understand. My family were up to no good and trapped, that is why I had